RHINOCEROS

JESSE SALVO

Blue

RHINOCEROS

– OR –

Pedestrian Verses

LIBRARY OF CONGRESS CATALOGING-IN-PUBLICATION DATA

Blue Rhinoceros *or Pedestrian Verses*
Authored by Jesse Salvo

ISBN: 9781737249184
LCCN: 2022934624

ANACRUSIS

If they would yield us but the superfluity, while it were
wholesome, we might guess they relieved us humanely;
but they think we are too dear: the leanness that
afflicts us, the object of our misery, is as an
inventory to particularise their abundance

—THE PLEBIANS, CORIOLANUS

If you wish to get rid of the rats
which make the walls of your house
their home, write them a note couched
in the politest terms you are master of,
requesting them to go to a neighbor,
and they will do as you desire. Be
careful, of course, to tell the rats which
neighbor you wish them to go to.

—UPSTATE PROVERB

BRIEF AUTHOR'S NOTE:

As I write this, I am locked down inside my home, and a half a million of my fellow human beings are sick or dying from a germ which seems to have only slightly more contempt for us as a species than we by all indicators have for one another. The year I am writing from is 2020, which is our society's poor way of trying to track how far away we have moved from the God we invented. People are always trying to calculate how far away God is, and what his face might look like, on account of we are obsessed with celebrity and he is the biggest celebrity we have.

If you are reading this account in 2021, in 2022, in 2050, or some other wholly unimaginable year, congratulations on mastering the mechanics of time travel. Congratulations too on surviving, as the odds did not seem particularly stacked in your favor, from where I was sitting.

It will be useful, I believe (for both expedience's sake and legal purposes) to list all of the people and works from which I have plagiarized below, so that you are not reading this book under any false pretenses (save, perhaps, that this is a work wholly of fiction). So without further ado, and in no particular order, here you have them:

The French playwright Eugene Ionesco
The fraudulent journalist Joseph Mitchell
The supreme authoress Jesmyn Ward
The inimitable Susan Sontag
The collected poetry of Leigh Stein
Pierre's Father's Funeral from *War & Peace*

The ending of *Love in The Time Of Cholera*
Nearly every line from *Coriolanus*
The scene at the Inn from *Don Quixote*
Yossarian's therapist from *Catch 22*
The music and lyrics of Katie Crutchfield
The lyric sanctimony of John Steinbeck (who was a monster)
The works of Raymond Carver (who was a monster)
The works of Diane Williams (who curiously manages
    to be a genius without ever behaving monstrously)
Three novels by John Irving
A Brief History of Seven Killings by Marlon James
Four novels by Kurt Vonnegut
Two and a half novels by Don Delillo
"Do You Hear What I'm Saying?" by Kori Waring
My sisters, in conversation

If you feel that you have been plagiarized, but you were not named on the above list, I am sorry. Legally, there is nothing I can do, as only the people mentioned supra are entitled to this book's royalties. It may be cold comfort, but please know that I suffer greatly, every day, as all of us do. Eventually all plagiarists get what is coming to them, and I am surely no exception in this, so it is only a matter of time until I am served my just desserts. Like I say: it is not a banker's check, but at least it is something.

I'll likewise mention something here, before it becomes readily apparent to you within the text, which is that I am an altogether different person, with different opinions and a different disposition, from the wretchedly jaded Thomas Entrecarceles. That if at times my voice seems to inject itself in the prose, I will endeavor to make myself known, by identifying myself as *"this writer"* as opposed to Mr. Entre-carceles' favored *"this journalist"* so as not to confuse your impression of the disgraced veteran newspaperman, who is very much his own person.

Now, I will address the elephant in the room, which is: there is a lot of pressure on me here, obviously. Considering the current state of global affairs, I may be part of one of the last generations ever to hold tenure on this planet. The clock is ticking! On top of which, consider that Isaac Newton, while sequestered in quarantine invented calculus (!) and that William Shakespeare (also here plagiarized), while hiding in isolation from the plague, penned King Lear (!!). To clear the air, I have no intention of writing King Lear, as it has already been written once to satisfaction, and as I never enjoyed it in the first place. I cannot even much promise that I will write a pure and unencumbered novel to anyone's satisfaction but my own. My mind is rabbitty and restless, apt to interject autobiography and editorial in the middle of books, which is a foible I have as-yet been unable to shake. You may chock it up to bad breeding or lack of discipline or white privilege or mental illness if you like. I promise, at least, to try and keep my interjections to a minimum, out of respect for the very real stories contained herein: those of the disgraced journalist Thomas Entrecarceles, the zoologist Sairy Wellcomme, the rhinoceros Beebop, others.

I will end this note with two stories I have always loved, about the French writer Honore de Balzac, who wrote a wonderful very large book called *The Human Comedy* and who was one of the great chroniclers of the weird undignified, butterflies-in-your-stomach experience of being a walking talking person in a badly constructed universe. The first story comes from near the middle of his life when Balzac had already achieved some level of renown for writing *The Human Comedy*. At this point in his career he was considered one of the sharpest and most prolific commenters on the human condition (in France at least), and one day a close friend asked Balzac why he harbored such critical contempt for his countrymen. Balzac, rather taken aback, replied that he felt no such way about his countrymen, as he'd had precious little experience of them. His friend was quite confused. Did Balzac mean to tell him that he never went out among the people? That he did not engage in modern French society? "Of course not," Balzac said self-importantly, "I am too busy writing about it."

The second story I quite like comes from the very end of Balzac's life. If I am remembering correctly he had fallen quite ill with some terminal disease, and in the course of his final decline became delirious with fever. The priest and doctor were both summoned to the writer's bedside, and Balzac, in the throes of his delirium, sat up, clutched the priest's hand, and went about peppering him with questions about the well-being of his own fictional characters. "Are they alright? Will they be well?" he demanded. The priest expressed that he did not know. The doctor, having no such occupational qualms about lying to a delirious patient, said that yes, they were fine, and Balzac, breathing a sigh of relief, died.

I don't know why I like those two stories so much, except that it has something to do with being alone and separate from the things you care about, and the things that can make you whole. So I am sitting here in my apartment, occasionally checking the death reports from around the world, inquiring after the well-being of my loved ones who are all very far away from me, and for whom I worry greatly. As I say, there is nothing original in this. It is all plagiarized from different sources. But I have written it down for you. It is not born of critical contempt for my fellow man, and it is not a fever dream either. What it is, in simplest terms, is a fairy tale. And what's more: it is the only way I know to bring you and I closer to people and things that now feel very far away, and hard to reach, and even harder to touch. So we'll start here, in 2030, with Thomas Entrecarceles of Lake Placid, New York, receiving a strange knock on his door.

CHAPTER 1

It is possible that I am not the ideal stenographer of these events. If you do not trust me I do not much blame you. I, having once possessed some station and privilege within my industry, appear to have lost all or most of both after having perhaps embellished my involvement in an armed conflict some years back as a foreign correspondent and being found out by a conservative journalist who, for her reportage, earned a national magazine award and Sunday show (for there is nothing we Americans revere more than the Troops; nothing we as a people despise more than Stolen Valor). After which I was roundly pilloried maligned sacked mocked and ridden out of my trade—asked in no uncertain terms to quit the only thing I had ever been any good at. For five years I tried, in some space adjacent to anonymity, to labor quietly as regular people do. First at a gas station, then a landscaping company. Both times I was eventually found out, recognized by someone, and it was decided that those same qualities which had made me unfit for journalism likewise made me unfit to count up the register at the end of the day, or properly fertilize a garden bed. So I was back to puttering around my cabin, inquiring vainly after work, and considering with measured dispassion the taking of my own life, when one spring day I received a knock on the door and the course of my life changed radically forever.

Sairy Wellcomme was not five years younger than me. Where I was rumpled, bag-eyed and dissolute she was a smartly dressed woman with short hair and nails, tall, horn-rimmed eyes and good posture. "I am a biologist" was the first thing she said to me.

1

"O.K." I said. I had been in the middle of rolling a cigarette and resumed my task with little delay as if I often received social calls from biologists to my little Adirondack cabin.

"Actually," she said, letting herself into my home. "I am a zoologist."

It was around three in the afternoon, which in the Adirondacks in late spring is a window of aggressively pleasant weather and pestilential insects. A little robin trilled in a tree branch at the yard's edge.

"Good of you to correct the record on that."

I fished through the papers on the floor for whatever I had been reading at the time (my memory is hazy). My dog Goober, who is an oaf, barked to signal that he was also a part of the conversation.

"I know who you are," Sairy Wellcomme said, eying me circumspectly.

"O.K." I said, "so then, return the pleasure."

"My name is Sairy Wellcomme."

"That's a strange name," I remarked, knowing as she could say the same for me.

"Well it's my name," she said.

"O.K." I said.

Several more seconds passed.

"I want to hire you," she said finally.

I looked up. As I looked at her she stared around at the squalid little cabin. Goober came to nuzzle her hand.

"You say you know who I am," I said.

She nodded.

"Nobody who knows who I am wishes to hire me," I said and began patting my coat pockets for a lighter.

She didn't say anything further.

I have a conversational disease where I must always be doing something with my hands whenever I am speaking to someone. Far from being an encumbrance, I have always thought it quite a happy necessity, as all conversation is very boring taken by itself. It is what made me such an effective alcoholic for so many years, before I decided to cut down on the small things that brought me pleasure in life.

I studied her fine clothes, the watch on her wrist, the frames of her glasses.

"You say you're a biologist."

"Zoologist," she corrected.

"Zoos must have had a robust last couple quarters," I commented, looking at her watch, then once again down at my busy hands.

She cleared her throat.

"As it relates to why I am here." Sairy Wellcomme sounded annoyed, which made her more interesting to me. "I'll confess I came into a very large sum of money, when both my parents died, when I was very young."

"So, what do you want to hire me to do, Sairy Wellcomme, independently wealthy zoologist?"

She looked down and pet Goober. Outside the screen porch, fat black flies buzzed psychotically hither and thither.

"I need you to solve a crime for me."

She looked up, embarrassed. I studied this woman's face. She looked, even in the dark of the cabin, to be under a great deal of strain. I shook my head.

"I'm not going to be able to tell you who killed your parents," I said flatly. "Much as I would love to rob a rich girl of her money, I don't suppose that I can, in this—"

She cut in, shaking her head.

"It's not my parents," she said.

"Who then?"

"It's not exactly a *who*," she said, "and I already know the party responsible for the, uh, death."

She paced the room in a circle, fingering her necklace like a fine society lady touring the hovel of a laborer. In earnest, the cabin wasn't all that bad. Just a little cluttered. Plus, there were socks hanging everywhere. I had a washer but no drier, which meant I hung my clothes up on a line outside. It also meant occasionally the inside of the cabin was decorated with items I couldn't fit on the line, airing out on any available hook or surface. You'd think the largest items would be the biggest pain but actually it is the small things, the socks and gloves and the like, which you cannot individually clip and hang from a laundry line without first letting go of your sanity and pitching headfirst into blackest madness, and so you end up hanging a thousand little socks everywhere all over the room like ratty woven charms. Or at least I do.

"Please," I said, "please please please, dispense with the theatrics."

Goober barked again, turned three times in a circle and began to gnaw on his own tail.

"Good boy," said this Ms. Wellcomme, then, looking up at me, biting her upper lip, "I'm afraid when I tell you it will sound very silly."

"That's alright," I said, "rich girls are allowed to be silly. That's one of the privileges wealth confers."

She shook her head, looking annoyed for a second time. She was not accustomed to being treated as an unserious person.

"It's a rhinoceros. It's the last blue rhinoceros on earth. Was."

"The last blue rhinoceros on earth," I repeated slowly. "And you think he was murdered."

4

"I know he was murdered," she said.

"How?"

"Because I murdered him."

I sat on my couch looking at this stranger. She did not appear obviously insane.

"You killed the last blue rhinoceros."

"Seventeen years ago."

"Seventeen years ago, when you were—"

"—Thirteen, or twelve, yes twelve. The same year that my parents died. I killed the last ever African Blue Rhinoceros."

"I don't understand."

Sairy Wellcomme smiled unhappily and her knuckles blanched.

"Well neither do I, I'm afraid. That's why I want to hire you."

"To find out why you killed the last Blue Rhinoceros," I said. "Did he owe you money?"

She made a face.

"Tell me what happened."

She inhaled then began to recite, as if by rote, what had happened to her.

"On June 30th, 2012, in upstate New York, both of my parents died in an accident. Two days later, I murdered the last African Blue Rhinoceros. I have no memory of how I got to the Zoo, or what I did in the intervening time. I have no idea how I hatched the plan or why. My memory is a blank. There are newspaper stories and all the rest, about the aftermath, but that is the totality of what I have to go on."

I said nothing. She said nothing.

Sairy Wellcomme seemed all at once to have a new compactness to her frame, a density summoned from I could not tell where. Most of us are simply party to history. It is like the weather. We walk out and if it is raining we get wet. But some handful of times I have had the odd experience of sitting across the table from one of the weathermakers. Some pill-mill oligarch or celebrated American war criminal. That was suddenly how I felt, hunched forward on my couch, staring at this anonymous zoologist.

"O.K." I said. "Very well. O.K."

"O.K. very well O.K. meaning you'll take the job?"

I splayed my palms.

"Why hire me?" I said. "Why not some credentialed, I don't know, private investigator?"

"Putting all cards on the table," she stepped sideways a little into the light. She was perhaps a half-inch shorter than me and startlingly good-looking in a remote patrician sort of way. "I am not unimportant in my field. I am, actually speaking, fairly well-respected, as zoologists go."

"And so," I said.

"And so I do not go around bragging about the fact that I killed the last of a species. It would not endear me to colleagues."

"I can imagine," I said.

"To be completely honest Mister Entrecarceles," she said, smoothing her face out, trying to affect a ruthless disposition, "it's compromising—could be compromising information. So, if I am going to hand over fodder for blackmail—"

"It might as well be to a famous liar," I completed.

"Well." She looked sheepish.

"I am flattered."

"Sorry. It's not personal." She let her eyes rove as she said it, "But will you take the job?"

"Well," I said, staring down frankly at Goober, then her face. "As my plans otherwise had consisted of selling Goober and then throwing myself into the ocean," I nodded, "yes, I will take your job."

Goober, hearing his own name, looked up excitedly.

"Oh dear," said Sairy Wellcomme. "I am so sorry to hear that you were considering that."

"Don't be." I waved my hand. "Worse things have happened to better people." She did not say anything. I felt suddenly energized, enlivened by this new sense of purpose, this rhinoceros murder.

"So to start with I'm going to need the name of the town where it happened."

"The town."

"The town, the city, in upstate New York where the rhinoceros died. The names of anyone who might have seen you the day your parents were killed."

"The town was called Littoral, New York."

"Literal."

"No." She spelled it out for me, then, as I wrote, and added, "It means *along the seashore*."

"Is it along the seashore?" I asked.

"No."

"Neat," I said.

A small pause settled between us where each began to turn over how little we knew about the other. I think she could tell I thought this was a sort of fool's errand because she said:

"I'll pay you quite a lot, Thomas."

"I'm sure you will," I said, but my mind was quite elsewhere at that point. After some more discussion of the job, my new employer gave me her contact information and departed. I stood alone in my cabin looking at my socks all drying on lampshades and doorknobs.

"Well," I said to Goober. He looked up at me, panting.

So that is how I cheated death by my own hand and began my investigation into the extinction of a species.

CHAPTER 2

Sairy Wellcomme's parents died in a gruesome accident on June 30th which you may or may not know as the 120th anniversary of the day, in 1882, when the U.S. government—We The People—executed the traitor Charles Guiteau by hanging him from a gibbet in Washington D.C.

The reason for this hanging, of course, was that Guiteau had, not-quite-a-year earlier, assassinated then-President James Garfield, for reasons I will get around to explaining later. The U.S. Government, being of a bloody and biblical mindset, was so aggrieved over the loss of President Garfield that the only thing it could think to do with his murderer was make theater out of his death. And so in 1882, the 38 states all got together and erected a gallows in the middle of Washington, and packed picnic lunches, and the lunatic Guiteau was made to hang for his crimes, while the crowd looked on and bayed with delight. The last words Guiteau ever spoke aloud were those of a poem he had written just for the occasion. The idea of the poem, he said, was "that of a child babbling to his mamma…"

Sairy who was twelve and did not much care for the violent stupidities of history, paid the date little mind (though it would come in due time to be burned in her memory forever). She occupied herself, instead, staring through a shop window on Bilbao Street which displayed a blue dress with yellow banana print, eyeing it covetously, noting how well it served the mannequin's unremarkable shape and speculating inwardly how it might work similar wonders with her own insanely apportioned twelve-year-old frame. Sairy was one of those people who is born, and goes through much of life Too Tall, and who always appears to those around her as a half-size too large no matter the company, no matter the room. This impression would last until well after college, I am told.

"Sairy," her mother said. "Sairy." The girl turned around and blinked twice. She took little note of her mother's face or hands, did not mark her voice or posture, as she did not know this would be the last ever day she saw her mother alive and there are ways in which the people we are closest to are the ones we pay the least attention.

Here is how Sairy's parents were slated to perish that day: in a slow-moving flood of exploding maple syrup. Here is why: a cost-saving effort to increase marginal shareholder value. But back to Sairy for the moment.

"Did you know," Sairy said conversationally, "that there is one Blue Whale who sings his song at 52 Hertz, even though all the rest of whales sing at 24 Hertz, so no other whale can hear this one?"

Her mother took off her headphones and stared at her strange offspring.

"What are you talking about?"

"I was reading about it," Sairy said. "They call him 52 Blue."

"O.K."

She said nothing. Sairy stared at the headphones around her mother's neck, looking deeply uneasy.

"It was just something I was reading," she said.

"And you felt it was imperative to tell me about this," her mother said, rubbing one eye. "This 52 Blue."

"What are we talking about?" injected Sairy's father cheerily.

"They also call him the loneliest whale in the world," Sairy continued.

"Do they," her mother said.

"Because nobody else can hear him, the whale."

"Sairy," her mother said, "is it here, swimming down this street, right now, your whale?"

Sairy blinked. "No."

"O.K. so then can we stop, please, talking about your whale?"

"It's not *my* whale." Sairy grew pink in the face. "It's just something I was reading." Her eyes began darting around the street nervously.

Sairy adored reading about wild animals, because she found that they alone could put all the peculiarities of being a human person into proper relation with one another. When you learned for instance that tortoises lived over 150 years, that walruses occasionally committed suicide, that male seahorses got pregnant, and pachyderms could sense impending tsunamis, it suddenly did not seem so strange to you that human beings should kill each other for paper money, or hack off the limbs of religious minorities for sport, or eat cheese whiz for nourishment. More than any other animal though, more than even 52 Blue, the creature Sairy best loved reading about was the mighty African Blue Rhinoceros. It was her favorite of all animals. When she was a girl, she'd dragged around a stuffed rhino everywhere she went, incessantly recounting rhinoceros facts to any adult who would listen, 'til eventually someone (her mother) informed young Sairy that stuffed animals were childish and silly and she must soon put away the trappings of childhood in order to properly transition to the unwondering nihilism of adult life.

"I'm going to go look at that dress," she announced loudly, not looking at her mother, who was herself not looking at her daughter. Sairy's father took his wife's hand softly in his own but did not say anything.

Emily Wellcomme was not a natural fit for motherhood. Part of the problem was societal: everyone from the Surgeon General on down promises women when they are pregnant that their hearts will swell and expand like The Grinch's with the holy gift of motherhood, that their chests will burst with a love unlike any they have known, trapped inside their DNA Helicases and X chromosomes. But the truth is there are all sorts of people born every day, and to assume they all conform to some normative brain chemistry based on what genitals they come out wearing is a fantastical bit of idiocy. Part of the problem was microcosmal: that Sairy's mother did not love her daughter, and had at moments, when Sairy was just a toddler, considered drowning the baby in the bath, or getting rid of it somehow, had nursed dark and morbid fantasies for a period, wept quietly in the shower feeling alien to herself, almost set the house on fire once, then went finally (at her husband's urging) to see a therapist, got her feelings sorted out, and now was resigned to living with and nurturing the mistake she had made, with a minimum of fanfare, 'til the strange creature was old enough to be cast out of the house. That this is not so distant a set of circumstances as you might imagine. That some shade of it has likely touched a person that you yourself know. And that to pretend otherwise is only to add yet more darkness to the private worlds of a bunch of people groping their way blindly through an already lonely-mad maze.

Sairy's father Miles was kind-hearted and rather doddering even for a relatively young man. Miles was always losing his car keys, overtipping waiters, accidentally giving people incorrect directions or walking in on his wife with other men. He loved his daughter, certainly, but not in a particularly astute way. He was a parent the way that certain people are fans of the New York Yankees. A sort of transient piece of his identity that meant different things at different times, and in different settings. As for his physical characteristics, I will go about describing them in Chapter 30, which concerns itself more fully with the events surrounding his death. Suffice it to say for now, that Miles possessed a sort of unremarkable handsomeness that did not add much in the way of character. It bears mentioning that despite these foibles, neither Mr. nor Mrs. Wellcomme were particularly bad at the physical *trade* of parenting, which is a lot of rote and routinization and does not require or even particularly expect passion from its practitioners.

Sairy went into the secondhand store (a converted bank building) that would soon save her life, as less than three quarters of a mile away a tidal wave of molten syrup roared down the street toward slow-footed onlookers, all clutching each other and screaming, and meeting death for the first embarrassing time.

Twelve-year-old Sairy, as I say, knew none of this. She'd already rucked and snatched the banana print dress off the plastic mannequin, accidentally knocked it (the mannequin) to the ground as she hurried past the mounted canoe paddles on the far wall and into the changing room to cry over her mother's bullying. In the small undisturbed quiet of the changing room Sairy wept, and recited the handful of really good curses she had learned, and wished her mother would die (she recalls this, her secret tearful wish, and feels in adulthood an incredible guilt over it, given what happened next) as she struggled to pull the dress over her body. Certain that it, like most everything else in her life to date, would be ill-fitting and strange.

But lo, providence! The dress was a perfect fit. It hung correctly at her shoulders, flowed down just past her scabby knees, she looked like Eleanor Roosevelt or an Olympian! She looked possessed and purposeful and strong and exactly the right amount of tall. It was at that moment, brushing past the curtain, emerging clutching some small handful of satisfactions from the secondhand store's dressing room, that Sairy Wellcomme made eye contact with first one, then another of her soon-to-be-late parents.

They stood very close to one another outside in the street, clutching each other's arms intimately on the sidewalk like the figurines atop a wedding cake, their mouths were pulled back from their faces, grim-set, their eyes very wide, muscles braced against some unseen blow, and then Sairy saw a flood of boiled-hot maple sap erupt from behind her mother's back, and she gasped as the person who'd birthed her was buffeted like a rag doll, knocked wildly backward, her skull dashed on a nearby brick wall, and yanked under by an unholy current, her father's body meanwhile pinned by some unseen weight against the plate glass of the secondhand store's display window, after a strained instant let go of the woman he loved, and she was swept away from him, as burns erupted all over the skin of his fragile little body, as he opened his mouth to voice some protest only to have scalding molasses flood down into his throat, gagging his lungs, bursting his stomach lining and blistering his esophageal tract, muting him instantaneously, pushing unbidden through his soft innards. Sairy crouched like some primitive forebear, way back in the Neolithic, an uncomprehending sapien flinch at the evolutionary violence unfolding before her twelve-year-old eyes, waiting with all muscles tensed for the plate glass to shatter, to share the same unhappy fate as her unhappy parents, but miraculously (likely, I have been informed, because the building was a converted bank, and because they never replaced the bank's plate glass) the glass of Littoral Secondhand held fast, never broke, strained beneath the flux and incredible weight of the sugary wave, but its panes did not crack, and so the whole unhappy scene appeared to Sairy through the windowpane as a colorful silent film, some cataclysm acted out on a lot already cast, and with a curious remoteness, like the burying of Pompei or the death of Christ on Golgotha, an image with no physical texture, created in tintype to teach you some abstract lesson about who Fate touches and why—and with that, Sairy Wellcomme's mind became a blank.

CHAPTER 3

I do not need to tell you, here in the 21st century, that you are probably being watched. This is not to inculcate some undue paranoia in your twitchy mammal brain. As with most other things, the security arm of the government is, by and large, indifferent to the citizens it claims to defend. Of course all surveillance states are not created equal—this is not to compare the authoritarian reach of, say, The Peoples Republic of China with more liberal technocratic governances like Finland—but it would not be unreasonable to say that you should expect you are under near-constant observation, should any high-ranking civil servant, or any private actor with a significant amount of juice, take even passing interest in your unremarkable (to them, I mean) life.

There is a probably-apocryphal anecdote about J. Edgar Hoover, at some point during his FBI tenure, summoning a cabal of rather powerful anticommunist reactionaries, business leaders and the like, to his office and explaining to them that the best, most assured way of defeating the Red Menace and the enemy within and all that, restoring peace and equilibrium to American life, would be the ability to daily itemize and track the miniscule financial transactions of individual agitators and political agents, to know their movements and intentions by way of micro-transaction, and so, the story goes, not one year later, the first Credit Card became commercially available as a domestic financial instrument.

Without getting bogged down in the particulars, the point I am trying to make here is not unduly complex. *In loco testis*—when you lack the person, check the tape. I do not know what became of Leanne Laura Swinburne, D.O.B. 1981, Irving County NY (though I do intend, in the course of my investigation, to try and find out). I cannot yet determine if she's died, disappeared, taken on a new identity, or gone to ground. I cannot find contemporaneous records that suggest she was ever picked back up or rearrested, though at the time it is not unfair to say there was a nontrivial amount of interest in ensuring she spent the next two-plus decades behind bars. I do not really care about delivering Ms. Swinburne to someone else's personal justice for her crimes. It appears to me that criminality, in this case as in many others, is a political designation without the appropriate political fetters. And I have always held that any incidence of politics where there is broad uncritical consensus is probably poisonous in some unseen way.

I do not have Leanne Swinburne, but I do have the tapes. I do, as part and parcel of a 2010 civil settlement in the case of *Littoral County Dept. of Corrections V. Chester Deal* (poor Chester, a low-level credit card fraud enthusiast who had a tendency when arrested to antagonize the people arresting him, had the bad luck of being the wrong person of color, mouthing off to the wrong psychotic corrections officer, on the wrong day of the calendar year, and ended up chained to a hospital bed in St. Lucius Presbyterian drinking his dinner through a straw for the next three months, and for this trouble was awarded a whopping $5,000 judgment by a county judge, which is to say $15,000 short of the cost of his legal and medical fees combined), have three hours of unsynced audio that corresponds with that tape (for you can compel a county to chronicle and store evidence of its own criminal incompetence but you cannot compel that county to do a good job of it), all of it available in the public sphere, for those who care enough to know.

I have the tape of the young girl speaking to the apparently blind woman, in a cadence very unlike that of any teenage girl I have ever heard speak. I have the tape of the woman in the jail cell hanging her head and reaching a hand out through the bars to clutch the girl's small fist. Then I have the cell door unlocking and the both of them leaving through the small atrium. The girl helping the jumpsuited woman into a battered old boat, then seating herself on the prow like coxswain, both of them gliding west toward the county line, a placid ship on untroubled toffee seas, serene tintype, froze idyll, on a day otherwise marked by massacre.

CHAPTER 4

I have begun reading up on amnesia, and trauma. You might remember that back in the 1990s there was a massive nationwide panic involving a scattered contingent of very troubled people who'd all for one reason or another been sent to hypnotherapists—going collectively public with revelations that they had been molested as children, many of them by their parents. That the instances of their molestation had been so traumatic that their brains had locked away the memories in some dark Pandoran box—repressed memories they were called—and that it was only thanks to the incredible perceptivity and professional savvy of these celebrity hypno-therapists that the individuals in question came to the realization that actually the ostensibly idyllic, Leave It To Beaver childhoods and pleasant home-lives they had all gone around believing they'd enjoyed, that in truth those were a great mental laundering of the horrific trauma of having grown up sleeping just down the hall from a monster, and, in many cases, that the *other* parent, while not out and out molesting the victims, had *known* and *protected* the pederasts who had preyed on these children, causing a psychological scar so deep and violent that the faulty recorders in the victims' brains had simply shut off, shoved the memories down below layers of pinkish neural tissue and gray matter, where they (the memories) would have stayed lodged forever, causing manifold neuroses and inexplicable harm, if not for the cutting edge hypnotherapy techniques that uncovered the whole horrific scandal. It was reported in The New York Times. It was the cover of Time Magazine.

Now it nearly goes without saying that the level of national opprobrium at these lurid medical revelations was profound, and that these married couples who had preyed on defenseless children, their own flesh and blood no less, were publicly destroyed, exposed, dragged, doggedly pursued and ruined by a polity that felt appropriately frustrated by the inadequacies of a slow-footed and unresponsive criminal justice system, that the hypnotherapists in question were appropriately enriched and enshrined in the green rooms of daytime television studios, that the courts, rushing to keep up with the righteous zeal of television jurists, threw an impressive number of people into U.S. Federal Prison, one of the worst places on earth for a child molester to end up, as America's prisons have a unique set of rituals specifically designed around what do with convicted pedophiles. And so it seemed for a time that while *happy* might be a bridge too far, that the Repressed Memory story and scandal had at least gotten itself a *Just* ending.

Until, that is, about fifteen years after the fact, evidence began to emerge that some mistakes had been made, some signals had gotten crossed. That the celebrity hypnotherapists had been caught more than once, implanting *false* memories in the heads of a bunch of angst-ridden people already in a highly suggestible state, that in truth there existed *scant-to-nil* medical evidence that memories could be repressed, let alone repressed-and-retrieved as claimed. That it was all an honest mistake. The hypnotherapists were over-zealous, the patients over-credulous, the national media overly excitable. But no one was made to give back their mansions or lose their Emeritus Chairs over it, obviously. Everyone was just trying their best, playing their small role, trying to eke out a living at the margins—though, obviously, all of the unfortunate sods who got swept up and convicted in the furor of the moral panic were left in jail, just in case. One of the truths of life in America, which you will not find written down in any of our amendments or congressional resolutions is that if you manage to commit a crime on a large enough scale, you are elevated, not punished, for it. And that conversely all the people you have wronged, by dint of the grotesque and horrifying size of their bad luck, get buried, willfully disremembered, for mass violence does not have a shaming effect on governments or people. Rather, violence aggrieves and traumatizes its practitioners in near-equal measure to its victims.

All this said, *caveat emptor*, I have no reason to doubt Sairy Wellcomme's claims that her mind went blank after witnessing her parents' violent elimination on June 30th, 2012.

Here are some things we *do* know about real cases of amnesia: The preeminent writer Oliver Sacks once made note of a man who'd been struck with herpes encephalitis of the brain, whose memory only lasted a few seconds at a time. The fellow in question kept a journal with time stamps, where all of the entries consisted more or less of the horrifying statement "I am awake." Over and over again. "I have woken." "I am awake." "I am properly awake now." Richard Wagner, the composer and anti-Semite, confessed in letters to being so overwhelmed with passion in the creation of certain projects that he would enter fugue states, losing track of hours or entire days of his life. We humans suffer certain very banal forms of amnesia all the time—the most famous example being Highway Hypnosis, arriving at a place without clear memory of the journey there, the full time that has elapsed in the crossing. Things as simple as lack of sleep or proper nutrition can result in memory gaps even in adults who are otherwise mentally stable. We likewise recall almost nothing of our childhoods before age seven or so, and this is completely unrelated to trauma, part of the very natural course of human cognitive development.

So it is not so difficult to imagine that a mind such as Sairy Wellcomme's, only recently (relatively speaking) come awake in the first place and suddenly put under abnormal duress, could resubmerge itself in the dreadful whiteness of pre-knowing. The term the Mayo Clinic has, for the sort of episodic un-awaking that Sairy Wellcomme says she suffered is "Transient Global Amnesia" which has a wonderful communitarian feel to it. A sense that one is a part of something much greater than oneself.

One strange thing about the diagnosis of Transient Global Amnesia in this case is that generally speaking, it is a condition confined to people of middle or late-middle age. Cases of children suffering Transient Global Amnesia without it being attributable to a chronic neurological condition are exceedingly rare (though not unheard of). The handful of neurologists I have talked to, however, have told me this is by no means some kind of an argument against the diagnosis. One advised me to "think of the human brain as a supercomputer that sometimes runs with the software capability of a 1998 Packard Bell."

It is of course possible that Ms. Wellcomme remembers perfectly well everything that transpired, everything she did, and simply wishes not to suffer the consequences for her actions, but I have my doubts. After all, the incident and her story were both buried in the past, unable to hurt her, until she came to my door and brought both to my sorry attentions. It is possible that Sairy Wellcomme suffers some sort of antisocial personality disorder, what low-information true-crime con-sumers would flippantly mischaracterize as "sociopathy" and that there is some, for lack of a better term, self-destructive drive within her troubled brain that compelled her to seek me out, to reopen the book on her strange past, but I personally doubt it. I would not be the first person to be manipulated by someone suffering narcissistic or antisocial personality disor-der, but something of my initial interview with her made me feel that she truly was upset by what had happened to her—by what she had done but did not remember doing—and that she truly was seeking out answers via the only avenue that she could work out for herself.

Turning all this over and over again inside a begrogged brain, I packed Goober into the passenger seat of my rusticate Nissan, and set out before sunrise the day of April 29th to turn over rocks in the town where seventeen years earlier a twelve-year-old had watched her parents boil alive in the streets, then inexplicably hatched a plot to kill a lonely rhinoceros. Anyone who's spent any amount of time in a more sensible part of the world could tell you that America is far too big to be one coun-try. It ought to be at least eight different highly hostile nations that are all constantly insulting one another and jacking up trade tariffs. Instead we are left with a gigantic hard-to-nav-igate amalgam, hugely flat in places, rock-strewn, desiccate, rusty, gorgeous, backwards, toweringly mountainous, sub-tropical, biologically diverse, inbent and insular, eccentrically ugly, killingly cold, and all over we are called Americans and we call our home America, and when we say it we mean the whole unwieldy project, with all its politics and massacres and fantasies and soda machines. There is no way to be sane and sensible and describe yourself with a straight face as an

American. It is a great joke we are all playing on one another. This is all to say that it took over six hours of driving with minimal stops to get from where I lived to the landlocked polity of Littoral, New York, and not once did I cross a state line, or make a wrong turn. Too big! When I arrived day had broken and the little hamlet had begun lumbering along at all its irrelevant businesses. I parked my car, got out, and went about trying to find someone who might have witnessed the 2012 molasses explosion, and who might have seen a Too Tall little girl, wearing a banana print dress, headed west with a deadly sense of purpose. And that is how I met old Mrs. Gina Barlow.

CHAPTER 5

Here is the thing Gina Barlow recalls most clearly about the day her husband and baby died: the temperature. Gina was born with a peculiar talent—it feels strange to call it a superpower, given as how little power she has been afforded over the actual facts of her own life to date—she always, always knows what temperature it is, within an eighth of a degree of Fahrenheit. There is no particular use in this heightened sensitivity, since the advent of the Alcoholic Thermoscope some five hundred odd years prior in the Medici court, no job on earth (at least in the present economy) prioritizes Gina's talent as useful or necessary. It is sort of tragic in a way. Still and all everyone agrees, it sure is a neat trick. On the day Gina's husband and baby both died of drowning, traumatic shock, pulverization, whichever took them first she does not want to know, it was exactly 38° Fahrenheit, give or take an eighth of a degree, in Littoral, New York (est. 1835 Y.O.O.L.)—which is one reason, among many, many, many others, Gina thought it so strange when she saw the little girl wearing the banana-patterned sundress, as the afternoon had not even cracked 40, that even in all the ensuing chaos and horror and bedlam she took note of the sight.

At the moment of their wholesale expungement from the ranks of the human race, here is, more or less, what Gina had been thinking about her husband and baby child: *Thank God They Are Gone.* This is not representative of some great streak of cruelty or callousness in Gina Barlow's personal character, mind you. Being a mother to someone and a wife to someone else (in that order) requires a giving over of yourself, even the parts of You you would like to hold fast to, the bits you wish could stay gummed to your soul to only share with yourself in the dead of night, even those are ripped away, all artifice ripped away, 'til you are walking around all the time sore and tired, the great Servicer Of Needs, you are a faucet that never quite stops running, as a mother, even when the tap is off, you are a steady drip-drip-drip of obliterated ego and happy obligation. This is the biological job we've designated for millions of human beings in the world and there is no way to do it correctly and nobody ever gets an award or sleeps an untroubled sleep over it and so when I say that Gina Barlow was deeply elated, in a real human way, that her dead (not that she knew) husband and dead (not that she knew) baby were gone, and away from her, that they had vacated her life for a holy half-hour while she allowed herself to do the slow, glorious, learned work of opening up her bakery on Bilbao Street to absorb into her pores the quiet of the empty shop and the way god speaks to us in the silences, I need you to understand that I am not saying she was a monster or a bad mom or a bad wife. That if the above rendered description leads you to believe that poor Gina was somehow deficient in her motherly, wifely duties, not up to the scratch of some fanciful standard you have decocted in your mean little mind, then both I and interviewee Gina Barlow would encourage you to catch the first train directly to hell. No version of life is easy, but some are harder than others. Try and remember that, the next time you ask to speak to someone's manager.

To address another concern head-on: I am not exactly in the intention of writing a book here (as I believe publishers and newspeople to be among the lowest forms of human life). Neither though, would I say that these notes serve simply as diary entries. It is true that I have always taken contemporaneous notes while researching a story (I have got nobody's idea of a good memory, and anything I do not write down becomes confabulated with the fictions of my mind or lost forever beneath a heap of irrelevant concerns) but also these pages do not read like my usual illegible journalist's shorthand. When I was a boy I was forced to retire from my School's archery team after accidentally fletching an arrow into the gam of an unsuspecting assistant coach. I have always had a poor sense of where the target is. So I cannot very well say what it is I intend to do with all this paper, these stacks of dead trees. At any rate I would need the Principal Subject's permission to publish her story and I do not foresee her giving it, nor myself pushing very hard. In short: I am writing this down, do not ask me who it is for.

So here, in plainest terms is what the about-to-be-widowed Mrs. Gina Barlow saw out her shop window the day that 80 people were killed in Littoral township, in relief of the high bright afternoon sun: She saw around 3:12 pm a wave of considerable size and amber color gush down Bilbao street, knocking over two food carts, sweeping the legs from under fleeing pedestrians, uprooting planted trees and spare chunks of gravel, pouring through gutters into alleyways, past all stop signs and red lights. She saw phantom limbs thrashing for desperate purchase above the churning current of the exploding wave, she saw scorched skin and contorted faces and heard through her cracked window the agonized screams and gurgled cries of neighbors and acquaintances. She could scarcely believe it was real—same as if you or I, one moment, were tending to the banal particulars of our daily routine, and the next, were playing audience to some violent massacre. Gina blinked through the windowpane, as some ticker inside her noted the temperature outside rise, by one degree, by two, by ten and fifty. She saw curled warbles of heat shimmer coming off the liquid's surface as buildings shook from the initial propulsive force. She braced. A minute passed. Nothing further happened. The current flattened out and the level of the molasses fell, leaving a sickly-scorched waterline on the sides of the brick buildings opposite. As it fell lower-still to around knee-height, and the current stagnated, Gina felt the temptation to peek her head out, to see how close the horrid brown river had come to the sill of her own shop's little window, until she saw Eugene Ionesco, two shops down, open his own front door and wade his way out onto the sidewalk. Gina nearly called out for him to stop, then alive with dread, saw his face change as Eugene looked down at his submerged knees and began screaming, feeling at once the temperature of the stagnant liquid, and, poor old fool, in what must have been a horrible amount of pain, pinwheeling his arms backwards trying to pick up his boiling legs, caught in the viscous soup, losing balance and falling sideways, facedown into a boiling sticky morass trying desperately to emerge again, attempting a sort of underwater pushup fighting against a profound surface tension and forms of pain you or I cannot well know, weighed down by the suffocating amber swamp, emerging briefly with patches of hair and skin missing, sloughed off, pink and ghastly, then staggering and falling in again, to lie quiet and drown in a horrible amber tomb, and Gina knew at that moment two things: One was that it would be hours until the liquid outside was cool enough that she could safely try and escape the shop. And the second was that her husband and baby were dead. That she was alone, alone, alone in the world. The scariest word in the English language by a country mile.

For a long time—perhaps two hours, perhaps six—she sat waiting, gripping her arms, shaking, occasionally moaning aloud in the quiet of the bakery, made suddenly horrible and satanic, like the living house of Mausolus, the quiet, she waited, alone, and how could she not make note, in that state, of the sight she caught next? Having nothing else to occupy herself, waterlogged with profoundest dread and doubting grief, certain images will stick in your mind, your whole long life, Gina Barlow saw a woman in an orange jumpsuit, coming down the street in a rowboat, leaning forward and pulling on the oars at a low, regular rhythm, looking fixedly at nothing, and there, standing with one foot raised on the boats prow, like George Washington crossing the Delaware, a little girl in a banana print dress.

CHAPTER 6

"You're fixed up real good now babykiller."

Leanne Swinburne, involuntary guest of the state of New York, is prone on the top bunk of an otherwise empty set of metal beds, laying on the chickenwire frame as there is no mattress, with hands laced above her belly, pretending not to hear the guard calling down the uninhabited block.

The ceiling is spotted with black mold. She breathes in and her breath catches inside a wet chest. The jumpsuit is scratchy, chafes at the underarms and ankles. Leanne has got these little patches of bare irritated skin that she stares at, touching them lightly with a cool finger sometimes to pass the minutes. She has not been allowed to read or write since being transferred here. There had previously been a television, playing reruns of some satanic gameshow, in the far corner of the hall, but its presence had upset a schizophrenic woman they'd brought in for spitting on a cop. They removed the television, then removed the schizophrenic woman. The television never came back in.

"I've talked to some of the guards over at Clinton, you know what they told me?"

Leanne can hear him walking up closer to the bars of her cell and stopping there. How much of a woman's life is spent pretending not to hear things she clearly was intended to hear? Catcalls, and sly workplace misogynies, the lurid importunacies of street perverts and the jokes that could end a marriage if you let them. How much of your life is spent in a sort of forced unlistening? Who inculcates this skill in little girls, right beside algebra and cursive? Against her better judgement Leanne turns on her side, glances over toward the hallway. County corrections officer Dan Bondurant, his badge all shiny and lapels straight as rulers, stands there leering through the bars.

Leanne sighs the tiredist sigh in the world. The smile widens.

"They told me it's like a bordello for the guards up there." He takes a hit from a vaporizer pen that does not, by its smell, seem like it contains tobacco, not that it makes a difference to Leanne. "You know what a bordello is Leanne?"

"Type of red wine," Leanne hazards.

Dan Bondurant's face stays frozen, trying to game out whether he is being mocked.

"It *means*," he says after a pause that lasts too long, "it's like a whorehouse for the boys up there. A different girl every night. That's what my friend said."

Leanne turns back around so she is facing the wall.

"You wake me when they're ready to transfer me, Captain Dan," she says flatly.

She can hear Bondurant deliberately-not-moving from his post directly in front of her cell. Can hear him playing with the change in his pocket.

"Maybe you want to get some practice in before they move you," he says slowly, drawing out the words, and she can hear that he is palming the cell key (which, it being the 21st century and all, is actually a key fob) jangling, clutching and unclutching. "Maybe you'd enjoy that." Leanne's heart begins to pump faster and her eyes start to rove around the cell for loose fixtures, something, anything she could use, if needs be, to fend off an attack. Cemented brick chickenwire metal frame window wall concrete floor metal toilet nothing, nothing. Everything here is bolted down, lugnutted together, to stop people maiming their bunkmates or hanging themselves with it. Leanne turns back around and tries to betray none of what she is feeling as she looks Dan Bondurant witheringly up, and then down. His carrion eyes rove her dowdily-clad body, lingering in places, standing on one side of the bars, she laying on the other.

"Or maybe you're already worn-in, like a baseball glove," he continues. It is incredible how much a man can look like a wolf. There is the sound of a truck backing up outside, some shouting.

"I have syphilis Dan," she says. "If you try and touch me, I'll give you syphilis." Time seems to be passing impossibly slow here, in this alone-cell in a concrete corridor, in a concrete world, would someone hear her yelling, or come if she called? Bondurant has got the key ring around his forefinger and he is swinging the fob so that it lands with a thwap in his palm with each revolution. She is higher up than he is. She could get the jump on him. Thwap. Claw out his eyes. Thwap. He shakes his head smiling.

"Nice clean girl like you? I bet not. I bet you're just fine Leanne." She will jump and land on him as soon as he walks in the cell. He is larger by one hundred pounds probably but she can use his weight against him, whatever that means. She will claw out his eyes and kill him. Thwap. Every muscle in her body is an electric wire. Leanne gives herself over to a fit of wet coughing. He has got the key fob in hand.

Then suddenly, a voice calls Dan Bondurant's name, faintly, from outside. Another man. The other guard, she thinks, the heavyset one. Calls to him, Dan, to come and take a look at this, as something fuck-all strange is going on outside at the refinery, right this very minute. And Dan Bondurant, glancing down at the key in his hand, then back up at Leanne, pauses, looking a bit rueful, and calls curtly:

"*Yeh, coming,*" and he walks slowly away from her, with Leanne's heart going about a thousand miles an hour, and is mercifully gone.

The door closes and suddenly she is gasping clawing at her own throat, having an honest-to-god panic attack for the first time in her adult life. She bites into the canvas flesh of her bicep and looses an animal bellow into the crook of her elbow. How can things have gone so bad, so quickly? This is the question poor people are asking themselves all over America at any given moment. How, how? She will not be assaulted. She will not be transferred to Clinton. She will murder that guard or murder herself. Die fighting like some starved circus animal. She will show men she has been listening all along, to everything, to all of it. That she remembers every word.

No telling how long until he will come back.

Take in these eight things with your eyes: Molded ceiling tile, leaky sink, half-dead fluorescent, painted brick, your laceless sneakers, a bedscrew fused to the frame by rust, video camera, crucifix above the door. How many fingers have touched and fashioned these objects? How many foreign hands' work have travelled through time and arrived in this room with you? To what purpose? None at all except that every room you ever walked into was built by hands, and before you never noticed. Accustom yourself to this ten-feet. Do not move through it right away but recognize that you could. That most of the rest of your foreseeable days will take place in this ten-feet or some other. The only things left in your possession are your body and the space it moves through. Maybe they are the only two things you ever owned. Guard these jealously, for the lease knows no guarantor. Only your conviction will fix it in the body politic.

Of course she could not know, Leanne could not, what queer designs the universe has outfitted for her. That she will not go to Clinton or to the grave, that she will in short order be freed by a twelve-year-old orphan girl in a stolen dress, that she is about to embark upon the strangest odyssey of her life, that these dark auguries only mark a beginning.

Outside the barred window she hears what sounds like sloshing water, and County corrections officer Dan Bondurant saying "What in fuck's sake—" and then a great and violent commotion draws Leanne's attention. She looks out the window, of course. She cannot help but look.

Herenow in Littoral, New York, in the quiet of County Holding, a barestrip truth suddenly exposes itself, insists rudely on being seen, with no one but poor Leanne Swinburne in her lonely concrete box to countenance it: some fates will come on you like a wave, catch you in the back, tumble you ass-over-teakettle, thrash and squeeze your little body until you could not begin to say which way is up, and then, just when you have been yanked all the way away from your moorings, just as you are done starving for air, that is when a horrible wisdom will flood into your heartsblood alighting your nerves with protean fire, every inch an agony, let no calendar record this passage, clocks will run backwards, every substanceless molecule combusting at once until in the dark a door slams and you are once again left alone knowing on your endings: how we revel in blindness, how we exit in pain.

CHAPTER 7

Here is the first thing the befugued Sairy Wellcomme noticed, after watching both her parents die violently in a sticky flash flood of molten sugar and tree sap: a pair of canoe paddles. The only other person inside Littoral Secondhand was the shop owner Ms. Laura Bronner. Bronner was painted pale with shock, gasping and blubbering and shaking her towish head back and forth on account of how deeply upsetting she found the scene she'd just witnessed. Sairy Wellcomme whose mind had gone offline for one reason or another, was the exact opposite. The little girl was, by Ms. Bronner's accounting, the picture of sangfroid.

"Have you got a canoe?" Sairy asked conversationally.

Laura Bronner who was still clutching herself, thinking of all her friends and family-members who might have been caught by the amber explosion, shook her head uncomprehending, not so much staring at this strange little girl as staring through her toward some haunted middle distance. Sairy, rather impatient with all this adult hysteria, pointed to the pair of paddles mounted on the rear wall and repeated:

"Excuse me Ma'am do those belong to a canoe?"

Mrs. Bronner (who it should be noted was having a very sensible and correct reaction to the massacre of her friends and neighbors) blinked and shook a few more times, limbs all atremble. Twelve-year-old Sairy Wellcomme tugged her earlobe, deeply annoyed by this, and walked over to the wall to try and fetch down the two mounted canoe paddles. She stood on tip-toes and hyper-extended her arms but even for a Too Tall little girl, the paddles eluded easy capture. She jumped, trying to swat the paddles off the wall but while her fingers brushed the worn-down handles, still she proved unable to get them down. Sairy Wellcomme began casting around the shop for something to stand on. And it must have been the physical juxtaposition of the girl standing in front of the paddles that prompted it, because suddenly some gear in Laura Bronner's grief-fogged brain caught, and all at once she understood what Sairy Wellcomme had been asking her, if not exactly why.

Littoral Secondhand *did* in fact have a battered-looking canoe sitting in the back storeroom closet. On slow days in the summer, Laura would close up the shop early and go with her fiancé to the lake to paddle aimlessly along the surface for a few hours, touching each other's knees and speculating wildly about lake monsters.

Laura Bronner walked stiff-legged into the back room of the store where large bins were piled high with recently donated, unlaundered clothing. She waded in past strewn articles and gaping cardboard cartons and finally arrived at the back storeroom closet where she kept personal items so as not confuse them with the donations for sale. Laura threw open the door and dragged the old boat out by its prow out onto the showroom floor. I have asked Laura several times now, why she felt it was incumbent upon her to follow the orders of a twelve-year-old girl, in the wake of a molasses explosion, Ms. Bronner's answer each time has been different and never entirely satisfactory, but here is one journalist's unlearned two-part theory on the matter:

1) There is nothing so nice after a catastrophe (and in general, frankly) as to be or feel *of use*.

2) One thing that seems fairly clear, after many muddled interviews, is that Sairy Wellcomme was not a normal

twelve-year-old and did not possess a normal twelve-year-old's charisma (or lack thereof). All the adults I spoke to who recalled interacting with her likewise recalled a real, almost unsettling sense of authority that emanated from the young girl in the banana print dress. Some seemed deeply agitated by the memory (and my questions in general), as if it cast into disarray several of the comfortable post-hoc assumptions around which they had all built relatively happy lives.

Laura Bronner dragged the worn-down canoe in front of Sairy Wellcomme, then got out a footstool and unmounted the two paddles hung against the wall and lay them down on the floor of the boat, as a cat presenting a mouse to its master. Sairy Wellcomme blinked.

"Thank you."

"Where will you go?" Laura Bronner said in an airy, unconcerned way.

"Down," said the little girl. "I have a very long way yet. I need to travel down."

"Where are your parents?" Bronner said.

Wellcomme gestured faintly toward the scene outside and the shop owner began to hyperventilate. Not wanting to turn and look a second time.

"The bottom of the boat might melt," Bronner fretted, her mouth very dry. "The fumes might kill you. You might die."

I have gotten a sense from speaking to survivors of various attacks and blights and pandemics over the years (this one among them) that this style of conversating is not so strange as it might seem to you or I. That this instant frankness or artless intimacy—or whatever you'd like to call it—predominates among survivors of any major horror, like as if the mass blood-letting both parties have witnessed has somehow managed to reach back into their histories, redraw family trees, so that they suddenly share some common ancestor and through that a more common understanding.

Of course, I should emphasize, we *do* all share a common ancestor. We all were born in Africa many Millenia ago, lay side by side in woven cribs, clutching each other's little fists. Our obligation to each other is written in our blood. Rings like a tuning fork through the marrow of our bones. But it is only in select groups—those privy to the very worst tragedies that can befall a community—that this soul-stirring seems to rouse, and stay roused, for a time at least. I don't know what to do with this information, or if it will be useful to you, whoever you are. As I have already expressed to my employer Ms. Wellcomme, my next plan after I finish with this mystery, is to swim out into the ocean, to keep swimming until I am so far I cannot get back. I suppose I just wish for you to know that while I was here I saw these things, and met these people. That there were moments when it did not feel so very alone.

"I might die," Sairy conceded, dragging the heavy canoe toward the entrance, pushing it heedlessly nose-first into the scalding, thigh-high flood outside the door.

"But death is not just an absence."

Laura Bronner, apparently satisfied with this answer, nodded, and began to help the little girl into her boat.

CHAPTER 8

I don't know if you recall your science teacher ever telling you, that the buoyancy of an object is proportional to the difference between the density of the object in question and the density of the liquid upon which it is floating. Put another way, as molasses or syrup is quite a bit thicker than regular old lakewater, that means that molasses would *push up* that much more on the hull of a regular old lake canoe than water ever would. In practical terms this also means that one could add markedly more weight to the *inside* of said canoe, without it being at risk of capsizing or needing to be bailed out at all. Unclear whether this calculus occurred to Sairy Wellcomme as she paddled down Bilbao Street under a high afternoon sun.

It is likewise unclear if Sairy set out from Littoral Second-hand with a very well-defined sense of purpose—or, rather, how she could possibly have done so. It is easy to know where you are going, reader—locate the sun in the sky, or sight some moss on a northfacing tree—it is quite a different matter to know *wherefore and how*. I know from the testament of Ms. Laura Bronner that the little girl, as she situated herself in the boat, averted her gaze so that she did not look at the remains of her poor father, lying limbs atangle beside the sturdy shop window. I know that Sairy, who had tried out for and been cut from her junior high school's rowing team a year previous, took the oars in hand with something approaching fluidity, and that she then, with barely a backward glance, began charting a steady westbound course, which would in due time bring her down the length of the frozen scene, to the bad end of Bilbao Street past the small County Holding building, the cash bail storefronts, past the strip malls and We Buy Gold outlets, toward the erstwhile source of the wave's explosion. The little girl did not seem even particularly to notice the incredible heat of the liquid through which she rowed (though I have been told by other witnesses that it was like to singe the hair off your forearms) nor the grisly forms trapped inside it, meekly stirring, wailing in pain, like some Hieronymus Bosch brought horribly to flesh. Sairy Wellcomme rowed calmly on, and if she had a plan, she kept her own quiet counsel regarding it, not that she had anyone to talk to.

She glided slowly through viscous ooze for perhaps thirty minutes or more, grunting from the strain of continuously picking up the heavy-coated oars, dropping them back down, when she heard a voice, and looked up.

"Hello?"

The little girl froze in her seat, ceased paddling, craned her neck around for a sign of a speaker.

"Hello is someone there?" the voice said.

"I am," Sairy said, straightening.

"Are you—Jesus Christ, who is there? Can you help?"

Sairy did not say anything for a while.

"I can't see," said the voice sounding distressed. Sairy looked around. There was no one on the street, nor the nearby rooftops. The voice came from her right, from what looked to be a drab, squat building with few windows and only a single entrance.

"I looked out the window and now I can't see anything."

The voice lapsed into silence. There was perhaps the unremarkable sound of sniffling adult tears.

"Flash blindness." Sairy Wellcomme cleared her throat.

"What?" came a dry cracked voice, from within the building's echoey guts.

"My dad was an ophthalmologist. He told me if you see something really bright it can scar your retinas. Like a camera. It's called flash blindness." Sairy studied the building. She was not too young to know the look of it. To know what it meant. "Welders get it a lot," she continued, hesitating.

"My name is Leanne," said the voice.

"Hi Leanne."

"What's your name?"

Sairy did not say anything.

"What happened?"

"Didn't you see?"

" . . ."

"An explosion. And, there's a flood now. Like oil or something." Sairy dipped her oar in the water and watched it drizzle back down in brown mucosal threads. "Hot oil maybe."

"Are people dead?"

"Not everyone."

"How old are you? You sound young."

Sairy could see a pair of fingers, pale and slender, stuck out through a barred window.

"What'd you do, Leanne?"

The fingers withdrew a moment as if they had touched a hot stove.

"What?"

"Why did they lock you in jail?" Sairy said, her tone becoming hard like she had heard her mother's tone become, in times of unpleasant decision-making.

"I." The unseen woman's voice faltered, she hemmed. "I stole. Bread," she said finally.

It is possible, even probable, that Sairy Wellcomme (only twelve please recall) was taken in by this lie. But we ought also to at the very least consider the possibility that young Sairy knew full well that she was being lied to, and either out of expedience, or pity, or as a result of some other curious private calculus, decided all at once to help Leanne Swinburne. That the apparently simple wholesale act of *deciding to help* another person, is one of the most underratedly potent political decisions you can make in the course of your relatively short tenure as a human being on this planet, capable of skirting any number of Newtonian laws, logistical crises, prohibitive logics, and that there exist vast economic and political structures erected solely for the purpose of discouraging you, reader, from making such a decision in your own life.

Either way—whether it was for the right reasons or for very wrong ones (and what those would even be)—all at once, and just like that, the fates of a blind convict, an orphaned twelve-year-old, a small town, and an unsuspecting African Blue Rhinoceros, were all morbidly intertwined, bound, one to the other, in some ancient and nameless sacrament that no church has yet been able to put the coin on. And if that recounting is not sufficient to your mind, then it is beyond my poor powers as narrator to explain it to you further.

"Please," Leanne called in the silence. "I'll starve in here. They've all forgot about me, and if you don't help, I'll starve."

I don't know whether she truly believed this or not.

Sairy paddled closer to the building.

"Where's the key," she said finally.

The fingers wrapped around the bars flexed and extended.

"Do you think I'll get it back?" came the voice.

"What?" Sairy said distractedly.

"My, uh." The woman seemed embarrassed at asking, at having to ask. "My *eyes*. Do you think—"

"—I don't know," said Sairy curtly. "Probably not, no."

She half-swiveled in her seat to survey the scene. Now she saw, not 100 yards away from where she floated, what she supposed was the source of the catastrophe. A great tank connected to five more tanks, with a limp hose slithering out between their struts. Ruptured open at one side, drooling yet more molasses at an unrushed clip into the street while a fire raged far off. The cooked skeletal exterior of a delivery truck, the tank cracked open like an eggshell, what had used to be the driver sitting inside the front seat of the cab, tar-black and rigid, permanently froze there, the nose of the truck half-way tucked into a drainage ditch. A few smaller fires still burned on the noxious brown surface. No living thing moved, for as far as she could see. The level of the liquid was deeper here. Sairy could see shapes, submerged in doorways or lying unmoving in intersections, lumpish shadows, wrapped around lightpoles, slumped against walled concrete, all drowned or burned or both. Gone gone. All in a sorry, fateless instant.

"I need you to tell me where the key is Leanne."

"The guard has it," Leanne said, finally bringing her voice down into a controlled register. All sorrow choked out of it, the temperance of her old self predominating. "Dan, his name was."

"O.K.," Sairy said, staring down at two slick forms curled in front of the jail entrance. "I can't exactly ask him his name."

She moved the canoe closer to the front door.

"He's the smaller one," came Leanne Swinburne's voice.

"Smaller, smaller," Sairy repeated, then jammed the oar underneath one of the laquered, unconscious forms and half-wedged it up near the lip of the boat. The creature was heavy. The thin cloth covering on its back fell away, disintegrated from heat and long soaking, revealing a troubled pink-red expanse patched together from exposed nerve and underskin.

Suddenly, the creature moaned. Sairy Wellcomme cried out, her throat closing up for a terrible second. The thing tried to stir, swinging fleshy arms toward the lip of the boat, keening blindly from a lipless carbuncled mouth. Sairy yelled and tried to push the boat away. The boiled creature reached out to try and grab the girl, scrabbling against her leg, hot, hot, unseeing, trying to pull her in, she brought down the paddle *thwap* on the creature's arm, it groaned again, it squirmed for her, trying to overturn the boat, send her sinking over the side. Sairy brought down the paddle a second, a third time, swallowing, trying in vain to gulp air down a throat that would not open. She sliced the paddle sideways, crashing down on the pink thing's hairless brow. *Thwap.* Finally, half in the boat, legs still dangling in the thickly ooze, the horrible humanish thing fell permanently still. Sairy, her throat finally dilating, wheezed, sitting there bent double, desperate for more air. She paused, stared for a minute, then reached out slowly, muscles still screaming alarm, to fish in the creature's pocket.

As soon as she touched the cloth with her fingers, sticky and hot as if it had just come out of an oven, it peeled and fell away, just as the man's shirt had, revealing a vast expanse of mottled thigh. A horrible stench rose up and filled Sairy's nostrils, the girl's eyes watered, she stifled a gag, breathed only through her nose.

"Hello?" called Leanne Swinburne's voice after several minutes, then quietly to herself, "She left."

"I didn't leave," called Sairy annoyed, saliva filling her mouth and itching the back of her throat. "I'm just getting the key."

And as if her words had made it manifest, suddenly, gloriously, Sairy Wellcomme felt a blue-gray fob on a silver chain fall into her palm. And with a little cry of triumph, she raised a sneaker and kicked the horrible form back into its liquid grave. It sunk with a heavy splash and for a second all was quiet and the only sound was her breathing. Then she announced: "I am coming inside."

The interior of Littoral County Processing & Central Holding was small and quiet, for it was a fairly uneventful little town, with a respectable-sized underclass to wage war on, but no great streak of criminality in its DNA. The one lurid story that had dominated the last month's news coverage in the county had been that of Leanne Swinburne, who now sat blind and frightened inside her small holding cell. The entrance gave way to a glass foyer with a single unmanned desk set beside a metal and glass door.

Beside the desk a boxy, VHS television, mounted on a stool, blasted competition cooking shows into the tomblike quiet. A half-finished bottle of Diet Coke sat with the cap off beside the keyboard of an ancient-looking desktop on a reddish-brown blotter, and Sairy nearly glanced backward at the entrance, thinking of the miserable creature she had battered with the canoe paddle, wondering if those blistered lips had not a half-hour prior sucked at the coke bottle's rim, absent any sense of foreboding. Sairy pushed through the unlocked door and found herself in the building's small interior cell-block.

The hall was dark gray and septic-smelling, with spaghetti-drains placed at intervals in the floor's depressed center. There were four rows of empty cells on the left-hand side facing toward the town's large sugar factory. To the right were three likewise empty cells, steel bars flung open exposing grim interiors, seatless metal toilets with attached greywater sinks and bunkless metal beds with no occupants. In the fourth cell, leaning, with arms crossed against one of the metal bedposts of the lower bunk, was a woman in an orange jumpsuit.

Leanne Swinburne was auburn-haired and athletic looking. She was not tall by any means, but neither did she strike a diminutive presence, standing somewhere around five foot eight inches tall, she had those pronounced shoulder and forearm muscles that are signature to nurses and mothers, women whose bodies are in a constant state of unpretty use.

Sairy Wellcomme took a single step forward. Leanne Swinburne's face moved at the sound.

"Hello?"

"It's me, Leanne."

"It's you," said the blind woman. "I thought maybe the guard…"

"The guard is dead."

"Oh," Leanne said sounding untroubled by the news, "what a Christian shame."

"Just me," Sairy said again, stepping closer.

"How old are you?"

Sairy did not say anything. Leanne tried again.

"What's your name?"

"I'm afraid," Sairy began slowly, "that if I tell you my name it will convey the wrong impression."

Leanne Swinburne scuffed the floor of her cell with one sneaker.

"What impression?" she asked.

"Of still being alive, at present."

Leanne straightened warily.

"How old did you say you were?"

"The problem is, your present doesn't exist anymore, Leanne," said the girl, ignoring the question, sounding very calm. Leanne involuntarily took a half-step away from the bars, her skin broke into gooseflesh at the sound of this strange little girl's voice.

"Your past is inert. It's like a weight, holding you here. Your future isn't born yet, and when it *is born*, the shape it takes will be stranger than you can possibly imagine. And here you are in a cell. And if I walk out, with this key in my pocket," Sairy Wellcomme jangled the key, "if it takes them a week, two weeks to come and find you, if no one remembers where you are, Leanne—what is your name *if it only exists* for you? That's my question."

One of the greywater sinks was not entirely off. It dripped into its metal basin to her right. The girl made no move toward the door that Leanne could hear.

"Are you going to do that?" she said, suddenly unsure what she hoped the girl's answer might be. Suddenly certain that this was not a conversation about opening a cell door.

"Am I going to, what? Leave you here?"

Leanne swallowed. Her throat was all out of saliva. Aridly dry. She remembered the rule of threes she'd learned while camping as a girl once. You could survive three weeks without food, three days without water, three minutes without air.

"Of course not," came the voice, impatient. "But it's not out of any great affection."

She was missing one. *Hours.* Three hours without what?

"Then what do you want?" Leanne said, her stomach knotted up with dread. The girl laughed. Not unsympathetic, the laugh, but still strange in this place. The key dangled from her fist.

"I don't want anything from you, Leanne. There's no trade you could make, commensurate in value to what's in my hand."

She heard the girl move closer.

"What I *get* in exchange is your name. Not some remote history in a police file, not some suspended present. I get *the eternity of you* stretching out blind in both directions, I get to *know your name* Leanne. And either I know it, or you forget it, that is the choice. I am offering you a choice now."

And for a moment Leanne Swinburne did not move or breathe or think but stood rigid and alone feeling the blood that beat in her ears loudly, wondering if it had always been so loud.

"My parents are dead," continued the girl. Leanne jumped as if smacked. "I am twelve years old, but I was just born. I am here on horrible business, and if you choose, you can come with me. And if you choose not, you can go your own way. It's not a question of being left in this jail cell, Leanne, it's really not. It's a question of would you even notice if you walked right into another one?"

Three hours without shelter. That was it. In untenable environs, exposed to extremes, a person can only survive three hours without some kind of shelter to protect them.

Leanne Swinburne, involuntary guest of a state that'd forgot her, reached a slender arm out through the cell's bars, closed her fingers around a small cold hand that did not flinch away, and opened her mouth to speak. Leanne was ready to speak, finally.

CHAPTER 9

"You understand what we do here, S—Mister Herbert?" one of the two interviewers asked brightly.

Neizar Muntasser said nothing, adjusting his fake glasses so they perched delicately on the bridge of a waxen proboscis. He loved elaborate disguise, Neizar did. He crossed his leg, observed in one corner a bust of Pallas (at least he believed it to be Pallas) looking deeply upset or pained in some way.

"Let us be clear," the other said. "We are, by market standards, a small fund."

"A fund within a fund within a bank, technically."

"Pierre personally recruited us while we were undergrads."

"We had no interest in any sort of a…"

As one trailed off a thought, the other would jump in, in that familiar manner of people who have spent far too much time with just one another inside a closed space.

"We're not materially oriented, by nature."

"Exactly."

"More like—"

"—But the *benefit* of working someplace with—"

"—Let's put it this way, our parent organization has assets roughly equal a quarter of the GDP of the country as a whole."

"Right. Except the country as a whole has all the responsibilities, the multi-pronged appendages, the bureaucratic moraxes, of, well, of a welfare state."

"You can quibble about the terminology if you like. Social safety net. Entitlement. Noblesse oblige. Public good. Post-war Liberal World Order. Information economy. But point being."

"If you were looking for, say, a more Fountainheaded—"

"—Or like if you're familiar with the works of Mr. Robert Nozick."

"The idea of *backing into* a state of nature, almost without meaning to."

"Those thugs in Zucotti Park can throw around the phrase 'Late Capitalist' all they like. But an organization with the resources to *conduct its own foreign policy.* Provide, obviously, premium healthcare and meet more than minimum living standards for those it deems worthy. A body with *no obligations* to those organizations that exist *without,* including your, whatever-you-call-it, parent state. An almost purely transactional creature. What you're talking about then is a *private nation* unconstrained by *common law. Geography* is irrelevant, and *regulation* is a euphemism. What a law like Dodd-Frank would be, in such a case, would be something close to a *tariff.* An attempt to correct an observable imbalance between discrete economies."

"A trade deficit, in other words."

Neizar nodded and thought idly about how he would begin to adopt these men's mannerisms over time, to build Herbert from the ooze of their id, the idiosyncrasies of their movements.

"I got it thanks," he said, trying to hurry them along.

"We're getting sort of far afield here but."

"Point being."

"The resources that such a nation has at its disposal. As long as your project can be compellingly pitched as *in the national interest.*"

"And the *nation,* in quotes, is an organism of unalloyed self-interest, see."

"We're talking about server farms the size of small cities. Cloud space. Computing power. Not to mention er, more *intangible* benefits."

"Yet," the one sighed in this effete way that Neizar quietly despised, "since our founder's unfortunate passing, some things have come to light."

"What sorts of things?" Neizar said.

"Well you saw that whole fracas with the Estate out in North Dakota."

"South Dakota," the other corrected.

"One of the Dakotas, at any rate."

"I'm sure that I didn't," Neizar said slowly.

"You must have, it was everywhere."

"An absolute fracas."

"Plastered across the—what do you call them. The running banners."

"Chyrons, plastered across every chyron in both Dakotas."

"And not a few here, I might add."

"I'm afraid I didn't see it," Neizar said dryly, then, leaning confidentially forward: "*What things*, exactly, have come to light?"

The two men exchanged a nervous glance.

"Communiques," one said cautiously.

"Communiques," Neizar repeated.

"The fund *without* the fund," said the other. "We've been receiving, well... instructions."

Neizar straightened. Crossed his leg.

He said slowly:

"You don't know who you're working for, you're telling me."

The men (boys really) exchanged yet another glance.

"Don't know," said one.

"Don't *want* to know," said the other, eyes widening.

Neizar resisted the urge to reach across and begin slamming the man's head against the tabletop again and again, until he ceased talking in circles. Perhaps seeing this, his interviewer hurried to explain:

"You already know the broad strokes, I expect. It's like a…" he searched for the right word "…Like a *co-op.* You don't so much own your individual unit, as you own a stake in the co-op, which owns *all* the units. So a fund may buy shares of, whatever, Coca Cola, but that doesn't mean that you, investor, own any part of Coca Cola."

"I just own part of the fund," Neizar filled in.

"Y—well, no. Not really."

Both shook their heads.

"It's not like a business you're investing in."

"More like a dissemination system."

"Like to dispatch a second analogy to buttress the first."

"Dispatch away," Neizar said, examining the bust again.

"If you, for some reason, have a ton of water stored in a tank behind your house. And you want to use it to water, whatever, your lawn, your garden, your crops. You have crops in this analogy. You want to put your water to its best possible use, rather than it sitting in this big rusty tank behind your house."

"Is the rust important to the analogy?" Neizar asked dryly.

The interviewer shook his head. "No, not germane."

"O.K. still following," Neizar said.

"What *we* run is a sprinkler system."

"Now, you are free to choose *not* to use our sprinkler system and instead try your hand at saturating the soil of your garden, the loamy earth in which your crops are planted, by hand."

"Using your, whatever, your small personal watering can."

"Right, *or,* you can give us about a liter a month and in return we make sure your water gets sprinkled in the places it does the most good."

"But just because your water is running through our sprinkler system doesn't mean you suddenly have some, whatever, some *ownership stake.*"

"It's binary. Use the sprinkler or don't."

"And we *can't,* by the way, guarantee that your crops will *grow.*"

"Right. Beyond our wheelhouse, as sprinkler purveyors."

"So what's the problem?"

The first man became excited again.

"O.K. so now imagine that there's this second sprinkler system."

"*O.K.,*" Neizar said.

"A system," the other chimed in, "only available to the people who are in some capacity involved with, employed by, helped fund, this first, initial sprinkler business."

"Exclusive," Neizar said.

"Yes precisely."

"A system within a system, within a fund, within a fund."

"Imagine, if this first sprinkler system, despite its best efforts, is guilty of some unavoidable marginal waste—let's say 35% of the water that passes through it ends up overshooting the lawn and sprinkling the asphalt, or the side of the house."

"Or else waters some tree that already gets plenty of rainwater and so doesn't benefit from the addition of your private water in any significant way."

"Thirty-five percent."

"An unfortunate amount of waste to be sure. But still the *efficiency and scale* of the sprinkler system far outweigh the losses you're taking at the margins."

At this, the one interviewer turned to the other, leaving Neizar to himself.

"Can I just interject and say?"

"Yes?"

"This sprinkler analogy is just delightful."

"Thank you there, Henry."

"Both apt and accessible to your layman."

"Something I'll consider recycling in the future. At your odd cocktail party."

Neizar cleared his throat. They glanced back toward him.

"Right, sorry there Sam."

"Imagine that, through various tweaks and sprinkler-industry secrets and minute water-pressure changes."

"Micro-adjustments."

"Imagine that that second, exclusive sprinkler system was able to bring its marginal loss down another 20%."

"So we're talking about an instrument that maximizes your water's effective use to the tune of 85%."

"And also imagine, if you will, that this sort of efficiency is simply *unheard of* in the sprinkler business."

"But here you have this second sprinkler system."

"Albeit a very small insular exclusive sprinkler system accessible only to a select few."

"Here you have a second sprinkler system, the putative value of which—"

"I'm going to interrupt you right here," Neizar held up a hand, "and say that if you are about to describe what sounds quite a bit like conspiracy to manipulate the market, that I would rather you held your tongues, and instead showed me to my desk."

The first man blinked nervously.

"We haven't done anything wrong."

"I am certain you haven't," Neizar said.

"We're not in any sort of trouble here."

"Not that we think, anyway."

"But it is concerning."

"Just something to be aware of, as you climb aboard."

Curious.

Neizar tilted his head at the statue again. He could not put it away from himself. It had a grotesque, a delicious sort of magnetism about it.

"May I ask," he said, "Did the sculptor make his face crooked on purpose?"

"Sorry?" Both men looked befuddled.

Neizar pointed, frowning toward the bust on the windowsill.

"Pallas. His face is lopsided."

One of the two interviewers craned his neck around, alighted on the statue.

"Oh that," he said dismissively. "Pierre is a nut for late antiquity."

"I see."

He squinted at the silver plaque on the base.

"It's Saturn, it says, not Pallas."

"Saturn," Neizar repeated, suddenly comprehending, "and so that makes sense then."

"What makes sense?"

"Why his face is lopsided," Neizar said.

"Why?"

"Dyspepsia."

The interviewer blinked. "Dyspepsia."

"Stomach trouble."

Neizar smiled.

"Something he ate, I'd imagine."

CHAPTER 10

It may or may not surprise you to learn that the Hudson River—actually the Hudson Estuary—flows in two directions depending on where precisely you encounter it. Starting in Manhattan Harbor and wending a path all the way up to the mighty Adirondacks, what you think of as a discrete system is actually a hundred tiny overlapping biologic matrices, all of them intensely sensitive to change, such that (this according to the NY DEC), "Should you stick a twig in the sand, in Troy, New York, and check back in twenty minutes, the water level will have risen or fallen, in concert with the tidal shifts of the Atlantic." That the river, which is not a river, can feel the ocean's pulse more than 150 miles away and respond to it. That these systems which appear so brutal to us are vastly more complex, infinitely more delicate, than the fantastically crude technologies stuffed inside our cell phones or television sets. That we lack even the vocabulary to adequately describe a Spring Day but fancy ourselves regents and curators of every living thing we encounter is a phenomenon far more horrifying (to this journalist) than most of the crimes written down in our brief unhappy histories.

The flood of syrup fell about a half-mile short of the beginning of the tributary system which skirted Littoral, and eventually fed into the Hudson. This can be supposed based on the contemporaneous accounts I have read, and the handful of witnesses I have interviewed. The last ever issue of *The Littoral Spectator* makes a point of noting, "While the river, three quarters of a mile away remains, thankfully, unpolluted by the spill, much of the town's sewer system has been overrun, and city planners worry what will become of the overfull sewage pipes as the molasses settles, cools, and most troubling of all, hardens."

I am not here to tell the story of Littoral, New York's overburdened sewage system, nor of the I-am-certain-hero-ic-men-and-women who eventually fixed it. I am, as I have stated, here to tell the story of a blind fugitive, and a young rhinoceros assassin, a mentally imbalanced insurance investigator, an accidentally rich anarchist and a corporate spy (et. al.). Of the country that birthed, then betrayed them all with startling efficiency. I suppose that might sound overblown or hysterical to some people's ears, but it is the truth as far as I can tell it.

Anyway, one can imagine that the girl and the woman were able with minimal difficulty to reach the end of the flood zone and, with scarcely more difficulty, to carry or drag the old canoe down the length of County Route 6 past U.S. highway 87 N-S down low-grade escarpment through ankle-high tangles of burr and thistle (I want to be transparent about the fact that I have spoken to no eyewitnesses who could attest to this route, but that it would cut the cleanest, most direct path to the water, and is not too difficult to navigate even with a canoe in hand, I have tried it) where they could ease the boat's prow into the steady current of North Siloam River and resume paddling toward their eventual rendezvous with the Hudson.

Sairy Wellcomme was by all accounts an unusually bright twelve year old but I have found no indication in all of my research that the girl possessed intimate foreknowledge either of the Hudson River Valley or its tributary system as they related to her eventual destination. Then again the girl's story is so chock-a-block full of strange open-ended questions, her navigation of a relatively straightforward river system does not rate as particularly high among them, for this reporter at least. From where Robert Vicaray encountered them both later on, we can surmise that Leanne Swinburne mostly allowed the current to pull the boat along at a lazy clip, only occasionally exerting herself with the paddles, and that the strange orphaned little girl as they drifted, would stare fixedly down into the water at passing fish, mouthing their taxonomies to herself as they swam under or past the boat.

Here is another extraordinary fact that we walk around all the time taking for granted: while exactly 3% of the total water on earth is freshwater, that 3% accounts for over 50% of all the fish species world-over. Any freshwater lake or river system in the United States is by nature almost maniacally fecund. Of course, we already more or less all know this innately. Or, rather, we know it without knowing it. We know for instance that when the people are all removed from the streets of Venice (as they have been here in 2020) the water in the canals suddenly runs clear, and the fish and birds return. We know about the abandoned temples in Cambodia where the forest overgrows the holy statuary. We know about ghost towns in the mountains where birds and squirrel nest in what had used to be the power station or village chapel, and that leads us to conclude, in an earnest and addlepated verve, that the relationship between humans and nature is de facto adversarial. That nature exists to conquer us and we to conquer it.

I have heard educated ecologically minded people declare, quite impressively, that human beings are a disease that the earth will at some point need to stamp out, just as we have cordoned-off and stamped out Malaria, say. The strange thing about this critique is it somehow manages to both vastly inflate our importance, and misunderstand our relationship and responsibility to nature. Indeed, the biologic world would continue to function fine if we disappeared, but it would not celebrate our absence anymore than it thrills at our presence. We are not apart from nature because nature is constantly acting through us. There are bacteria in your brain right now, that substantially alter cognitive ability, mood, disposition, that change their behavior based on the exterior temperature of your environs. We think of ourselves as having an incredible quantity of control over our own cognition, our impulses, over who we love, or choose to sleep with, or what we have for breakfast, scarcely ever considering that we are, at the end of the day, just high-end apes, being acted upon by everything from the pollen in the trees to the plants we have ingested. This is no minor point. The reason certain people refer to humans as a disease, a cancer on the planet, is because they crave a biological judgment in place of a moral one. But nature does not glory in the preservation of a penguin nor weep at the clear-cutting of a forest. That is up to you, reader.

I don't mean to get preachy here. My reason for taking you down this winding side path, while our protagonists sail like uncanny messengers athwart the sleepy banks of the Siloam, is that all these issues—of stake and equity, guilt and judgment—had lately dominated the brain of an Ozark anarchist named Robert Vicaray. That as Sairy and Leanne angled their small, sticky canoe toward the river's westward fork, as they sat not ten miles east of the North Hudson River Junction, as Sairy mouthed to herself the Latinate names of fish she did not remember learning in the first place, a spiritually imperiled Robert was barreling down the highway in the opposite direction, bound purposefully for the disaster the two of them had just got done escaping. We will cover Robert Vicaray's own personal anguish and how it found expression, in due time, for right now I would like to return momentarily to the river valley, to the countryside and its history, on the off chance that it lends you, the reader, some fuller picture of these people and their lives. For just as some certain brain bacterium can dictate whether or not you get a tattoo, or how you feel about Jesus Christ, so too do landscapes shape their people, in deportment and habit—their sensitivity and fatalism and independence of spirit. So I will present you with a (brief) survey of these lands, their private history.

Stretched between Lake Ontario and Waterford, just north of Coxsackie, cheek to jowl with Oneida Lake, sits the manmade trough called the Oswego Canal. Begun in 1823, finished in 1828, then demolished and redone in the 1880s and finally expanded to permit the passage of larger trade vessels in 1917—the year it was officially subsumed by the Erie Canal system. To study the gently undulating surface stretched 24 miles long with its seven near-equidistant locks, you'd hardly suspect that the surrounding territory had been witness throughout history to parades of European savagery and greed, and that the soil there has been watered, and glutted, with native blood, but it was and it has. The first French expedition in the region took place in 1615, personed by the intrepid Samuel Champlain (after whom the great lake is named), traveling alongside Algonquin and Huron tribesmen. On that first journey, the party kidnapped 11 Onondaga women and children whom they had encountered working in the forest, then landed on Lake Oswego's far beachhead, hid their canoes in the woods, and snuck through the trees with the stated goal of exterminating the Onondaga entirely. This collegiate attempt at genocide was rebuffed, the party suffered several losses, and an injured Champlain had to be "carried several days on the back of one of our Indians, thus tied and imprisoned...in a sort of hell" back to where the party had hidden their canoes, in order to escape.

In 1654, the French landed on the beachhead once more, this time with apparently every intention of impressing Christianity on the Iroquois rather than kidnapping them (Iroquois, in case your history is rusty, is not the name of a tribe, rather it is the historical name for the confederacy of five tribal nations—the Onondaga, Cayuga, Mohawk, Oneida and Seneca—that formed a single governing structure, well before representative democracy was a gleam in pallid Europe's eye), but then, as the New York Tribes proved less than susceptible to this particular brand of salvation, elected instead to settle down and make themselves at home in someone else's backyard.

Certain aspects of Iroquois culture—the insistence on self-determination for one, the fact of its being a matrilineal society back when the most consuming debate between educated white men was whether or not God had created European women with souls—deeply troubled the French missionaries and their eventual English successors. This is not to claim that the tribes of the Americas were perfect—after all, you have already read how the Algonquin and Huron made war against the Iroquois. Nor is it to deposit you in a sort of morally entropic soup where history appears as nothing more than a stochastic distribution of state-sponsored violences, which (to this journalist's mind) only serves to embolden the sorts of people who would like to see an increase in state-sponsored violence here in the modern era. But it *is* to say that there is a long, insidious tradition of ethno-European interlopers, in this region, coming in and offering indigenous peoples salvation with the one hand and smallpox blankets with the other.

There are precious few Onondaga left on the land now. Precious few Seneca or Cayuga or Huron. We do not make significant mention of the Indian Removal in our history books—save as footnote in the profiles of our Great Men—we do not make mention of the treaties we signed and then violated with impunity. Our land grant system for public Universities largely consists of territory stolen from people who were here first but that is not brought up at Baccalaureate masses as far as I know. Native Americans were not legally recognized as human until 1879. Not recognized as citizens until the 1920s. Were not guaranteed access to the franchise until near to 1950. Even in professedly liberal sections of the country, we do not study the death march of the Nez Perce, the mass graves out West, the kidnapping of Indian babies, the scalping of Native American civilians on government contract—nor any of what David Truer describes as "a concerted strategy" here in the 21st century "to control Native Americans via debt, dependency, threats, and force"—perhaps because it doesn't seem appropriate to teach to children. In any case, we elide a serious adult reading of our history by consensus, we do not discuss how we got this land or who from, and so we walk around, a brittle people with a frailish spirit. We jealously guard the snowglobe of our precious national fantasy and whenever we feel history begin encroaching upon it, time and again, we reach back to blood. Our past is not some remote series of regrettable missteps—it is happening right now, all over again, forever and for the first time.

The families in upstate New York nowadays are, by plurality, people whose fathers' fathers went to work on the canals and never left. The construction of the Erie, which took a little more than eight years, mobilized mass segments of the early U.S. population. At a given time there were over 50,000 men employed on this public works project. The jobs, which were good paying if dangerous, were given near-exclusively to white men and allowed white families to build early wealth. Some linguists theorize that this huge, exclusionary endeavor, accounts for the fact that the South Philadelphia accent is not all that different today from certain New Jersey or rougher-hewn New York accents, that all these populations absorbed a way of speaking to one another while working together on the Erie. That you can map a Philadelphia stevedore's cadences onto a New York teamster without very much divergence, phonologically speaking, provided both men are white. This is not an effort to degrade east coast people. It is the same story all over the place. It is the history of the country in miniature. It is what we sow our crops with and how we talk to our babies. Bad history does not make bad people, but it can turn good ones to liars.

CHAPTER 11

I went and visited Oscar Louder, lately of Erie Pennsylvania, 12 March 2030, and he threatened to shoot me. Not in so many words, of course (he is a former insurance man after all) but the point certainly was got across.

It nearly goes without saying that Oscar is no longer an insurance investigator, nor a disaster-response expert. In fact he is no longer much of anything. He is in his late 50s with early arthritis and bad chest congestion from a lifetime of smoking cigarettes. He watched his mother die two years ago from her own bad habits and has been a victim of persistent melancholy ever since. His wife comments on it in a rueful tone that makes you think she has tried to tackle the problem every way she knows how.

"When Oscar gets an idea fixed in his head, however."

I had lied and told her I was an investigative reporter doing a retrospective on the insurance industry, and she had told me she would speak to her husband, then got back to me about coming to visit.

"He never talks about his work for them," she said. Her name was and is Jessica. Jessica sensibly elected to retain her maiden name when she and her husband married, so legally she goes by Jessica Stoltz though she does not bristle when people assume otherwise.

"Its very strange to go your whole life called one thing, and then suddenly, overnight, you're supposed to be called something else." She waved a hand. "Senseless."

I said I agreed and that that was why I never changed my name for any of my wives.

She made a charming, exasperated face, then asked if I wanted anything to drink from the fridge. I expressed to her that I would take a seltzer if she had one. She offered to go get it and disappeared into the house. There is something about another man's wife that makes her (I have found) easier to fall in love with than the average person. Something about the strength of her negotiating position relative to yours. I sat on the sofa, rearranging the contents of my pockets on the table, waiting for my interview with one of the only people who could tell me about the 2012 Maple Syrup Disaster in Littoral, New York. The resulting standoff that ended with a rhinoceros and several people being killed.

"Hello," came a voice from the front hall, and a thin man emerged looking at me.

Oscar Louder had light brown skin and a scrub of gray-black hair cut short to expose a still-full hairline. He had a sort of languid posture and slow intelligent eyes that hardly seemed to blink. One was rather reminded of a cartoon owl.

"Oscar," I patted myself down furiously, pretending to cast around absently for my thoughts, which I have always found is a useful tack to take as an interviewer, "here is just a—would you mind if I record on my phone? Sorry," I said.

I continued to pat myself. My phone was already recording turned over on the table.

Oscar Louder leaned, with both hands pocketed, in the doorway to the front hall. His body had a strange economy to it, expressive of a sort of contempt for the unconsidered or mislaid.

"Do you want to tell me what you're doing in my home, first?"

"Well I—" I scratched my chin, still rummaging with one hand in an empty pocket.

"I called ahead. I spoke to your wife."

He nodded.

"I know that you called ahead. I know that you spoke to my wife," he said. "Try not to answer me with things I already know. My question, again, is what you are doing in my home?"

"Well I'm a journalist," I said, standing, offering him my hand.

"I would hardly call you that." His eyes were looking over my head toward the mounted wall-clock. His breath sounded labored.

"I recognize you from the news a few years back," he said. "They didn't seem to think you were much of a journalist then, I recall."

My stomach lurched. I chewed on the inside of my cheek, staring at him.

"Ah. Drat. Well." I sat back down. "You can fool half the people half the time," I said. He did not find this charming.

"Remind me of your first name," he said, still not moving.

"Thomas," I said.

"Well Thomas," he said, "now that we both know each other, tell me what you're doing in my house."

"I told Jessica, I'm investigating the insurance industry."

Oscar Louder shook his head.

"Nobody," he said slowly, "nobody nobody nobody is paying someone with your history, to investigate the insurance industry."

My jaw twitched unpleasantly. He came a little farther into the room.

"Are you working *for* the insurance industry, Thomas?"

I raised my eyebrows.

"No."

"No," he repeated, smiling. "You know what a furtive movement is, Thomas?"

"I know what the words mean in combination," I submitted.

"It shows up all the time in police reports. Justification for the use of force. Against people who look like me, mostly. Subject made a *furtive movement*. Plaintiff gave a *furtive glance* toward the glove box. Subject *lunged furtively*. You were a writer Thomas, how does one *lunge furtively*?"

I shook my head, ignoring the use of the past tense.

"One does not," I said.

"One doesn't. But courts afford extreme latitude to police in such cases," he said. "Courts afford a lot of latitude to homeowners too. Castle doctrine is what they call it. Think of that. Every bloated mortgagee, in every suburb across America, Supreme Regent and Lord Protector of the world's humblest kingdom."

I shifted in my seat.

Shot by a retiree would not be my preferred way of exiting this material plane, though I am not usually particular about aesthetics.

"Are you threatening me? Do you have a gun in the house?" I said, keeping my voice even.

"No," he said briskly. "I don't like guns. Would you turn off the recorder on your phone please?"

Mrs. Jessica Stoltz returned and handed me a seltzer and, as if on cue, said glancing to her husband:

"I have to go and drop off the papers with the notary, Oscar, if you want to join me."

"Well," said Oscar glancing between his wife and me, "it sounds like we have to go and drop off the papers. With the notary." He laughed without much humor in it. "Thank you for coming to visit, Thomas."

"I am not working for the insurance industry," I repeated, making a show of turning off my phone.

"Good. I wouldn't recommend it," he said, looking point-edly at his wristwatch.

"I'm working for a woman named Sairy Wellcomme."

Oscar stopped in the middle of his living room, wheezing softly. He did not take his eyes off the clock. Made no sign that he recognized the name.

"I don't know a girl named Sairy Wellcomme," he said finally.

"Woman, I said." I stood again, buttoned my coat. "Girls grow up and become women, Oscar."

I studied him closely. His face was a carved mask.

"Some never do," he said.

"You'd better go," said Mrs. Stolz to me, glancing at her husband's face.

"I'll walk you both out," I offered.

"Best if you didn't," she said, not unkind. I could not tell if she too knew the name. If he had told her about that strange short period in his life. Perhaps not. We do not promise each other our histories. As the alumnus of two marriages, I can attest, we promise our futures, never our pasts. It is a calcu-lated risk on the part of the other person, that the one does not outweigh the other.

She smiled and took her husband's hand standing there in their small living room. You might never expect that this waifish specter of a man had been involved in something extraordinary. That he had once helped a girl with the strang-est most gruesome sort of favor.

"Well," I said, taking exaggerated steps toward the door.

Mrs. Jessica Stoltz, called the same thing all her life, fol-lowed me to the front door and pushed a seltzer into my hands as it swung closed in my face.

"Goodbye Mister Entrecarceles."

CHAPTER 12

There is nothing useful to say about the suffering of Oscar Louder.

As with so many of us, Oscar's distress was primarily the result of an interior tension he could not get any relief from. As in most cases of people afflicted with this sort of tension, that made him a particularly unpleasant person to be around, which led to him being quite lonely for quite a long time.

He had grown up as what passed for middle class, in the part of the country still known colloquially as the Black Belt. His father, an autodidact, taught music for the diocese. His mother was a professional alcoholic. Here is something peculiar: Oscar, when he was a boy, became obsessed with the moon. Oscar was a regular font of information regarding earth's only satellite. He knew, for instance, that over 90% of the moon's surface comprised just four types of rock—breccia, basalt, anorthosite and loose regolith. He knew how to identify the Sea of Tranquility versus The Sea of Serenity (versus The Sea of Crises versus the Aitken basin). He knew that the moon completed a synchronous rotation once every 27 days—which was the reason it appeared, from his vantage point in the Black Belt, never to move very far one way or the other. The reason Oscar became so obsessed with Earth's pet dead gray rock is this: when he was five, he'd looked into a telescope and seen a man's face up there. Of course, young Oscar hadn't actually seen a face, or a man, as no one actually lives on the moon save exiled chimpanzees from early NASA experiments. The face he saw was the result of pareidolia. Pareidolia is a Greek word that means human beings are always seeing faces and patterns in places where there are none. The human brain is so excitable and confused all the time by everything it is experiencing, that it is constantly imagining things that are not really there at all—like crop circles, or sailing stones, or masonic covenants or true love. This is all documented scientific fact. But as Oscar had no one around to tell him the documented scientific facts, or what pareidolia was, and as he hadn't the words at age five to ask for himself, he went around for a long time, laboring under the silent impression that he'd seen the face of God. While that might seem a terrible prospect to you or me, reader, to five-year-old Oscar Louder it was wonderfully exciting to know approximately what God's face looked like, and that thanks to the miracle of synchronous rotation, it never ever seemed to turn away.

As a grown up, Oscar was an insurance investigator for American Fidelity Insurers—a conglomerate owned by a conglomerate owned by a Fortune 500—which insured something like ⅙ of the homes on the Eastern Seaboard (more or less depending on where you drew your lines) of the United States. He hadn't gone to school for claims adjusting, Oscar hadn't, nor home insuring, nor even customer service. Oscar (who was the first person in his family to ever go to college) had gone to Cornell and studied liberal arts. He could not, of course, get a job in the liberal arts after graduating, as the existence of such jobs is largely a fiction confined to college brochures and situation comedies. This being the lay of the professional landscape, his degree was effectively useless to him and all the people in his family who counted on him.

Now, when I say that Oscar Louder's liberal arts diploma was *effectively useless* I do not mean in a literal sense that it had zero uses. After all you can use a liberal arts diploma to decorate the walls of your personal study, or browbeat your social rivals. You can light it on fire and use the warmth to heat yourself in the winter like the fellow in La Boheme did, or you can auction it off anonymously to some bored internet millionaire. Those are all literal uses for the liberal arts degree that Oscar Louder and his family had taken out five figures in private loans in order to attain.

What I mean when I say that Oscar's degree was *useless* then, is that when the very bright seventeen-year-old Oscar Louder was sat down by a bunch of very clever vice-rectors and bank executives and made to sign papers guaranteeing payment on bundle after bundle of high interest loans in exchange for the chance to receive a post-secondary-school education, when Oscar, with no one in his family to tell him otherwise, went off shield-in-hand to Cornell and chose to study Liberal Arts, as he aced his classes and worked part time in a sandwich shop as he desperately pursued unpaid internships and queried his professors about post-college employment that they all sheepishly one-by-one had to admit did not strictly speaking exist, that it had never been made explicitly clear to poor naïve Oscar Louder that what his Liberal Arts diploma *actually was* was a very pricey status signifier, a class marker for a class that didn't particularly want him as a member in the first place.

It is that when Oscar went away to college, he (foolhardily) believed that the purpose of a giant education factory like Cornell was to prepare its students with the tools that qualified them for materially and spiritually more rewarding work than someone without a college degree (like one of Oscar's uncles, say) could attain. This was fundamentally not the case. What Cornell's role was—what it *saw* its role as—was to continue to turn a profit, regardless of the vagaries of the job market or the long-term well being of the students it graduated. That in an age of calcified income immobility, this profit motive scarcely ever intersected with the actual rubber-meeting-the-road prospects for someone like Oscar Louder, and that the University, applying its own fumbling inverse logic, had long ago *begun telling itself* that its role was not actually to graduate people with the best employment prospects, nor even the Pollyannaish-but-at-least-internally-justifiable-mission of graduating a bunch of students who shared some common moral framework, some binding utopian ethos—no, Cornell continued to churn out rich kids of incredible indolence, and unscrupulous nihilists bound for the financial sector, at the same clip as it inexplicably graduated hapless Oscar Louders, students whom it swore up and down it had "taught how to think," that Cornell had long ago decided that the role it played in the U.S. social fabric, beyond obvious rent-seeking, was to serve as a sort of national Human Resources Department, year after year graduating a panoply of ideologically diverse men and women whose single identifying characteristic seemed to be the things they considered gauche, as well as a precious sense of personal destiny instilled in them by the school's Spirit Committee.

Oscar Louder for his part had been disabused of any heady sense of personal destiny. He had been, at this point in his life, disabused of most of the notions that had made a nest in his unserious heart when he was still an undergraduate. He did not feel that Cornell had "taught him how to think" in any meaningful way, save in the narrowest possible sense that he now knew which books other Cornell graduates considered Important, and perhaps that it had pried open just enough skepticism inside of his noncompliant brain to make him an ineffective and miserable employee, without ever equipping him with the tools to actually alleviate any of his own misery. (Even this last part Oscar could not be certain of, as he had on occasion—especially in the years following the Great Recession—bumped into men and women of little-to-no formal education who seemed to have the same glum internal sense of corporate and governmental structures in the United States as he did, if a slightly less precise sense of the locus from which those most direful influences flowed, without ever having read, like, a single advanced course syllabus.) So Oscar, knowing how silly he would be made to feel if ever he articulated some of the pain and unease he experienced on a daily basis, took an entry level job with an insurance company, and set to work on the lifelong project of suffering quietly. And for a while there, it seemed he could more-or-less survive on spiritual table scraps, put away the unproductive parts of himself in some attic box, clock in and clock out with the florid indifference of a deckhand on a ship whose captain he will never meet. For a while it seemed like that.

Then Oscar met Phillip Bell.

Of course, displaying the sort of acumen that can earn you a seat at an institution as prestigious as Cornell in the first place, Oscar quickly rose through the ranks of American Fidelity Insurers until he'd achieved the lower-rung position of Insurance Investigator, at which point his career progress became mired in internal company politics and stalled out. He did not seem to mind the position of Insurance Investigator, Oscar did not, at least not for a little while. After all, it meant he got to receive forensic training and travel hither and thither all across the wild country. He got to survey flood plains in North Carolina and the wreckage of cyclones in Mississippi. For a while there, everything was shiny and new and peachy and keen. Enter the doomed Phillip Bell.

Bell was one of those rare examples, so deeply confounding to orthodox American liberals, of a person of color whose political disposition seems hellbent on contravening his own basic self-interest. A Philippine-American veteran of the Armed Services who'd started a pet store in Florida called Bell The Cat.

Bell The Cat, besides being a cute name for a pet store, refers to an old fable about a bunch of church-mice who are being terrorized by a stealthy, murderous tomcat. In the fable, the mice, deciding enough is enough, all get together and convene a mouse council to try and determine what ought be done about the foul and evil-tempered predator that plagues their waking days, creeping up on them from behind without so much as a sound, eviscerating their comrades for mere sport. Many suggestions are made to the council, none holding significant promise, then one very clever mouse pipes up "I have a solution!" The other mice clear a space for the clever mouse to speak. "I've cracked it," he says. "What we must do is affix a bell to the cat's collar. That-a-way whenever he is nearby, we will hear the trill of the bell and know to hide ourselves."

He finishes. The other mice applaud. Everyone thinks it a splendid plan and they resolve to go about enacting it forthwith and posthaste. Then, just as the mouse council is winding down and congratulating itself for its innovative plan, another voice wafts in, from a crack in the nearby stone, a very different voice indeed, not belonging to any mouse, full honey and menace. *"Ah yes,"* the voice purrs delightedly outside the council walls. *"But tell me, little friends, who among you will bell the cat?"*

Hard to know why this particular fable so appealed to Bell. Perhaps as an ex-soldier in a country where less than 2% of the population elects to wear a uniform, to go and fight in useless desert wars that have lasted more than four decades between them, with no clear aim or benefit or terminus in sight, he found something darkly funny in the hapless mouse council legislating solutions they had no idea of how to enact. Perhaps the sense of menace in the fable appealed to his general disposition, or he thought that it said something about collective appetites for solutions being in tension with concrete individual sacrifices. Then again, maybe he just liked that it was a story about talking animals. I really could not say, and I doubt that Oscar Louder could either. But the pet store was called Bell The Cat, all the same.

"I don't believe in handouts," is how Bell greeted the clipboard-toting Insurance Investigator, already sweating through his shirt in the midday heat.

"Uh." Oscar thumbed the clipboard, scanning the document for Bell's name. "Phillip."

Bell plowed on, "If you think I'm looking for a handout, just that you're mistaken. I'm just seeking what is owed on this policy I bought."

"Yeh O.K.," Oscar said, shaking the man's hand. He had travelled to over fifty disaster sights in his time with American Fidelity and was more or less accustomed to this sort of aggression from people who resented the idea they must ask or beg for anything. Who resented his, Oscar's presence, in their lives, as a sign that there were great deposits of treasure all over the country whose distribution was determined by some esoteric regulatory set, a Goldbergian contraption whose trigger mechanisms had been purposely obscured from their view.

"I just need to go and see the pet store myself, if that's alright," Oscar said apologetically.

"Suits me down to the ground," sniffed Bell, getting into his truck and beginning to drive away. Oscar followed behind the wheel of his rental car.

Bell led him to a glass-pane storefront on Port St. Lucie Boulevard and opened the door on a showroom full of empty cages, wet dander, mold spores creeping along the walls and ceiling tile. The carpet was soggy. The showroom wall had a line of yellow grime a little above knee height.

"Flooded, obviously," said Bell while Oscar plodded around. "Had them pump the water out of pocket, so it wouldn't sit stagnant."

Oscar said nothing, peering at the empty cages, ignoring the smell.

"Lost my shirt on it though," Bell continued, "and I like animals."

Oscar looked up from his printout at this. "What?"

Bell looked awkward, standing in his flooded pet store, surrounded by molted plumage and woodchips, smelling of hamster shit and swamp water.

"Just—if the form has a space for Why Did I Open The Business, it's because I like animals. Better than most people." He smiled.

Oscar said, slowly, "There's no space on the form for Why Did You Open The Business."

"Oh," Phillip said, suddenly becoming very interested in an empty fish tank. "I talked to one of the FEMA people this week. They said if I'm insured through National Flood Insurance that I still put the claim in through you guys."

Oscar nodded. "Yeh," he said, "you can't individually contract with the government, even if your policy is NFIP, it's always through some intermediary. That's Florida state law, not federal."

"I told the FEMA lady on the phone: I disagree with her employer's right to exist, but thanks all the same for her help. She was a good one, she got a kick out of it, what I said."

"Yeh," Oscar said mildly. "So you've got a policy through NFIP, and you've got your tailored Professional Liability coverage, your B.O.P. Do you have any other policies not through us, Phillip?"

"Phil." Bell shifted. "Should I?" He put his hands in his pockets, then decided against it and hooked them in his belt loops.

"Not necessarily," Oscar said. "Only thing that matters is the Flood Policy, nothing else covers an Act of God."

"Active god," repeated Phillip Bell.

"Act Of," Oscar enunciated. "It's the insurance company's term for no-fault accidents. Floods or wildfires or..." He gestured.

"Didn't know insurance companies had religion," Bell said amiably.

"They don't," Oscar said looking down. "Just the policies."

"So how long between putting in for an Act of God," Phillip Bell seemed to like the sound of the phrase, seemed to derive some pleasure or comfort from deploying it, "and when the policy pays out?"

Oscar see-sawed his hand.

"You're gonna find in the wake of storms like this, everybody's answer is different, depending on how they go about the process. Some policies can take months to pay out. Sometimes FEMA will send their own people over here and decide to try and haggle-down your payout. The state also needs to give everyone the green light to rebuild. Sometimes the insurance company and the government will play footsie with the claim because no one wants to pay out. If you want it settled quick, a lot of people have success with public adjusters."

"Well I've got a maximum policy here. And the damage was maximum. So the policy should pay out the maximum right?"

"That's what the rules say as written," Oscar said carefully, looking at the man, his handsome friendly open face. "Just be prepared for some red tape. There's three stakeholders here. You. The company. The government. You've all got competing aims. You're all essentially engaged in a mutual divorce settlement."

"Well I'm not asking for any handout," Bell said.

"I know that," Oscar said.

"Just that the policy has to pay out. I mean I spent fifty thousand dollars purchasing the fucking thing."

"I'm putting in your claim today," said Oscar. "If you have more questions, you call me O.K.?"

Phillip Bell did have more questions. Three months later when he had received no word from anyone, he called Oscar in the middle of the day.

"Hello."

"Hi, Oscar. Phillip. From—"

"Sure, of course."

"Hi so I haven't heard anything."

"Sure, let me check for you."

Oscar started to search through the byzantine electronic claims-filing system.

"I don't mean to bother you," Bell said into the staticky silence.

"No bother," Oscar said.

"Just that I've got my small business loans. I've got a mortgage. And I still haven't been able to rebuild the fucking storefront. Every day I'm hemorrhaging money. And I've got the animals out back."

"Sorry—You're keeping the animals out back you said?" Oscar shifted in his seat.

"Sure, in the yard. Some in the garage."

Oscar blinked. He hadn't thought about what had become of the animals in this interim period. He pictured Phillip Bell's modest suburban backyard teeming with caged pets, squawking and yipping and sneezing while Phil sat there on the phone.

Oscar found the claim, followed the link to the Claim Status, downloaded a PDF of the Claim File Negative.

"My wife hates it. I try and walk them all every day. I don't like them being just in cages like this. I mean so O.K., so they'd still be in cages in the store, sure."

Oscar continued reading the PDF. Bell seemed to be arguing with himself. "But this is different," the store-owner concluded.

"Phil," Oscar said finally, "I'm not lying when I say I put the stamp on your claim the day we spoke. I'm seeing that FEMA paid it out."

"Oh."

"I'm going to call around. Hold tight O.K.?"

"Yeh O.K."

Oscar put him on hold and called around until he found someone in the southeast regional office.

"This is Greg!"

The voice on the other end of the receiver sounded like it was being held at gunpoint.

"Hey Greg, so."

"Hi there," said Greg.

"So I'm Oscar."

"Hi Oscar. What can I do you for?"

"I'm calling because—"

"—sure—"

"—Because I went and investigated a business down in your neck of the—"

"—Um hum—"

"—of the woods, and I'm seeing obviously the guy's claim paid out by FEMA."

Oscar related Bell's information.

"O.K.," Greg said. "O.K. I'm looking at what you're looking at."

"So the guy hasn't seen a dime," said Oscar.

"Right," said Greg in a chipper explanatory tone. "Well, we're collecting on the policy, obviously."

"Yeh," said Oscar, "but the guy can't rebuild his storefront, he's drowning in his SBA loans."

"Oh jeez," Greg said, sounding devastated. "That is terrible."

"Yeh," Oscar said, impatient, "so I'm wondering why this is being slow-walked."

"Well so *he's* not actually the claimant. *We the insurer* are the claimant, in this case."

"Yeh."

"You can't individually contract with the Federal Government for flood insurance. That's Florida state law."

Oscar massaged one cheekbone idly, staring at the blinking light on his office phone.

"Yeh no I understand how the claims process works."

"O.K. well, great talking to you Oscar. Have a—"

He could hear the man move the phone toward the receiver.

"—No Greg—wait—Greg?"

"Still here," came Greg's voice, happily unchanged.

"Yeh no, Greg, I'm *asking when* he, who has paid us for his policy, will *see* some of that money, so that he can rebuild his store."

"Um," came Greg's voice. "Difficult to say. We are not a phil-anthropic organization here. Has he gone through an adjuster?"

"Why would he go through an adjuster?" Oscar said loudly, losing patience, glancing around.

"On the level. What the hell is going on down there?"

There was a pause on the other end of the line.

"Listen I am going to level with you here," Greg said, sud-denly adopting a soft tone. "With stuff like this, on the ground, FEMA is the State Government, is Us. I don't know if you've ever met an elected official from the Florida Republican Party but the swamp makes these people strange. They are not men of women born." He paused as if carefully curating what he intended to say next. "In *some* cases," he said, "it has been *par-ticularly* hard to ascertain where discrete departments begin and others end."

"What on earth does that mean?" Oscar said.

The man, who sounded young, maybe just out of college, cleared his throat.

"It means," he somehow made his voice even lower, "that we're not putting in individual *claims* here. We're putting in *claim bundles*. And we're getting *bundles paid out*. And it means that brass, people higher up on the food chain than you or I, have handed down an edict, that says first and foremost, we need to see the *total projected amount of revenue for the region* paid out to AFI before we start distributing checks to Peter and Paul."

Oscar leaned so far back in his office chair that the base nearly snapped.

"You're telling me you're slow-walking all claims in the regional southeast in order to make sure the branch manager gets his Christmas bonus?"

"I'm telling you," Greg said, "if I *wanted* to move heaven and earth to get this guy Bell his payout *tomorrow*, that I'm not even sure we *have* his money."

With that, the southeast regional office, in the person of Greg the chipper deskman, unceremoniously hung up. And Oscar was left staring at the blinking light that signified Phillip Bell, sitting, waiting with a phone pressed to his ear.

"They paid it out," Oscar said, "but I don't know how long it'll be. If you need the money, your best bet might be an adjuster, or an advocate to force everybody's hand."

"I don't understand," Bell said. "Adjuster is for like... If I want to settle out of court, or—?"

"Sort of similar, yeh. It's not a legal proceeding."

"But I paid the policy," Bell said, sounding, for the first time since Oscar had spoke to him, strained. "It's right here in front of me, *I paid*. It's an *Act of God* like you said."

"I know," Oscar said, "yeh, I know."

Bell made a strange stifled noise on the other end of the line. A voice called his name in the background. Then he laughed, a forced levity returned to his tone.

"My wife says I'm turning into a democrat," he said. "Sitting around here, complaining about everything. Waiting for my check."

"Yeh," Oscar said uneasily.

A fuzzy silence. "Well." Bell breathed heavily.

Oscar said: "Phil, call me back in a week, I'll keep asking about this."

"Yeh?" Phillip Bell seemed relieved at this. "Thank you. Really, man, I thank you."

"Sure, just call me in a week."

And he did call. Every week he called, and every week Oscar had to report that there was nothing new. And perhaps he should have detected some change in the man's tone over time. Perhaps he shouldn't have taken it for granted that a person can hold out as long as you need them to.

"I shot a snake," came Bell's voice, flat and altogether different than it had been the previous months.

"Sorry?" Oscar laughed despite himself.

"Don't laugh. It's not funny." Phillip Bell's tone was ink black and affectless.

"I apologize Phil," Oscar said.

"It was a boa. It was starving. I shot it because it's a crime to release them."

"Listen Phil," Oscar said calm and tremulous, "I'm getting internal bulletins that they've started to pay out some claims finally. Yours has got to be near the top of the list."

Bell said nothing.

"Phil?"

"Yeh I'm here."

"I said your claim's got to be near—"

"—What does that mean?" Bell's voice snapped. "I'm fucking broke. So what does *top of the list* mean, Oscar? Explain it to me, please."

"Listen, I know it's been a bad year."

"Actually hold on, I'll put the receiver up to the snake I just fucking bored through with my M9. You tell the snake O.K.? I've got fourteen rounds left, by the way."

"Phil I am truly sorry about all this."

"No you're not. Don't—"

"Yes I am truly, I—"

"*No, you're not*, because *sorry* is something you are if you *feel guilty* for something. And you don't feel guilty Oscar. And I know that because I can hear it in your voice *when you talk.*

And I know it because if you felt guilty, if you *felt actual guilt,* you wouldn't still be calling me from a company phone."

Oscar didn't say anything then.

"The snake was yesterday," said Phil into the silence. "Today I'm calling up kill shelters about the dogs."

"They're mailing the checks. Just hang in there a little—" Oscar said.

The line went dead.

He made more calls. Checks were being mailed, yes. Did people know about *this particular check*? No, sorry. Everybody was busy and tired. They were now being investigated by the same Florida Republicans who'd pumped and dumped company stock over the past 9 months. The head of Southeast Regional had pulled the cord on a golden parachute, moved back to Stamford Connecticut and could not be contacted. The company was being audited. Nobody had headspace for one more favor.

A week went by without Phil calling. Then two. Oscar began to feel relief (then guilt, for his relief) at this respite from the sour desperation of Phillip Bell. The check must finally have come, he told himself. That was the reason for this newborn silence. After months of slow-footedness the company had done what was right, paid out. That must be it.

Then, one slow day at work, Oscar had decided to call. To check in.

"Hello?"

"Hello, hi—is…? Sorry, do I have the wrong…?"

"Who is this?"

"I was calling Phillip," Oscar said, his mouth going dry.

"This is Detective Bruinessen with the Broward County P.D."

"Oh."

"Could I ask you to please identify yourself."

"Is Phil—"

"Mister Bell has passed away unfortunately," came the voice, sounding like it didn't consider Bell's passing particularly unfortunate.

"What?" Oscar heard his own voice, sharp and irritable in his ear. It seemed to suggest that only an idiot could pronounce Phillip Bell dead when he still had a working phone number. "How?" he asked.

"We are not allowed to comment on an open death investigation," said the detective, also irritated.

"What?" he said again. Then: "Was he murdered?"

It was as if his brain had been overexposed to sunlight. As if he had stood up too quickly.

"Sir, could I please *for the third time* have your name."

"Oscar. Louder. I'm with the insurance company."

"Well, Oscar Louder with the insurance company, Phillip Bell has passed away. We are investigating the circumstances surrounding his passing. And this is the best number to reach you?"

"Yeh," Oscar said, then: "No. Let me give you my cell."

Oscar gave the man his number. Detective Bruinessen promised he would be in touch and hung up. Oscar sat there with the phone still against his ear.

This is what happened, in as simple detail as possible: Phillip Bell of Broward County Florida, who was in almost 80,000 dollars of personal debt to various banks, strapped to an overdue mortgage he could not walk away from, woke up one morning in mid-March, dressed himself, put on a pot of coffee, then unlocked his service revolver from the living room cupboard, went up to where his wife lay sleeping, and shot her four times in their shared bed. Then Bell went down to the backyard where he had his remaining animals stored in cages and one by one carried the puppies upstairs and drowned them in the tub. The birds he had already set free. The hamsters and other rodents had all starved or begun eating each other. Bell left the small waterlogged bodies of the dogs there in the bathroom, piled atop the drain.

Then, just as the Broward P.D. began arriving in cars and armored trucks, to investigate reports of gunshots on a quiet suburban block, Phillip Bell stuck his military issue semiautomatic in between his teeth at the top of the bedroom hall. There was one last bang from inside the house, and Bell's suddenly-limp body went tumbling down the carpeted staircase, 'til it sprawled drooling jawless blood on the bottom floor landing. That is where the Broward P.D. found him with his service pistol still in hand, just as the coffee in the kitchen began to burn.

One more thing: On the bathroom tile Bell had scrawled in his wife's lipstick, above the lip of the tub where the pups lay piled, the phrase Acts Of Man.

Two months later the check from American Fidelity arrived in the mailbox, for half of the total amount owed on the policy for Bell The Cat LLC. One of two installments. Neither ever got cashed, which suited AFI just as well.

Oscar Louder, the day after he learned all of this—over the phone, speaking with a reporter for the Sun Sentinel—got up and went into work, same as he would have any other day of the calendar year. What would *you* have done? This is not an extraordinary American moment. This is not some parable for you to glean from. There is no salable end, no secret median to solve for. Just that these things happen, people are spun off on different trajectories. That Oscar Louder's was one such trajectory. A body reeling madly over eternities of silence and dead space. If you are itching, reader, for some solution, some busybox or easymaking phrase, then I suspect that you already know the answer. When belling a cat, after all, the question is not *how*? The question is *who*?

CHAPTER 13

By the time Leanne Swinburne and the child Sairy Well-comme came slouching out of the water, tugging their battered canoe up onto the narrow laneway running parallel the paved road, dusk had already begun to fall and the temperature with it. Recall that this was well past sundown in one of the coldest regions in the contiguous United States, which even in summer can be perilous. Both the girl and her companion trudged up into the bushes and stored the canoe in a thick collection of undergrowth, to come back for if they needed.

Leanne of course could do precious little planning on her own terms, being only vaguely cognizant of their physical surroundings. Sairy Wellcomme seemed supremely confident of their path forward, as if she had seen it all in a dream. Leanne would recall in passing that those first hours did indeed have a shocked and dreamlike flavor to them. As if no horror, no change of fortune, however bizarre, was outside the breadth of imagining. The air was cold, she could feel that acutely through the thin, short-sleeved prison shirt, a little damp in back from the exertion of rowing.

"Hold still," commanded the little girl's voice softly. Leanne complied, standing straightbacked and silent, just downhill from the bushes where they'd hid the canoe. Up above where she stood, Leanne heard a car. Moving quite fast around a turn. Leanne flinched but the car made no sign that it could see her standing on the slope, nor that it considered her particularly close to its path.

"This will be uncomfortable," the girl said from several meters down, sounding like she was fishing around for something. Leanne braced, hearing the small body drawing closer, expecting to be hit with something, a paddle maybe, she did not know, what she felt instead was a great cold heap of slime on her breastbone. She felt the girl's little hands smearing the cold back and forth against her chest. She gasped. "More," muttered the girl, either to herself or Leanne, unclear.

Leanne heard her plod back down the slope, then return with yet more wet fistfuls which she deposited liberally on Leanne's belly, her back, her biceps and thighs, slathering her head to foot in the dark. Leanne began shaking from the cold. Her teeth began to chatter. She did not cry. She did not ask why the little girl was doing this. She was beyond both of those impulses at the moment. For ten more minutes the girl dumped mud (for that's what it was) all over Leanne's body until she'd lost control of her muscles, shaking violently like a flag in high wind, trying to grip herself with numb extremities, nearly losing her balance on the slope.

Then she felt the girl's soft small hand take hold of hers, tug her by the arm uphill toward where the cars passed by. Leanne staggered up the slope, cutting her hand on something, until they both came over the edge of the hill and her cold fingertips registered the hard sharp dimpling of highway shoulder. Leanne stuck out her hand, groping for a metal crash barrier, the girl was still tugging her gently along. The ground underfoot finally became level. Leanne walking forward accidentally banged her knees on the anglised metal of the guardrail, nearly fell forward on her face. The little girl stopped, standing beside Leanne, still holding her hand. They both stood there for several minutes, quiet. They heard a car approaching.

"Raise your hand and wave Leanne," Sairy said. "Raise it and keep waving."

Leanne did, snapping her wrist back and forth overhead like some mad socialite, she heard the machine's snarl, perilously close, moving toward them.

"It's going to crash," she said over the din of the engine.

"It's not going to crash," replied Sairy calmly over the combustive roar drawing nearer each second to where they stood. Every nerve ending in Leanne's body screamed for her to move.

"It's going to hit us," she said, certain this was true.

The sound was a godless drone, not ten feet away, bearing down on the both of them there in the dark.

"It's not, Leanne. It sounds closer, because you can't see it. Just keep waving. Don't stop—"

She did not stop. And just as she became certain beyond doubt in her heart that they would be struck, as she braced, as her muscles tensed, imagining the sudden rending pain of being slammed by a car at full speed, flying broken-boned through the air back down toward her final cold resting place to snap her neck on the river's muddy bottom, to die on impact or slowly drown, just as Leanne Swinburne awaited the quick strange end to this frail short-lived adventure, that's when she heard the vehicle begin to slow, then roll easily to a stop, and she heard a driver's side door thunk open, and a man's voice saying "What in the—" and the little girl at her side, in a voice wholly unlike the one she'd been speaking in up to that point, began screaming, a horrid pulse-shattering sound:

"Please my Mom she needs help—please I think she's blind something is hurt idonknow somethinghappenedidonknow please help she's blind, mommy, mom, please help HELP HER!"

And whether it was the vertigo of that moment, or composite shock from the day's events, or some superb bit of acting she hadn't known she'd had inside her, Leanne, still shivering, felt herself grow dizzy and begin to slip, and suddenly her body was plunging over the divider, through an echoey unknown while, at the last possible moment, she wrenched her shoulder, turning sideways toward some paler calumny, and a new floor rose up to meet her, all the air inside her lungs departing with a rough *thud*. Leanne's mind drew backwards down foreign gantries, and she pressed her cheek against the pebbled ground, hearing muffled footsteps approach, head turned sideways, breathless silent, as if listening for the histories of a cold and ancient earth.

CHAPTER 14

Leanne startled awake on a cot, in a chilly, cavern-ous-sounding room. Turned her head left, then right, cricking it in the place she had fallen. She yelped inadvertently, sent her hands out searching down the edges of the bed, ran her palms across the fibers of the blanket covering her waist. Blind she was blind she could not see. Leanne breathed in and breathed out and her breath was loud. She could hear people moving across hard flooring. She tried to sit up, then, exhaling again, lay back still. Think think. Have a brain Leanne. Do not panic.

Her hands continued to roam, taking in data without necessarily registering it as such. Her clothes were all gone. Leanne ran her hands up and down her sides. She wore clothes she did not recognize on top of her gray underwear.

As if reading her mind, a voice said, "They cut the clothes off you when you passed out."

Leanne swallowed once. It was the little girl. She had not dreamed her. It was not some hallucination. This girl, however old, really had come and opened her jail cell and bound her neck with some strange invisible leash. Really *had* smeared her body in mud and—Leanne without thinking reached for her wrists, her pulse alighting.

"You're not cuffed," said the little voice, low and calm. "All the mud made it look like you were just wearing scrubs."

"Scrubs."

"They didn't notice the inside-color, with me screaming. I told them you were a nurse."

Leanne paused, trying to piece together all this informa-tion, being delivered in such a frank tone.

"I *was* a nurse," said Leanne finally, softly.

"Good then," said the voice, sounding indifferent.

"Wh—" Leanne sat up a little, "where are we?"

"An abandoned auditorium, looks like," sniffed the girl. "Convention center or something, maybe."

"*Who...?*" Leanne started to ask, then stopped herself. She was not arrested. She had escaped imprisonment. If this strange girl was not concerned, she needn't be concerned either, for now.

"Do you want something to drink Leanne?" said the small, even voice.

Leanne nodded and a cup was pushed into her hand.

Leanne drank deep, without hesitation. It was juice. Tart and sweet. It is funny, without visual cues, how for a little while you are uncertain even of things that might seem obvious.

"Is it apple juice?"

"Yes, do you want more?"

Leanne nodded. Her cup was filled and handed back.

"What is your plan for me?" she asked after a long time, head angled awkwardly into the silence.

She heard the little body near her begin rustling, busying itself with some work.

"Don't have one," she said, sounding preoccupied. "You do not factor greatly in my designs, Leanne, I'm sorry to say." Then, slowly: "I am hoping you will help me with what I aim to accomplish."

Leanne opened her mouth to say *And what is that?* But just at that moment she heard some large noisy body drawing close.

"Welcome," a voice boomed from what sounded like fifty feet away, "to the Pavilion of the Abandoned Future!"

The body drew nearer. It sounded like it was hobbling. A second set of steps, lighter and quicker, seemed to accompany it.

Leanne heard the voice, now scratchy and warm in closer quarters, say:

"Been haunting your bedside all night."

"What?" Leanne said, disoriented.

"Your daughter."

She opened her mouth to say she didn't know what the voice was talking about. Her heart was beating very fast. Then she felt the girl reach out and squeeze her hand. *Daughter. Daughter.* Her mind absorbed the lie, she tried to arrange her face so as to look unsurprised.

"You gave us a scare there. Jesus."

"Who are you?" Leanne said, tilting her heard in the direction of the man.

"I'm the fellow whose car you laid down in front of." The voice sounded friendly and considered. "My name is Vicaray."

"O.K."

Leanne ran her hands over her torso all covered in coarse mohair or wool.

"You and your girl have names?" he said after a few more moments had passed, trying to make it sound jocular.

"My name's Sairy," said the little girl. "This is my mom, Emily."

"Sairy, that's a nice name, pleased to meet you," he said. "Emily."

Leanne did not respond. It was the first time she had heard the little girl say her name.

"You feel alright Emily? I'm no great shakes at First Aid. We got a doctor coming."

"I feel fine," Leanne said maybe too stiffly.

"Well good," said the voice, sounding sheepish somehow.

"Who are you?" she said slowly, becoming less nervous by the second. "Government?"

"I'm." Robert Vicaray seemed to consider this question in real time. "We're a group—not the government—you know what mutual aid is, Leanne?"

"No."

"Well we're here to help. That's basically it. We're just here to help."

"What's in it for you?"

Robert cleared his throat.

"Sorry?" he said.

"I mean, what're you helping for, if you're not the government? What's in it for you? You're like a charity?"

"No, not a charity."

"What then?"

"We're—" Robert's voice began, but another voice, strained and wobbly, cut in.

"I don't think—Robert—we don't need to be going around telling people about our intention to break the law, here."

"Who are you?" Leanne said, angling her head toward him.

"Sorry, this is S—"

"—Don't tell her my name."

"Take it easy, it's safe, she's a nurse. It's her and her kid here. This is Sam Herbert."

"Are you sure?" The girl's voice cut across the adult bickering and the conversation halted. Leanne's pulse jumped a little. She heard Vicaray's body move slightly, like maybe he was turning to face the girl.

"Am I sure what?" the man, Vicaray, said kindly.

Sairy Wellcomme did not speak for a few seconds, seeming for her own private reasons to want to stretch out this silence.

"Are you sure," she said slowly, "that it's safe here. For us."

"Oh," he laughed.

Leanne heard Vicaray rubbing his chin, heard the rasp of a beard against skin. "Yeh, you'll be safe here, you've got my word." He sounded touched at the girl's question.

Beside him, the other man, Herbert, seemed to be fidgeting busily with something, some piece of equipment or detritus that required his fullest attention.

"About what?" said Leanne, feeling dull-witted and clumsy, as if all the participants in this conversation were several steps ahead of her already.

"About the explosion," Vicaray said. "About what happened to you. About what the hell is going on in this town."

CHAPTER 15

Hark! Wheresoever there is trouble, so too will you find the prepper. They flock to catastrophe as moths to a wooly flame. Natural, born of man, it is all the same to them. They are wandering hands, searching the dike for finger-holes. Robert Vicaray was just such a hand.

He had always been (his term here) "an ideocrat," Robert, long back as he could remember. Growing up on the Oklahoma side of the Ozarks, just north of Salisaw. It was not so much a *mistrust* of government he experienced wandering around the woods there as a boy in the early '90s, witnessing the shale companies crack open the earth, dynamite the mountains, strip the foothills and poison the water table, all on contract with the Clinton government, it was not so much that as a friendly incredulity towards those forces that claimed *governance* or *oversight* in the first place.

Behold I come as a thief... And all that.

Robert had grown up a solitary child, largely solitary at least, walking WPA forests, paying the pipe at BLM sites near St. Francis with his mother. His father had a happy family somewhere in one of the Dakotas (his mother never said where exactly) and he didn't want anything to do with either of them, which was just as well. Robert's Mom was mountain rescue, among other things. In season she worked two service jobs and on weekends painted with oils. Having herself grown up in the midst of the Depression, watching men plant those same forests she and her son now traipsed, there was never any sense from her like she felt things ought to be much different. Like any of them deserved any better. The great play went on, you simply sang your verse and waited for the shepherd's crook to pull you offstage. You worked and eventually you died, and in between perhaps you were lucky enough to finish a few oil paintings.

In the summer she would take him up to the lean-tos and A-frames for weeks on end. They would put in sweat equity, repairing them for the seasonal hikers there. She taught him the Muslim proverb about digging the well for the man who comes after you. They would stain the houses, patch the roofs, go for walks in the woods. At night he would read by lantern light. This was the business of being an alive person, he thought, laying prone in the woodloft listening to his Mother's soft snores, nothing more complicated than this.

Recall one night as he lay on the wood planks inside his down bag, in the creaky summer quiet.

"You awake kiddo?"

"Yuh," he said.

"You know I love you."

"Yuh Mom," said Robert.

"I'm gonna tell you something because I think you're old enough to remember now O.K.?"

"O.K. Mom."

"You know what a delta is kiddo?"

Little Robert flipped through all the cardstock in his brain for a few moments.

"Part of a river," he said feeling confident.

"No," she said. "I mean yes. But also, it's a triangle. You learn it in math. It means *changes*, or it means *difference*."

"Oh."

"You know I think you could be anything?"

"O.K. Mom."

"I mean it," she said. "You're so smart, you're so *quiet*. You *listen good*, Robert, you don't know how rare that is, but it's really rare. Even for children. For anybody."

Robert said nothing. Outside the cabin something moved in the bushes but he was not scared.

"Here is something though: when you're old, whatever the *delta* is between what you *know* and what you *do* Robert, that's how happy you're going to be O.K.? Do you understand?"

Robert did not understand but he felt this was such an important lesson to his Mother that to express his confusion would be to disappoint her somehow. She seemed to sense something of this in her son's quiet.

"I'm gonna tell you because I love you, but I don't think Moms can love their sons into being happy. Even though we'd die to be able," she said. "And probably you'll be happy anyway and it's all fine," she added with what sounded to him like false heartiness.

"But just remember if you're looking around, and you're not happy. If you know things that are true in your heart, don't ever let anyone treat you like those things are silly or not worth attending to. If you're ever unhappy, you just look at the delta between whatever you *know*, and whatever you're *doing*. O.K.?"

"O.K."

"You don't have to understand what that all means right now but I want you to try and remember *the words*. Try and remember about deltas O.K.? For me?"

"O.K. Mom."

"Also kiss me on the cheek."

He did and the skin on her cheekbone was damp, but in the foundering darkness of boyhood he could not figure why his mother's cheek should be wet from this conversation, or what it might mean for his life. So it always is with parents and babies. And yet we assure ourselves in adulthood that we do not believe in ghosts, or in messages from the dead. Robert would look back and recall this conversation with his mother not as a whole unit, but as an iterative pulse, a sort of geologic engine with its own mysterious logics shooting up to the surface of his present like a geyser without warning. Who says the dead do not speak? If you listen with your ears you hear nothing. The dead talk to us constantly. The problem is that we only start to listen once they're in the ground.

The shepherd's crook came for her when Robert was still in high school. Cancer, obviously. Imagine this: One member of every household on Robert's block growing up passed away from cancer. What a strange coincidence. Now imagine returning from your Mom's funeral a legal adult who cannot yet grow a beard, and staring across the way at the refineries, their flare stacks never burning out, imagine standing in your yard watching those flare stacks burn all night, standing vigil so long that you catch a cold, and spend the next lonely week puttering around your house trying to kick it. Imagine growing up all at once. Imagine your life turning out quite different.

Robert finished high school because it felt like the thing to do, did a bunker on college for the same reason. There is this sensation of belonging only to yourself and the world. It is an incredibly lonely feeling. But loneliness can, on rare occasions, be its own sort of gift. Like having prepaid table stakes on every bet you will make for the rest of your life. Suffering does not naturally confer great wisdom on those it touches but sometimes it can at least help explain your situation to you. Robert's situation then, in starkest possible terms, was that there was no one left with his best interest at heart, no orderly system of governance left in his corner of the world, no one who particularly cared whether he lived or died. You can be upset by this conclusion but you cannot take issue with the underlying facts.

He had always liked to read, as a boy. This tendency redoubled in grief. He inhaled theory, the same way, when he was young, he had first torn through Robert Louis Stevenson. He wolfed down entire bibliographies. Millet, Bookchin, De Beauvoir, Bakunin, Gramsci, Rachel Carson and Gil Deleuze. To know who exactly your enemy is, to be able to put a name to him, is another kind of freedom, though not without its constraints.

Take note: The human heart has a finite repository of useful hate. You can instantly tell when someone has exceeded their natural capacities in this arena. Their brain begins to atrophy, they cannot distinguish their allies from enemies, and their heart becomes ill. Likewise, if someone (on account of deep-down cowardice or excessive comfort) elects to disengage totally with the part of themselves that usefully hates, you can usually ascertain without much difficulty the softish pettying contours of their personal outlook, the things that it would be easiest to exploit. To give yourself over to nothing is to choose enslavement to the moment. Even Jesus kicked the traders out of the Temple.

He became, for a civilian with a high school education, unduly conversant, unhealthily fixated on energy sector realities. Volunteered with the Sierra Club, NRDC, Green Peace. Oil and gas. Carbon output. This was in the early aughts, recall, when Deep Engagement on climate issues consisted of sharing pictures of brown polar bears and reading Jon Franzen. Robert became what your average professional policymaker might term "politically insane." His reading of the Keeling curve became steadily more apocalyptic. All the measures being advocated by the nominally rational actors in the conversation seemed divorced from mathematical reality. Robert would read an article or research paper, then email its author, questioning the study's underlying assumptions, about growth rates or the efficacy of carbon capture. Sometimes he would receive polite-if-glib responses, sometimes offers to call on the phone or meet for lunch. When this happened he would drive across-country, sometimes all night, show up bag-eyed with reams of paper in hand, which gave the dual impressions of being both mentally unwell and ready to prosecute when in reality he was desperately seeking rebuttal, wanted someone to tell him he was wrong, innumerate, or that he didn't understand the science. But time and again, the authors would simply stare at him, shift uncomfortably, finally admit, as one scientist did: "You want me to say it? O.K. I will say it. The trajectory we're on now is not sufficient to preserve anthropologic life on earth."

This was crazy to him, that he could be sitting in a coffee-shop with these supposedly rational actors, these adults in the room, and they could be admitting to his face that the measures they were advocating were nowhere near significant enough to preserve life on earth, but that anything beyond what they advocated was far too radical for them to support. Patently bizarre, like listening to a war criminal sigh ruefully over the fates of future victims. Not that Robert blamed any one individual he confronted for the totality of the problem, but whatever happened to digging the well for the man who comes after? He recalled, when he was young, his mother telling him about Buddhist monks lighting themselves on fire in the Mekong. He recalled vaguely, Irish dissidents on the news starving to death in English jails. These were his reference points for personal investment in a cause you believed in. But some part of him knew, innately, that all the people he questioned and sat across from (even the other volunteers he'd met at Sierra) would consider such acts uncouth or politically immature somehow in the way they failed to prioritize individual personal comfort. He could tell, in the conversations he had, how you could be counted right on each of the individual facts you marshaled for your argument and still somehow convey to another person a deep sense of being psychologically unwell.

Robert began to suspect, very strongly, that he was living through the commission of a new form of genocide. Born of the new century. That no one had yet put the word to it. That the truth was they'd inoculated against the disease two generations back, when it came wearing knee-high boots and bad haircuts, and once it was gone, they'd never spared a thought for the possibility it might mutate and return.

I am not saying that this is a fundamentally accurate way of viewing the world. Just that these are the (perhaps-overly-operatic) terms in which Robert thought. Young men, particularly ideological young men, have a very limited vocabulary for expressing their discontent. This is primarily because they have absorbed decades worth of psychological messaging, from advertisers and historical documentaries and the like, telling them that if they couch their concerns in a certain specific way, those concerns will receive a more serious hearing. What these young men do not perhaps apprehend (or maybe they do viscerally apprehend, some of them, but see no easy way of shuffling the deck on) is that by adhering to this narrowed vocabulary, a vocabulary that's been deliberately circumscribed by a bunch of well-paid and competent consultants acting in what is fundamentally bad faith, that they trap their complaints within a preciously narrow window with a broad margin of error. One where the people who oppose them can rebut the exactest possible version of their claim as a way of throwing the baby out with the ideologic bathwater. This is, it bears reiterating, by design. A method of discourse control devised by powerful reactionary forces in the culture. A sort of industrywide ideological price-fixing. Not that Robert did not have a decent point in arriving at the conclusion. The baleful words: *genocide, fascism.*

After all, if there is a solid or articulable center to the terms at all, it is in a mutual tension: between a grotesque violence being visited on a discrete minority, and a sort-of *forced unknowing* in the remainder of the population, some twilight of passive guilt, collectivized accession diffuse enough never to rise to the level of actual civic resistance, but egregious enough to have a sort of anxious constancy, a ceaseless unabating sickly feeling of social disease, like a blanket you can never quite kick off. Both of these elements already prevail in the minds of a whole boatload of people where manmade climate change is concerned—just ask a fisherman in the Maldives, or one among the more-than-100-million people who suffer from Climate Depression. Robert Vicaray was one—his brain got broken by grief, and, after that, he couldn't think right. This author is another.

Anyway, point being, these are not organic ideas. They were put into the national bloodstream by a bunch of people who professed to lead us, they were installed, as all unnatural ideas are, through violence, or the threat of violence. You can know and not-know at the same time. You can know something part-ways or all-the-way-through. But there is a great danger in that, reader. On account of sometimes when you know a thing all-the-way-through, as Robert Vicaray did, it suddenly seems batshit insane to you that people could go on living any other way. The danger of this all-the-way-through-type knowing is that, once it possesses you, no response seems too radical to consider, no bedfellow too strange. Which is how extremists are born.

So Robert Vicaray became what you or I might consider an extremist, formed from this soil, this land. In mind at least he was disloyal to the civic peace, which is a great crime for a civilian with just a high-school education to commit. This is what Robert's disloyalty mostly looked like: he lived by himself on the edge of the woods reading odd books and building chifforobes for his neighbors. Meanwhile in Washington D.C. and all over the country, the great play went on. The great companies cracked open the land, pumped water and sludge through its veins, extracted their treasure, poisoned the water and the people drinking it, belched acrid black smoke into the air children breathed, and all the while the flare stacks kept burning. People sang their verses and died, some of them too soon. Robert Vicaray was radicalized, whatever that means, and so it is very possible, had already doomed himself before he ever set foot in Littoral, New York. Imagine that. Is it so hard?

. . .

2009 came and out of the blue Robert received a call from a lawyer in North Dakota. "I'm calling in my capacity as executor, for Allen Vicaray's estate." Apparently, the father that hadn't wanted Robert now wished to give him something, one last thing, in passing. It is hard to describe the feeling of going from having no father, to having a dead father with no stopover in the Living Father camp. It is a most vertiginous and cerebral feeling. "You know what an escrow is, Robert?"

"Whatever it is I don't want it," Robert said over the drone of a belt sander. "Give it to charity."

"I'm going to fly you up here and we'll meet," said the lawyer, "then you can decide if you want it given to charity."

He was by that time 23 and essentially aimless. Not quite a drifter, on account of he still lived in his small childhood home. He did day labor, carpenter's apprenticework, whenever he got hard-up but it was not a nine to five and he had never in his life had healthcare or lived above the poverty line (not that he thought in these terms, exactly). It is quite possible he was still a virgin. Given his happy lack of prospects, Robert decided there was no harm in taking a meeting up in North Dakota. Freelance carpentry would await his return. He could find someone to feed his cat. He would meet with this mysterious lawyer, if only to get a better sense of who his father had been. He had never before traveled outside of Oklahoma.

"How was your flight?" asked the middle-aged lawyer that greeted him in the lobby of a big blue building in downtown Minot. The man brought him up the elevator, through a sleek, murmury office space, and set him down in an empty conference room. "Would you like something to drink? Water? Something?" Robert did not answer, he stared around the conference room as if searching the building for code violations.

The man pressed on.

"Listen Robert, I worked with your dad. For your dad. He was a good guy, and he felt bad about, um, never being able to see you, growing up." The fellow leaned forward slightly in his chair to accompany the euphemism. His face was smooth and friendly. Robert reassessed the man's age. On closer study he looked to be only slightly older than Robert himself. Maybe only 28. It was evident in picayune details. How his suit still fit to his body awkwardly as if he were playing dress up. How his cadences still bore the solicitousness of relative youth.

"They make you wait a long time," Robert said.

The man's open friendly look did not fall away from his face.

"I'm afraid I don't—?" he said searchingly.

"In the movies they make it look like you just sit down and take off. But they make you wait a long time. On the tarmac."

"Oh," the man said, his face adjusting back into a sort of default of relaxed quizzicality. Like this was all just an interesting jigsaw he was determined to put together.

"Doesn't he have a family, with kids?" Robert said finally, feeling awkward about broaching the subject of his own legitimacy in this very clean conference room.

The lawyer nodded, leaning forward and massaging the side of his head with one hand.

"Yes, I mean to be—that's what makes this all so—excuse me but—so fuck-all strange here, is that Allen—your Dad—he has two children, a son and a daughter I mean, by his wife—his *new* wife—and yet…"

The lawyer's gaze was pulled into some middle distance, as if certain legal formalities were too haunting to be able to speak about in polite company.

"I mean," he straightened, studying Robert, "can *you* figure why he'd name you as the will's sole beneficiary? Why he'd…" the man tapped the table gently "…draft a will in secret in the first place?"

Robert just sat there. The lawyer continued to study him, his ragged thrift-store appearance, as if there must be something exceptional about this young man, to warrant his receiving the amount of money being discussed. Robert felt like reminding him he'd never so much as met his father, and so had even less of an idea than everyone else about what had made the man tick, but instead shelfed this impulse and continued to say nothing. He was preternaturally reticent, Robert was, noticeably soft-spoken for an ideologue, one of those types of radicals that Dostoevsky warned against with such alacrity as the ones who do most lasting damage.

"This has been a sort of hell for me," confessed the lawyer with a start. "I knew Allen. I know his family. His daughter and son, his wife. They just—it's caused them a lot of pain. We all have secret hearts, maybe." The lawyer conceded, leaning back, looking vaguely dyspeptic. He eyed Robert. "To get *nothing*. They didn't deserve that. I don't understand why he…"

The lawyer worried the knot on his tie. Robert cleared his throat. He still had not seen a picture of the man who'd left him all this money. Did not know what he'd looked like, or how he'd sounded.

"I mean," Robert crossed his leg in a way that felt unnatural for him but natural for the room, "surely if he's given it to me, to someone who *didn't mean* anything to him—"

The lawyer looked like to interrupt, to say how Robert's father had probably cared for him a great deal, in his own insufficient way. Robert made a gesture to signal he did not need to hear it.

"—then that's your answer. That's him giving you the answer right here."

The lawyer straightened, blinked.

"The answer is that nobody *deserves*. If I got it, and I am *by nature* undeserving—" The lawyer tried to interrupt.

"Listen," Robert gestured, feeling he wasn't explaining very well, "I don't know him from Adam. I don't know if he was a kind man, or a hard-hearted son of a bitch or what. Seems like it's not mine say."

Neither of them dwelt on this irony.

"But everything about the way he lived signals to me that he didn't think I was worth very much. And everything about the way he died seems to indicate maybe this was his way of saying that the money was worth even less than I was. Like maybe he was telling his family that they shouldn't measure him by an escrow. I don't know. You can tell them that, maybe," he offered.

The other man seemed to find this answer far from satisfactory.

"It just seems cruel," mused the lawyer.

"Well maybe there's points you can't make without being cruel," said Robert impatiently. "Or maybe there's no point to any of it. He was your friend. You'd know better than I would."

The other man did not answer. He began to read down a list of assets and accounts Robert had recently come into, by dint of his late father's cruelty or addlepated ideology or what-have-you.

"So you're rich, basically," concluded the lawyer, tapping the ledger he'd just read off twice in a row.

"Yeh," Robert said.

"You have any questions?" he said.

"How'd he die?" Robert said staring at the man's face.

The lawyer mouthed the question back to himself softly. Then said:

"He fell off the roof."

"Oh," Robert said.

"He was cleaning the gutters and he fell off the roof and he died," said the man busying himself with the papers on the table.

"Right," Robert said.

"So nothing hereditary," said the lawyer.

"Um," Robert said slowly, "what if I gave them half?"

"What?" The lawyer's voice signaled some minor agitation. "Who? Half of what?"

"His family if I—"

The lawyer's puzzled look re-returned.

"You don't have to give them anything, the will is not ambiguous."

"Yeh, I know," Robert said.

The lawyer looked quite touched, then.

"Well I think, yeh of course you could, you know. I can draw up the waiver. If you're sure?"

Robert nodded. They both stood.

"You know I bet this was a test," the lawyer said, his whole demeanor brightening to a childish verve.

"I don't think it was a test," Robert said, but the lawyer did not seem to hear him.

"I'll file in probate court for the full estate, deed half to you, then half of it to the intestate heirs. Some taxes will come off the front end."

"O.K." said Robert.

"I'll draw up the waiver," said the lawyer again. "Can you stick around a few more days?"

Robert said that he could.

"I wanted to see Mount Rushmore, anyway," he said.

"Wrong Dakota," said the lawyer, briskly standing up.

"Oh."

"We've got a Scandinavian Heritage site."

"O.K."

"It's pretty good," the man said and shook his hand goodbye.

Robert waited around for a few days in order to put his signature on the documents, then flew back to Oklahoma to go back living more or less the same as he had previously, having never visited the Scandinavian Heritage site.

Of course, in the same way that certain quantities of wealth can cause otherwise rational people to ascribe complex and variform meanings to the petty caprices of a rich old man, so too can it have counterintuitive effects on his living family. Rather than be heartened or touched by Robert Vicaray's choice to divest himself from half the estate he had inherited, the widowed family instead seemed, if anything, to bristle at the perceived high-handedness, and contrary to that lawyer's Pollyannaish good cheer about the human heart's reciprocal charity of spirit, the payment seemed to provoke the family further, as if his voluntary concession of half the money had awoke the widow and her children to the notion that the other half was up for grabs. They immediately took what Robert had conceded and used it as collateral to hire an absolute bulldog of an estate litigator.

Of course, as the lawyer in Minot had said, the will was fairly airtight. It had been prepared in the presence of two witnesses who could vouch for the testator's soundness of mind, and at the end of the day the dead man was entitled to do what he liked with his own money, however cruel. Still there was more than one way to skin a cat. The family's new lawyer called up news outlets and gently encouraged them to pursue all leads about the sordid contestation of a vast Dakota fortune (What assignment editor worth their salt would pass on such a story?). Why would such a Great Man, family man, pillar to his community, decide as his last act, to thumb his nose at his devoted wife and children? Who was this mysterious interloper who flew into town just to collect on other people's Wills? Who voluntarily gives up half the money they are owed, to a family they've never met, without ulterior motive? Without that they feel guilty, or know that they are in the wrong somehow? What kind of emotional duress might a man have to be under in order to change his will to exclude its rightful heirs? You can tell a whole story just by asking questions and pretending not to know their answers.

The widow and her children were destitute—double-mortgaged and living on shoe-leather and sawdust sandwiches, the high-powered lawyer told cable panels. The story was tailor-made for television news. It lent itself naturally enough to flattening and political retrofitting. Its characters could be reduced to broad archetypes, reporters could parachute in, caked in bronzer, and sort everyone into Venn diagrams. There was money and death and a contested will and a mysterious illegitimate son. It was King Lear in the Dakota suburbs, and it cracked open the door for people in television studios in New York and D.C. and Atlanta to sneer at the petty machinations of hayseeds in the breadbasket, as if people all over the earth were not scrambling for money to salve the wounds of grief. As if this irrationality and misshapen pain were of a unique local color, specific to those they considered Flyover People.

At the story's height, one of the major networks had on a person they labelled a Body Language Expert, who assessed that Robert's posture was "that of someone who is haunted by his crimes." One cable panelist speaking to a picture of the boy onscreen pronounced: "Nobody's innocent that's got teeth that look like that." Which made him feel very self-conscious about his teeth. Robert received marriage proposals and death threats. His mailbox got vandalized. He built a shoe-tree and a back deck and a dining room table for the family down the block. He was 24 now.

Luckily for Robert (and rather unluckily for a certain Junior Partner at a certain Minot Law Firm) according to ND state law, the executor or executrix of a will disperses estate funds "*at his or her own peril*" which meant that while Robert had already received his share of the will's contents, the widowed family, as part of the civil suit, painted a broad financial bullseye on the back *not* of Allen Vicaray's mysterious bastard son but on that of the Will's poor Executor. This was a relief to Robert as it meant he did not have to fly back and forth to North Dakota for a series of civil proceedings he did not understand. Still he did not touch the money, sure as he was that some court would one day weigh-in and say he must give it all back. No court ever did so.

His estranged Father's family were embroiled in the civil suit for more than a year before a North Dakota judge finally stepped in and dismissed the case as "profoundly spurious," taking the unusual step of lecturing the plaintiff's lawyer from the bench that he "ought to be disbarred, for the circus you've made of this family's grief," (the ND bar association, it should be said, evidently disagreed) upholding the validity of the original document, the correctness of the executor's actions, and mandating (perhaps unfairly) the family cover the full legal costs of the executor for more than a year's worth of civil hearings. It was an unqualified mess for everybody involved, practically nobody was well-served by its having happened, and the television media, just as they had at the conclusion of the repressed memory scandal, just as they are so often wont to do, packed up their microphones and flew home 'til the time came to pursue the next story, no worse for wear than they had been.

Recall that this was in the summer of 2010 that the civil suit was finally settled. As soon as he was able, Robert liquidated everything he'd inherited. A quarter he paid that poor lawyer in North Dakota, for the inconvenience he'd endured, and to advise him about what he should do with the rest of it.

The lawyer set up a call between Robert, himself, and a colleague in New York who worked in wealth management.

"You can pretty much do what you want," the New York man said. "If you like, I can set you up a couple meetings with some mutual funds here in New York."

Robert demurred.

"You could always buy property somewhere and rent it out," he suggested.

"That's, uh—I would prefer not to."

The man sounded truly perplexed at the idea that someone might not want to become a rentier. "You've got the sort of money currently, where, if invested correctly, it could reliably generate more and more income for the rest of your life. Hell, you could live off the interest alone Robert. Your *children*..." It sounded like he was typing something as he spoke.

"I don't have any children," Robert said.

"For the future, I'm saying."

"I don't want to give my money over to a stockbroker," Robert said.

"Wealth manager."

"What's the difference?"

"Listen," sighed the man, "you have your moral convictions or gag reflexes or whatever, but at the end of the day these are the guys that determine who is well-off and who is not. They don't care about your politics and you shouldn't care about theirs. The U.S. Treasury is currently *minting money* to line their pockets, under a *Democratic* administration. They are going to be fine regardless of whether you invest in their fund or not, regardless of how many drum circles there are in Zucotti Park. This is *suprapolitical* Robert. It exists *outside* politics."

"Not my politics."

"Well," the lawyer cut in, sounding despondent.

"What about, er, energy," Robert said slowly.

"Yes…" The man's voice brightened. "Yeh, that's always a sure bet. O&G shares are trading near—I'd have to look—but low right now. Well, I mean, *everything* is trading low," he laughed, "but if you wanted, sure you could buy up shares, wait for the price to double and sell off, that's a pretty good bet in the short term."

"I'm not talking about B.P. or Exxon or whatever."

The man's audible good cheer dissipated nearly as fast as it had come.

"O.K. What then?"

"Panels."

"Panels," repeated the man flatly.

"Solar panels. Or wind farms."

"No major funds are investing in solar right now. The technology isn't there. Solar batteries aren't sufficient to get you through an overcast weekend, let alone a rainy season. Plus they're ugly. Homeowners don't want to stick them on the roof and hurt their property value, especially now with half the world remortgaging."

"Well, what about wind?"

"Also ugly. Rich people don't like it."

"Don't like wind?"

"Don't like the farms."

"Well," said Robert petting the cat on the porch with the back of his hand. "I don't like rich people."

"First of all, you are rich people. Second of all, when rich people don't like a building, they stop construction on that building. It's not even ideological. The freaking Kennedys killed a wind farm off Martha's Vineyard for Christ's sake. Nobody likes them."

"Well, I like them," said Robert.

"Bully."

"This is still my decision to make, is it not?" Robert snapped. A pause. "Yes."

"Good," Robert said. The cat, startled by him raising his voice, had padded a little ways away and was staring.

"Listen, I've got to go. We'll speak soon."

The man hung up, sounding on the whole displeased. It was just Robert and the lawyer now.

"You think you could find me ten companies that do wind and solar work, that I can give half my money to?"

"I'm not a financial adviser," said the lawyer. "That's a completely different skill set."

"Now you are," Robert said. "I've just paid your retainer."

"I don't have a broker's license. I can't invest in any publicly traded company. I can't buy or sell stock."

"Find someone who can."

The lawyer didn't say anything. Robert scratched the cat beneath its chin, it rumbled delightedly.

"This is basically the one thing, short of chucking the money into a deep dark well, that anyone would tell you *not* to do."

"Yeh."

"Hell, you don't like real estate or mutual funds, buy a burger franchise, Robert."

"You guys do this sort of stuff all the time, I feel like," he said, barely listening. "Due diligence. I just need due diligence on ten companies is all."

"And someone to invest for you."

"And someone to invest for me."

The lawyer made some turbulent noise into the receiver.

"What about the other half?" he said.

"Of the money? Don't worry about it."

"You're going to leave it in a savings account, I hope, for when your giant pinwheel farm goes belly up."

"Don't worry about it, I said."

Robert hung up.

The next call he made was to the Oklahoma City chapter of Food Not Bombs.

"Hi."

"Hello who's this?" came a voice.

"Hi I'm wondering if you folks take donations."

"Sure do," the voice said cheerily. "Are we talking about canned goods, or perishables here or what?"

"I mean money."

"Oh," the voice on the other end paused. "Yeh that's fine," she said in a way that sounded right on the border of being un-fine. "Can you drive over to drop it off?"

"It might be a little too much to drop off," Robert said.

The voice on the other end hesitated. "I don't understand, is this a joke."

"No joke."

"Because people are starving, so if it's a joke it's not super funny."

"No joke," Robert repeated. "No strings or anything."

"How much money?"

Robert told her. He heard the person on the other end put the phone down. He waited.

"We're going to call you back," said the voice when it returned.

They did call him back, after, Robert surmised, some pro-bono consultation with a tax lawyer.

"Our 501c3 status is still pending so it's a bit complicated, but he's setting us up an account. We should be good to go within the next couple weeks."

"I don't care about any tax deduction or anything," Robert said.

The man coughed. "Thanks so much for this," he said.

"Yeh well." Robert felt his face begin to flush. "Solidarity not charity."

"Right," the voice said half-heartedly. "Solidarity not charity."

So that is how Robert went right back to having almost no money in his bank account, after inheriting a sizable fortune from an estranged dead man. Or it would have been.

Save mention for a middle-sized federal program that had gotten buried underneath thousands of pages of TARP stimulus, a couple of paragraphs barely anyone noticed empowering the Department of Energy to begin distributing grants and zero interest loans to clean energy startups. By federal standards the program was tiny. Compared to the defense budget, or even the budgets for Social Security or Medicare or Education, it represented an infinitesimally small portion of total federal spending, which is why it got practically no traction in the press. In a three-year span that featured major healthcare legislation, precipitous financial collapse and the rise of Facebook and Amazon, it was hard to find column inches for a decidedly modest federal grant program. But from the perspective of green energy companies it was massive. The largest one-time investment in Solar & Wind in the history of a global energy market otherwise dominated tip-to-tail by federal oil subsidies. That beleaguered lawyer came back to Robert with due diligence on ten small firms working on high-altitude wind energy, or on improving battery storage on energy farms, or on increasing the yield on solar cells, and Robert signed off on the investment sight-unseen, hoping at long last to be rid of the money, which, as long as it stayed with him, seemed some importunate specter, demanding that he reassess the life of a dead man he cared so little for he could not even properly hate.

This was the creeping sanctimony of the rich insinuating itself into his life: as long as the money stayed with him it made shrill demands on his attentions, beggared his sympathies. Perhaps the lawyer had been right, perhaps, after all, it *was* a test: The bigamist returned from his unhappy grave like a poltergeist, refusing to budge from the lives of those he'd left. The children he'd raised, the poltergeist made greedy and litigious, and the one he'd abandoned he taunted with gifts, trying to upset some fragile equilibrium in his life. This was why these men collected money in the first place, it seemed to Robert, to further impose their bilious humors on the world long after it had dispatched with them. With enough money you can reanimate your own corpse, you can never leave, your children or grandchildren will hear your footsteps in the upstairs hallway, pacing between terra-cotta soldiers, softly proclaiming, *How nice how nice, only a nice man could have bought such nice things, no?* The same deranged fixations that drove you in living to hoard what you had, may leash their souls, yes, *that* was the test, whether the lawyer knew it or not—the test was, *are you quick enough to outrun the vainglories of the dead*?

But with a handful of words spoken over the telephone, Robert had banished it. The lawyer all but assured him the money was sunk. Any reliable financial observer would say as much. Of course, that just goes to show. Nobody knows anything. For the second time in less than three years, Robert Vicaray became an accidental aristocrat. Only four of the companies he invested in panned out, but apparently in the context of the market, a failure rate of over fifty percent represented remarkable acuity for an investor. Because he was investing *not* through a quantitative fund, but a know-nothing in personal wealth management, Robert's yield on his haphazard investments was massive. He kept trying to be rid of the money. Kept instructing his lawyer to invest more and more recklessly in different improbable energy ventures, and kept, to his chagrin striking gold. He donated yet more but could not be rid of it fast enough. He tried to withdraw all of it from his original investments to donate or burn or bury in the woods, but on investor calls was advised by these now-quite-well-staffed firms that his principal investment was large enough, that withdrawing it all at one time would destabilize the firms, and in a shakily-recovering economy, cause mass layoffs, pay-cuts, and could put the companies in danger of being bought and stripped by some larger fund with O&G priorities. Robert was miserable. The lawyer was nonplussed.

"What'd you imagine would happen?" he asked.

"I don't know," Robert said, feeling a strange ache in his neck, "I don't know."

"You're just like your Dad," said the lawyer, happily dismissive. Robert stood frozen in his kitchen, letting the words reverberate down inside him. The lawyer seemed to realize his error.

"I meant it as a compliment," he said. "Like a sort of mercurial thing."

"Mercurial," Robert said. "Saturnine."

"Listen, if you pull out of any of these ventures, you risk destabilizing a lot of firms that are doing really good work," the lawyer said. "They're finally able to compete on a head-to-head basis for household electric grids. Solar's almost at a price point where it's outcompeting petroleum. Nobody would have predicted this a year ago. This is a coup, Robert, that your investments, in part, made happen."

"And what next," Robert said slowly, "after we convince everybody that—what?—that composting their own orange rinds and buying local, and whatever else, will save people on the coasts from drowning. What happens when the water keeps rising, then?"

The lawyer laughed the way you do when you're tired of having the same argument with the same person, over and again.

"Everybody's got to do their part," he said. "You're doing more than most."

Robert noticed a pile of sawdust collected on his sleeve. He flicked it with a fingernail.

"Robert?"

"I'm here."

"I said you're doing mor—"

"—Yeh," Robert said cutting him off. "I look forward to my merit badge."

He hung up, standing in his small workshop, feeling suddenly claustrophobic. Unable to shake a feeling of deep disgust, with the unfinished furniture, and the piles of sawdust, spare nails and rusted machines. His bootprints on the floor and the sound of his body here. With himself. Robert went out in the yard to breathe. And that is when the quake hit.

CHAPTER 16

Perhaps it would be best if we just address the question head on, yes? This question of *Why?* Why would a little girl, whether in possession of her faculties or no, be so hellbent on killing an endangered rhinoceros, one she had never before had occasion to meet? It seems to me that to ask the question in the first place either betrays the narrowness of your parameters for historical interrogation, or else, conversely, the inconspicuous radicalism of your outlook. For in the same way that Americans talk like Jeffersonians but govern like Hamiltonians, so it also appears that Americans think of their history in terms that more closely resemble Zinnian incredulity regarding their politics' various sacred cows and third rails, while at the same time still expecting the future to pan out in staid, Burkean fashion. Perhaps this is what certain, very silly people mean by The End Of History, or when they refer to U.S. citizens' peculiar optimism as a *fait accompli* of the national character—that all that lies behind us appears as madness and yet we expect some certain quantity of order and decorum from our future selves. This is not me using a handful of fancy lecture-hall terms to hang the lampshade here, reader, this is a trap I myself have fallen into, time and again. For as much as we claim to be jaundiced by or inured to the facts of our history, it is quite another thing to see our neighbors acting it out all over again in line at the grocery store.

We know from historical documents that the Dutch exterminated the Dodo out of rapacious and unabating hunger for its flesh. We likewise know, or can read, that we humans extinguish roughly 150 species per day, for various reasons of economic convenience, mobility, whimsy, confusion, simple ignorance. We are apt when hearing that number, 150-per-day, to shut down our brains, as thinking about it represents a highly uncomfortable, and intellectually dissonant experience for any halfway intelligent, halfway decent person. We know there are fewer than 20,000 Asian elephants remaining on the planet, around 400 wild Siberian Tigers left (these are, admittedly, cherrypicked examples, rhetorically lazy on the part of this journalist, on account of it is much harder to get people to care in the abstract about the extermination of a certain insect or reef fish, even though both species may have a vastly outsized effect on the ecosystems they inhabit, as compared to big, colorful animals like the elephant or the tiger) but we are not starved for want of elephant steak or Siberian tiger meat. We kill elephants for the ivory in their tusks. We kill tigers, as far as I can tell, because they are big and have stripes. If this seems markedly more justifiable to you than a disturbed young girl needlessly executing a Blue Rhinoceros I would ask you to please run through the math again.

You might, though, remark that the thing that distinguishes this instance, in terms of strangeness, from those other, far-off animal deaths, is that it more closely in character resembles a sort of a targeted assassination than your typical death by deforestation, or big game hunting, or poaching, or overfishing, or food-source depletion or what-have-you. On this point, I agree with you. There seems almost a sort of personal animus (if you'll pardon the usage), some bad blood, between the little girl and the rhinoceros. After all he was the *last* Blue Rhinoceros. He did *have a name* and everything. So then I suppose we must go about trying to articulate what constitutes a political assassination and why.

For the very phrase comes loaded with a series of unexamined underlying assumptions—value judgments, for lack of a better term. The death of President James Garfield in 1881 at the hands of Charles Guiteau seems a clear-cut case of Political Assassination. Guiteau killed Garfield in order, more or less, to protect the Spoils System (as in: to the victor go the spoils) of civil patronage, which Guiteau feared under assault from Garfield's professed belief in the countervailing Merit System. We are ruled here in the 21st century largely by way of meritocracy, for not even a bullet could halt the progress of Garfield's utopian dream. The men and women who today deny our bank loans, determine the paucity of our wages, reorganize our society around sensible and efficacious aims, all attain place and purpose on the basis of merit. And it is on the basis of our own merits that we are judged worthy of love, or charity, or attention, or relief from pain.

The assassination of Medgar Evers by a white coward seems roughly to conform to this same notion, of a larger structural argument, working its conclusions through a rogue maniac with a weapon, to produce horrific results. Moving through modern history, the attempted killing of Ronald Reagan by a man who wished to impress the actress Jodi Foster seems a little less clear-cut, as examples go. However, the assassination of Israeli Prime Minister Yitzhak Rabin in 1995 by an ethnonationalist, after Rabin began pursuing a peace agreement with Palestine, seems more or less a textbook case of politically motivated assassination. We could go on like this: the killing of Indira Ghandi by a Sikh extremist, the execution of Congolese Prime Minister Patrice Lumumba, a former mail carrier and leader of the Pan African movement, at the hands of the American and Belgian Intelligence Services.

But the next step becomes particularly difficult. We prosecute assassins for the obvious reason that they are murderers. But no one ever prosecuted segregationists George Wallace or Lester Maddox for the killing of Medgar Evers. No one ever suggested throwing Benjamin Netanyahu in jail following Yitzhak Rabin's death (despite Netanyahu's hosting right-wing rallies where the crowds promised to "rid the country of Rabin with blood and fire," despite anti-Rabin rallies where Netanyahu appeared alongside a mock coffin). No one ever would.

It would likewise be treated as patently absurd if the Congolese government were, tomorrow, to go to the Hague and demand the extradition and trial of the men responsible for assassinating Patrice Lumumba, all of whom are presumably still alive, comfortably retired, in the suburbs of Fairfax or Ghent. For a Yemeni widow to demand justice be visited on a drone pilot, or a U.S. government official, is an even more fantastical prospect, somehow.

All of this is true, and verifiable, and I know of no useful place to put it. There seems no room for it in our politics and no patience for it in our art. It is not exactly germane, here, except that each of these examples casts into deeper and deeper uncertainty (for me at least) what precisely we mean by words like "assassination" or "criminal" or "guilt" or "murder" or "conspiracy." I will call Charles Guiteau a madman if you will. I will call John Hinkley a madman if you will. I would happily call anyone who leverages violence for political benefit mad if you would, but I suspect if we did we would constitute a minority in this.

For we show no appetite as a people for institutionalizing or otherwise imprisoning CIA agents, or drone pilots, or Benjamin Netanyahu, or John Ashcroft, though all would seem to fit that category naturally enough. If you think it mad that a young girl of twelve would take it upon herself to kill a rhinoceros—less mad perhaps than John Hinkley but more so than a Belgian Intelligence Officer—I imagine that I would need you to define your terms more clearly. It seems the whole world has gone mad, or else the whole world is sane, and our diagnostics are broken. But either way I would not presume to pin it on poor Sairy Wellcomme. (I *will* say that Sairy herself disagrees with this assessment—that she herself says, softly, when asked, "It's crazy, so crazy, to want to *kill a rhinoceros...* Why?" but I think that by doing so she gives over the country she grew up in, the times she was raised in, to short shrift and speedy doom.) To declare something mad is to abrogate the conversation about that thing, shrug off your responsibility to try and explain it. William Shakespeare, capable typist that he was, put it like this:

> *Lovers and madmen have such seething brains,*
> *Such shaping fantasies, that apprehend*
> *More than cool reason ever comprehends.*

That is my favorite thing that he ever wrote, reader, I don't know why. But it is the thing that has often anchored me when I've felt myself teetering right on the edge of spiritual dissolution. When I've felt my whole life and outlook to be wasted or wrongheaded or strange. That lovers and madmen often apprehend more than cool reason ever comprehends. So if this seems to you to be a story about people who are unwell, who are strange and crooked-souled, or people or events which appear to you as quite mad indeed, it is because those people, those events, have always made heaps more sense to me than any of the best practices or morally hazardous guidelines or algorithmically optimized virtues that each day dominate more and more of our public life, crowd out vile heterodoxy, and each day redraw the lines regarding who gets to be viewed as fully human.

For nowadays you can crack open a history book and find that American drone pilots set off bombs at civilian weddings out of love for their country, that Yitzhak Rabin was killed for the benefit of Benjamin Netanyahu, Patrice Lumumba was disappeared to stem the tide of Pan-Africanism, John Hinkley shot the president to impress the actress Jodi Foster, that some of these are the acts of madmen and others the acts of reasonable and blameless functionaries. Charles Guiteau shot President James Garfield on July 2nd, 1881 and 119 years later, on the same day, at the same hour, Sairy Wellcomme killed Beebop the rhinoceros in his enclosure in the Littoral County Zoo. You can decide for yourself where the lines are drawn, what a crime is, who is mad and who is guilty. I am merely here to relate the facts, as I have learned them. To the victor go the spoils.

CHAPTER 17

"I don't know," said the woman softly shaking her head. "I don't know."

Robert bit his lower lip and looked over at Sam Herbert who didn't seem to know what to do with his hands. Sam was useful and good-hearted but almost unanimously hated by the people setting up shop around them in the Pavilion. He had a peculiar talent for making people near instantly dislike him, and then, a moment later, forget he existed entirely. It was a strange sort of negative charisma the likes of which Robert had scarcely known existed.

"Why don't we start with you telling me everything you can think to tell," said Robert, looking between the woman and the girl. The woman in the bed—Emily Wellcomme—sat up but for a moment did not speak.

"It was a truck," she said finally. "I saw out the—I saw it as *Sairy* and I were walking down the street together. I pulled her in toward me and... her face must have been pressed against me so she didn't suffer any f—any flash blindness... like I did." She paused, waiting to be asked something, but they all waited for her to continue. She did: "The far end of Bilbao has the refinery. Molasses has fumes the way jet fuel has fumes. I guess the safety systems failed and a spark must have caught and all of the tanks erupted."

Robert had a knot in the back of his neck that he kneaded with two fingers.

"Molasses."

"Well, maple. But they cut it with molasses."

"Maple."

Emily Wellcomme nodded.

"As in syrup. The town's flooded with syrup."

"The tanks are vertical. They run...maybe 50 feet tall where they boil the water off. So if one of them failed, or if they all failed at the same time, that's a lot of weight pushing down at the same time, plus the heat from boiling the sap. And it's all hitting the ground at once, it was like a wave, like a tsunami, you could hear it *roaring*."

Oscar Louder's eyebrows went up, he inclined himself forward slightly.

"So what did you do, exactly?"

The mother's mouth twitched, she turned her face toward him.

"Sorry?" she said.

He took his glasses off and cleaned one of the lenses with his shirttail.

"If it was like a wave, like a tsunami, happening in front of you. And you drew your daughter against your chest and you couldn't see anything, from flash blindness. What did you do to save yourself? Why aren't you both burned, or dead?"

Robert looked over at Louder, annoyed. He almost said: *Why are you grilling a teenager and her blind mother about an industrial accident?* But did not.

"I," said the woman slowly, "I don't know."

"We hid inside a store," provided the girl. She had an odd name. What was it? *Not Sarah*. Robert thought: *Rhymes with dairy*. Sairy, her name was Sairy. "I pulled Mom into a store with me, and we hid there, and the syrup couldn't break the plate glass."

She paused.

"Was that the wrong thing to do?" she said.

The girl (couldn't yet have been in high school) looked scared—rattled and uncertain and pale. Robert's throat hurt to look at her. He could not bring himself to ask what had become of the father. Whether he was drowned somewhere beneath a sea of viscous chemicals.

Oscar Louder stared perplexedly at the girl a few moments longer. She did not return his gaze. She stared concernedly at her mother, touched her hair a little. The mother was so shaken still that she nearly flinched at the girl's touch.

Robert cast a pointed look at Louder, then said:

"That was a very smart thing to do, Sairy. You probably saved your Mom, by doing that."

"Oh good," said Sairy Wellcomme. "Oh good."

Oscar shrugged and fiddled with a cigarette. He looked at Sam Herbert, then Vicaray.

"Robert," someone called.

"Yeh." Robert kneaded the top notch of his neck again, not yet moving from where he stood.

"Need you to come look at this floor plan here."

Robert shifted his weight on and then off of his orthopedic cane.

"Yeh," he said again.

He smiled at the girl and her mother, gave a little jokey half-bow, and took his leave of them all. Oscar Louder, Sam Herbert, Emily Wellcomme and her daughter. Hobbling off toward another corner of the Pavilion where he was needed.

CHAPTER 18

Robert was still out in the yard when it struck. It was late, maybe nine or ten in the evening and he was availing of himself of the last of a pack of cigarettes he'd had kicking around his kitchen drawer for the better part of a year. First it seemed it must be some great gale, an uncontrolled wind blowing through southwestern reaches of the country, knocking over yardsigns, bending the land's features to its will.

Then he felt the shaking underfoot, the great pregnant rumble, as if finally the rage of some titan had been provoked, some horrid golem awakened not to be put back to bed. Robert found he could not move. He crouched, watched his woodshed jumping fretfully right to left, watched the asphalt of the street outside protest and snap, brittle as graham-cracker, fell to his knees and threw out his hands wide trying to gain purchase on his back lawn, clutching vainly at yardgrass and loose soil coming up in his hands. He heard the faraway BOOM! of some structure splitting to pieces, he saw his septic tank shoot insistently to the surface of his yard and begin lazily flooding the ground with liquid waste. Of course, he saw all of this and none of it. For his whole animal brain was overridden by an ancient and thoughtless imperative. There was a threat now to his being. Suddenly it was very important that he keep being. Nothing, nothing was more vital. Should he cease, so too would Oklahoma and God.

Robert, knocked flat, cast his eyes up searching wildly. The great oak in his back yard leaned unnaturally forward, the roots pulled up from the soil like the tentacles of some gigantic land-octopus. It lurched grinning toward him, the cancers of its bark seemed to fly through the air hungry to club him in the chest and face, the boughs flew madly forward wishing to knock the wind from him, the tree groaned in anticipation ready to crack Robert's skull open, water its newly-grown tentacles with his blood-yolk.

Robert, looking up at the massive body falling toward him with such speed, could think of nothing else to do: he rolled. He rolled and rolled and rolled dirtying the back of his shirt, smelling the grass-stain on his clothes, recalling this sensation from back when he was a child and would throw his body sideways with abandon down the slope of Carroll Hill, he rolled and heard a THUD and CRACK and suddenly was not moving anymore, was breathing very heavy, on his back.

"Oh," he said, relieved. "Oh. Oh. Jeez." His whole body was numb with elation at having escaped and Robert decided as the shaking finally abated, to stand himself up, but found curiously he was unable.

Odd odd. Well-met body, you've done good work, stand up and take a bow. His thoughts sailed across the lobes of his mind possessed of a sort of lunatic mirth. Again Robert sent the message from his brain to his legs, *I say, stand,* and again was met with mutinous indifference by his lower half. *Come now old fellow, please, be reasonable.* Robert, impatient, braced his abdomen and sat up on the ground, breathed, looking down.

Hum-dee-dum. Curious. Curious. Legs don't usually look like that now do they?

His closest neighbors were a quarter mile down the way. Somewhere very far off he heard a couple voices faint and directionless, calling. *"Is anyone alright?"*

Ha-ha! Ho-ho! Quite right Captain Robert! Usually, recall, the kneecaps face the other direction entirely.

Trapped underneath one of the tree's long, heavy boughs, the branches snagged against his pantcuff. Robert had a vague flashing memory of watching this angled branch come straight down on his legs impacting on the bone with such force that the kneecap shot sideways. He could see it with violent clarity, and he was not sure if it was a memory or his imagination filling in blanks. A far-off person was shouting.

"Is anyone alright?"

This tickled Robert and he bit down on his tongue to stifle a bray of laughter, feeling wracked and queasy. He tried calling out.

"Is anyone—?" The voice asked haltingly.

Robert thought of calling out to them (if they could hear him) in a hoarse voice. To set them straight. The correct question was "*Is* everyone *alright?*". Or else "*Is* anyone *hurt?*" This business of asking if *anyone* was alright would take all day to sort through, he thought. He tried shouting once more but found the effort made him dizzy and tired. His ears were warm. He lay back on the ground and closed his eyes. He would rest his eyes just a minute. He counted the seconds. Sixty seconds, fifty-nine seconds. He opened his eyes again. The light was much different. Murkier now. Dark dark.

Robert stared uncomprehending at the shadow of his right leg in the dusk, stuck out at a geometrically dubious angle like some cubist rendering, the liquid in his stomach began to pitch and rise like the spume of a soda fountain. He felt his pores break out into sweat. He vomited onto his own lap.

"Sorry," he apologized to no one in particular, wiping tears and sweat and spittle from his face, the stench of his stomach's contents wafting up into his sinuses.

Seems you've met with a spot of trouble eh young Robert?

It was getting cold. He could not hear his own voice calling out for help (if that was what he was doing). He might be shouting or he might be silent he could not for the life of him tell. He could feel, in some imprecise way, muscles being used, as if on autopilot but could not process their ends. He fixed his attention on the tree and not on the temperature dropping around him. He ought now to extricate himself from this *fucking cunting no good* TREE he decided.

Sitting up, he leaned himself as far forward as he could go, so that his stomach folded like an accordion and the muscles above his tailbone stretched so taut he feared they might snap from the tension, that his spine might explode in pain and wilt like a cut fishing line leaving him stranded here in the yard. His arms were extended as far as they could go, his head hovered somewhere above his pinned knees, the stench of his own vomit still clouded his nostrils as he grit his teeth, breath hissing in and out at an uneven pant, with both hands he gripped the bark, it lay heavy on his leg, he heard coming from between his clenched jaws a sort of a gurgling *moan*—(so he had not been calling for help after all)—a furious *whinnying* that came out in stuttered aerobic gasps. Robert, feeling the muscles of his neck bunching, every tendon in his shoulders screaming with the impossible effort, *lifted* the tree and, still in a sitting position, *heaved* it away from his body like a shotput. It thudded once more to the earth.

With that Robert fell backward into the dirt and lay there a moment with eyes closed, breathing, making a high, triumphal noise in the back of his throat. He opened his eyes. Something was different now. What, what?

The voices. The voices had gone away. Fallen silent. How long? The yard was fully dark now. How quickly had the sun gone down? How much time had now elapsed? Robert summoned all his energy and screamed.

"Hello?"

He waited. The voices did not return.

He screamed again. *"Hello? I need help."*

Waited, sitting, panting.

"I am not alright!" he shouted as loud as his voice would reach, shouting from his belly, laying on the hard ground, smelling of vomit, the sewage flooding his front yard. Perhaps he had imagined the voices, just as he had imagined seeing the tree come down on his kneecap. A half-mile, certainly, would be on the outside edge of shouting distance. Maybe his brain had just filled-in the voices, as being the sort of thing you hear after an accident.

He sat up again. He was shivering now. His stomach muscles were sore. His body had coated itself in sweat in reaction to the pain, and now the cold was setting in. He stared down at the mangled shapes below his waist in the dark. He wiggled his toes inside his boot, imagined that he felt his toenails touch the steel toe's roof but could not see. He thought that if the bones were broken in the wrong way, the blood vessels crushed, his legs might become gangrenous and need amputating if he did not reach a hospital soon.

Come on. Come come come on Robert.

He began, gingerly, to lift and drag his torso, with both arms. He pulled himself tentatively, a half-yard, away from the tree. As he did so, he eyed his legs, those scamps, to see whether they might try another kneecap-switching trick. Instead what he saw was one of his boot's toes falling limply to the right as it dragged, and with that, suddenly, the pain came, radiating up through his body from the mangled nexus of his impacted knee. Robert moaned, his vision went spotty, then white, *comeoncomeon no*, he willed his mind to stay awake, held onto consciousness by a thread *nononono*, he sat breathing deeply, watching his knees like they were venomous snakes, the initial scream of pain receding to a horrible throbbing, as if there were some unseen power-drill steadily droning into Robert's kneebone at a rate that was just at the edge of consciously bearable. He stared up, first at the darkened interior of his house, then around his yard. The back door, the one closest to him, was up a flight of wooden porch-steps. Then up a metal sill to enter the kitchen, where he'd left his cell phone. Robert chewed the inside of his cheek, sucked the cold air steadily in and out of his chest. He could not drag his legs up those steps, not as they were. He would lose consciousness again, and it was growing darker and colder, his legs (he imagined) more necrotic, by the minute. Robert's mind, usually so calmed by nature, began conjuring animals out there in the woods.

People here kept their dogs inside for fear of coyote and black bear. And mountain lion. Robert had never seen one, but he had seen their tracks, and every year the park rangers warned that they found one or two backcountry hikers dragged somewhere off-trail with their throats ripped out, their bellies pillaged. They said once you caught a glimpse of one, it was already too late, that that signaled it had already been stalking you for hours. That it had already decided on you, and that no other dinner would do.

How quickly did a mountain lion move? How quickly could Robert drag himself up the porch steps, open the kitchen door, pull himself across the tile floor and shut the screen? *Not fast enough, darlingbaby.* He mustn't dawdle. He must have a brain. O.K. so he could not go up the porch steps in his current state. So then what other options? He briefly peered out over his lawn, could hear the sewage still bubbling to the surface. But what then? Drag himself through the waste to get to the road? To wait on the arrival of a passing car? It was dubious, he thought, and unpleasant. He swiveled his neck around, trying not to move his torso. *Tree, porch, house lawn, shed, lawn, house*—he stopped himself.

Shed. Of course. It was not ten feet to the unlocked shed door. He could drag himself that far without fainting, inside he had planks of spare timber, rope. He could tie down and splint his legs to the wood to stabilize them, then drag himself up the porch-steps and inside. He braced himself, lifted his buttocks up off the ground with his two arms, flexed his jaw and pushed himself backwards along the grass. Again the nerves in his legs seemed to erupt in fresh waves of pain, travelling up the whole length of him, causing his torso to convulse, scrotum to shrivel, hair to stand on end, and his mouth to make a voiceless gagging sound in the dark, fat pendular threads of spittle dangled from his chin. He felt them there. Without waiting for his brain to prepare itself for the pain again he lifted himself once more and *pulled* his waist another couple of feet. Tears sprung unbidden to his eyes, his entire body was slick with sweat, he loosed a sort of mammal bellow, leaned over himself, his vision swimming, waited, breathing, 'til his pulse receded in sync with the throbbing in his legs.

God jesus god pleaseplease.

He was close now to the shed. Robert straightened a little, sitting. Not two body lengths away, yes very—*hold on.*

He sat, staring, not blinking, in the dark. *Was the door always open?*

Robert sat staring at the mouth of the shed, hung lazily agape on a cantilevered hinge.

"Must have been," he said aloud, nearly startling himself. He must have left it open earlier. Or.

He picked his body up and dragged it infinitesimally closer, strangling some protest within him.

Or it must have swung open during the earthquake. Yes that was it. For it had been closed when he had first walked out in the yard with his cigarette. Just as—

(Hello.)

Robert slowed his breath, staring into the dark of the shed. *Just as you remember it being closed after the shaking stopped.* No.

Just as you remember the tree coming down on your knees, and turning your head sideways and seeing the shed door, still closed, still shut.

(Hello Robert, I see you.)

No, he had just—it was all very confused what had happened after the tree had fallen. It was all quite unclear. He hadn't even heard any voices, maybe, he was alone all alone.

"Hello?" he called, and immediately he cursed himself for a fool. As soon as he heard the words in his ears, he nearly laughed. *Who was he calling to?*

His eyes fixed on the dark interior of the shed.

No one. Ha-ha. There was no one, and nothing here but *him, but Robert.* Calling out like a fool to the nothing in his shed. Nothing stirring in the liquid shadow of the fusted interior. No purr of a great cat lying in wait for him there. There was no shape, no sound of a creature breathing, no cloud of vapor rising gently from inside the murkish frame in cold evening air.

Cowboy up, old Robert. Only one more push and—
And what?

And you'll be inside. He batted away a dread-soaked vision, plagiarized from some childhood comic book, pale gray arms, extending out from the shed, grabbing him by his neck and pulling him into the dark, some leering slack corpse-face with blackened gums breathing fetid clouds into his mouth as he struggled in vain.

The jaws of a great cougar sinking into his leg as the claws slit his belly open like an envelope. You are alive when they eat you, he seemed to remember someone, maybe a park ranger, telling him.

Well?

His thoughts screamed. His pulse in his neck throbbed, threatened to burst his carotid with its pressure.

Buck up. Don't be a child.

Well?

He lifted himself and slid inside the shed. His broken knees complained again. He stifled a moan. Then sat motionless on the shed's plastic floor, horror creeping through his chest, waiting, there, in the dark. He held his breath, ready, at the faintest sensation, to ram his elbow backwards, begin thrashing, and moved his left hand slowly along in the sawdust, searching for a hammer.

But nothing stirred. Robert exhaled.

He tried peering around in the dark but it was no use. Instead he sent his hands out as blind emissaries, to fetch what was needed. He came across the planks first, as he had some idea where he had stacked them. He selected two long thin cuts, shorter and wider than his legs, not so thin that they would flex beneath his weight.

It took a long painful while to lift himself up, and place his legs back down sitting on each plank. Then he sent his hands out searching again for the next component. *Rope. Rope.* His hands scoured the walls, then the floor but found nothing but sawdust. Robert now felt almost merry to have such a concrete project laid out before him. He could not believe he had got himself so worked up, nearly pissed his pants, staring at a shed door. *So what* if it had fallen open? It seemed so silly to him now. Was that really so strange that he had had to create some lurking ghoul in his mind? The coil still eluded him. Robert, making an irritable noise in his throat, leaned backward to search the shelves directly behind him. Rummaging with oustretched palms. Something moved behind him, overhead.

And that is when he felt the hand fall on his shoulder.

The hand was light, the fingers coarse, caressing the hairs on his neck. *Hello lover.* He heard it now, whatever it was, panting loudly, making its hunger desperately known. Robert tasted copper on his tongue. He pitched sideways, throwing his elbow out in the darkness cursing *nonono,* his skin crawling as his elbow connected with the shelf and he felt the whole structure shudder. His forearm caromed off and he shot out the arm to stave off the creature, to hold it back, wherever it was, whatever it was, panting, trying to scream but the sound got lost in his throat, and all that came was a boyish sob. Robert felt something heavy land on his head on the back of his neck with a *thwap* and then, *jesusgodnopleasepleasenotpleasenotlikethis* snaking down, coiling itself around his neck and Robert gasping in the dark struck out at it with both hands knowing nothing but this moment where eternity hung over him like a pendulum, the thing's coarse, dead, skin wrapping around his arms as well as his throat, ensnaring him. Robert punched at it feebly in the dark, trying to stave off what he knew came next *pleaseno-godpleasehelp* writhing, unable even to scream, and then, as if hearing his prayer, suddenly, the hand fell away.

Robert, his neck still in the clutches of the creature's unseen appendage, launched himself out from the mouth of the shed, his legs exploding once more. The tentacle came with him but there was no weight behind it now, it seemed to have been severed somehow. He dragged his body out into the night air, and it was there, laying in the dim entrance panting, that he spotted the work glove laying on the floor of the shed, and suddenly understood.

Robert let out some noise halfway between a laugh and a scream. He put his hands to his shoulder and exhaled, guffawed "You moron." The glove had fallen off the shelf and onto his shoulder. He put his hands up to his neck, untangled the rope that he'd managed to wrap around himself in his idiot panic. The rope that'd fallen off the shelf when he banged his elbow against it. His legs still throbbed. The breathing in his ear had been his own hyperventilating. He began to laugh, relieved, threading the vilest curses he knew into great gulping breaths.

You whoreson you shit-for-brains you dumbfuck peckerwood Robert.

Then, slowly, gingerly, he saddled himself back up on the planks he'd arranged, lashed his broken legs to the wood as tight as he could manage, groped around in the dark for something to cut the line after cinching it. Then deliberately, calmly, he dragged himself back across the lawn in the dark, sitting atop his makeshift sled, up onto the porch, into the kitchen, and, finally, called himself an ambulance.

The paramedics were if nothing else, entertained by Robert's makeshift medical stretcher. "You're inventive I'll give you that," said the fellow, winking as they lifted Robert up into the bus with them. "Wouldn't mind having you around in a pinch."

While the bones were shattered and Robert had to have pins inserted all up and down his legs, miraculously, no blood vessels had been damaged, and the doctors seemed confident that he would walk again. "You'll be in traction a little while," the surgeon told him after the anesthesia wore off, "you'll be limping for longer."

He *was* in traction for a while. And then physical therapy. And then limping around with an orthopedic cane. Eventually they let Robert head back home, to deal with the septic tank, and the insurance, and all the rest, to sleep in his own bed, finally. They gave him the number of a Physical Therapist who did house calls and Robert arranged for the PT, a musclebound perennially cheerful woman who'd gone to the Tokyo Olympics on the Pommel Horse, to come and visit twice a week.

He limped back in the house, surveyed the rotten contents of his fridge, hesitated, standing in the kitchen, and went out into the yard. Robert eased himself down the porch steps and went three paces toward the enormous felled oak. Blinked, looked around. He spotted the butt of the cigarette he had been smoking when the quake struck.

It was around this time that he started thinking about disasters. About laying broken-legged in his yard in the dark, and how the whole apparatus of government had seemed so far away from him then. And how, contrary to his bookish dogmatism, it had filled him not with libertarian joy, but with profound terror. About how he could finally use up his ill-gotten, accidental fortune, once and for all.

He limped a little farther along, pulled by some strange instinct. It was a blue-bright day and the sun shone loudly in the yard. Robert hobbled toward the mouth of his shed, grinning at his own idiot foolishness not to be able to let a thing go, he reached the crooked door and hung from it, peering inside. There was the shelf with its assorted bric-a-brac, and there the white work glove that had given him such a scare, and the rope coil he'd used to splint his legs. He nearly laughed. He bent down to pick it up. As he did, his gaze travelled farther along the floor. Robert stopped.

There on the floor, carved in the sawdust, sat two sunken impressions—as of feet, as if something had been standing there a long, long while. They did not look human, not to Robert. They were not a man's footprints at least. He cursed. He felt his face flush. If he had had anything in his bladder, at that moment, he suspected he might have pissed himself. In front of the two prints, whoever (whatever) it was had carved a triangle (*Delta*, he thought *you know it's a delta*). Within the shape's three lines, a crude drawing had been rendered, a stick-figure hangman, like you'd do on the blackboard in middle school. *Fill in the blanks.* A little stick figure with no discernible features, save a neck crooked back at an unnatural angle, hanging from a childishly drawn gallows. *Try and guess.* Robert's eyes returned a moment to the rope on the floor. Had something, some horrible visitor, hovered there in the shed's back reaches, in the dark, just outside of view? Had it stood there, caressing his neck? Playing with him?

He looked back down at the ground, his skin erupting in gooseflesh, and tried, stiffly, to drag the sole of one medical boot across the triangle, to sweep away the drawing, its message. He nearly lost his balance but caught himself. Robert dragged his foot again, obliterating the contents of the triangle. He heard himself make a noise he did not recognize. Underneath the image, the words, scrawled in childish capitals,

GET UNEXT TIME

CHAPTER 19

"Mister Vicaray?"

The man stood on Robert's porch with a duffle bag slung over his shoulder and a hand extended. Robert made no move to take it.

"Yeh," he said.

"Um," said the man withdrawing his hand after a moment, "are you going to invite me inside?"

He was wearing a starched collared small-checked shirt, wool tie, glasses and a pair of dress pants with high olive socks.

"I don't know you," Robert said. He wiped his hands with a pink towel, as he'd been in the middle of doing dishes when the doorbell rang.

"My name is Sam Herbert," said the man, "and I want to come and work for you."

Robert looked this very clean young man up and down.

"To do carpentry?" he said finally, perplexed. The man on his porch blinked as if he suspected he might be getting razzed.

"No," he said, "not to do carpentry. Let me—do you mind if I come inside?"

Robert stepped back from the door and allowed Sam Herbert to enter his house.

"You want a beer or something?" he said.

Sam shook his head no and began speaking with that tip-toing deference that people idiotically show to visionaries and very rich men.

"I was on a desk at the Boerum Hill office next to Pierre," Sam said, seeming sure that all of these words held significance for Robert.

"Oh," said Robert trying to be polite. "Was it nice?"

Sam Herbert gave him a strange, puzzled look.

"It was, um, fine," he said. "I'm here now." He nodded for emphasis.

"Yeh," Robert agreed.

"You're doing something really special here. And I'm not the only one that thinks that," averred Sam Herbert.

"Well, I've gotta take a belt-sander to the legs before I'm finished," said Robert, still, for some reason, convinced the young man was talking about his carpentry.

Sam Herbert nodded, either not understanding what Robert had said, or convincing himself that it was some type of abstruse metaphor for financial instruments.

"Listen." He opened up the duffle bag he'd brought in with him, and began pulling out reams upon reams of paper prospectuses, laying them face-up on the coffee table in front of Robert where he stood.

"I'm getting out a little over my skis here, but I figured if I was going to show up sight unseen, I'd better not show up empty handed." He laughed at this, even though Robert could not discern what was funny about it. "You don't have to look at any of these right now. Just that I wanted you to see that I've got a vision for our project—*our*, sorry, *our*, presumptuous— that I've got a vision for things going forward."

Robert picked up one of the booklets from his coffee table and thumbed through it not really reading.

"The stuff you've done already. I mean other funds— even smaller, more agile ones, they're maybe a year behind where you are on this stuff. Six months ago *nobody* was talking about a solar boom, *nobody* was talking about carbon capture as *lucrative, ground-floor* stuff. But now." He blinked. When

Robert said nothing he plowed on. "Not just that it's the right thing to do, but that someone like you, *went in and did it.* Put your money where everyone else's mouth was. The prevailing knowledge was that the first guy through the wall would get bloody. And now here you are, Robert, on the other side of the wall, and all these really smart guys are scratching their heads and noticing how there isn't a drop of blood on you."

Robert still said nothing, and so Sam leaned forward talking at an excitable canter.

"People are calling up Pierre. Big players, are calling and asking this no-name PWM-guy for *advice,* for *interviews.*"

"Listen, I'm really sorry, you're—?"

"—Sam," the man nodded several times in a row at the question.

"Sam, I'm gonna be straight with you, I don't know what you're talking about."

Sam Herbert smiled what Robert privately thought of as a Client Dinner Smile.

"Right I'm kind of arriving out of the blue here, I understand that."

"Maybe you've got the wrong house."

"Is your name Robert Vicaray?"

"Well yeh."

He shook his head. "Then I don't have the wrong house." At this he seemed to look around for the first time at the interior of Robert's modest ranch with appraiser's eyes.

"Not exactly flaunting it are you."

"I don't know what you've heard," Robert said.

"I suppose I get it," Sam continued. "Buffet still drives round in the same 1998 Dodge Dart, from what I understand."

"Is Buffet Pierre?" Robert asked.

Sam Herbert blinked at him. "Warren Buffet," he said.

"Ah yeh right." Robert flushed.

"You don't know who Pierre is?"

"The investment guy. Oracle. The something Oracle."

"He's handling a—well I don't know how much—but a substantial chunk of your wealth."

"Buffet?"

"Pierre!" Sam Herbert said, nearly shouting.

"Oh," Robert blinked. "Is he doing a good job?"

Sam looked anew at the handmade furniture, the frayed carpeting which hadn't been replaced since Robert was a baby. He seemed to be rapidly recalibrating his impressions.

"Listen, could I get you a beer something?" Robert tried again.

"He made it sound like you were working hand-in-glove on this."

"Pierre," Robert said, this time confident he knew who they were talking about.

Sam Herbert suddenly clutched his head in his hands, looking fretful and strained.

"I quit my desk at Boerum Hill," he said.

"Congratulations," Robert said, sensing almost immediately this was not the correct thing to have said, for the young man seemed to intensify his grip on his own skull. Not particularly knowing what to do, or how to comfort him, Robert limped hurriedly out of the room, came back holding a Coors and pushed it into one of his visitor's fidgety hands.

"O.K.," said the man drinking a little from the beer, "why don't, O.K. why don't you tell me what exactly your process is here, if you don't know who Pierre is, for how you invest?"

"Well," Robert said, trying to think what precisely his process was. "I guess I like to read."

The young man, Sam, leaned all the way forward, anticipating some stroke of insight, *coup de main*. When, after several
seconds none came, he repeated:

"You like to read."

"I guess," Robert continued, thinking aloud, "if I read
about some solar energy company or something that I think
is interesting, I jot it down. Then I send along instructions to
put some money into it."

It is difficult to know which concept might be more offensive to the sensibilities of a young financial sector worker: the
idea that a non-genius with a high school degree could do well
in their industry simply by unsystematically reading a handful
of magazine articles, or the idea that that same person's success could be chocked up simply to blind luck—that great
success or failure in their industry was equivalent essentially,
to correctly calling a series of coin flips and, after having done
so, being lauded as Someone Who Deeply Intuitively Understands How Coin-Flipping Works. At any rate Sam Herbert,
torn between these two equally unappealing options, stood up
and paced nervously around the room. He was one of those
people who picks savagely at the label on his beer while he
is drinking it, and Robert, glancing down, noticed the long,
horrible furrows his itchy fingernail had made criss-crossing
the logo.

"You don't even know Pierre," muttered Herbert again, as if
the idea that someone might not know Pierre was rather offensive.

"No," said Robert, adding, "sorry." Turning something
over in his mind.

"Everyone's so full of shit," the rabbity young man spat,
suddenly full of vinegar.

"Well not everyone," Robert said. "But Pierre maybe."

The young man did not respond. Robert thought a little longer, recalling the feeling he'd had limping around his backyard with his orthopedic cane, his new plan.

"Listen uh, Sam, I know this isn't what you expected, maybe, but I've been thinking about something and maybe— it's not exactly what you'd hoped—but I may have a sort of job for you, where you might be able to help me out."

Sam Herbert looked up, kneading his knuckles in the silence.

"The good news," he said, "is I *do* need somebody to handle all the investments I've got."

Sam Herbert's countenance brightened considerably, the worry seeming to depart a little.

"What I need," Robert said nodding, "is for you to withdraw all my money."

Sam Herbert's spiritual dyspepsia seemed to return all at once.

"What do you mean *withdraw*?" he said.

"I need it back," Robert said simply.

Sam shook his head. "It's not—" he made an irritable noise "—Listen, it's not as if it is sitting in a savings account somewhere. It's in companies' bloodstreams. It's out there *moving around*, constantly."

Robert nodded. "Yeh well, I need it," he said. "All of it. And I need somebody who can get it for me without hurting any of the companies—having them layoff workers or anything, I mean."

"What're you going to do with, conservatively," Sam estimated aloud how much money he imagined Robert currently had invested. "Bury it in the yard?"

"Nope."

"Then what do you need it for?"

"It's sort of hard to explain," Robert said.

"Try," deadpanned Sam.

"You ever see those videos from China," Robert said slowly, "where they build, like, a skyscraper in 30 days?"

"No."

"Well, there are videos," Robert said, slightly irritated by this interloper's skepticism. "Time-lapses where they'll make like a forty-five-story building in four weeks. Two floors a day, or something."

"O.K."

Robert continued, scratching his jaw. "Usually to build a skyscraper, like here in America, you'd have to build it brick by brick, right? But these Chinese builders what they've done is create these *modules. Uniform modules.* So while we're all toiling putting one brick on top of another brick—"

"—they just slide in the modules," Sam completed, sounding impatient.

Robert snapped several times excitedly.

"Right, they just slide in one block on top of another block. Two floors a day. And in 30 days they've got a skyscraper."

"O.K.," said Sam Herbert, sounding confused. "So, you want to build skyscrapers?"

Robert shook his head, no.

"Have you ever been part of a disaster?" he asked.

Herbert shifted in his seat. "What?" A look flashed across his face that Robert could not discern.

"Like an earthquake or a hurricane, or..." Robert gestured.

"Oh," Sam said. "No."

"Well I have. We had an earthquake here, from fracking. Bad one. And I've been reading up for a little while now on Hurricane Katrina. Did you know that the majority of the rescues that took place during Katrina, were done by New Orleans residents unaffiliated with a federal or local authority?"

"No," said Sam dully, blinking the way you might when being accosted by a street preacher. "I did not know that."

Robert did not notice the other man's absent enthusiasm, became excited now himself, hoisting his weight to his feet, lurching for his cane, going to try and find the book he had been reading.

"You know the largest in-person presence in New Orleans, after Katrina wasn't the Red Cross and it wasn't the Feds, it was a collective called Common Ground. 25,000 people doing mutual aid work, this *against explicit orders* from state and local authorities."

Herbert seemed to be torn between his brain's natural inclinations toward curiosity and an ingrained blue-blooded skepticism of any form of charity uncircumscribed by established politics.

"So you're going to—sorry." He held up a hand, either to stop Robert or himself. "*What you want* is to make the pre-form-block-skyscraper equivalent of Federal disaster relief, is that it?"

Robert, perched on top of his cane, felt a blush travel across his face. He said nothing, feeling silly, hearing it said aloud like that. Sam Herbert stared.

"Do you have any experience, in nonprofit work, waste prevention, resource management—in actually *doing disaster relief?*"

"No," Robert admitted.

"No," Herbert said. "Do you think maybe we should *find someone* who's maybe been *involved* in the response effort to a natural disaster or humanitarian crisis, in the past, Robert?

Before we start going town to town with our little tent-city on wheels?"

Robert did not know whether Herbert had used the words *we* and *our* intentionally or not. He opened his mouth and then closed it again.

"I'm not saying one way or another whether I'll help you," Sam Herbert said, suddenly sounding markedly less jumpy, more confident than he had when he thought he was auditioning for an investment role. "But if you want to cause the least amount of disruption, what you do is you contact other shareholders. Every stock sold is a stock bought. You gradually, piecemeal, sell off your stakes to various parties, starting with the least volatile stocks and threading in the most volatile ones over time. You don't *withdraw* anything. And you definitely don't make it look like you just *juiced* the alternative energy market with a pump-and-dump scheme."

"O.K.," said Robert, not knowing what most of these words meant.

"You know what the dangerous thing is, Robert, about trying to build a skyscraper in 30 days?"

Again, he said nothing.

"It's that if the math is wrong, your building collapses on top of the people inside it."

Samuel Herbert fully peeled the label off his beer and left it there on the handmade coffee table. He got up and shook Robert's hand, letting himself out.

"You got a place to stay?" Robert asked, feeling a sudden, nervous intimacy with this person.

"Motel 6," Herbert said simply.

"Good then."

"My advice, and it's free: Get to searching for somebody who's been on a hundred disaster relief sights. Who knows where they get—I don't know—portable toilets, how to transport bottled water across state lines. Basic stuff."

With that, Sam Herbert left for his roadside motel. And so began Robert Vicaray's search for a third partner, someone who knew disasters inside and out, which soon before long would lead him to the doorstep of one Oscar Louder.

CHAPTER 20

As I was walking down the length of Bilbao street rather aimlessly for the third time in as many days, my telephone began to ring. The screen showed a New York City number and I halted in the street to stare at it, let it go to message, organize myself against different possibilities, then called the number back.

"Lo."

"Tommy." The voice was soft-sweet and frightening.

"This is he."

"What's this I hear about you sniffing around New York backwaters, chasing down old industrial accidents?"

I cracked the knuckles on my left hand then flexed the fingers, for no particular reason. Above the intersection the traffic light changed to yellow, blinking yellow, red.

"I couldn't attest to what you hear on a given day," I said finally.

I switched the phone to my other ear and used my dominant hand to tug Goober, who'd sat down in the middle of a zebra crossing like an idiot, back to the sidewalk. He pushed his cold nose against my free hand for attention and I patted his ears which only seemed to increase this need in him.

"You're a bad liar Thomas."

"Which is why I've sworn off it," I said. "It's the straight and narrow for me, *mon petit chou*. A pedestrian's life, in good civic standing."

"Going around pestering church widows and digging up their husbands, from what I hear."

"I'm just stopping in at a little boutique town in the Hudson valley, savoring the fruits of retirement is all."

"Of graft you mean."

"You do me dishonor, Misia."

I scanned the intersection. There were four people on the street with me, that I could see—one young couple at catty corners, one old woman running a newspaper stand, and one, a homeless man who appeared to be asleep on a bus stop bench. Of the four it seemed most likely to me that the homeless fellow was a plant, by which I mean not particularly likely.

"How do you know where I'm going or who I'm talking to besides?" I said.

"You beautiful dumb baby boy," she cooed. I felt the blood come into my face. "You know how easy it is to clone a cell phone with the correct equipment? Leave your phone on the bar for two minutes while you're feeding the cigarette machine. Leave it on the bedside table next to someone you've slept with. You haven't been to any bars lately have you Thomas?"

I took the phone away from my ear a moment, looked at it, put her on speaker.

"*Kidding*. It's a joke, Thomas. I got a tip. A phone call."

"Who from?"

"Anonymous."

I said nothing.

"Oh, now you're cross," she said.

"I would have thought *News Of The World* had chastened you people a bit," I said.

The light changed again and the little crosswalk man began blinking into and out of existence.

"What does some limey hacking scandal have to do with me?" she said, her tone flattening.

"It doesn't necessarily. Just the fellow cutting your checks."

"I don't like how you talk to me."

"Good, call less."

"How about you come to New York City and I'll buy you dinner?"

"Can't do it, sorry."

"Of course you could."

"Prior engagement. Another time maybe."

Goober, it's possible sensing my unease, growled at nothing in particular, then barked.

"Is that my Very Good Boy I hear?" she said.

As if he'd heard her question, Goober rolled onto his back to have his stomach scratched.

"Yes," I said. "He's begun tearing a neighborhood child limb from limb."

I tried to make him roll back around with the toe of my boot.

"What neighborhood would that be again?"

"I have to go Misia," I said "Pressing antiquities to buy. Did you need something?"

"Do you remember the first thing I ever said to you Thomas?"

I did not say anything in response.

"I walked up to you at a party and I promised something, you remember?" She sounded almost tender or nervous, like she herself could not recall. Like without me, the memory might disappear forever.

"I have to go," I said again.

The keel of her voice returned. Or maybe had never left. Maybe it was affected, like she was working a source.

"You have to go," she said, sounding like she found this very funny.

"Take care Misia."

After I'd ended the call, I took out my pad and copied down three telephone numbers. Paused, thought a second, then copied down a fourth. Then I walked over to the park bench where the homeless man sat with his head hung in his lap.

"Hi," I said.

His head jerked awake and he squinted at me in the sunlight.

"Are you following me," I demanded.

He smiled. The look on his face seemed absent any guile or nervous agitation.

"You want this phone?" I said.

He looked at me, said nothing.

"I don't need it anymore. You could probably sell it. It's worth near to 500 dollars." I handed the device over. He looked down at the phone, then back up at me.

"Well, if anyone asks you to follow me, don't," I said. I stood there a moment, expecting something more maybe, but there was nothing more, and soon Goober became restless again.

We walked away from the bench, crossed the intersection, him straining at the leash in order to smell different parts of the pavement. Then I heard a muffled cry. I turned.

The man was on his feet in front of the bench, gesturing broadly and smiling. His mouth was open and he was looking at me, trying to yell something across to me.

He nodded a few times, gestured to the shiny phone in his hand. He was trying to say Thank You. Over and again. *Thank you thank you.* He tried but each time it came out garbled. He opened his mouth wider and pointed so I could see the problem. You always read news reports about people abducting, attacking, maiming homeless men. Some long-ago wound. He pointed with a dirty forefinger. Someone had cut out his tongue.

CHAPTER 21

It is an old saw within the mutual aid community that one of the main obstacles to disaster relief, after physical resource scarcity, is embarrassment. Truth is, a lot of the time, the only thing keeping folks from getting what they need in otherwise dire situations, is a combination of learned-helplessness on the parts of the people who could otherwise be lending a hand and deep shame on the parts of the people who could *use the hand* to start with (Robert's own mother's phrase regarding this sort of moral sloth was that "idleness in crisis is the original sin of stupid men" something her son may as well have tattooed on his forearm, for the amount he thinks about it, day to day in his own life), and that in order to make an impact in the life of a stranger, often, all you have to do is 1) show up and 2) ask what they need.

Yes it is true, that given a medium-sized resource budget, you can appropriately prepare for certain constants. There will always—as Oscar Louder says—be a need in the wake of any crisis, for bottled water, canned goods, hospital blankets and chemical toilets. But also that so much of becoming part of the solution to any major problem lies simply in being bodily attendant and unafraid to ask. That in our current atomized reality, the simple act of being present is vastly underrated as a social force, as is the profound human anxiety that impedes most peoples' doing so in the first place.

So here is what the anarchist Robert Vicaray, the disgruntled Oscar Louder, the fake wealth manager Sam Herbert (and many others) did in order to radically reshape their collective reality in the wake of a series of avoidable disasters: they showed up and asked what they could do to help.

Often the requests were so simple it was vertigo-inducing that they hadn't already been met. Elderly or handicapped people needed groceries but couldn't make it down the stairs of their apartments. People needed to shower but there was no running water. People needed garbage removed from the road, but the garbage trucks were not travelling down their streets. Once you begin asking to help, the question itself has an incredible intrinsic momentum, it carries you along so that you are saying *What next? What next? What next?*

Sure there is, especially amongst the crunchier members of the political Left, a certain unavoidable quantity of bullshit you must take on the chin. Of Facebook narcissists who spend the majority of their time posing for pictures, or factionalist ideologues who can only ever envision themselves as Leaders of Men. There is unaccountability, and theft, and vanity and petty territorialism that can drive you near-mad with frustration. Still at-center there is the project. There is the chance to work hard at work worth doing. At not having to settle for some diffuse intellectualized theory of the common good or categorical imperatives or whatever. That you can measure out the work you have done in piles of trash cleared or pallets of water delivered or planks hammered into place by nails. That contrary to what you once believed, to be able to subvert your ego in service of some collective material good is not indicative of that personal fecklessness or weak moral DNA you once thought. That actually to be able to patiently respectfully work alongside others with whom you disagree on any number of things, in service of a worthy project, can often be an act of herculean strength of character.

Oscar Louder's main stroke of genius, once he'd joined the team, was to have them, for lack of better terms, beta-test and scale up so that, organizationally, everything they wanted to do got done in concert with their increasing competency at doing it. And so, it started with a dozen of them showing up to flood zones and towns that'd been hit by hurricanes. Trying to figure out what worked and what did not. Vicaray was insistent on a few frustrating particulars—for instance every important role was to be occupied by not one but two people, one male and one female. (His logic apparently being here that if you did not *explicitly* make gender parity a goal in every single administrative position, in every single leg of the process, that structures would default to being male, and have deleterious second-order effects somewhere down the line.)

While resources were shared and while nearly all decisions were made by voice-vote, the group was *not necessarily* as hostile to hierarchy in Deed as they professed in Thought. There was natural, inevitable, specialization, expertise and division of labor. Eventually, as they slowly over time built out and up, they even went as far as to appoint men and women responsible for addressing criminal complaints—an internal police force essentially—not based on the letter of the American criminal code obviously, but on basic fundaments of shared ideology, a sort of primitive contractualism.

It was not uncommon for the group—which Vicaray had jokingly once referred to as The Rude Mechanics, though nobody seemed to remember precisely what joke he had been making at the time—to have a tense relationship with actual local police forces given the former's happy disregard for rules about looting, theft, drug use, sex work—given that a non-trivial portion of Rude Mechanic's gender-equal hierarchy-that-was-not-a-hierarchy comprised *enthusiastic* looters, thieves, drug users, and sex workers, that police cruisers that parked themselves within 500 feet of whatever Field Hospital or Temporary Shelter or Supply Warehouse the RM's had set up on the ground there, would often find themselves or at least their vehicles, egged, covered in spray paint, or bologna, or with their tires slashed or some piece of produce wedged in the tailpipe. This hardly endeared Robert or the organization to local law enforcement, and not a few State organs of the Patrolman's Benevolence Association had begun agitating for the RM's (which, again, was not actually the name of the organization, but a joke Robert had made that had somehow snagged purchase in the mind of every bloviating right wing radio host and police advocate in the lower-48) to be designated a Hate Group notwithstanding zero recorded incidences of actual violence against police officers, zero statements of intent to harm police officers, the completely peripheral relation of police officers in general to Robert's or Oscar's, or Sam Herbert's or Murray Bookchin's or anyone else's stated goals. Notwithstanding all that, it was soon seen as a threshold, red-meat issue in certain more conservative localities to advocate measures running the gamut from Resolutions of Censure to the Firing Squad whenever Robert Vicaray or his little group were brought up (which is how, eventually, he came to the attention of one Police Sgt. Dan Volsky, of Irving County NY).

Their first bite at the apple was a 500-year flood in a town called Lawrence, two feet below sea-level in the Mississippi River delta. The RM's showed up in station wagons and rented U-Hauls and school busses bought for a song at a firehouse auction. They went door to door with water bottles and cell phones. They got threatened a lot, shot at some, chased by evil-looking dogs, cursed for fools. But they also—not to be saccharine about it—experienced an extraordinary outpouring of gratitude from people, for basic human kindnesses that you wouldn't think twice about lending your neighbor. The first things that became apparent, after that initial experience in the flood zone, were 1) exactly how extraordinarily poor the poorest people in America are, and 2) just how violent the relationship between U.S. Police and America's permanent underclass is.

On his second day in the delta, Robert heard police driving around announcing via megaphone that anyone seen outside their house would be considered a suspected looter and anyone suspected of looting would be shot on sight. On the fourth day they came across a dead boy on the street, looking lonely in repose, nobody around to explain him. On day six Robert witnessed two police officers nailing a schizophrenic man inside his small house with four-by-fours while inside he screamed "Help! Help!" Robert made eye contact with the two white officers who nodded. They said nothing, and left carrying the four by fours, looking annoyed and indignant. Robert eventually pried the man out, but could not convince him to leave his home.

Even if his personal philosophy was not reflexively hostile to firearms, Robert would never have anticipated how much of Disaster Aid consisted of physically protecting people from cops. He and his merry band had come with emergency blankets and cell phones and water pumps and ace bandages, not anticipating in their most fevered imaginings that they would also have to build literal bulwarks protecting Americans from the men who professed to guard over them. Poverty is a form of violence same as wife-beating or kidnapping. No amount of bookish theorizing can prepare you for the visceral reality of rigidly enforced privation. As everybody from Marilynne

Robinson to the Dalai Lama could tell you, there exists no actual scientific reason why, in an age of abundances, in a post-scarcity economy, in an ostensibly developed nation, anyone anywhere should have to be poor. It is a choice that we wake up and continuously re-make every day, to allow the criminal mismanagement of resources in service of state-planning for various equity outfits and NGOs while people go hungry. Just because something isn't written on the books, doesn't mean it's not a crime. They'd left the flood zone battered, victims of significant and avoidable theft, with confidence shaken and egos bruised, but determined to be more effective.

"This is why we started small," Oscar Louder said. He alone seemed enervated by the experience. He alone was greatly pleased.

"The best thing in the world is to find out about your biggest liabilities on the smallest possible scale."

Perhaps it was Louder's natural grimness, his inborn pessimism. Perhaps it was seeing the way the police treated a bunch of people who shared his skin tone when he himself never seemed to talk about where he came from or who his family was. Perhaps it was a sort of joyous rage he felt at being allowed to see the contours of the thing, the outside lines, finally in relief.

"It's like walking around carrying a body," he commented dryly once, to Robert. "It's like having to carry a body around with you everywhere you go. And no one can see it but you're dragging it around everywhere, on your back, all the time, and it is *exhausting*."

Robert had nodded, without ever asking Louder the obvious follow-up: whose? Who was Louder dragging? He never seemed to talk about how or where he'd grown up. You could tell in a vague way, by how he talked, the words he used, that he'd been raised in someone's impression of the black middle class, if such a thing could be said to exist. But it was as if he were an orphan or had walked out of the sea at the age of 30, fully formed. No mention of parents, or siblings or childhood friends. No mention of whose body it was, that taxed him so, everyplace he went. And Robert, perhaps out of cowardice, perhaps out of thoughtlessness or self-absorption, never asked.

The next time around, they increased monitoring of the reusable tool stores. They had a sign-in-sign-out book. It would still be easy enough for a determined grifter to walk away with a pair of bolt-cutters as they were not actually *running down* the tools that went missing. But the *very act* of checking them out, the *very act* of putting down one's name (this was another of Oscar's brainstorms which bore fruit) seemed to have some rippling psychological effect on the lightness of peoples fingers, the rate of pilfer. They made more mistakes, took more manure in the teeth, said thank you very much, got more organized, and naturally and steadily became more hostile toward local and Federal authorities. Toward even the other non-profits who would show up and offer someone a FEMA trailer with the one hand, and a no-knock raid from immigration with the other, who seemed to think there was no viable daylight between taking Federal money and fully aggressively complying with every know-nothing Federal jackboot. It wasn't just the undocumented either. Every municipality where a local D.A. was looking to polish his/her bona fides fighting The Drug War, fighting Sex Trafficking (which is generally D.A. code for locking up sex workers), fighting the scourge of Homelessness ("strange" Oscar remarked once "that the only way we know to talk about suffering is the language of war") represented one more locality where the big Aid Organizations ended up striking a hundred little devil's bargains with the government, all in order to get ice water to folks in some fresher hell.

It was unceasing, attritive and attractively dumb. They (the cops) would sweep through the relief tents with flex-cuffs and assault rifles 'til they'd met whatever quotas they needed to get raises or revenue bumps or lead the evening news. Until word began to get around that all the same problems you'd had before the disaster struck—harassed by Social Services, parole violations, shook down by the police, bench warrants and unpaid fines— all trailed you into the Red Cross tent, intensified by cops' boredom, by enclosed space and time, and wasn't that a steep price to pay, just for a shower and a hot meal? These mammoth organizations knew this. Knew they were neutering themselves, making themselves less effective at distributing aid to the people who'd needed it most, and still did it anyway, because it was more important to them to maintain a salaried organizational roster, year round, than it was to thumb the nose at their heavily armed benefactors.

Study this: Any non-profit sufficiently large for you to have heard about, is also afflicted with mass quantities of bureaucratic incompetence and waste, even if organizationally its heart is in the right place—which most of them are. By the time Rude Mechanics'd hung out their shingle at their third-ever disaster site, they were somehow receiving major cash infusions from Direct Relief and All Hands International. It wasn't that those organizations were actively malicious, though Robert had his issues with both. Indeed, they wanted to connect people with resources *so badly* that they were willing to essentially hand-off a sack full of unmarked bank notes to an uncredentialed anarchist and his weird disaster collective, and deal with the consequences later—it was that one of the attendant woes of being a Big Cultural Institution like the Red Cross, or All Hands, was that you were *also* constantly mired in labyrinthine administrative moraxes and slow-footedness and one-hand-washing-the-other-it is that accompany all Big Cultural Institutions in the U.S.

But the RM's benefit was that of a Chinese skyscraper, lean and uniform and concerned primarily with the elapse of time. Time was the only nonrenewable resource in a crisis. Time could be measured out in avoidable deaths and rotten food, in hospital beds and headlice. And the collective's modus operandi—though they would bristle at the comparison—was that of the big box stores, the Walmarts of the world, to move as many units of aid at as low a cost a possible. Even with no hierarchy and two people in every position, and doing things by voice-vote, they were *still* able to distribute aid at a much more rapid clip than anyone else with boots on the ground in a given disaster area. And as news of them travelled from city to city, that they went into communities and did not care for the criminalization of vice, and did not work with police, and did not hand-wring over the dreaded Waste-Fraud-Abuse nexus, that they instead got you what you needed as quickly as possible and asked if there was anything else they could do, so too did their name get passed around in mutual aid and direct action circles, by word of mouth or online, in the same way that other names and places got passed around like storybook characters or dead congressmen, Malik Rahim, Cheran, Mexico, Jackie Sumell, Marinaleda, Spain, the same way people would later talk about the women of Rojava. You can take issue with a bunch of ideologues who inveigh against organized worship, then nominate all these people and towns for secular sainthood. It is a valid critique. But if pressed on this point, Robert Vicaray would likely shrug it off. You may choose your master, is the consensus, but do not kid yourself thinking you are no one's slave.

They were well known to a certain set, dialed-in and on-call for whenever, wherever the next catastrophe would strike. A rolling Marinaleda. Patching holes in the dyke and, so doing, becoming part of it. Replacement planks on the ship of Theseus. Then word came down one day that there had been some kind of accident in upstate New York, an industrial explosion of some sort, massive and out-of-nowhere. Nobody had any information yet. Everyone was still monitoring police scanners. So Robert and his little circus of lefty weirdos piled into their station wagons, and their rented U-hauls and their school buses bought for a song at auction, and they pointed their noses north, never imagining what strangeness might lie waiting for them there.

CHAPTER 22

After the blind woman and her daughter had explained what little they knew, Herbert and Vicaray dispersed. So then it was just Oscar Louder, standing in front of the two of them, and fiddling with an unlit cigarette. The auditorium, which had capacity for perhaps 400 people (though there were fewer than 200 hospital beds) was not yet a quarter full, volunteers were still going out into the town with headlamps, heat-resistant waders and kayaks, calling out trying to find people trapped inside their homes or else (dreadful) who'd been caught in the initial explosion but survived somehow.

"So," the blind woman, the mother, cleared her throat and Oscar startled. Evidently she knew he was still here, could sound him out, from the noise of his breath or his fiddling with the cigarette. "What's next?"

"Next." Oscar repeated slowly as if the concept had never quite been articulated to him before.

"Are you—do you have to discharge me or?"

Oscar glanced from the woman's face to her daughter. The girl was staring at him now (was it possible?), smiling a little.

"You don't worry about that," Oscar said. "No one's kicking you out of here. Just focus on—" he stopped himself. He'd almost said, "Focus on getting better," then realized what a meaningless sentiment that was, that people were always insisting to one another. Like as if infirmity were a result of a failure of will.

"What's going on in town?" the woman continued.

"Power's out," Oscar sniffed. "If what you say is right, about the syrup, then probably the sewage lines are all fucked—excuse my language." The mother looked puzzled as if she could not ascertain why he would ask to be excused. He tucked the cigarette behind his ear. The girl reached out and squeezed the woman's arm again. Oscar once again glanced between the two of them. Something off, something strange was happening here.

"We've got two engineers here plus a lot of journeymen who used to work for Con Edison, but getting the power back on is going to take a long time. The Governor's declared a state of emergency just an hour ago and formally requested Federal help, but there's no way of knowing how long it'll take FEMA. After Katrina it took them five days to get into place, National Guard took six, but New York isn't Louisiana and the head of FEMA isn't a horse trainer." He rattled all this off glancing around the room at the collapsible beds being rolled in, electing not to wonder where they were getting the beds from and if it was through legal channels.

She muttered something that sounded to him like: "—*daze-out water*."

"What?" Oscar looked sharply at this white woman whose name eluded him. What had the girl said her mother's name was? Ellen? Emily?

"Just something I learned," said Ellen or Emily. "People live three days without water. Three hours without shelter."

Oscar nodded. "Some people," he said. "Old people can't live three days without water. Babies." He gestured. He saw the woman tense at the word. *Babies.* "Chronically ill people, any stress is going to exacerbate their underlying conditions. But that's not the worst-case scenario yet."

"What…" the girl, who'd been quiet up to this point, spoke up now, looking at him with wide eyes. Oscar could not say why this girl's eyes made his skin crawl. "…is the worst-case scenario?"

Oscar met her gaze, deciding whether or not this was appropriate conversation for a non-adult. He supposed she was about thirteen, and her mother did not seem to object.

"The worst case scenario," he said, "beyond something like Katrina where it takes the government five days to arrive, is that town officials try and maintain civic order but don't have the resources or manpower to distribute what people need, and so people are trapped, and desperate, and the power stays down. And then—"

Oscar's attention suddenly was tugged sideway as two medics gurneyed in a horribly burned man, his eyes bulging, darting around, his mouth wailing (they shushed him), blistered skin still strapped to the gurney, transferred him gingerly to a nearby bed. *Jesus.* Oscar looked back toward the girl, and saw that she too was looking at the burned figure, her eyes bulging alarm.

"Hang in there honey," one of the medics said softly to the man, then glanced around looking almost embarrassed at having said it. The man clearly did not have much time left on the clock.

Oscar's stomach wobbled. Children were not supposed to be party to these grotesques (not that Oscar knew, Sairy Wellcomme wasn't exactly present or accounted for, mentally or spiritually or whatever). The girl recomposed her face and returned her attention to Oscar. The mother, Emily or Ellen or whatever—who could not obviously see the poor specimen who'd just been brought through the door—leaned forward, confused by Oscar's long pause. "And then?" she repeated. The burned man seemed to be looking over toward the woman and the girl, staring fixedly at both of them. Then one of the medics jammed a sedative into his arm. His eyelids flew wide, then began to droop.

"And then," Oscar continued, reclaiming his own attention. He suddenly itched to light his cigarette inside, to take the wispish industrial smoke inside himself to sink its grey clouds into the soft pink tissue of his lungs, 'til it was absorbed and his brain began to buzz, "because we have bad luck… it starts to rain."

With that, he left them, the mother holding limply to the daughter's hand, as the girl stared fixatedly across the gymnasium floor at the burn victim with his eyes medicated shut.

CHAPTER 23

Police Sgt. Dan Volsky was not a particularly evil-meaning man. As a public servant, maintainer of civic order, security guard of the world, he was essentially a fastball pitched straight down the middle strike zone of the American male disposition. If his personal politics leaned revanchist at all, it was in that knee-jerk way of nearly all cops in that he thought broadly about Bad Guys and Good Guys, in that he did not particularly care for the opinions of non-police on police matters, in that he believed in the efficacy of holding one set of ideals in your head, and another more durable set, in your hands—which is a cognitive dissonance only ever afforded the white and the powerful in America.

Unlike most cops, Dan Volsky actually lived in the community he policed. And unlike most cops, he did not particularly care for the thousand political belligerencies of the Thin Blue Line. But again, Dan was not some mythic hero cop. As the majority of his time was spent interacting with poor whites, their chemical dependencies, their domestic disputes, their negligence and fraudulence and late child support payments, Volsky held no great love for the people he policed, and had acquired as most cops do an essentially jaundiced view of human nature that stopped just short of the water's edge where his own personal tribe was concerned. He was, by all knowable metrics, a decidedly mediocre police officer.

Now it may have been earlier mentioned but I will iterate for clarification, that at the time of the explosion on the north end of Bilbao, the Mayor, Deputy Mayor, Police Chief, Deputy Police Chief, Fire Chief, County Comptroller, Head of the Arts Council, and all their various Chiefs of Staff were neatly assembled (as ill fortune would have it) shoulder to shoulder on a woodblock rostrum draped in matte black skirting and stage carpeting, sitting with hands in their laps, on collapsible metal chairs straining beneath the weight of all these bedecked, dress-uniformed men of great public account, posed underneath a banner that read REMEMBERING FALLEN HEROES. The event was to commemorate a horrible fire that had burned through the town in 1972, where various officers and firefighters and local actors had perished pulling regular civilians to safety from the blazing remains of the Littoral Community Playhouse, which had been putting on a local rendition of Shakespeare's *Coriolanus* wherein midway through, a fake cannon was meant to go off shooting ticker tape and confetti over the heads of the unsuspecting audience (it being the 1970s and all) but, on the last night of the play's run, the disgruntled director (who was at the time in the middle of a messy divorce, and who had just received word that his Fellowship at the nearby Arts Council was set to be eliminated by the its board of directors, on account of student agitators unaffiliated with the Arts Council had disliked some comments he (the director) had made regarding Secretary of State Henry Kissinger's secret bombing campaigns in Laos and Cambodia and, what was more, that he (the director) felt the dissolving social mores of the Sexual Revolution, the rise of Radical Feminism, the fight for the ERA, that all these great horrors had done was brainwash and rob a bunch of otherwise lovely girls of their femininity and disintegrate the social fabric, and that basically the whole of Women's Lib and the Antiwar movement had been an unmitigated crock and complete failure from the outset was this august community theater director's from-the-hip assessment of the current state of America—that upon losing both his long-term fellowship and his long-term wife, in a span of less than 3 months, the deranged theater director had got it into his head to, on the last night of the show, load the stage cannon with six gallons of the town's most famed export (knowing as he did that both the president of the Arts Council and the wife who was in the process of leaving him, were both sitting out somewhere in the crowd) not intending to hurt anybody, he swore afterwards, just to give them a nice little scare and soil their pristine churchclothes. And so, the act break of *Coriolanus* had come and the unwitting stagehand had lit the cannon and pointed it up toward the catwalk as he had every night previous, except that this time it was filled with liter upon liter of thick maple syrup. The syrup might well have exploded out into the air, and given everyone a good scare. Certainly that might have happened were it not for the fact that the stage cannon they were using was not sufficiently equipped to propulse any sort of viscous liquid (or really anything of significant weight) out into the air. That what happened was that the quantity of syrup in the barrel instead caused the pressure inside the cannon to, slowly, build and build and build, and that, after several seconds of waiting with fingers plugging ears, as a disappointed sigh began to pass through the audience (all of whom had after all, expected the confetti) that the stagehand who had first lit the cannon edged forward still plugging his ears, and, using the toe of one boot, nudged the barrel a little, and perhaps that little shift, the small jostle or the pocket of air it let in, caused the pressure differential between the cannon and the air around it finally to tip past some critical threshold, and, in a barely perceptible instant, the stage cannon exploded into pieces. Syrup and flame shot out in every direction, and almost at once the stage, the curtains, the walls, the mezzanine balconies and proscenium arch were set ablaze as a roaring fire crept across the ceiling. People stampeded for the closed exits, trampled elderly ushers, and the theater director watched in horror from the stage as his little prank unfurled into an unmitigated disaster. He was charged, obviously, and thrown into jail, after the proper authorities had reconstructed what happened. He eventually died in prison, which is as senseless a place to die as any other.

At any rate, that is why such a heady assemblage of local bigwigs were all gathered together in the exact same place, at the exact same time as less than a quarter mile away, tank after flimsy tank at the Littoral Maple Co.'s storage and refinery complex, began without ceremony to fail, in a way not dissimilar from how that long-ago cannon had failed, and that is why as the huge boiled churning wave rushed down the street toward the flapping banner REMEMBERING FALLEN HEROES and the accompanying flag at half-mast, as the Mayor, lamented the "Extraordinary failures of past fire-safety regulations," clueless as to why all the people in the folding chairs in the front row before him were leaping to their feet and scrambling away—quite rudely it seemed to him—from the stage, as he continued to speak, never once glancing back over his shoulder at the liquid brown wall that signaled his and everyone else on stage's impending doom, learning that we are always fighting the last war, so that today's mayors shake their heads disbelievingly at the fire codes of mid-century community playhouses, so that tomorrow's mayors will marvel at the regulatory lassitude of Maple Refinery Safety Requirements but more than anything, more than the ghosts of angry bit-players, the prevarications of local leaders, more than history as metaphor, or catastrophe as theater, what this incident signifies beyond the obvious Numbering of the Dead, is how a vacuum forms in space, and how nature learns to abhor it, and how it can swallow up your life and the lives of those around you, launch you suddenly along paths you have no way of coming back from, atop hierarchies you never consented to or thought about in a serious adult way, the way Sergeant Dan Volsky by dint of his decided mediocrity became suddenly the highest ranking member of the Littoral County P.D. thanks to a disgruntled theater director, a negligent syrup company, a shoddily constructed rostrum, a buildup of industrial chemicals, a tax loophole—stupidity masquerading as luck and luck masquerading as fate—how Dan became aware of a murder, showed up guns ablazing demanding that Oscar Louder and the rest of the folks at the Pavilion turn over a wanted criminal, and came to a bad ending one night in late June, underneath a black and parturient sky.

CHAPTER 24

The three nosey young men adjourn, and Robert is quickly called away to examine some supply store that the field medics have set up. Oscar Louder lingers in front of the woman and her daughter who's lost in her own thoughts. Sam Herbert, looking flushed, clears his throat and wanders away in no particular direction. Herbert's role here is, primarily, to ensure that if they need to access a lot more money, on very short notice, they can do so without fuss. The other side of that coin, however, is obviously that, once on-site, he, Herbert, is effectively useless for anything beyond handwringing. His evident pedigree and style of dress do not endear him greatly to the rest of the Rude Mechanics. He reeks of private school and moneyed indifference. Some people, behind his back, even refer to him as The Narc. Chief among these uncharitable surveyors of conscience reigns David Boggs, the group's resident drunk, a man whose peculiar genius regarding anything with four wheels and a motor, makes him a near matchless value-add to the operation, enough, at least, to justify paving over his pretty obvious personal shortcomings.

As Boggs' father, a career construction foreman, was known to show up to his building sites on Monday mornings still profoundly under the weather, and incidentally managed to pitch himself dead of a heart-attack at the ripe old age of 42, it would be fair to say that Boggs comes by his dipsomania honestly. He's well-liked by most everyone (even the phlegmatic Oscar Louder, who doesn't seem to much like anybody) on account of it is rather hard to dislike somebody who wears his biggest flaw on his sleeve, and on top of the fact that, for all his bluster, and besides his one peculiar vendetta against Herbert (who, in addition to "The Narc," Boggs sometimes refers to as "that walking Brooks Brothers mannequin"), he is essentially harmless.

No one is 100 percent sure how Boggs came to be part of the Rude Mechanics in the first place, nor how he gets from location to location. The consensus seems to be that he just sort of showed up one day, on some or other disaster site, and started tinkering. He is fiercely loyal to Robert and Robert alone—though he rarely, as I have said, causes trouble with Oscar Louder. His accent is unplaceable (people like to take turns guessing). Boggs himself seems to relish his non sequitur status here, to jealously guard any bits of biography that seem to slip past the censors. He is of course *sine qua non* rather shiftless. If you're caught in the unenviable position of having lent him five dollars or a pack of cigarettes, you'd be better served cutting your losses than trying to recuperate them. His favored poison is red wine, which Boggs himself acknowledges begrudgingly is "lace curtain." He is partial to Spanish reds, sips them out of an expansive array of portable coffee mugs. He swears that he works best with a hangover and so is kept well stocked, whenever someone needs an engine fixed or somesuch. His politics are illegible. Anyone who studies Boggs' conversation for some sort of ideologic cogency does so in vain. Robert Vicaray has, in the course of knowing him, heard Boggs assert the following semi-political things:

He thinks baseball should be taught in schools

He thinks federal milk subsidies are a blight on society

That he hates "the so-called congress"

That an individual should be allowed to fish in any body of water, public or private, anywhere in the United States, provided they bring their own rod.

That "All licensing is a racket"

These, combined with Boggs' semi-regular paroxysms of naked contempt towards various corporate functionaries, public servants, artificial coy pond owners et. al., make for rather difficult placement on the traditional Left-Right axis of American politics. As far as anyone can tell, and insofar as he has any ideology whatsoever, Boggs is an enemy principally of Bigness, but also thinks Smallness is underratedly baleful.

"Where'd you get the horse, Boggs?"

Glen Aurech, sitting sandwiched on a picnic bench between the fat asses of Messrs. Arthur Dewell and Devon Hitchcock, regards the swaying David Boggs with what could be described as cautious amusement. They are taking a five-minute break in between fetching pallets of dry goods from the back of a U-Haul before the very last light leaks out of the sky. In addition to the horse, Boggs is inexplicably holding a plastic coffee thermos that reads I'D RATHER BE IN RENO. That jumpy little pencilneck, Herbert, whose specialty seems to be minding other peoples' business, emerges from the front of the building and lingers, just outside the ring of their conversation.

"So it's illegal to own a horse now?" Boggs hiccups, leaning against the flank of his new friend, a chestnut mare with a bridle but no saddle to her.

"It's definitely illegal to own somebody else's horse," says Glen mildly.

"Go to hell."

"Suit yourself Boggs."

The drunkard seems unsure of whether he wants to stay and argue some more or move on with his new friend in search of better grazing. Unfortunately for Herbert it is at this moment that Boggs catches him staring.

"What are you looking at?" probes Boggs as the three men on the bench half-turn in the direction of Herbert, who stands completely still, not saying anything, looking from Boggs to the horse and back again.

"You got something to say to my horse here?"

Art Dewell laughs, which you should never do in the presence of a drunk since he will near-to always take it as encouragement.

"Boggs, let it alone," Glen says.

But Boggs does not look of much a mind to let it alone. He stabs a finger in his own chest.

"Anything you got to say to my horse, you can say to me." The mare urinates in the grass to emphasize the point. Sam Herbert has yet to say a word.

"What is it you do here?" Boggs asks witheringly. "Besides standing around like you're trying to win a uselessness competition?"

Glen is torn between his desire to preserve the civic peace and his desire to see someone take the mickey out of this straw-haired rosy-cheeked hedge fund man, who is always hanging around, gawking, never lending any sort of hand, never saying anything to anyone—who seems somehow to resemble everyone who ever denied you a bank loan, or outsourced your job, or complained to your manager about your tone.

"I handle the money," Sam Herbert says finally. The sentence is a probing, sheepish concession, as if it were arrived at by committee consensus. This is one of the many problems, Boggs thinks, about sending these little boys away to college. They come back little men, unsure of basic facts.

"You handle the money. No." Boggs shakes his head. "The money handles you." He gestures profoundly, like he is the first man to ever saw through the Gordian knot.

The drunk's whole face glows orange in the last vestiges of the dying sun. Herbert seems frozen. He keeps glancing at the horse as if for guidance.

"What do you keep looking at?"

"Is that your horse?" Hebert says accusatorily, looking around for support.

"Is it *your* horse?" Boggs says.

Herbert shakes his head, no. Boggs lays his palm ostentatiously on his sternum like a declaimer of late antiquity.

"My grandfather was a groomer on the racing circuit. He lost all the fingers on his left-hand to a mean Filly. He loved the horses even after—you can't blame an animal. They would sleep rough a lot of the time—the groomers. Or in lofts above the stables. He'd had to fend off intruders. He loved Franklin Roosevelt. I used to ask him why, and he used to say, 'Not all Democrats are horse-thieves, Dave honey, but it is my experience that all horse-thieves are Democrats.' Do you understand?"

No telling if a word of this story is true. Anyone studying the oral history of David Boggs' family tree would notice the number and composition of his bloodline appears continuously to evolve depending on what point he is trying to emphasize.

Herbert shakes his head that no, he doesn't.

Boggs looks as if he has just won a great rhetorical victory against all odds.

"Of course you don't."

Sam Herbert clears his throat with what seems like herculean effort.

"If you took that horse from somewhere you have to give it back," he says.

Boggs' eyes narrow suspiciously.

"You want my horse, you foul little rat?"

"He doesn't want your horse Boggs," Glen says after what seems an eternity, feeling annoyed at having to intercede on the accountant (or stockbroker or whatever)'s behalf.

All is quiet except for the mare's breathing.

Boggs clutches the horse around the neck for emotional support.

"The Narc can say what he wants for himself, no? Or else what was all that college for? You want this horse?"

Sam Herbert, wide-eyed and noodle-armed, shakes his head a third time, *No.*

"Good because I've killed for less," Boggs says.

"Who have you killed Boggs?" Art says.

"Shut up," Boggs admonishes again.

It's around this moment Oscar Louder emerges from the Pavilion of the Abandoned Future. He wanders over toward the group of men sitting or standing around the picnic benches.

"They run out of work for you fellows out here?" Oscar asks dryly.

The men on the picnic benches exchange sheepish looks, get to their feet, curse their lower-backs as they two-step limpingly back toward the rear bumpers of the trucks dragging twin pallet jacks behind them in the dirt.

Boggs is still staring at Sam Herbert.

"Where'd you get the horse Boggs?" Oscar asks, not much caring about the answer.

Boggs, who as a matter of habit for some reason dares not trifle with the veteran insurance investigator, pulls his eyes away from Herbert, and says, mildly:

"Found it."

Sam Herbert looses a high, incredulous laugh. Boggs looks daggers.

"Well, ditch it with someone," Louder instructs. "We're taking a boat toward that town."

Herbert straightens to attention, turns to Oscar:

"Which town?"

"The one where that mother and girl came from," says Oscar Louder. "The one covered in syrup."

"It's getting dark," says Sam Herbert, and Louder turns and eyes him like he is a particularly ugly decorative sofa or something.

"It's a good thing I'm not afraid of the dark then."

Boggs nearly guffaws, then sets off to find someone dumb or soft-hearted enough to hand off the horse to.

"Leaving in five minutes, Boggs," Louder calls at the back of him.

"Well," sighs Sam Herbert, and Oscar Louder cannot help but feel some measure of disdain rise up in his throat, looking this overcoiffed feckless Andover boy up and then down, thinking of a bathtub full of drowned dogs, and how it always seems like the same few people get stuck belling the cats of the world. "I'll come with you then," says Herbert, nodding determinedly.

Oscar Louder blinks, taken slightly aback by this pronouncement. Then he recovers, shrugs, silently remonstrating himself that he doesn't know everything, all the time.

"Suits me down to the ground," he says.

CHAPTER 25

AN UNSUBSTANTIATED AND ALMOST THOROUGHLY
IMPOSSIBLE ACCOUNTING OF SAIRY WELLCOMME
AND LEANNE SWINBURNE'S CONVERSATION IN THE
PAVILION OF THE ABANDONED FUTURE, FOUND
IN THE NOTEBOOK DRAFTS OF THE DISCREDITED
JOURNALIST THOMAS ENTRECARCELES

"Leanne."

She felt a small hand on her cheek.

"Wake up Leanne." The hand's fingers were soft, tapping out a rhythm on her cheekbone.

"Leanne wake up, we have work to do now."

Work. She ran her hands along her body. Why was she wearing these strange clothes? And why was it so dark? And where was—? The hand tapped her cheekbone once more.

In the fuzz of her brain Leanne connected the hand with the voice and the voice with the girl. *The girl.* She shot up in bed, flinched away from the hand's gentle touch.

"Hush. You'll be O.K. Hush now. We have work to do."

The hand reached for her again but she batted it away.

"Who are you? What are you?" Leanne said sharply.

The girlish voice ceased cooing. It sat quiet a moment.

"I already told you my name Leanne. It's S—"

"That's not your name," Leanne snapped, confused.

"Sure it is. Keep your voice down," the girl instructed.

Leanne complied uncritical still.

"That's not your name," she said again, "so what are you? Are you a girl?"

The voice sighed, sounding impatient.

"If I tell you that I'm not, will that help?"

Leanne did not respond. She would wait. She would not move. She would not take instruction until the voice explained itself to her satisfaction.

"I've got the memories of a girl. I've got the body of a girl. My *name*." Somewhere far off, someone knocked over what sounded like a bedpan. "My name is my name, the one I have got. As for what I *am*—"

Her tone indicated that the girl seemed to consider the very question quite trivial. "—*There is a world elsewhere* Leanne. Colors your eyes cannot adequately see, sounds you cannot adequately hear."

Leanne cleared her throat, refused to move. The girl sighed again.

"I'm not lying to you. I am trying to explain how I got to be here: When that explosion happened, there was a tiny little hiccup in the fabric of things. Nothing you would have noticed. But I happened to be—at that moment—in a sort of transition-state. So your little explosion punched a hole in the place where I'm from, and I accidentally slipped through the hole, and I accidentally fell inside the body of this little girl. So I am trying to get back where I came from, basically."

"Are you a—Jesus what—a demon?"

"There's no such things as demons," sniffed the voice flatly. "Or underfiends or what-have-you. I'm—it doesn't matter what you call me. Call me a plant. I'm as value-neutral as a plant, where I come from."

Leanne touched her own face, softly. The girl continued:

"I just am what I am. And I would like to not be here anymore. The girl will be fine, once I'm gone."

"So how are you going to do that?" Leanne said slowly.

"Do what?" said the voice, sounding preoccupied.

"How are you going to get back?"

"You're not going to understand it, if I tell you."

"I already don't understand," Leanne said.

"You're going to *really* not understand. Just come with me, there's a lot of work we have to do. I have seen the way."

She tugged on Leanne's hand but the latter stayed sitting in the hospital bed.

The girl sighed.

"The town has to consent to let me kill their rhinoceros."

Leanne shifted in her bed.

"What?"

"I told you that you wouldn't understand."

"You have to kill a rhinoceros."

"The town has to *consent* to *let* me kill the rhinoceros."

"Like an animal sacrifice."

"Sure."

"And that will—what—that will punch another hole in the... fabric of things, for some reason?"

"Listen, I don't make the rules here."

"You're insane," Leanne said softly. "You're an insane little girl."

Leanne was of course correct. Sairy Wellcomme was laboring under the sorts of shaping fantasies exclusive to people who ought to be locked in the loony bin. There are no such things, after all, as spirits, or magic, or fate, or miracles, or life beyond death. We mostly make up such notions out of boredom, or desperation, or broken-heartedness. Sairy might as well have been saying she could control the revolutions of the heavenly bodies, or talk to animals, for all the sense she was making. Yet, once you have fixed a story in your mind, about who you are and what your purpose here on earth is, it becomes, dangerously, almost impossible to forget. That's why so many people all over the world end up in such tough spots all the time—because some other damaged person at some point sold them on a story that wasn't hardly true, about the way their life would turn out, and they couldn't shake it loose. We humans think, because we're so clever and advanced and have mastered the periodic table of elements, that storytellers have control over the elements of the tales they tell, but it is actually quite the opposite. Stories act on the people who tell them. Fairy tales existed long before we invented them—sat, like dinosaur fossils, waiting to be undusted.

"We really don't have time for this right now. We have to go. There's a lot of work we still have to do."

Leanne shook her head.

"I won't go with you."

"This plan doesn't work with just me by myself. I need you to follow my instructions or we're both pretty much cooked."

"Kill a rhinoceros."

"It's not so crazy, is it? You've heard of—what? Rumpel-stiltskin. The Pied Piper. All I require is one single rhinoceros in a zoo, Leanne. As appetites go, you could not wish me milder."

Still Leanne would not climb out of bed, so the girl made an impatient noise, and said:

"The badly burned fellow they carted in just a little while ago is the Corrections Officer from County Holding. He's alive and he's recognized you, and as soon as his sedative wears off he's going to tell someone who you are, and what you did, and they are going to hand you back over to the police."

She paused, letting this news sink in. Then said:

"Leanne, I'm going to whisper in your ear some things I would have no business knowing otherwise, and then, once you're sufficiently convinced that my situation is just as I've represented it to you, you're going to come with me and help me with the next leg of my plan, which includes saving you from that Corrections Officer. Either that or you can sit here alone, and wait for the men to come take you away."

And the little body moved close, the head inclined towards Leanne's ear, and she nearly flinched again, as the girl, or the creature with the girl's voice, began to murmur of things it had no business knowing otherwise, while Leanne held her breath, and wondered inwardly whether she herself believed in spirits, in demons, in sacrifices and fairytales, block-grants of phantasmagoria, whether the characters in storybooks asked themselves these same questions, just before the hex took purchase, and whether people's rational disbelief is a matter of indifference to the ghosts that come to haunt them.

CHAPTER 26

Of course it should have been easy for Robert to spot, had his judgment not been so occluded by his own idealism, he should have recognized right away that he had been duped. Hadn't it been, after all, far too easy to convert this supposed Wall Street trader, abruptly, to a life of mutual aid administration? Hadn't it been a bit convenient, after all, that Samuel Herbert should have happened to find out all about Robert Vicaray's personal environmental investments, to quit his job on impulse sight unseen, travel halfway across the country, all in order to solicit a job from a man he'd never so much as *met*? If Robert had been thinking critically, it is almost certain, in retrospect, he would have apprehended there was something strange going on. But instead he was blinded by the courage of his own convictions. Fixated like a madman on this new idea of his—that through direct action, he could build, or help build, a little society in those vacuums where the old one had broken down.

You see, Samuel Herbert was not named Samuel Herbert at all. In actuality, he was Neizar Muntasser the orphaned child prodigy and infamous (in some circles) corporate spy. Muntasser had been hired by Allen Vicaray's old firm after that drawn-out civil court case in the papers had caught their attention.

It was not strange enough, thought they, that Allen Vicaray should have given his whole substantial fortune over to some young man in Salisaw, Oklahoma whom none of them had *ever met* but that the young man in question, *also, should then* strike it rich investing his inheritance in alternative energy? This seemed, in the firm's eyes, a bridge too far, quite preposterous on its face. Something was rotten in Denmark, and they were determined to root out what precisely it was. And so, Muntasser's retainer was paid, no expense spared. He was given clear instructions to monitor, and if necessary, destroy Robert Vicaray and whatever best-laid plans the young heir was concocting out on his little Oklahoma ranch.

Of course what the firm did not know (not that Neizar was volunteering) is that they were not the only ones to have approached him about this case. That he had taken another meeting, made another covenant, with quite another party, less seemly still. It was not so much that Neizar was a *double agent*—he was not thwarting the intentions of one employer on behalf of the other. It was rather that where the eccentric circles of his two patrons aligned, Neizar completed his commission swiftly, brutally. That where one fell off in ignorance, the other continued in obscurity.

A little bit of biography concerning the notorious corporate spy: Neizar Muntasser had been a world-class pianist bound for the conservatory and afterwards classical stardom, until one day when he was 16 he had gone up with his father and mother in a private helicopter and crashed into the side of a seacliff. While Neizar's parents had both been killed on impact, the young man had launched himself out of the vehicle's side door, gone plunging 500 feet into the water, been dashed against the cliff face by the angry waves, fished out of the water by a nearby pleasure boat and somehow miraculously survived—though he had lost several toes, and had to spend most of the next year in traction in St. Swithun's Recuperatory Center For Medical Unfortunates.

While Neizar eventually recovered movement in all his remaining limbs, his prodigious ability on the piano never returned, and so Neizar Muntasser, at 17, dedicated himself to being ruthless at business instead. His first very lucrative business opportunity came not a year later, when he was approached by the head of a major telecom company to seduce and then blackmail a British entertainment mogul. Neizar, who had neither moral qualms about blackmail nor personal fears about seducing a 50-year-old man, performed his function well and was paid handsomely for it. He used the connections he made performing this first job to arrange an interview for Harvard business school. He aced the interview, being an intensely capable interviewee, possessed near-perfect standardized test scores, explained away his grades with his tragic backstory and soon before long was the scourge of Cambridge, MA.

All the while that he was in college, he maintained his contacts in the corporate sector, doing work whenever it didn't interfere with his studies. And as the lines between working for a large multinational, and working, directly or no, for the American Intelligence Services, could often get quite blurry, it was more than possible that Neizar occasionally committed crimes on behalf of our CIA and NSA. For much the same reason narcotics dealers on the street will often give the jobs of most legal precarity to children, who the court will not try as adults, so too was Neizar's smooth babyish face, his comparative youth, a boon to the unseemly multinationals that—needing unpleasant things done for unpleasant reasons—hired out and referred him each to the other.

It is probably true that Neizar was on the high-functioning end of the spectrum of Antisocial Personality Disorder. That this side of him peeked its head out occasionally. On one occasion, for instance, a fellow Harvard undergraduate had remarked at a party on Neizar's penchant for fine dress, "Neizar loves nice things, don't you Neizar? Don't you love nice things?" the idiot boy had kept repeating the phrase, looking around for laughter, or support, several more times. At which point the seventeen-year-old Neizar Muntasser, budding corporate spy, had fixed his bright blue eyes on the other young man and smiled, "No," he said, "*You* love nice things. What *I love* how much wealth thrills you. How afraid you are of it. The power it holds over you. That's what I love. Understand?" The other young man, a scholarship case from Pennsylvania, had excused himself from the party and not come back for the rest of the night.

Still I do not want to give you the mistaken impression that because Neizar was afflicted of this psychiatric handicap, that he was out and out incapable of feeling. Indeed, what made him so effective as a corporate spy was that he *deeply felt* each and every fraudulent role he took on, as if the truth of it burned at the very core of him. When he took on the identity of the fretful simpering Sam Herbert, for example, he *really felt*, in nearly all public settings, both fretful and simpering. It was only in a very few quiet moments, reporting to his shadowy bosses on the phone, or sitting alone on his bed considering the events of the day, that Neizar's face muscles relaxed, his affect flattened, and he was able to slip back into the languid state that felt, to him, most natural.

When, as Sam Herbert, Neizar first came across the girl, this Sairy Wellcomme and her fainted mother, blocking the one eastbound lane of Highway 87, his reaction was panicked concern, fumbling solicitude, checking the mother for hypothermia, checking the girl for shock, calling ahead to one of the volunteer Medics already setting up shop in the empty

Pavilion, while beside him Robert Vicaray jammed on the accelerator and shot eastward. That was as Sam Herbert.

As Neizar Muntasser, though, he felt a feral curiosity pawing at him just beneath the surface. He felt some keen hyena-ish interest peek its head up, unbidden, inside him, begin niggling at the folds of his brain. Neizar, not Sam, was the one to notice that the young girl's eyes, far from panicked or flooded with tears or disassociated from shock, darted around, taking in data as they drove, even as her face and voice expressed anguish or worry for this woman she claimed was her mother.

And when the mother was finally awake, sitting up drinking juice, and they approached her bedside, all hail-fellow-well-mets, it was Neizar who noticed that she hardly seemed to react upon hearing what was supposedly her own name. It was Neizar who noticed the little girl, staring (did he imagine it?) fascinatedly at him—no, at Sam Herbert.

When that down-home idiot rich-boy Vicaray said, "This is Sam Herbert." It was only Neizar who noticed that the little girl, looking directly at him, seemed to smile with some impossible secret knowledge. That she said:

"*Are you sure?*"

And when she did, Sam Herbert, and Neizar inside him, shifted without meaning to. Barely perceptible unless you were studying his face, as this child now was, fixedly, with a cold sort of reptilian intelligence flickering behind her gaze. Neizar picked up some medical apparatus and set to work pulling it apart with his hands, still staring at the girl.

"Am I sure what?" Vicaray said, oblivious.

The girl did not speak, held Neizar's eye for a long quiet moment, not blinking. Then, finally, she said, looking at Robert earnestly. "Are you sure that it's safe here? For us?"

So then. So she would not expose him, at least not immediately. Or perhaps he had imagined the whole interaction. Neizar put the medical apparatus (some kind of hand-operated oxygen pump) back down on the bed, still pulled apart.

"Why don't we start with you telling me everything you can think to tell," said Vicaray looking between the woman and the girl. The woman in the bed, whom Neizar had up to that point paid very little attention, straightened and began speaking with a sort of alacrity Neizar had not anticipated.

"It was a truck," said the woman. "I saw out the—I saw it as *Sairy* and I were walking down the street together..."

An obvious lie, Neizar thought.

Vicaray massaged the back of his neck, oblivious. When she'd ceased talking he gripped his orthopedic cane and said,

"Maple."

The woman in the hospital bed nodded.

"As in syrup. The town's flooded with syrup."

The other man, the sad chain-smoking insurance investigator that Vicaray had hunted up from some fluorescent-lit office park somewhere, drew close, listening to the woman's story. Neizar had noticed how discomfiting people found his gaze. The white people around him especially, something about the morose acuity behind that stare—as if it were a horror for them to be looked at.

Neizar returned his attention to the woman in the hospital bed. She was saying:

"And it's all hitting the ground at once, it was like a wave, like a tsunami, you could hear it *roaring*."

The insurance man has a habit of fiddling with unlit cigarettes. Neizar would not call it a nervous habit because the man so rarely seemed to exhibit nerves. But a psychological gesture certainly.

"So what did you do, exactly?" the man, Oscar his name was, said calmly. The woman's mouth twitched, she looked at him.

"Excuse me?" she said.

He, Louder, took his glasses off and rubbed one frame between his thumb and forefinger, pinched beneath the cloth of his shirttail.

"If it was like a wave, like a tsunami, happening in front of you. And you drew your daughter against your chest and you couldn't see anything, from flash blindness. What did you do to save yourself? Why aren't you both burned, or dead?"

"I," said the woman slowly, "I don't know."

"We hid inside a store," said the little girl, jumping in too quickly, it seemed to Neizar. "I pulled Mom into a store with me, and we hid there, and the syrup couldn't break the plate glass."

The girl looked between the two men, Louder and Vicaray, pretending confusion, Neizar thought.

"Was that the wrong thing to do?" she said.

Robert Vicaray gave the Insurance Man a look, as if to say Has This Child Answered To Your Satisfaction? Oscar Louder stared perplexedly at the girl a few moments longer. She did not return his gaze as she just had Neizar's, instead looked fawningly at the woman she called her mother, sitting up in bed.

Vicaray said:

"That was a very smart thing to do, Sairy. You probably saved your Mom, by doing that."

"Oh good," said Sairy Wellcomme. "Oh good."

Oscar Louder shrugged to himself. He turned and caught Neizar watching him, and grinned in a guileless way. As if he was saying: *Old habits die hard.* Or perhaps, Neizar thought: *Strange and getting stranger.*

CHAPTER 27

They have cast off and set sail atop the dark resistant sea of the Littoral Maple Flood, Oscar Louder sits backwards in the prow of a three-man skiff that Boggs managed to scare up seemingly from nowhere. They have got two pairs of hand paddles that they must reach for at intervals to supplement the loudly straining motor.

"We got to shut the engine every twenty minutes or so," Boggs had explained, leaning over the rear of the boat in the dark, "otherwise it'll overheat in this christing soup."

Boggs coaxes the boat propeller along intermittently, gentle and solicitous as a lover whenever they're running the combustion engine.

"Like trying to use a Magic Bullet to mix fucking cement," he snarls, sweat beading on his upper lip in the dark.

Oscar has got a small flashlight clamped in between his teeth. He has already sweat through the back of his work shirt. Sam Herbert is doubled over an oar with his knees bent.

The liquid underneath and all around them radiates an oppressive swampish stench. Sickly-sweet and unremitting. Their progress down Bilbao Street is slow.

As any beleaguered Chemistry Post-Grad could tell you, liquid viscosity as it relates to heat-transfer is, like many other elements of nominally simple thermodynamics, anything but. For one, while you are probably at least *conscious* of the fact that any viscous liquid will become thicker with cooling, you'll like as not have a slightly *harder* time of it figuring out the relationship between heat transfer and stagnancy. For, while standard physics says that the power drawn by any agitator should be simply subtracted from total exothermic heat transfer in order to determine net cooling (i.e. that if you mix something around a lot, it will get colder faster, like for example blowing on a hot spoonful before tasting your soup) the truth is that the rate of heat transfer in a viscous liquid initially *increases* with increased agitation speed. That's to say: if a superheated, high-retention-high-viscosity liquid were the subject of a one-off, very violent agitation (like, say, an explosive syrup flood resulting from the gaseous pressure buildup in a faulty storage tank) you would initially, counterintuitively, see the heat of that liquid *rise*, not reduce, to the tune of up to 20% of your baseline temperature (represented visually it looks like a sort-of drunken lognormal distribution) as competing laws of physics impelled your superheated high-retention-high-viscosity liquid rapidly, violently outward and upward, all at once.

Likewise, trying to ascertain precisely how long a given liquid will retain heat can invariably be a much harder question than it might first appear to your not-steeped-in-thermody-namic-lingo layperson. Like the old joke about the boy who tells his Professor that he wants to know the name of the liquid that can hold the most heat for the longest time and the Professor proceeds to pull out a map and point to the Pacific Ocean. It is all a matter of what questions you ask. The list of common liquids that possess the greatest *specific heat capacity* is topped by none other than good old liquid water. Liquid hydrogen has higher *specific heat per gram* than water, but as liquid hydrogen cannot independently exist at ambient temperatures, the whole discussion is rather academic. Substances such as ethyl glycol or mercury both have high boiling points, low freezing points, and a fair amount of chemical stability over a wide range of temperatures (which is why they are so useful in things like automotive antifreeze and thermometers, respectively) but this knowledge is not as useful as one might think, in determining how rapidly a roughly 6.9 million gallon admixture of xylem sap, water, light treacle, heavy alkalis, triglyceride oil, phosphoric acid and variform refining chemicals will shed heat. The truth is that between the Rude Mechanics' five decently qualified bachelors of Chemistry, there were at least three conflicting estimates regarding how long the chemicals might stay dangerous, each factoring in different variables of chemical volatility, ambient temperature, initial heat shedding and the continuous unimpeded burning of liquid industrial fires in several different locations throughout the city. And that even as late as two days hence, when the FEMA rank and file properly got set up on the ground, their actuarial people were *not willing to stipulate* that the level of personnel-risk represented by the stagnant syrup batch was sufficiently low as to allow them to begin launching rescue efforts. The syrup people, for reasons of public liability or incompetence or some other unseen inducement, could not (or would not) confirm to the government that it was safe to go in. And so, this was yet another way of saying that the people of Littoral, the people inside the Pavilion of the Abandoned Future, were very much on their own. That they would be on their own for a very long time yet.

David Boggs, who himself is almost wholly ignorant of the abstruse calculus of chemical engineers or federal actuaries or syrup consultants, says this, leaning over the side of the boat:

"Pretty fucking hot, huh?"

Neither of the other two men respond. Oscar Louder, squinting in the dark, takes the light out from between his teeth and twists in his seat, shining it before them.

"We're here," he says.

Herbert and Boggs relax their respective grips on the oars.

"Where is here, exactly?" Herbert says, looking around wide-eyed. In the dark with the power down, the buildings of Bilbao resemble formless masses, hulking over their small boat. Like great dark sea monsters rising up to eat them.

"This is where the little girl said the explosion happened."

Louder picks up the oar and paddles a little. On their left sits a line of three crooked-looking light poles, one with a human-shaped lump wrapped around it. The submerged two-lane auto-road runs straight, kissing the semicircle of the syrup refinery at a tangent. The diamond-wire gates have been blown over, knocked flat, presumably by the explosion, jutting half-submerged from the still syrup like the great fins of meshpole sharks. There are still several fires burning on top of the noxious surface, but with (mercifully) little-to-no wind, they have not yet crossed the wide breadth of street or spread licking up the walls of the rundown buildings.

"What did you want to see?" says Herbert, his voice too loud in the liquid quiet. Absent the calls of voices, the glow of electric lights, hum of televisions in living-rooms, or the fluorescent leak of all-night diners, you suddenly realize how much the night is given over to the stars. How much space lies between you and them. And how fragile certain types of peace are. Oscar shines his flashlight around pushing down this feeling inside himself, employing his brain as Witness and quiet catalogue of verifiable things. The light passes over more dark organic shapes lying mangled or facedown underneath the flood.

"So the little girl and her mother are walking up on the sidewalk this way," he runs his flashlight on an east-west axis. "Which side of the street are they standing on?"

"If you're walking that way," gestures Herbert, "usually you're on the right side of the street." Louder makes a noise like "Hmm" and tries to paddle their little boat over toward the submerged northern sidewalk. Boggs, seeing this, picks up a paddle himself and helps it along.

Louder tilts his flashlight upward.

"You see a problem here?"

"What problem?" says Herbert, sounding irritable.

"If you're walking up this side of the street, you can't see the syrup refinery."

"So."

Louder blinks.

"If you can't see the refinery, you can't get flash blindness."

Herbert sighs heavily. Boggs thinks idly about shoving him overboard.

"O.K. so they were on the other side of the street."

Louder begins to try and paddle their boat back over to the south side. Boggs, still not understanding why precisely they are here but quite enjoying this strange little detour and how much it seems to irritate Sam Herbert, gamely assists.

Oscar is peering around with the flashlight trying to make sense of things, shining the beam along wrecked facades, shattered vitrines and uprooted awnings, mouthing the words to himself as he reads *We Buy___, ____cksmith & Key 24 Ho_r, 4-in-1, __ohn The Evangelist Bail Bonds &c &c.*

"County corrections," Boggs says as Oscar's flashlight passes over an ugly brick façade. Oscar hardly listens. He is following his own wending suspicions down toward their natural endings. All pulverized glass and inbent edifices covered over in sticky sap, drowning interiors, obscuring their floors.

Why are a Mother and daughter on a Friday afternoon, trav-elling by foot down this derelict street abutting a Maple Refinery, away from the center of town? Then: *Why don't you trust them, Oscar? Everyone else trusts them, so why don't you? What jarred thing set loose on the eddies of your brain won't stay put? What about their story doesn't—?*

Oscar Louder clicks his tongue against his teeth.

"Where's the storefront?" he says.

"What?" Says Herbert.

"The girl says there's an explosion, her Mom goes blind, so she—the girl—she drags Mom inside a plate glass storefront to hide. She specifically says *plate glass*."

Oscar raises his eyebrows, looking at Boggs then Herbert.

"Do you see any intact plate glass storefronts around here?"

Boggs blinks, peering around in the dark. There are brick porches and cellar steps and the collapsed interiors of a couple office spaces. But there are not any storefronts like the one described.

Sam Herbert straightens and begins craning his neck all the way around.

"There's a store just there." He points to the glass display window of a jeweler on the north side of the street.

"But they can't have been walking on that side," says Oscar. "We already—"

"—So then they ran over," Herbert interrupts. Boggs growls like an attack dog. "The girl hears the explosion, grabs Mom, runs across the street."

"A flash flood, a slow one, can move about nine feet per second. A fast one can move up to thirty-five miles an hour. That's fifty-one feet per second, about," Oscar says.

Boggs whistles admiringly.

"How do you know that?" he says.

"I used to work in a lot of flood zones." Louder itches an eyebrow. "Numbers stick in your head."

Hebert says nothing.

"Okay, we'll do some back-of-the-envelope math. I'm assuming, because this was an industrial explosion powerful enough to knock out the power and waterlog an entire town, it was probably moving pretty fast, but we'll table that. So you've got a wave of syrup moving, conservatively, over twenty feet per second. At that speed, six inches of water can sweep a person away. *Two feet* of water is powerful enough to lift a car. This little girl with her blind mother, hears an explosion, turns heel, and sprints going—what? Twelve miles per hour? She has the presence of mind to beeline straight for this plate glass storefront, let's say, at a diagonal, while behind her a thirty or forty-foot wave is rushing down the street, ripping up all these lightpoles and awnings over here, enveloping everything in sight. We think she makes it to *that* jewelry store in time? *That's* what we believe happened?"

"Must have," The hedge fund man says stiffly.

Boggs shakes his head. "I don't believe it."

"Or maybe she just got mixed up and said the wrong kind of window," says Herbert.

"She *specifically said* the glass protected them."

"Then maybe she was *specifically* confused."

Oscar shakes his head.

"There's too many weird little incongruities."

Herbert smiles incredulously.

"Why on earth," he says, "would the little girl lie? Why would the girl, her mother, both lie?"

Oscar Louder peers back toward the ruined maple refinery, the dark slithering hose hung like a severed tentacle from the side of one strutted tower, the looming tanks, now empty, having drowned a city of people with the contents of their sloshing bellies, having knocked the power out, glutted the sewers and turned the stars back on, all a function of some titanic caprice.

He has finally been presented a value he cannot solve for. He shakes his head wondering, then says:

"Let's go and see the explosion site."

CHAPTER 28

I called up my employer after myself and Goober returned to the small squat hotel where we'd both taken up residence for the duration of our stay.

"Who is this?" Sairy Wellcomme's voice sounded crowded out by flurry and harry.

"Thomas Entrecarceles, your intrepid private gumshoe."

"What is this number you're calling from?"

"It's the room number," I said. "Listen, I had to get rid of my cell phone."

In the background I could hear some sort of metal rattling.

"Is that a jackhammer?"

"It's two bearcubs," she said. "They're suffering some sort of intestinal distress. Every day we have to rub their butts."

"I see."

"To massage the anal glands I mean. So they'll eliminate."

"Who says zookeeping isn't glamorous?"

"Zoology is not zookeeping. I would ask you not to conflate the two."

"Well, whatever it is then."

"Why did you get rid of your cell phone?" she said over the distressed yowling of the bearcubs in the background.

"I got a call from an old friend."

"Oh, is everything alright?" she said.

"Yes," I said. Then, "Well, no. Someone else is looking into your story."

The other end of the line went silent a moment, then I heard her excuse herself to someone, and the sound of the baby bears receded from the background.

"What do you mean?" she said, sounding now much more focused, more quiet. I cradled the phone and began scratching words on the hotel pad. Stray impressions, doodles.

"A former, hmm, colleague called me and asked about what I'm doing here."

"A journalist?"

"If you loosen the ambit a little," I said.

"Don't be cute."

"I can't help it."

"Hmm."

I said: "She doesn't know your name. She just knows that I am going around asking questions. And by virtue of the fact that I am interested, she is now also interested. In the most general terms."

"Who does she work for."

"She works for a cable news channel."

"Which one?" she said stiffly.

"I'll give you three guesses."

She paused again.

"I knew this was stupid," I heard her worry softly. "I knew. I knew. I shouldn't have pushed the issue. I shouldn't have hired you."

"This is not me telling you to be worried," I said, after a moment. "This is me telling you to prepare yourself to be worried in the future."

"What does she want?"

"What do any of us want?" I said. Goober thumped his tail on the floor. Sairy made an impatient noise. So I said, "She wants me to sit down for a dinner with her. She just wants to gloat, probably. Or maybe, I don't know—" I caught myself in a stare, fixing dully on Goober's tail thumping mechanically against the hotel carpet.

"—Listen, I have no intention of sitting down with her. And she's certainly not donning a deerstalker and running down the story herself," I said. "Some obscure insurrection up in a Hudson Valley backwater twenty years ago, it's not naturally telegenic. In a week's time, it's off her radar, and you with it. She's a television journalist, which means distractible."

I said this hoping it was true. Every notable lie I have ever told has boiled down to an attempt to wish things into existence that were not so.

"Well."

"I'm not trying to make my nut here, Sairy. I promise you, whatever I find, stays your and my business."

"So what have you found out?"

"Breadcrumbs," I said. "Detritus. Little things that won't stick together. I tracked down the store where you sheltered when the accident first hit. The woman still owns it. She remembers you a little. Not much, just a girl who borrowed a canoe. She was surprised when I talked to her. I think she'd convinced herself that you were a hallucination. And, let's see here."

I began to leaf through my notes.

"Another woman, who owned a bakery, she saw you as well. Later the same day, with an adult woman she couldn't identify."

"Well," Sairy Wellcomme said, "mightn't it have been the one from the clothing store?"

I shook my head even though she could not see.

"The store owner swears she stayed put. She says you set off in that borrowed canoe and she stayed and waited for help. Anything's possible, she could be lying, though I can't imagine why. But I suspect not."

"What did the woman look like?"

I flipped back a page.

"Hard to say. People forget, memories fade with time. Even if this baker, her name is Barlow by the way, even if she swore she knew exactly what this mystery woman looked like, I'm not sure I would trust her description."

"Right," she said, sounding disappointed.

"Right but it almost doesn't matter, because we know where you ended up. We know you landed at a makeshift field hospital on the western outskirts of town. Some converted exposition space or I don't know. We know that because I tracked down someone who'd been brought there himself, and who remembers you. The man said he thought it was a Red Cross hospital. But—and here's where things get strange so bear with me—"

She said nothing, listening.

"—Every contemporaneous source I can find says that the Red Cross wasn't on the ground there until day three. Ditto FEMA. Ditto any other major aid organization."

"Couldn't it have just been the town? The town leadership, or whatever?"

"That's what I thought," I said, frowning, "but I've been going back through every article written during that time. The town newspaper shut down, obviously, but papers from the surrounding area covered the whole thing. There's an article—hold on I'm pulling it up—"

I pulled out my laptop and ran through my browser history while Sairy waited.

"Vischer's Ferry Observer, fifteen July, twenty twelve," I read into the receiver. "State audit finds death of Mayor, other local leaders, played critical role in Littoral disaster."

Outside in the parking lot I saw headlights flash. I heard a car ease into a slot near the front office and someone get out.

"Apparently," I continued, "all of the town bigwigs were gathered together for some outdoor ribbon cutting, the moment the tanks began to fail, and they all died in the flood. So some local police chief was suddenly the last living member of the town organizational structure. The only guy who knew where the light-switches were hidden."

"The papers might just be wrong," Sairy suggested.

I heard the person outside in the parking lot kill the engine, heard the car door thunk, the sound of footsteps walking towards the front office.

"It could be the Red Cross was already on the ground, or something, like the guy says they were."

"Could be," I agreed.

"This fellow I mentioned, Drum, ended up in the field hospital. He seemed on the level, and he had a pretty clear memory of everything. He was the town librarian. He didn't suffer any burns or anything, he caught a blow from a falling shelf, when the explosion hit and shook the building, broke his collarbone. The explosion collapsed the front archway but an assistant librarian pulled him up to the second floor roof. The library has one of those flat multilevel roofs. They sat there all night on the roof, waiting for the police or somebody. A group came down with stretchers and flashlights and he ended up in this auditorium. But here are the two most salient things he recalled to me about that day: One, he said that when *you* came in you weren't alone. You were with a woman who *you called* your mother. He seemed quite sure. She was hurt, also unburned. Also she was blind."

"Blind."

"As in could not see."

"But I *saw* my mother," she said slowly, sounding upset. "I mean *I saw* her—"

"Die, yeh," I said. "And the woman at the secondhand store seemed to corroborate that. So the two possibilities are: maybe she wasn't killed after all. People survive tsunamis, nuclear explosions. The human body is incredibly durable. Maybe you rescued her and brought her to that hospital with you and she passed away there. *Or...*"

Sairy finished the thought.

"Maybe there was a woman I was calling my mother, who wasn't."

"Right, yeh."

The door to the motel's front office opened once again, I heard the footsteps in the parking lot return, then draw nearer. I stood up from the bed and began to cross toward the window. Outside was too dark to see much. A few overheads soaking the parking lot with orange light but not well enough for me to see anything moving about outside.

"Traumatized people, people who suffer a shock, do all manner of bizarre things. Displaced loss or anxiety. I'm no psychiatrist but I don't know, it doesn't seem so far-fetched to me."

The footsteps outside paused. I wondered if they could hear my voice. If it travelled that far, out into the lot.

"What's the second thing," Sairy said.

"The second thing the fellow remembers is the name of the person in charge—or who seemed in charge at least—of coordinating resources at the field hospital. I checked with the Red Cross and he was never on their payroll. Ditto All Hands, Salvation Army, UNICEF, SBP. Hell I even checked with Team Rubicon. Nada. What I found instead was he used to work for some insurance company, doing Flood damage payouts. I tracked down his old manager from the insurance company, the guy said he was an oddity, Ivy League whiz kid with attitude problems who quit without giving notice to go work for some millionaire in Oklahoma."

The footsteps outside resumed, closed the final distance.

"Millionaire in Oklahoma," she said.

"Yeh."

Someone began knocking very loudly on my door. Goober began barking at the sound.

"Someone's here," I said. "I'll have to go."

"What was the man's name? The insurance guy," Sairy said.

"What? Oh. His name. Louder. Oscar Louder," I said. "He threatened to shoot me."

"Oh dear."

The knocking continued. I told Sairy I would call her in a few days' time and hung up the phone.

I stood in the hotel room a moment, listening to the knocking, unsure of whether I should answer the door. Though there did not seem to be an alternative.

CHAPTER 29

"Careful—careful."

"Your saying 'careful' don't do anything," Snarls Boggs.

Sam Herbert makes an indignant puppyish noise in his throat.

Oscar ignores them both, peering around at the ghastly forms jutting out on either side of their little boat, like the skeletal masts of shipwrecked boats. Dark ferries moored along the serpentine meanders of Styx, awaiting new commissions, new passengers.

On his left periphery there is a truck, like a cement mixer, jutting out madly from the drainage ditch, only its cab and hose still visible, a horrible licorice-black homunculus hunched forward in the cab's front seat. As they pass it a sickening stench reaches Oscar and his eyes water. He hears Boggs gag. He catches Herbert peering intently, without apparent fear, at the shape in the cab. Herbert tilts his head. Then, catching Louder watching, rearranges his face's shape into a watery, sheepish grin. The cab is too charred for anything inside to be salvageable.

"There's a ladder up here, Boggs."

Louder shines the small flashlight in the direction of one of the exploded towers and they bring the boat closer.

"Careful," Sam Herbert says once again as they glide alongside it. Louder reaches out and grabs the rung of the ladder. Not too far from them there is some chemical fire burning steadily in its place, showing no sign of wavering.

"Looks like pockets along the surface are still flammable," Herbert observes to no one.

"It's like a scene out of hell," says Boggs hoarsely.

Oscar, peering up, rattles the ladder a bit. It groans. He peers up underneath it.

"The whole bottom's ruptured, blown out," he reports mildly. "Platform is still intact though."

He gets to his feet slowly, careful not to rock the boat, places his foot experimentally on one of the rungs, places his hand on another.

"Why are you going up there?" Sam Herbert says sharply, annoyed.

"Dunno," Oscar says, hoisting his other foot into the air.

Oscar will admit the other man has a point. How does he, Oscar, know the whole ladder will not collapse beneath him as he climbs? What will be gained by his climbing up to survey the maple still? He does not know, but he knows that he feels drawn to it. Compelled as by some rich and boyish mystery. He sets foot on the second rung, then the third. Soon he is midway up, and the ladder seems to moan and wobble unpleasantly with each new step he takes. Oscar does not stop. The air is colder up here. There is a wind that cuts across the night's sky and rocks the top of the tower, turning the sweat on Oscar's back icy against his skin. As he tops the ladder, he hears something, and glances down to see a shape moving up the ladder beneath him. It is Sam Herbert. He clambers up the top rung, lays his palm flat on the grating.

"Hello."

Oscar watches him, saying nothing. Herbert peers around at the darkness. He does not have a flashlight with him.

Oscar takes a few tentative paces forward, then a few more, listening to the metal creak underfoot. He turns his back to Herbert and traces the cylindrical belly of the tank with his flashlight. He steps slowly along the walk, bracing himself against the wind. The handrail is not quite up to his hip. Wind slams against the side of the empty tank, rocking the structure, causing the thin metal to flex and tremble. It is only from below that these gigantic creatures look serene.

Oscar walks further along, further still, suddenly his foot strikes something hard, there is a loud clatter, the something goes skittering, Oscar curses, half-lunges for the object, but feels the platform wobble underneath him. He almost loses his balance, goes pitching over the side, heart slamming in his chest, the moving object, still spinning, flies off the edge of the catwalk, goes plummeting down into the blind darkness with a *thunk!*

He hears Sam Herbert, behind him, shift at the sound. The hissing of the fabric of his coat as he draws near.

"*What was that?*" says Herbert sharply, and Oscar realizes that the other man must be standing very close behind him, for he feels his breath on his neck. "I hit something with my foot," he says, annoyed, then adds, "Would you back up please?"

A pause.

Herbert shuffles backward a little. "What did you hit?"

Oscar tamps down his anger with himself for having been so clumsy.

"Some sort of container."

"Did you get a good look at it?"

"No," Oscar says shortly.

"Oh."

An uneasy silence settles between them both. Herbert says:

"When you say 'container' do you mean more like a lunch pail some worker forgot up here, or do you mean more like a gasoline can?"

"I don't know," Oscar says stiffly.

Herbert says nothing. What is the other man thinking, at this moment?

"It had some kind of animal on it," Oscar says finally.

"What?"

"It had," Oscar halts. "It looked like a zoo, with an animal on it. A gray animal."

"So like a lunch box."

"I've already told you I don't know," Oscar says, working to get his temper under control. *Fucking idiot.*

He clears his throat, takes a few more steps forward. Shining the flashlight further along the curving wall of the storage tank. Checking his footsteps carefully this time.

Annoyingly, Herbert has closed the distance between them again. Oscar can feel the other man's eyes on the back of his neck. Some underdeveloped primitive part of his brain is screaming alarm, at having another shape so close behind him in the dark, generating noise, little chuffs of air, the sound of Herbert's hand reaching out blindly in the dark as if to grab at something, brushing the loop on the back of Oscar's shirt— what children at his middle school used to call a *fag tag.* Older boys would reach out and hook Oscar as he walked down the hallway. Yank him backwards by the loop on his shirt. Tell him they heard his mother was a drunk. Tell him they heard she'd fucked the priest while his dad watched, playing along on the organ. That she'd fucked a boy scarcely older than Oscar himself, they heard, and wasn't that neat?

Oscar breathes in sharply, the cold air catches in his rib cage.

"There it is," he says.

There, more than eight feet across, sits the mouth of the rupture, the hole from which the original explosion would have poured. Oscar hesitates, draws closer. He eyes the hole in the tank, staring into the pitch dark. He knows that the bottom has dropped out, but is unable to see from up here. Unbidden, his brain begins at once to picture it. To imagine the pitless chimneying free-fall that would welcome him like an empty embrace if he were right now to trip. *Or if—*

"So this is where it happened," Herbert says quietly, just behind him. Oscar's pulse leaps a moment at the sound.

He understands that this is something people do when they are nervous, articulating the obvious. He does his best not to hold it against Herbert.

Oscar doesn't respond, simply stares into the tank's brown belly, hoping some voice will echo out from the inside, explain these jarring uncertainties in him. He pictures it again. Some violent lurch, and his brown body sailing through dank air, wind muffled in the dark. He pictures pale hairless arms flayed with flame, reaching out from below this chasm to draw him down into the hot blind earth. To sink into the horrible fetid quiet in their fleshy embrace. He is sweating again, despite the wind. Is Herbert drawing closer to him or is he simply imagining it?

"If it were arson," the voice behind says lightly, quietly probing, "as an insurance investigator, what would you be looking for?"

Oscar half-turns to look, his light still trained downward into the disemboweled tank. The other man is no more than a muddled shape to him, standing there. A rough silhouette from which senseless interruptions spew forth.

"Didn't do that kind of insurance," he says in clipped tones.

Is he imagining it or does he see Herbert smiling, the glisten of his white teeth, in the dark?

Then Oscar sighs, relents, feeling that he is being irrationally short with the finance man:

"From my limited, civilian understanding," he says, "you would look for streamers, anything that would have been used to ensure the fire spread to nearby areas, you'd look for whether the fire had multiple points of origin, for combustible liquids left on the floor, if, for instance, the markings on this hole were consistent with an explosion punching *into* the tank, as opposed to an industrial explosion which would rupture *outward*."

"O.K."

"If the arsonist left anything behind," Oscar continues.

Herbert shifts in the dark.

"Like a container with a zoo animal on the cover, you mean?"

Oscar shrugs noncommittally.

"Maybe like a container with a zoo animal on the cover. But there's nothing to indicate anything like arson. The direction of the explosion, for one, argues against it. As far as I know."

"Unless someone added something to the tank to make the things already inside it more volatile. Then walked away and forgot their little jerry can."

Oscar stares at the outline of the boyish Wall Street trader, made somehow sinister by mere proximity to this boiled cataclysm.

"I suppose," he says, "but you'd be fitting a lot of square pegs into round holes in order to reach the conclusion you want."

"As far as you know."

"That's right, as far as I know."

He shifts his weight and the metal creaks underfoot again.

"Well," Oscar sighs, gesturing back the way they came, "shall we?"

CHAPTER 30

I am going to confess something to you now: Earlier in this story I evaded description of Miles Wellcomme (Sairy's father's)'s physical features. You may have assumed (in good faith) that I was just avoiding overwriting, or purple prose, or that I was trying to prioritize the most germane details for you who do not have an infinite repository of spare time or attention to dedicate to all the pettiest details of the Littoral, New York disaster, but the ugly truth, reader, is the omission of Miles Wellcomme's physical characteristics was purposeful on my part, an act of craven deception and self-preservation.

You see, due to some bizarre stroke of chance, or idiot coincidence, or some other strange engine of galactic caprice, the 45-year-old Miles Wellcomme was born and grew up to look almost completely identical to me, the author, Jesse Salvo, D.O.B. 10-14-92. I know how it sounds, believe me. I was just as baffled and incredulous, when I found out, as you surely are now. But oftentimes our realities make a mockery of our fictions and I am chagrined to say that this is just such a case. Miles Wellcomme, the 45-year-old ophthalmologist resembled—due to some scrambled genealogical powerball, some certain finite set of genetically circumscribed possibilities for the facial features of men of Mediterranean and ethno-european descent, perhaps some wayback common ancestor whom we both share and owe a great evolutionary debt—dead to rights, not the narrator Thomas Entrecarceles, but Me, the authorial I.

Which is partly why I lied to you, sinned by omission, and buried mention of Miles' looks altogether. Truth is, writing a book, even a nonfiction account such as this one, is a delicate tightrope walk. You have to choose what to leave in and what to take out. But beyond that, and most importantly, you must *establish trust*. I felt that, on top of everything else—the syrup disaster, the dead rhinoceros, the amnesiac girl—if I were also to casually mention that the Subject's father just so happened to look, dead to rights, like yours truly, that you, the reader, would throw up your hands, shut the book, and pronounce our whole contract together voided. As I had (I felt) some fairly important stories to tell you about disgruntled insurance investigators, prison breaks, exploding space shuttles, vicious mobs, and Samuel Champlain, and as Miles Wellcomme's otherwise unremarkable facial features did not rate particularly high on that list, I confess, I shelved the whole issue, made no mention of this peculiar resemblance, out of respect for Thomas Entrecarceles, and Sairy Wellcomme and Oscar Louder, and their stories. But no charade can sustain itself indefinitely. The time has come to unmask! So Miles Wellcomme, who died in Littoral, New York, not one day after his wife and only love, had eyebrows and a chin that were identical to mine. He had the ungainly apish arms and barrel stomach that I have. The same blockheaded handsomeness that went out of vogue alongside the Thunderbird. And I suppose too that he had my nose. And I suppose that he had my face.

Neizar Muntasser, the expert corporate spy, adjusts his wig, mustache and fake glasses, shifting his body in the rear of the motorboat while, inside, the Insurance Man and that idiot mechanic shuffle through reams of paper records, looking for anything that might indicate what caused the explosion. It's a fine bit of idiocy, of course. They will not find anything tossing the office of some Maple Refinery middle manager. But it gives Neizar a moment to think. Sweat slickens his brow in the dark. His fake nose begins sliding precariously down his face. Neizar reaffixes it in a preoccupied way.

There had been a moment, up atop that Maple Still, when Neizar had nearly done something quite silly. The man, Louder, had been standing on the edge of the walkway, standing, teetering before the charred black hole of the storage tank, looking down, the rent-metal exterior wall folded back on itself like wilted parchment, its jagged edges flowering darkly out on either side of him. Louder had been standing with his back to him, and Neizar had nearly reached out and *pushed*. It would have been so simple. One hand between the shoulder-blades, a mild shove. Why had he not? Why had he wanted to? Some feral part of him—the part that made him exceptional at what he did—had sunk its teeth into some secret knowledge to which he was not yet privy.

Neizar takes off Sam Herbert's glasses, polishes them pensively. So the girl was lying. He understands now. He had seen what Louder had missed—two shapes lying motionless in the entrance of a County Jail. The woman was blind, the girl was not. Suddenly it made sense to him: The mother had been locked away for something. Drugs maybe. The little girl had come and rescued her. Maybe they had killed the guards, though Neizar privately doubts it. Like as not, whatever explosion had flooded the town had also caught those two wretched creatures laying on the jail's doorstep in its blast. He thinks back to the Maple tank. The walkway. That idiot insurance man's clumsy foot connecting with some metal container—Neizar had just barely glimpsed it, spinning through the flashlight beam, it was not a lunch box. Perhaps Louder had seen it too. Perhaps he is not yet prepared to admit it to himself.

One skill Neizar has learned, in his years of taking up various corporate espionages, is how to radically curtail his curiosities. For, when adopting some new self, becoming (for all intents and purposes) a mole, one must needs have an expansive intellectual appetite at all times, for all things, one must needs never be satisfied with pat answers or assume that one understands the mechanisms of hidden power, but to turn that same curiosity over on his, Neizar's, employers and beneficiaries, would be an act akin to professional suicide, cannibalism, a recipe for disaster.

For in Neizar's world, certain things were known and never said, e.g., that certain firms and financial institutions had a long, easily traced legacy of sharing a bed with American intelligence. NOCs they were called—non-official covers— that is, people at private companies, receiving private salaries from those companies, as a cover for CIA (or NSA, or NIS, or some other acronym-rich sub-department of Uncle Sam's) business. The firms were eventually reimbursed by American Intelligence for the salary expenditure—whether it was in cash or another sort of *quid pro quo*. This was a sort of open secret. That this Robert Vicaray, barefoot anarchist or whatever you like, had had an estranged father who'd ranked very high indeed at a firm known to have significant dealings with obscurer parts of the U.S. government, that he (the father) had died under less than convincing circumstances, that one of the men who sat on the board of this firm was the erstwhile head of a certain Maple Syrup conglomerate in Littoral, New York and that *then*, if this were not all suspicious enough, that the boy who claimed not to know the father who'd named him as his sole heir, had dumped all of this inherited money *back into* the hands of a Private Wealth Manager, a fellow named Pierre Ironsides who before going into finance had spent six years doing doctoral work at Georgetown's SFS. It was, of course, entirely possible that this all represented a force no more sinister than coincidence. That this anarchist with his para-governmental NGO rushing around the lower 48 was a True Civilian. But if that was so, he had attracted the attention of only the wrong sorts of people. Not six months ago, Senator Feinstein had all-but-publicly-declared the CIA a rogue agency after intelligence agents had broken into her Senate office, planted and stolen documents, and threatened one of her top congressional aids with treason charges.

At any rate it was none of Neizar's affair. He thought back to his first (only) in-person meeting with his employer—a ruddy-faced man, body and countenance betraying that he was much taken to excess, who Neizar recognized vaguely from television. The man never spoke. His flack or handler or whatever instead did the unctuous business of talk talk talking to Neizar, about how highly recommended Neizar came, about how he (the flack) recalled meeting Neizar's parents once, before their accident in the helicopter, about all that idiocy in Zuccotti park. Neizar nodded along politely with all of this but his focus was solely on the other man, hunched at center.

"I am just wondering to myself," Neizar had said softly, near the end of their dinner, his bright blue eyes fixed on the silent, red-faced fellow before him, "whether this job monitoring this, hmm, young man, makes me eligible for a government pension, somewhere down the line." The old fellow either scowled or grinned. And the talker at once leapt in, his tone stiff.

"I don't know where you got the impression that we're affiliated with any sort of government organ, Neizar. That is our mistake if we gave out that impression, but it is certainly not the case. We are, simply-put, private actors here on private business."

Neizar smiled.

The other, speaking for what was perhaps the first time and the last time, said

"Dinner is over now."

Both men paid for the dinner in cash, bizarre for a Manhattan brasserie, and stood.

"I'll expect a call," Neizar said. When neither responded, he worried perhaps he had been too cute with his prying. These people prized discretion above all else. What did it matter to him really, *who* he was working for? It never had in the past.

But the call eventually did come, telling Neizar to ready himself for a Potemkin job interview with some shop out in Boerum Hill—a quant fund or something. It was not of course any sort of job audition, he knew. The job itself was already secured. It was instead an entrance interview, some kind of debrief, given unwittingly by two poindextrous men who—if they had anything to do with the CIA—Neizar would have voluntarily eaten his own shoe. Ponderous boy-men snatched from some campus out in Mountain View. So much of private espionage—of spycraft in general, he felt—was this, above all else. Actors who do not know they are in the play. The right hand purposely obscured from the left.

Picture this: A quantitative fund with a black box at its center. Some dark object they all revered like cultists but none could see. A firm that did not know who was running it or to what ends. Receiving anonymous instructions via text, complying uncritically so long as it meant they got to keep playing spaceship. *Assets roughly equal a quarter of GDP. Server farms the size of small cities. Cloud space. Computing power—more... intangible benefits.* Neizar had sat in that office for three months and everyday looked over at the desk that read *Pierre Ironsides* and every day the chair had remained empty. He'd begun to suspect that there was no Pierre. That the name existed to obscure the person, rather than to label him. And whether that two-headed creature that had conducted his entrance interview knew as much, whether they too were in on the joke (for it was a great joke, he was beginning to see now, its outlines) did not seem particularly relevant.

Now, 11 months hence, he sits in the back of a boat in Littoral, NY, listening to Louder and the other lackwit rifling through the desk drawers of a deceased maple company employee. While, back at the Pavilion of the Abandoned Future, unseen by him or anyone else, a strange girl in a banana print dress walks slowly toward the burn victim they'd carted in less than an hour prior. The girl has not been able to keep from glancing at the bed since the new person arrived. Now she draws very close, studying the sedated man's face.

Where did this girl, her mother-or-not-mother, fit in, in the swirl of exclusive funds and rich recluses and mysterious deaths and syrup companies? Neizar does not know, nor does he particularly care. But he still feels he has some role to play. That until his window makes itself known, he will wait, patient as a housecat. He will watch and he will wait. And when the chance finally comes to fulfill the obligations of his contract with the red-faced man, his peculiar covenant, whatever it is, he will know it, and he will not hesitate again.

Neizar Muntasser, disguised servant to an obscure master, sits in the back of the boat, rocking gently from the distribution of his weight. Not far off, the chemical fires atop the surface burn a bright barium green. The moon is a fat siren not yet full, just beginning to peek her head up above the horizon, block out the twinkling stars and impose her gaze on the evening's business. Neizar wonders idly, as he reclines, whether he will have to kill the little girl, or the insurance investigator, or Vicaray himself. But if it were as simple a business as a murder for hire, he feels, he would not have been called in the first place. He watches the moon and wonders idly if its pull extends beyond natural bodies. Whether this flood of syrup too would respond to the levy of its tides. It occurs to Neizar that for all his formal education, he never learned it in school.

Then a light shines in his eyes, and a voice calls out in the dark, and Neizar, as Sam Herbert, holds very still.

CHAPTER 32

Inside the office, idly thumbing through signed invoices and carbon copies of timesheets, David Boggs says, "Hey Oscar."

Louder does not look up from his reading, his small pocket flashlight trained on the document before him.

"Yeh Boggs."

A cannister? An explosive device? And who exactly would want to blow up a maple still? A disgruntled employee, maybe. Or. Or the obvious alternative. Surely someone high up in some law enforcement office was probably already considering the possibility. Surely, it was not just Oscar to whom it had occurred.

"Has anybody ever called you the N-word? Like a white person, I mean."

A terrorist attack, that's what you're thinking.

Oscar wishes he could smoke a cigarette without risking collective annihilation via industrial chemical explosion.

"Yeh, Boggs."

"They did? Like a white person?"

He nods yes, still reading.

"Like a white person."

"Jeez," Boggs whistles. Then, as if he cannot help himself, "How did you feel, when they said it?"

Oscar is scanning the words of the internal memo, but not absorbing any of it. He's suddenly been struck with this strange new fear, unbidden, rushing through his pulses, veins dilating. Something he cannot admit to himself. Trying to tamp it down—all fear, anxiety, paranoia, is just the same thing, Oscar thinks, which is, at root, an inability to exercise adult control over your own imagination.

"Didn't really feel like they were talking to me," he says mildly.

"Well if anybody ever said it in front of me I'd kick their fucking teeth in," Boggs volunteers.

"Thanks there Boggs."

Of course, Boggs would think this quite heroic. It was such a grimly natural thing, for a people who'd been granted—had granted *themselves*—dominion over the whole wide earth, over the levers of all power, staked paying claim over God's creation, that they should eye those two syllables so covetously, as a privilege to give up. Who were denied access to nothing and still could not seem to stop cataloguing their losses, marinating in earthly grievance, sowing their own crops with salt.

"Do you like white people, you think?"

"I'm trying to read here Boggs," Oscar says.

"Right, sorry."

Oscar pauses. The sentence in front of his nose reads: *Improper density management can lead to two suboptimal flavors, namely: fermented and scorched.* He says slowly:

"It's like Sista Souljah says, 'If there's good white folks, I haven't met them.'"

"Come on," Boggs says.

We use three tools to measure density, the hydrometer, the thermometer, and the refractometer.

Boggs makes an incredulous noise, smiles disbelievingly.

His face says: *Well I'm white, aren't I? And aren't I good Oscar? Don't I deserve to be ranked among the good?*

Oscar thinks but does not say that as long as David Boggs—be he Italian or Irish or Pennsylvania Dutch—as long as he needs his own whiteness to exist, as long as he needs Oscar to be black for him, Oscar cannot vouch for his goodness.

But then, Oscar thinks, glancing over at Boggs, perhaps something has changed. Something is slipping that they cannot get back in-hand. He thinks of how darkly Vicaray ruminates on his Keeling Curves and flare stacks, on the gradually warming earth. Had he not been born with the badge of white skin—that ultimate ticket of admission? Did he not have white money, begot of white power, begot of a white bloodline. But still try as he might, this Ozark boy, he could not make the levers move. That the system of dominion they'd for so long employed was durable. They'd done something incredible: created a parasite that was larger than the host it fed on, and never anticipated that the creature might at some point grow strong enough to turn on them.

He thinks of that object caroming off the toe of his shoe, flying crazily off the catwalk spilling liquid in the dark. He thinks of standing before that spilled maple tank, gasping its idiot hunger in the screaming wind. Of a hand laid flat on his back, pushing.

He reads: *Often the paper with the scale printed on it can slip, resulting in the wrong brix reading. Often the hydrometer can become coated with film, resulting in an inaccurate reading.*

And now—

Maple, but they cut it with molasses.

Oscar hears a loud noise outside. Suddenly flashlight beams blare, criss-crossing through the window slats.

"*Don't move please,*" he hears a voice command loudly in the dark.

One of the flashlight beams trains itself on the entrance. The other is fixed on their little boat, bobbing just outside.

"I'm not moving," he hears Sam Herbert's voice call back stiffly.

"*Stay where you are,*" booms the voice.

"I am doing that too," says Herbert's voice.

Oscar looks over at Boggs, who is moon-eyed in the quiet office, then sighs and walks out with his hands both extended in front of him.

"Who's that?" The flashlight beam snaps right until it lights on Oscar's face. "Don't move."

Boggs emerges behind him. The beam jumps nervously to Boggs' own face. The drunk holds up a hand in front of his eyes.

"Get that idiot thing out of my eyes," Boggs snarls.

"Calm down please, what are you doing here?"

"Conversing with a cancerous lackwit," says Boggs.

"I said to cool it with the insults," says the voice behind the flashlight.

"Not doing anything," Oscar responds in measured tones. "Just having a look around."

The flashlight beam travels back towards Oscar, then snaps forth at once to Boggs.

"That's better," intones the voice. "See how your friend is calm? You be calm."

"My friend is humoring you because he can tell you have suffered some past brain injury," Boggs says. "I am less sentimental."

The man behind the flashlight sighs.

"I'm not getting paid enough to have this conversation," he says.

"If you're a cop, you're getting paid vastly too much," says Boggs.

"What are you doing here?" says a second, deeper voice. The flashlights draw closer. The man is indeed wearing a police uniform. He and another patrolman are sitting in the hull of a boat that reads SILOAM RIVER RECREATION.

"I've already said, we're just having a look around. Now we're leaving."

"Not looting."

"Sorry?" Oscar cocks his head forward a little.

"We got reports of looting," says the cop.

"Who's reporting to you? The phone lines are down you mendacious gasbag."

"Insult me one more time and I will hog tie you in the back of this fucking boat," says the voice calmly.

Boggs falls huffily quiet.

"We are not looting," says Oscar.

"Well we've had some reports."

"Of looting," Oscar says.

"Yeh."

"What were people looting," he says, credulously-he-hopes.

"Different things. Valuables. Local riding club had a horse go missing." Boggs shifts imperceptibly, just outside the flashlight beam. "We had a couple pharmacies broken into by some alternative-looking folks."

"Alternative-looking," Oscar repeats.

"Is there an echo in here? Yes, alternative-looking, I said."

"Meaning what."

"Meaning not from around here."

"You know everybody who's from around here?" Oscar says flatly.

"We know when someone's not from around here."

"O.K.," says Oscar. "Well we haven't passed any pharmacies unfortunately so we can't really help on that front."

"You mind if we search your person?" says the second cop.

"Sorry?" Sam Herbert says.

"*Do-you-mind,*" the other police officer says slowly, as if speaking to an unbright child, "*if-we-search-you-to-be-sure.*"

"You come any closer to me and I will throw your hat an illegal distance," threatens Boggs. Louder lays a calming hand on the drunk's chest.

"Can you control him please?" asks the first cop, annoyed.

"Unfortunately, we are going to decline your offer to search us," says Oscar.

"It wasn't an offer," says the second cop.

"I am aware of that," says Oscar.

There is a pause where the flashlight seems uncertain of what to do with this statement.

"If you're gonna be difficult we can always call over some more officers and arrest you right here."

"I'd prefer if you didn't do that either," says Oscar.

"Has anything else gone missing?" says Herbert.

The police officer on the right does not seem to have anticipated this question.

"What?"

Sam Herbert straightens importantly in the light.

"I said has anything else been stolen, that you know about? We're a Mutual Aid Group. We've got a running list of criminal and civil complaints we're taking down from people in the field hospital to follow up on after the crisis."

"Oh," says the cop slowly.

"For instance, we've got the owner of a private boat house and tour company back at the field hospital, who says that several of his vessels have gone missing from out of the dock."

Herbert lets the bluff sit in the air for a second. The cops say nothing. The flashlight lingers on his pleated pants, oxford blue dress shirt, stained unseemly with sweat. He says:

"You officers haven't seen anyone going around looting boat docks, have you?"

Again, neither man responds. He adjusts his glasses.

"Of course it would be easy enough for me to explain to him—the owner—that in the course of crisis-response, sometimes, first responders need to get their hands on resources as fast as possible, like insulin, say, or rescue boats, or what-have-you. If you fellows would like me to take care of explaining that to him when I get back to the field hospital, and see if he would go so far as to sign some sort of waiver, I'd be happy to do that for you."

And probably if it had been the slurry David Boggs or even well-dressed, polite, Oscar Louder, telling this brazen lie, these two august officers of the law would have put them in bracelets, or, at the very least, adhered to the old bureaucratic adage to trust but verify, but likely because of what Sam Herbert looked like, and how Sam Herbert spoke, the man behind the flashlight sighed again, shone his light back on Oscar Louder, and said slowly:

"You tell your people if we see anyone else breaking into a rite-aid I don't care if they're carrying the fucking cure for cancer we will shoot them on-sight."

"I'll try and remember that," says Oscar Louder.

"I know who you all are. I know what you do. I don't like your organization's politics, I don't like that you're here, and if you don't hand over that field hospital in the Pavilion to the Red Cross or FEMA or whomever, *as soon as they're set up on the ground*, I will blockade you like it is a fucking 16th century siege. I will block supplies from reaching you until you are starved for resources, understand? Until you are *screaming out* for relief. And then, one by one, as you emerge with ribs showing, I will arrest you all on a battery of larceny and public menacing charges. I don't care how many little old ladies you deliver dementia medication to. You are not going to run roughshod over my town, this isn't fucking New Orleans."

Oscar purses his lips.

"Thank you for explaining that Officer."

"Volsky."

"I'm sorry."

"My name is Dan Volsky, I said."

"Well thank you for taking the time Officer Volsky, and now if you don't mind we'll be on our way."

"I don't mind Oscar, not one bit." Sgt. Dan Volsky smiles at him in the dark.

"Let's go Boggs."

Boggs clambers into the boat, grumbling murderously to himself.

"And Oscar?" Louder looks back as their little boat begins to putter away from the two cops, standing there silently, amidst green fires burning. Boggs is right, the scene recalls something ghastly premodern dreamscape, some Alighierian hell. Dan Volsky raises a hand, "I just cannot wait to see you again."

CHAPTER 33

The man who let himself into my room was tall and well-muscled, silver-haired, with bright blue eyes and uncommonly handsome eyebrows. On his face he wore, what seemed to me, an obviously fake beard and fashionable frameless glasses.

"Mister Entrecarceles," he said, eyeing the hotel's chipped crown-molding, his mouth moving a little beneath the fake beard. His eyes did not dart. Their progress around the room was painstakingly deliberate and his gaze hung a long moment on my journalist's notebook, left open on the bed. I reached over and shut the cover.

"Present," I said.

Goober, laying on the ground, growled at the interloper. The man scratched at his fake beard, staring back at Goober.

"You should keep him on a leash," he said dryly.

"He's well trained," I said. "He just doesn't like unexpected guests."

Goober's black jowls peeled backwards to present his canines, but he did not rise from the floor.

"He looks quite nasty."

"Who are you?" I said.

The blue-eyed man nodded a little at the question as if it accorded with some impression he'd had of me. His finger-nails looked well-manicured. The left underarm of his suit-coat bulged with what I imagined was a shoulder holster.

"I am the person who tells you things you do not want to hear, Thomas."

"I have enough of those, thanks," I said.

The tall blue-eyed man, perhaps my age or a little older, blinked, and I looked in his pupils and saw a reptilian opacity. A dead stare. My arms broke to gooseflesh. The man reached his right hand across into the left fold of his coat, the gesture slow, untroubled, the long, manicured fingers tugging at the object clipped into the underarm there. My pulse began to thump in a way it hadn't even when Oscar Louder threatened to shoot me—this man, I felt, could eliminate me right here, put a bullet through my heart, sit with the powder-burn steeping his nostrils (it's a very distinctive very acrid smell, burnt powder), walk out of here and never be caught. I had visions of myself lying on the hotel carpet, drowning in my own blood, a hole blown through the center of me, of my chest, while Goober licked mildly at my palm. I should throw myself at him. I should tackle this man. But I did not. I was frozen in place by some glacial horror. I would feel the first bullet punch my sternum, rip open the meat of my heart. I would feel some agony so acute it had needed to be reinvented and glossaried by doctors—at the end, my heart would hurt more than any previous injury had hurt, in a way that so dwarfed all fell agony, all screaming duress that I should have never known pain in the first place, for all the relation it had to this last feeling. I was suddenly able to conceive quite clearly of endlessness, of a pain as wide as heaven, this blue-eyed man could make me feel and not think twice and never know regret or recompense, and I felt some remote thing, some terror in abstract, grow closer and larger and looming to me, like a mighty cetacean appears as a speck in some Pacific distance. As all titanic things in growing closer awe you, I felt awe, finally realizing the dream of my own death.

The hand, withdrawing now from the coat, held my phone.

"You should be careful where you leave this," he said softly. "People go mad for these things."

He tried to push my phone into my hand but I shook my head.

"Finders keepers." My voice came out phlegmy and soft. He continued holding it out, seeming not to have heard my refusal:

"Some people would kill just to get their hands on one," he said.

I thought of the homeless fellow who'd waved his arms so ebulliently earlier, the severed tongue wagging in his open mouth. Tried not to let on any of the nauseous terror that suddenly had swept through my gut and back, arms and rectum. My palate was flooded in saliva and copper, my clamped teeth starved for warm blood and air. I took the phone almost without realizing I had.

"Tell me," purred the man, "who you are working for, and why you are going around asking the questions you are asking?"

"I'm an independent journalist," I lied. "I work for myself."

"No," he said flatly. "You don't. Lying to your friends won't do you any good, Thomas."

He emphasized my name a second time.

"Are you my friends?" I said.

He nodded, looking at the closed notebook again.

"I am the only thing standing between you and certain protocols designed specifically to deal with people like you. So I am the best friend you have ever had," he said.

"I like to know my friends' names," I said, sitting down on the bed now. If this sort of man was going to kill me, I felt, he would not waste time with cell phones and miscellanea. "I like to know who precisely my friends are."

"Who. Who." He pursed his lips. "You know the parable about the man and the river?"

I did not say anything.

"A man wakes up one morning, goes for a swim in the river, goes home, goes to bed. The next morning he wakes up, goes for another swim. Is it the same river? Is it the same man?"

"There are almost no words," I said, "for how unimpressed I am by fortune cookie bullshit."

"Let's begin here:" he said. "I am perhaps the only living person in a position to be honest with you about the events you are asking after, seventeen years ago."

"And what events are those, sorry?" I said. He offered another chilly smile.

"Do you know what *Korisne Budale* means Thomas?"

"Afraid not," I said.

"It's serbo-croate."

"Oh, well, how did I not know that?"

"It comes from a political theorist out of the eastern bloc. It's the phrase they had for true democrats, liberals the communists considered *confused and misguided sympathizers* the ones who'd collaborate with the proto-Stalinists for the sake of Democracy, in quotes."

"Useful idiot," I said.

He see-sawed his hand and nodded.

"Except like so many elements of our discourse it's been mangled in translation. The original phrase hews closer to *useful innocents*."

"Well, I crave to be of use, so," I trailed off lamely, and, without meaning to, began thumbing through my phone. I found my audio files, voice memos, photographs and interviews had all been deleted.

"I am not talking about you," he said.

I looked up from my wiped phone.

"Just so I'm clear," I said, "am I conversing with the man, or the river, at present?"

He stepped toward me, sitting on the bed. Goober rose from the floor, hackles raised, snarling but not moving.

"I'm here to tell you," he began, "that you are *vastly stupidly* underestimating the strength of will, of the sorts of persons who can bury a history."

I inclined my head forward. "Is that you? Do you work for a person like that?"

He fingered his throat, dead blue eyes wandering up toward some heaven I was barred from seeing. "Not currently. But I have, from time to time, had the cup pressed to my lips. Seventeen years ago I thrilled at the taste, Thomas. You would thrill at it too if it found you worthy."

"What kind of work were you doing seventeen years ago?" I said, curious despite myself. The back of my throat was swollen, like it was being pressed on, air barely travelling down through the trachea.

"Work that was not so different from the kind you're doing now," he said, glancing at my notebook again. I covered it with one hand, as if it were some intimate organ I could not bear to have others see. "I was selected as a worthy instrument by a Power, I do not know why it chose me. Perhaps because I have never hesitated. Because I proved myself unsqueemish. I do not even know if I worked for some jockeying faction, or as an avatar for the whole. Perhaps my hire was simply this Power's way of conversing with itself."

My mouth was very dry then, hearing these dead eyes speak with such pitch and verve. Of being close in aspect to some organism of scale. Or standing in the shadow of some gothic fate.

"What were you hired to do?" I said.

He sat down on the bed then.

"Would you believe me if I said I am not sure?"

He brought one leg up to his knee and pulled off the wood-soled dress-shoe. He let it drop, then brought up his second foot, unlaced and took off the second shoe. Let it drop to the floor. He took off a sock and I saw he was missing three toes on his right foot. I did not know if this had anything to do with the story I was pursuing, with Sairy Wellcomme's rhinoceros, or if it was just meant to unnerve me. He took off the beard finally. The fake glasses. Laid them on his lap. His face was smooth and beautifully patrician, in the same way as Wellcomme's had been.

"At first," he said, "I thought my job was to monitor this *Korisne Budale*. A boy who didn't know he was being used. To watch him. To kill him maybe. The son of a man that vast swathes of wealth had previously moved through. The Power didn't need the man anymore, he'd become an encumbrance, and so he met an unfortunate end. He'd invented a system, though, a sort of *camera obscura*, black box, a new instrument, Thomas. They still needed the box, and the system, but they didn't have its inventor, they needed a useful innocent."

I guessed: "Some Okie boy who gets rich overnight."

His head tilted forward just barely.

"Some poor friendless Okie boy gets befriended, recuperated by someone pretending to be his father's lawyer. Who sends away his money and assures him in dulcet tones that it's all being put into Wind Farms and Soylent Fields. A boy who isn't so educated or curious that he asks to actually see receipts—who's temperamentally erratic, stupid enough, to constantly be moving the money around, so that it's near impossible for even a sophisticated observer to track. All this so that he can jet around the U.S. to different slums and play white savior with a band of people that he imagines are fellow disciples of the cause. And it gradually comes to light that he is not so innocent after all. And because of that, of course, he becomes gradually less useful. Meanwhile his father's black box keeps getting fine-tuned, keeps getting more complex and building outward. I thought maybe they wanted blackmail. I didn't realize they were staging some great play, a farce out in the open, for everyone to see who cared to look."

"You're telling me—Maxwell Smart or Robert Moses the Robber Barren or whomever cuts your checks—you're telling me they created a fake Disaster Relief Nonprofit, without the knowledge of the person who was the founder of the Disaster Relief Nonprofit. And for what?"

He didn't say anything but I continued down this line. Unspooling the yarn of my own thoughts. Set at once to articulating the shaping fantasies of this seething paranoiac.

"To run cover for mass transfers of money, to run guns, or boost widget sales, or something, within the national borders?"

He smiled at me, sitting down on the bed, wiggled his toes a little and inclined his head toward the phone in my hand.

"I would never suggest to you that the U.S. intelligences service or private military contractors commit crimes on American soil. *But Brutus is an honorable man.*"

"What precious national interest is served by the killing of a rhinoceros?"

He extended his palms up towards the ceiling.

"I can only speculate. One hand washes the other. If a man's wife dies under mysterious circumstances and it turns out the man took a policy out on his wife the week before she died, you'd imagine those things were connected, yes?"

"Goldman Sachs or whomever doesn't take out life insurance on rhinoceroses," I said.

He made an obvious gesture.

"Mortgage-backed securities, CDOs, Credit Default Swaps—none of these things were products until suddenly they were. Wherever there's a dollar to be made, have you ever known us to leave it for someone else to pick up?"

I said nothing. The embarrassing thing was how it did not seem so far-fetched to me. If death is the engine of all evolution, what would be the putative value of mass death—of the death of a species? All checks demand a balance. Could extinction be commoditized? Surely, yes, to that last question. Surely the significance of its happening ascribed its own value. An asset-backed debit. A tontine for the end of the world.

I tapped the inside of my wrist with my forefingers. I could not ask him the thing I truly yearned to know. Could not say: *and what about Sairy Wellcomme?* Was I to believe that someone was training twelve-year-old Manchurian candidates? *Korisne Budale.* To what end? But to ask would be to give her up, to bring her to his attention. He was not planning on shooting me this instant. But perhaps he would not show such restraint where my employer was concerned.

Then again, perhaps he already knew about Sairy and was playing with me, the way cats play with their food. The thought swung back and forth inside my brain, needing to know, afraid to say. I could not. I had promised I would protect her privacy. He continued.

"Or, as I say: Some favor owed. A sick fantasist. A game," he said. "Power in conversation with itself, Thomas."

I straightened up on the bed, the part of my brain that had used to report stories had kicked online.

"I still don't have any tangible reason to believe you," I said. "If it was for money, where's the money? If it's a crime, where are the witnesses? *Cui bono?*"

The man blinked, then began, slowly, to pull on his socks, to slip his remaining toes beneath the leather tongue of the shoe.

"This is your last exit ramp." He stood, reaffixing the beard and glasses. He began walking away. "The next time it will not be the man outside your door. And rivers don't knock."

And with that, the fellow disappeared.

CHAPTER 34

As it is often quite hard to divine an author's intentions from the rather crude tea leaves of the events taking place on the page, and as I, in my capacity as storyteller, am fully committed to transparency and aboveboardness in this instance and all others, I'll now go about explaining why I killed-off each of the following important characters, to put to rest any niggling doubts you might be experiencing, about intents or purposes herein:

In no particular order:

Police Sgt. Dan Volsky I killed off as a punishment for moral sloth.

Robert Vicaray I killed off as a lesson about the limits and astringencies of ideology.

Beebop the rhinoceros I killed off in order to save Sairy Wellcomme's life.

Sairy's Mom I killed off to highlight the dysfunction of American families.

Police officers Tim Green, Leonard Dormer, Matt Foley, I killed for crass political purposes and street credit.

Charles Guiteau I killed in order to highlight the cruel allowances we afford ourselves when we believe God isn't watching.

Thomas Entrecarceles I killed off because he gave up on the world.

Sairy's father I killed because he reminded me of myself.

All this will hopefully have been made clear in the meat of the text. However, if, at moments, it seems to you that I, the author, am meting out gratuitous violence without a clear overarching moral framework, or simply in order to cover

over plot holes in the text, or if it ever seems, even more gro-
tesquely, that I do not share your exact identical set of politics,
then let this primer stand as a reminder for you to refer back
to whenever you need to assuage any fears you might have
about consuming a piece of art that is not adherent to popular
moral orthodoxies, or styptically self-assured in how it views
the world, or the people in it.

I'll now go about explaining, in simple, verifiable detail,
what Sairy Wellcomme did after she had convinced Leanne
Swinburne that she was possessed by an evil spirit:

She took the convicted felon by the hand and led her
down the West Corridor of the Pavilion of the Abandoned
Future toward the closet where medical supplies were stored.
The Pavilion, which Robert Vicaray's crack operatives had
broken into and begun fixing up as soon as news got to them
about the industrial explosion that had so rocked the nearby
town of Littoral, New York, had been built for the 1992 Exposition, a gigantic-budgeted multi-city affair, that the state
government had put together in order to commemorate the
500th anniversary of Christopher Columbus's arrival in the
Americas. Columbus, a part time sailor, was also a notorious
slaver, murderer, rapist, and villain of the tallest order. He is
celebrated every year on a day in October—this author's birthday, in fact. There is a city in Ohio named after him as well.

The theme of the 92 Exposition was A Future Of Dis-
covery, A Future Of Hope. An enormous slush fund of
public-private money went toward the construction of brand
new, hulking, event spaces, like the Pavilion, all fashioned after,
standing as testament for and paean to, what the future looked
like from the relatively sunny vantage point of 1992. Outside,
bisected by a cylindrical steel rod was a 75-foot model of the

Challenger space shuttle with the once bright-blue NASA logo washed nearly invisible due to acid rain. The exterior was surrounded by a complex sort of channel system of shallow fountains reminiscent of the variform irrigation canals of a rice paddy, save for the frontmost entrance, and an enormous flat expanse of paved asphalt designed to serve as the Pavilion's main parking lot.

The acute irony that, as soon as the 92 Exposition was over, the state government had picked up stakes, gone back to business as usual and completely abandoned the enormous structures it had made to represent the future of its citizens is almost too heavy-handed to comment on without embarrassment, but there you have it.

So it was that a gigantic, strange-looking auditorium, a brutalized geometric amalgam of chromatic glass, breezeblocks, Moorish fountainry, stainless steel and rebarred concrete, had sat quiet and largely unregarded for a long lonely while, before local activists had broken in, fixed up the interior, and begun using it as Headquarters for all manner of not-quite-legal events and initiatives. It had served, over the course of its second lifetime, as unlicensed homeless shelter, unlicensed methadone clinic, illegal music venue, illegal Narcan distribution site, unlicensed battered women's shelter, hippie squat, art warehouse and more. The plumbing was not hooked-up, the lights were off, and it grew deadly cold in the winter, but if you could bring your own heat, your own toilets, and came equipped with a lantern or two, the venue was in decent enough condition.

In less than six hours since the initial explosion (under Oscar Louder's weather logistical eye), the merry band had set up fifty chemical toilets in the asphalt parking lot, had wheeled in and blanketed over 200 hospital beds, had set up six generators, had assembled a full mess with portable stove, oven, even a spice rack, had illumined the main amphitheater's interior with floodlights, had stocked medical supplies and dry goods, and had set about pulling people from the wreckage of the industrial accident which had flooded over half the town and started about a dozen (thankfully isolated) fires burning all over, while nobody was quite sure who, if anyone, was in charge.

Sairy and Leanne padded down the building's particolored hallways, unsure always of where they were in relation to the entrance, until they came upon the door to a great, hot room. Inside, a half-dozen people in tied aprons clattered industriously about while food sizzled over modified camp stoves on metal stilts, hooked up via rubber hoses to a butane gas line. Back against the far wall of the kitchen sat perhaps thirty more big butane drums waiting quietly to be of use, and another five used-up tanks tagged with yellow duct tape sat tucked in the corner. Sairy slipped into the room while Leanne waited outside. Leanne muttered nonsense to herself while she waited. She liked the babble of nursery rhymes, Leanne did. Right that moment here is what she was repeating to herself: *Sana sana colita de rana.* Leanne had learned the little nursery rhyme from one of the nurses she'd worked alongside at the hospital (this was before the state had decided that the most useful place for Leanne to be was Jail). She—the other nurse—would say it to little children after they received shots, or suffered some minor injury, to keep them from crying. *Sana sana colita de rana.* Leanne did not know what it meant but she liked it as she liked the sound of the Apostles Creed or certain Christmas Carols.

Two people passed her, standing alone outside the kitchen and, if there was anything odd about her presence there, neither of the passersby ever made any sign of it. Leanne waited and waited and finally Sairy Wellcomme reemerged, saying nothing, taking her by the hand and leading her further down the hall.

"What happened?" Leanne said.

"I stole something," Sairy said quietly.

"What for?"

"That burned man they carted in."

"Captain Dan," Leanne said vaguely. "The one who recognized me."

"He is a problem we are in the process of solving," the girl's voice said. Leanne did not ask what this meant.

They walked for another ten minutes in silence, then took a sharp right turn. Sairy spotted a busy-looking woman in floral scrubs and began following her at a distance, tugging Leanne along like a skiff at her side. The woman was walking toward a door cracked slightly ajar. Sairy halted suddenly, already knowing what she would find behind the door. After ten more seconds passed she tugged Leanne closer, closer still, until they could both hear the woman moving around in the room just on the other side of the door. Sairy squeezed Leanne Swinburne's hand.

"Say that you have to use the bathroom," she instructed in a whisper, then sidled around the corner, just out of sight.

Leanne, processing without understanding, cleared her throat loudly enough that the woman in the supply closet could hear, and said in a sharp voice, "Excuse me."

The woman peeked her head out of the medical supply closet. She was (not that Leanne could see) a beautiful West Indian doctor with soft, brilliant eyes.

"Yes there honey," she said.

"I'm sorry," Leanne said, "but would you mind showing me to the bathroom."

The woman, taking in the awkward cock of Leanne's gaze, her eyes unmoving stare, leapt at once to graceful action. "Of course I can." She took Leanne by the small of the back and led her down the corridor toward the outside area where the portable toilets were all lined up one next to another. As soon as she was gone, Sairy Wellcomme slipped back around the corner and into the supply closet. She was tall for twelve but still had to stand on tip-toe in order to reach a box of plastic plunger-flanges. She cast around, and found, nearby on the same shelf, a black permanent marker, a barrel, needle hub adapter and shaft and finally a three-inch bevel which she carefully covered in a plastic cap. Sairy clutched all these components between her fingers behind her back (since they do not make many girls dresses with pockets, on account of the patriarchy) and hurried out the open door of the supply closet, nearly barreling into none other than the disguised Neizar Muntasser, recently returned from the site of the Maple Explosion.

Neizar, still affecting the nervous disposition of Sam Herbert, leapt backwards, nearly knocking off his fake glasses, spewing effusive apologies while the little girl stared shamelessly at this peculiar form of kabuki.

"Dear," he declaimed hurriedly. "Dear I didn't see you there." Then, straightening, "What are you getting up to, inside that supply closet? That's no place for children."

"Do not waste my time," Sairy Wellcomme said flatly.

Neizar-as-Sam gave the girl a puzzled look.

"I'm afraid I don't—"

"Nature teaches animals to recognize their friends," the girl said.

Neizar tilted his head.

"Beg pardon," he said.

"You may beg," she nodded, "but do not trifle with me Neizar. I know what you found, out at that still."

Neizar finally, unable to help himself, let his affect flatten, the mask fall. And he looked for the first time, with his unnatural and clinical interest, toward this girl-thing.

"What did I find, little girl?"

The girl smiled.

"You found out who did this."

He pursed his lip, his nerves rattled, his eyebrows went up.

"I am here on peculiar business," she said, "and you are going to help me."

And Neizar began to listen.

CHAPTER 35

Not five minutes later, as Leanne Swinburne was being guided back from the toilets and into the Pavilion of the Abandoned Future on the kindly doctor's arm, Sairy Wellcomme walked slowly up to the unattended hospital cot of the badly burned man, just then coming out of the grog of opiated sleep. She glanced around once more, to ensure that she was not being observed, drew close until her nose hovered not an inch from his face. The eyelids fluttered, watered, widened with recognition.

"Hello Dad," Sairy said.

The daffy ophthalmologist Miles Wellcomme stared at what he imagined to be his daughter in medicated silence, his eyes began to brim with joyful tears at the sight of her. Sairy, or the creature controlling Sairy, drew from behind her back a syringe, recently constructed from stolen medical supplies, and, without second thought, jammed the needle into her father's leg.

Now you have probably been told, via television brainwashing or Hollywood films, of the idea that a syringe filled with just air, injected into the bloodstream of an unlucky patient, will like as not cause what is called an "air embolism"—that is, a blockage of the heart or other major organs, leading to cardiac arrest, and, shortly thereafter, death. The truth, this writer is chagrined to say, is a bit more complicated. While it is certainly true that, given unlimited time and fair malice aforethought, someone with proper motivation and a standard issue medical syringe could prompt in a restrained patient a fatal pulmonary embolism, the problems in the realistic execution of such a plot are, to your enlightened medical professional, manifest and manifold.

For one, the sorts of hand-waving armchair pathologists who assert the perils of accidental oxygen bubbles in the blood, often neglect to mention the sheer *amount of air* that'd be required to kill a given organism. For instance, in order to cause an air embolism large enough to kill, say, a rabbit, or your grandmother's toy poodle, you would need to inject between 40 and 60 cubic centimeters worth of oxygen (Quick side-note for the curious: 60 ccs is equal to 60 ml, they are for all intents and purposes identical, duplicative measurements) into the poor creature's bloodstream in a concertedly small window of time. (For frame of reference, a 50cc syringe resembles more or less a large turkey baster.) Morbidity and mortality rates from a venous air embolism in a human adult are dependent on four factors, to wit:

1) variability in the *amount* of air entrained
2) variability in the *rate* of entrainment
3) the position (as in, physical posture) and cardiac status of the patient in question

and

4) his or her physical size.

These numbers only scale up, realize. So where 50 ccs of air will adequately bump off a housecat, the sort of embolus you would need to claim the life even of a moderately-sized dog would be somewhere closer to 100-120 ccs. More than two oversized turkey basters. While obviously no one has approved experiments to see exactly how much air it takes to cause myocardial infarction in an adult human, the estimate from documented euthanasia cases sits somewhere between 200 and 300 ml. Point being: short of dragging a bicycle pump to the bedside of the person you're trying nefariously to murder, there is no very effective way to entrain enough air in a fully grown man or woman to stop their heart. Whether she knew all of this or not is unclear, but what Sairy Wellcomme had done *instead* was this: Sairy had ducked into the Pavilion's galley kitchen and without any of the very busy chefs noticing, palmed a great large jar of nutmeg from the spice shelf, then slipped right back out the way she came, the whole kitchen staff being none the wiser.

Now, while powdered nutmeg (taxonomical name *myristica fragrans*) is a perfectly innocuous spice when imbibed in any reasonable quantity, you may be surprised to learn, reader, that the seed of the nutmeg tree actually contains small amounts of a very potent narcotic called myristicin—rather the same way that all apple cores carry trace amounts of cyanide, or poppy seeds opium—and that myristicin can be quite poisonous indeed to humans if ingested in amounts greater than just three teaspoons. Normally this wouldn't rate as a problem, on account of, who on earth would want to consume four teaspoons of powdered nutmeg in one sitting? But as life in America is exceptionally long and exceptionally strange, there have of course been examples of persons—thrill-seekers, spice fanatics, bored teenagers—who consumed myristicin in such high concentrations that they (the persons in question) required hospitalization, or, on rare occasion, a plot of ground.

One such very sad example had taken place in Sairy Wellcomme's hometown, just the previous year, and had been splashed all over the local news so that it would have been near to impossible for young Sairy not to have seen. In the example in question, an elderly man and his wife, both of whom suffered differing degrees of progressive dementia and neither of whom had a full-time caretaker or any family to speak of who loved them very much, cooked one night for dinner an enormous pot of pasta and—by all accounts completely accidentally—in the fog of mutual dementia, added heaps and heaps of *myristicin fragrans* to the sauce in the saucepan, stirring it in and eating voraciously with expansive appetite and great gusto, never noticing the dish's peculiar taste until their bellies and bodies and bloodstreams were so full up and distended with myristicin that their blood became toxic, their minds went crazy, and their hearts stopped working. The county coroner ruled it an accidental death and most everyone shook their heads and moved on (save for a few consumer advocates who staged various events and die-ins outside the offices of local legislators and spice company executives, demanding that a larger, more explicit warning label be added to all bottles of nutmeg sold in the state of New York, a demand that never got any real traction on account of how expensive it would be to recall and retrofit all the bottles that were already out there flooding the market and—these activists averred—endangering an unwitting public) muttering how strange and macabre the whole thing was that these two octogenarians with degraded tastebuds and disintegrating minds had shoveled so much of the wrong spice into their bodies, and that, to borrow a phrase, "you never hear the one that kills you" (*the one* in this case being six tablespoons apiece of pulverized nutmeg).

But while four tablespoons, when orally administered, are usually enough to cause a human body to go into toxic shock and renal failure, the human stomach—contrary to Meninius' famous speech to the Plebians—is actually a fairly poor delivery vehicle for any narcotic, myristicin included. That is why tortured drug addicts are always trying to circumvent the digestion process with cold coffee filtration, and

skin popping, exploding their nasal membranes and so on—
that, actually, if one were to fill a single 50cc syringe with a
mixture one part water and three parts *myristica fragrans*, to
bypass the digestive tract entirely, mainline it directly into the
bloodstream of the intended victim, almost without exception, such a mixture would prove lethally effective. And so
that is what Sairy Wellcomme did as Leanne Swinburne was
being led by the hand back into the Pavilion of the Abandoned
Future, unaware that she had just served as accomplice to the
murder *not* of a villainous Corrections Officer but of Sairy's
own flesh and blood father, all while the disguised Neizar
Muntasser set about making the sordid preparations that the
young twelve-year-old mystic had tasked him with. As Sairy
leaned very close to her unrecognizably burned father, not
long for this earth, his eyes wide and watering, she clasped her
small fingers around the short hairs of his neck and jammed
down the plunger flange of the syringe she had put together
from spare parts, sent the ground fruit of a tropical evergreen
harvested from the Spice Islands shooting through her Dad's
veins. As the toxic spice was delivered efficient as clockwork
from Miles Wellcomme's healthy, vigorous 45-year-old vena
cava into the right atrium of his strong pink 45-year-old heart,
as it filtered between atrium and ventricle and his body began
to realize something was very wrong, his heartbeat became
arrhythmic, his skin broke into a sweat, and the unstoppable
evolutionary momentum of cardiovascular biology overrode
all ringing alarm bells. As his body sent the poisoned blood
flooding into his gasping lungs, his heart became tachycardic,
his brain began to panic, and his body began to seize as his
poisoned, oxygen-rich blood flooded back into his veins and
arteries seeking out each furthest corner and organ and crevice

of his badly damaged body. His pupils dilated, his autoimmune system began to attack itself, his temperature began to rise, his daughter's face in his visual field oscillated rapidly, his body slipped into toxidrome, as Sairy spoke softly in the ear of the man who'd played the role of father to her, much the same way certain men play the role of New York Yankees fan. Sairy leaned toward him, kissed him on the cheek, and whispered comfortingly, "Our hearts are too great for what they contain." And then our intrepid subject Sairy Wellcomme straightened and slipped away across the auditorium, leaving her father Miles Wellcomme, who reminds this author of himself, shaking in his hospital bed alone. Miles died like that, shaking. And I suppose that he had my nose. And I suppose that he had my face.

CHAPTER 36

After Sairy had done away with Miles Wellcomme, her doddering father, she ditched the syringe of nutmeg in her and Neizar's predetermined hiding spot and crossed the length of the auditorium so that she was standing in line behind several agitated looking men and women who were waiting for the chance to borrow a cell phone and make a call. The volunteers had fashioned what looked like little old-fashioned curtained booths, as if for voting, or taking funny photographs, in order to give people some semblance of privacy while they made their phone calls. Sairy, waited patiently in the line, ignoring the couple of strange looks from people, suspicious of this twelve-year-old girl waiting by herself, unattended, in the emergency cell phone line. But the young man behind the table displayed none of this hesitation, handing over the cell phone for Sairy to use. "Here you go," he said cheerily. "We ask that everybody keep their phone calls to under five minutes, if you could." Sairy nodded and slipped into the booth, pulling the curtain shut behind her. Then she dialed 911, found the lines were flooded, hung up, counted sixty seconds, called again, and managed to get a harried-sounding operator on the line.

"-mergency response."

"Hello," Sairy said.

"Howcunni help you?" said the operator briskly.

"I just—gosh I am so scared. I think I just saw a murder." She heard the operator pause a moment.

"O.K.," said the operator. "O.K. are you safe?"

"I don't know," lied Sairy Wellcomme. "The man—we're in an emergency hospital. The man walked up to another man, in a hospital bed. He injected him with something he—god, I think he killed him. I think they're euthanizing people here. Please help."

"Do you know the name of the man you saw?" said the operator. "The killer?"

"I think he says his name is Vicaray," the little girl said softly. Someone in the next booth over coughed. "I think he calls himself Robert Vicaray. He seems to be running things around here."

Once she'd finished her call in under the allotted five minutes, Sairy Wellcomme thanked the bearded volunteer, handed back the phone, and headed back over to find Leanne Swinburne in order to enact the next part of her plan. She found the Wanted Woman milling around the snack table picking up and putting down various candy bars.

"It's you," Leanne said when Sairy touched her hand, not altogether thrilled-sounding. "What do we do now?"

"Now Leanne," said Sairy, "we begin to reveal ourselves."

Leanne straightened.

"Doesn't that undermine whatever other things you're trying to achieve here?" she said.

"I am only trying to achieve one thing here, as I've told you Leanne."

"But you can't do that if you're locked in a rubber room, I'm assuming."

"Your problem," said Sairy sweetly, "is that you lack vision."

Leanne said, "Flash blindness."

Sairy opened her mouth, then shut it again, and caught Leanne by her hand. They traveled down more of the Pavilion's tortuous alleyways, 'til they happened once again upon Robert Vicaray, this time by his lonesome, laying a line of colored tape on the floor behind him, slowly, painstakingly, shifting his weight on and off his bad leg, clutching occasionally to his orthopedic cane. He looked up, caught sight of them and grinned, saying proudly:

"Red goes to the bathrooms, yellow to the kitchen, green goes to the medical supplies, blue goes to the emergency exit."

Leanne said nothing, shifting uncomfortably. Robert, waiting another moment, shrugged, then looked down at Sairy Wellcomme, who gazed levelly at him.

"What can I do you for, ma'am? You two getting along good?"

Sairy Wellcomme nodded, not saying anything, took out a permanent marker, and knelt down on the floor. She leaned over, slashing three bold black strokes onto the tile, then slowly drew a circle, an oval, and several more rude intersecting lines. She straightened, smiled, held out her hand palm up, as if presenting a science fair project to a county magistrate. Robert's face went white, his jowl muscles strained, sickening, his molars ground against one another.

On the floor Sairy had drawn a delta, and in the center of the large black triangle, a gallows and a hangman. The same as in Robert's shed that night, long ago. The girl walked ten paces away to a nondescript door, tried the handle, and the door swung wide. The interior Robert could see was a cramped closet someone had repurposed with janitorial supplies. There was no functioning light inside. The girl gestured that they should all step inside to talk. Her face indicated that they three had much to talk about. Robert feeling his pulse ram against his neck, swallowing some low moan, took a few wobbly steps forward. The girl and her mother disappeared into the closet. He hesitated, then, against his better judgment, wrapped his knuckles around his cane, and closed the five more paces so that he was hovering in the entrance of the supply closet where he could see the woman and her ward standing in the low seep of the intermittent hallway lights. His hairs stood on end, his flesh erupted in goosepimples. Still, he did not speak.

"Robert I'm going to give you a chance to save your own life," said Sairy Wellcomme, "by helping me to kill a rhinoceros."

CHAPTER 37

Now perhaps you have already guessed what anyone checking the fine print would have been able to tell you: gigantic pavilions on the outskirts of towns do not just sit, abandoned and underutilitized, for indefinite periods of time without that there is a reason. Perhaps this was yet another example of Robert Vicaray's peculiar credulity, his ideocrat's incuriousity, where the nuts-and-bolts operations of the organization that he'd helped found were concerned. Robert like as not assumed (wrongly) that someone—Sam Herbert, one of the on-the-ground volunteers—anyone had done the reading, and that the property had no secondary or tertiary functions, no stakeholder with a vested interest in how it got used or by whom.

But had Robert—again had *any person*—checked the real estate files, waltzed through the unlocked doors of the now-flooded county records office and pulled the manila folder out of the drawer, the truth would have become readily apparent: that the state government—saddled with the task of slowly paying down an enormous amount of debt owed to various contractors, financial lenders, big architecture firms, accrued in the heat of supreme hubris, heady postcolonial fervor, as part and parcel of the 500-year celebration of the first ever European to leave a trail of blood on this continent's fair shores—the state had, in 1994, begun the undignified process of selling off various rights, licenses, stakes and deadweight public properties to any interested party who had two cents to rub together and make a third. Chief among these public financial sinkholes ranked the Pavilion of the Abandoned

Future. And it was in that year, the year of the ascent of America's Moral Majority, that a small Nonprofit Trust had bought up the Pavilion as a method of offsetting its already very high insurance deductibles.

Of course there is not—never has been—a unanimous professional consensus regarding the best Disaster Response practices of Licensed Menageries & Zoological Parks where their animals are concerned. That might come as a bit of a surprise to hear, but it is the plain honest truth of the matter, that no one is quite sure of the right thing to do. Throughout human history, zoos as institutions have weathered just about every form of catastrophe you could think of. The semi-famous (in certain circles at least) example that springs to mind is that of the Parque Zoologico del Bilbao which, in the 1980s, due to river pollution, suffered a massive flood with waters high enough to put pressure on, and eventually break the glass enclosure of a 900-pound Polar Bear. As polar bears are (perhaps uniquely) the only mammal in the animal kingdom known to actively hunt-seek humans as prey, the newly liberated bear had already made short, unpleasant lunch of at least one slow-footed American tourist by the time zoo staff were able to track down and (unfortunately) shoot her. The tourist, a supply-side economist and visiting lecturer at the Universidad de Bilbao, was identifiable only by the bits of Hawaiian Shirt and Birkenstock still stuck in the she-bear's teeth, and in 1990 the Spanish national government made a formal apology to the man's family for the whole unpleasant incident (the bear's family received no such apology). Likewise, and to bolster this argument, the vast majority of the fish in the New Orleans Aquarium died in the aftermath of Hurricane Katrina. This might seem obvious—that the nonhuman denizens of any highly regulated environmental enclosure require both electricity and running water in order to survive, and that absent those two things, they will very quickly cease surviving—but aquarium fish are far from the only captive animals who exist in states of such precarity. Certain very large zoo animals for instance rely on daily shipments of fresh food. When those supply lines are cut off, those animals can starve and die in a startlingly short time.

As zoos are insured in rather the same way an art museum or pet store would be insured, they are as much slaves to policies and deductibles as any medium-sized business. And the peculiarities of zoo insurance make for a tangled weave of perverse incentives—after all when an art museum insures a Van Gogh, it is insuring the painting itself, it is not concerned about the Van Gogh leaping off the wall and devouring one of the museum's patrons. It is not irregular for such businesses to have Emergency Evacuation plans drawn up, rather the same way the late Phillip Bell kept his living wares in cages in the backyard, until the pet store was no longer flooded, as a way of decreasing their deductibles for certain high-risk animals (for zoo insurers do not view all animals as equal, nor write their policies from behind a Rolfean Veil Of Ignorance) at the margins.

You might think that closes the book on what zoos ought to do in the case of impending disaster—that is to say that they should, *de minimus*, do *something*, but then consider the quite unfortunate example of Zoo Miami, a private park situated deadeye in the center of the portion of South Florida known colloquially as Hurricane Alley. In 1992, with Hurricane Andrew fast approaching the state's East Coast and predicted to make landfall near-to-smack-dab on top of the zoological park, Zoo Miami made the controversial decision to attempt the emergency evacuation of all 4,000 of its living attractions. This wasn't some fly-by-night chewing gum and twine endeavor, mind. The zoo board, which had one of the more substantial endowments in the continental U.S., had drawn up, in concert with several logisticians and biologists, an extensive, rapid-response Hurricane Readiness and Evacuation plan. Overnight they mobilized over 500 trucks and threw together over 1,000 portable cages and enclosures in order to transport their more than 3,500 biologic wards to a secure bunkered location in adjacent Northern Peace River Florida. Unfortunately for the staff of Zoo Miami though, all the best laid actuarial plans of mice and men cannot account for the sheer whopping size and scope of certain types of bad luck. First, the stress and trauma of moving some of the zoo's more sensitive and exotic creatures resulted in over 200 species' deaths. Secondly, an additional 50 *deaths* were attributable to a 35-foot-long Bolivian Anaconda named Daisy in an improperly secured latch-tank which someone had mistakenly loaded into the back of the container truck carrying the majority of the zoo's Aviary and Exotic Bird show, so that when the truck driver (after ten mind-numbed hours on gridlocked Florida highways) finally pulled into the parking lot of the zoo's secondary storage location and released the latch on the back of his container truck, the sheer horror of the vista of blood-soaked plumage and dismembered wings, as well as the gorged, satisfied looking snake, that greeted him as he raised the metal door, was apparently so affecting that the truck driver in question—no one's idea of a fragile man— eventually ended up *suing* Zoo Miami for long-term emotional distress, and still, to this day apparently cannot stomach most poultry dishes.

On top of all that initial catastrophic ill-fortune, and almost as if someone upstairs was playing a cruel joke on them, as the staff of Zoo Miami finally finished loading the last of the large animals into the secured underground bunker, cataloguing their losses, reporting accidents, licking their wounds, just as they had begun to settle in, the Hurricane in question rapidly changed course, streaked up Florida's coastline and slammed directly into West Palm, Acadia, and eventually, Northern Peace River, flooding the marshlands and rivers, choking off the highways and supply-chains, downing the power lines, and, a black cherry on top of a gruesome sundae, flooding the secure underground bunkers where Zoo Miami had just locked their poor doomed animals. The losses were extraordinary, several employees resigned in protest, but because the Hurricane had done so much damage to the State in general, the plight of the animals of the Miami Zoo never broke through the news cycle, glutted as it already was with stories of such gross human misery. If all this seems needlessly, gratuitously digressive, reader, I want you to know that it is not without purpose. What I mean to impress upon you, by telling you about the catastrophes of businesses such as Zoo Miami is that: as far as I can tell, the companies that insure zoos such as the one in Littoral, are no more experts on what to do in extraordinary circumstances than the zoos themselves. That when catastrophe strikes—true and abject disaster—it turns out that everyone is an amateur and has been the whole time.

So the Board of Trustees of the Littoral County Zoo, in compliance with a blanket policy underwritten by Cretch & Pulchre All-Risk Specialty Insurance, had raised the capital to purchase an empty amphitheater on the outskirts of town. They had drawn up an emergency evacuation plan, for all the animals therein, in the unlikely scenario that some precipitous natural disaster should throw the safety of the insured animals, the zoo as a whole, into financial jeopardy. Now as the zoo did not have an enormous endowment to start with, and as the staff it *could* afford to employ was already quite small, the evacuation of all 514 of the Littoral County Zoo's involuntary guests, was to be carried out principally by local volunteers under the strict supervision of the few paid experts the zoo did have on staff—the trust had arranged to conduct two separate interactive weeklong symposia, dry-runs for the real thing, a group exercise called Philozooic Emergency and Response Training, for which the unfortunate acronym was PERT and so that was why, on the evening in question, as Dan Volsky and the officers of the Littoral County PD arrived in force outside the walls of the Pavilion of the Abandoned Future, as Sairy Wellcomme prepared to enact her byzantine plan, as Robert Vicaray's unhappy chickens all finally came home to roost, a parade of specially outfitted Straight Trucks, Stake Bodies and trail-hitch pickups bearing the logo LITTORAL COUNTY ZOO on the doors, dragging behind them oversized horse-trailers, and piloted by an array of wild-eyed, frazzle haired PERT volunteers, motored obliviously onto the scene, wedging itself tragically in between the Littoral Police and the Mutual Aid group that the Littoral Police had showed up to assault. That is why, when bedlam finally erupted and the hounds of hell were finally let to slip, as the charred flotsam of some Past's starry-eyed Future was sent jettisoning violently into an indifferent Present, as flame shot dancing in horrid tongues around the building's entrance, and as poor Robert Vicaray cried out in anguish, Beebop The Rhinoceros was set accidentally free. It is why Beebop, who had been born in captivity, who had never shown any indication that he was suited to life beyond his enclosure, went galloping half-blind out into the moon-soaked evening, and became the subject of a county-wide capture-and-kill order, a commission taken up by a strange little girl who had uncovered a mystery, delivered the townspeople a terrible secret, and so staked some peculiar claim over their secret hearts, coveted their bloodiest whims. Because of an insurance policy, and blind coincidence. A trick of fate if you believe in that sort of thing, or something perhaps more sinister. Confluence or conspiracy. That the little girl so hellbent on killing Beebop should be there to see him released, to capitalize on his escape. Poor Beebop did not know he was being used or manipulated or framed or moved against. He did not know what a Capture and Kill order was, or why anyone should desire his blood. He did not know, and could not, that certain types of freedom can be quite lethal indeed.

CHAPTER 38

Here is how Sairy Wellcomme convinced the town of Littoral, New York to let her kill their prized Rhinoceros: she made three haughty predictions and told the townspeople that, if all three of the things she'd prophesied came to pass, they must let her kill Beebop the Great African Blue Rhino. The townspeople of course scoffingly brushed off this mad little girl, making her speeches among the hospital beds in the Pavilion of the Abandoned Future. Then, when all three of those things came to pass, they were all so affrighted of Sairy and the power she must represent, that they agreed to sacrifice their decrepit old rhinoceros to the girl's insane bloodlust.

Here, without pomp or circumstance, are the three predictions that Sairy Wellcomme made in her terrible hortation that night, what is referred to as the second night of the Littoral Country Maple Syrup Disaster.

1. That the space shuttle outside the Pavilion of the Abandoned Future would erupt in a fiery holocaust.
2. That the beasts of the land would be let to run free over the Pavilion, to kill their captors.
3. That the moon in the sky would turn away from earth.

Of course, after Sairy gave such a long, insane, villainous speech to the nonplussed citizens of Littoral, she finally enacted her plan to neutralize Robert Vicaray, take over the Pavilion of the Abandoned Future, imprison those who appeared in any way disloyal to her, and execute Beebop once and for all. There was no sense in waiting, after all her cards were on the table. In fact, I am ashamed to say, it was almost *exceptionally easy* for Sairy Wellcomme to arrest and hang Robert Vicaray, to consolidate all the power he'd set so hard to diffusing, to realize her terrible destiny. There are several different reasons for this and here they are, in no particular order:

1) Most people do not, as Robert Vicaray had, set themselves to being useful as a way of avoiding thinking about God—rather the opposite. Most people sit and think about God as a way to avoid being useful, and this personality difference made Robert Vicaray seem quite alien to the townspeople of Littoral, NY. They found him, to a person, annoying and self-serious, so that, as soon as they were furnished with a reason, they weren't surprised to find themselves more than willing to believe any number of grave accusations against him.

2) Sairy Wellcomme so efficiently dispatched with Sgt. Volsky and the Littoral Police Force that the people of Littoral couldn't help but be a little impressed, monstrous though her actions may have been, by her savoir-faire. It was thrilling to see a crime so efficiently committed, and there was rather the niggling urge for some reprise, to see what other neat crimes Sairy could cook up if given a leadership role.

3) Once she had won over Oscar Louder, Sairy Wellcomme essentially had control over entire supply chains of food and medicine and toilet paper, and people. Even decent, right-minded nonviolent people need food and medicine and toilet paper.

4) Sairy was, at the end of the day, correct in her prediction that, when the chips were down (as old Burt Orley put it right before the final voice vote, in characteristically unadorned terms): "Nobody gives a toss for a goddamn rhinoceros in a zoo."

You would not know it to interview the townspeople now, of course. They all remember things quite differently. They have every right. This is not the first draft of some foul history. What passed in Littoral, NY in July 2012 does not belong to our national conversation. It is theirs, and they keep it a closed loop, an unholy covenant. It is a rock I wish I had not overturned in the first place. I have never been innocent but I know that innocence is a word necessarily defined by its own absence. I do not know what to call the absence of history. It is not death. It is the great eye turning away from us. Of course I have always despised the eye, I had never known what it was looking at or why. It always seemed to be looking directly, menacingly, at me. Ever since I was a boy, I felt this, and since then I hated all history as the purview of hobbyists and dilettantes. But I am nearly through now, and I will set down the rest for you, as clear as my fingers can write it.

CHAPTER 39

Here, according to contemporaneous notes of the journalist Thomas Entrecarceles, are the minutes of the conversation that took place between Robert Vicaray and Sairy Wellcomme inside that supply closet, on the first night of the Littoral County maple syrup disaster:

"I drew that shape," Sairy said, staring levelly at the limping anarchist, his slight starboard list quite pronounced in the shadowed relief of hallway lights. "I was in your shed that night. I wrapped the rope around your neck. It was all me Robert. I am the thing that goes bump in the night."

He shifted his weight to his better leg. The woman, the mother, just stood there behind the girl. Letting her talk. Exercising neither control nor admonition.

"I'm not going to hurt a mentally-ill little girl just because she draws a shape on the floor," he said finally.

The muscles in the little girl's face went slack. The eyes looked impatient.

"Can I ask you a personal question?"

He did not reply. Her face had a peculiar sort of cunning about it that he found deeply repulsive all of a sudden. It was like a creature flitting in and out of an affected childishness. One that had no business pretending to be a child.

"Do you think you would feel *absolutely safe* in the hands of the divine Robert?"

She looked up at the row of dead fluorescents above, as if perhaps the divine she referred to were hiding inside it.

"Dunno. Haven't met them," he replied in a clipped tone.

His back was to the nearly-shut closet door. He felt a peculiar dread steal over him, sink into his limbs and spine 'til they felt waterlogged and slow. He must *keep her in front of him*, he thought without reason, knowing how absurd he would sound, if he were to breathe his thoughts out loud. His fear of this child, or of whatever inhabited her, not five and a half feet tall and he, Robert, a fully grown adult *afraid for his life* here staring across the room at it—at her. Or, no, that was not quite right, not *his life*, though that was the only standard he'd ever been taught to measure fear against. Staring at this small creature, it was some other inching horror, some strange and wordless peril he felt.

"Because I don't think that you would," she continued. "I think that you've spent your entire life up to this point telling yourself that *useful* is a synonym for *happy*. I think that, if I could offer you a machine that had the power to make you *stop thinking*, there is practically no limit to what you'd be willing to do."

He pictured himself sitting broken-legged in his shed. He pictured this thing standing in the shed behind him. Not some girl in a dress but whatever had left those imprints on the sawdust floor.

"I think you would *throw your body over a fire for me*, Robert, if I could do that for you."

He smoothed his face, trying to indicate none of what he thought on it.

"Don't believe in God," he said with false brio. "And I dunno what you're talking about."

"Sure, of course you do," she purred, waving a hand. "Not capital-G *God*, no, you don't believe in *that*. Some parochial conception of a Unity. But in *immortality*? In *a design of creation*, you believe, Robert, even if you can't admit it to yourself. You believe in things that *are not objects of knowledge*. That *do not have sense-content*. Every day you walk around *acting as if* you believe in them. And in the *acting as if*, you fabricate these things, this set, of which no mind can form any concrete notion. You're a *secular Pharisee*, Robert. That's what you are."

She smiled and he could sense scorn dripping off her. That this emotion fit much more naturally than the playacted innocence of earlier did not escape his notice.

"Fraudulence isn't even the right word for it. You *create things* and take *no responsibility* for their existence. *What punishment* could I dispense equal to that?"

He did not speak. Unbidden, the image popped to his mind, of the stick figure hanging by a crooked neck. Drawn on the tile floor just outside, just out of view. The little girl, who talked with such calm authority, waved a dainty hand dismissing her own point.

"Well there is no such machine, so you needn't worry," she said, picking up an extension cord, examining it with cursory disinterest. He inched his cane behind him, trying to keep his balance, holding her small eyes' stare. There was nothing obviously abnormal about them. They could have been anyone's eyes. But they were not.

He said: "I don't know what's wrong with you, if there's medication you need, that we can get, but you and your mom—"

"—She's not my mother," said the creature in its banana print frock. "I have no mother." She grinned at him and there was something unnatural in it. "I popped right out of God's head."

Robert, keeping eyes on the girl, reached back with his cane and wedged the door open a crack. She noticed this.

"Are you scared of me, Robert?"

"I just think you need help," he said slowly. "Something is wrong with you. And I want to be able to call for help in case something happens."

"*Don't lie.*" The little girl's face changed all at once, the incisors poking out beneath her forelip. Her mother, or whoever it was behind her, jumped at the venom in her voice. "*You think I don't know when you lie, but I do.*"

Then, as if someone had flipped a switch, she recuperated her temper, tugged at the hem of the dress.

"You think, because I found you in your shed, that I can only get you when the lights are off," she said. "Like a ghoul. Like a monster from a storybook. Listen," she looked at him without blinking, "if I decide to come for you, Robert, it will be in broad daylight." The door was wedged partway open behind him. "If I get you, it will be where people can see. O.K.? I will eat your heart in the marketplace."

"O.K. then," Robert said flatly.

"But I don't want to have to do that, Robert. What I want, instead is for you to help me. I want you to convince the people in this encampment to let me kill the rhinoceros in the Littoral County Zoo. I need you to put it to a voice vote, like you would any other line item. If you put it to them, they will vote for it. If you do that Robert, you will save your own life."

Robert opened his mouth to reply, and heard rather than felt, a great booming laugh erupt from the back of his throat, looking at this girl and her not-mother. Suddenly he did not feel so afraid. He was gripped by absurdity.

"You said a rhinoceros?" He laughed.

The girl looked displeased.

"This peculiar incredulity you all have, I find it quite boring," said the girl.

"As in from Asia."

"He's African," said Sairy, "but yes."

"Why on earth would you want to hurt a rhinoceros?" said Robert laughing a little, finally. Unable to believe he had been frightened by this strange girl.

"That's my business," bristled Sairy Wellcomme. "Call it a political gesture. Or," she continued ponderingly, "like the broke aristocrat who slits her wrists in the bathtub before the Repo men come. An aesthetic decision."

"Well it's insane," said Robert shortly.

"Very well," nodded the girl. "Very well it's insane. So then put it to a vote. If it's so insane it should be easy. These people are creatures of rational self-interest after all, aren't they, Robert? So put it to a vote and they'll rationally, self-interestedly, vote to leave the poor rhinoceros alone. I'll go home, defeated. And you'll have saved your own life."

Robert kept the grin fixed to his face but said nothing.

"Unless," the girl said, studying him, "you're afraid that these people you've got here are *not* rational, not even necessarily *self-interested*, at all. Unless you're afraid that at-center, every human heart suffers a touch of madness. And that if I were to put it to them a certain way, in *just the right* way, that the people here in your little encampment might vote to kill an innocent rhinoceros just to relieve their thousand pettying troubles, or to revenge themselves against the myriad indignities everyone goes around cataloguing, that there is no non-profit, no salve, no coalitional politics for. But you're not afraid of that are you?"

Robert Vicaray did not reply. Sairy opened her mouth to speak, when suddenly there was a rap on the door. Robert jumped without meaning to, cursed himself. The girl half-turned, her eyebrows raised.

"I think," she said, looking past Robert toward the door, "that will be your insurance expert, just back from the flood site."

He said nothing.

"I think," she said, "he will have some uncomfortable questions for you."

Robert licked his lips, half-turning toward the door himself.

"I can protect you Robert, but this is your last chance. You need to speak up now. I need you to say you will help me. Otherwise," she shook her head sadly, "otherwise I am going to have to tell people what I know, what *he* knows, what *you* know to be true."

"Robert." The voice outside the door was indeed Oscar Louder. *"Robert I need to talk to you* now."

The little girl stared at Vicaray, who said nothing. Finally, she shook her head, took the hand of the woman who was not her mother, and pushed past Robert Vicaray, leaving him alone, paralyzed beneath the enormity of his own sorry fate.

CHAPTER 40

"You'll be late to your own funeral, Thomas."

"Street parking in New York," I sniffed.

"I've been here for about twenty minutes in case you were wondering." She eyed the menu. "Don't preoccupy yourself. I already ordered you a drink."

"There is, Misia," I said, "a special circle in hell set aside for people who mock those in recovery."

She waved her hand.

"I didn't realize you believed in hell."

"How could I not believe, when I'm there right now."

"Was it one of your twelve steps?" she asked.

I leaned forward. "Do you know what all the twelve steps are?"

"You know that I do," she said, sounding bored. "You know my father—"

"—so then you know I've got to say that I'm no sort of expert on any kind of twelve-step program," I said.

She squinted at me as a busboy filled my water glass.

"What?" I said to her.

"You look fit, don't you?"

"Thanks," I said, then flattened my fabric napkin over my lap, smoothing the creases at the sides. "The reason I agreed to come—" I began.

"—The last time I saw you, let's see," she interrupted, affecting pensivity. "I was—that's right—it was the night before my story about you broke. I asked you for comment, and you called me a Nazi."

"Actually I called you a Nazi sympathizer," I said. "Actually, I shouted it."

"I left out some of the more charming details," she said.

"I shouted it because you'd pushed me into the Hudson River, in March," I said.

"I was very upset. You put me in a horrible position Thomas, you really did," she said. "You have to see things from my perspective."

"From the banks of the river, meaning."

She made a face.

"Don't be cute, Thomas. It's like seeing one of those tiny dogs on fifth avenue wearing a sweater."

I drank my water. "Your show last week had a segment where you heroically dispelled the notion that Santa Claus is Black," I said. "Do you think that's what they had in mind when they handed you an Ellie?"

"I couldn't really say what they had in mind," she sniffed. "It's not my business is it? Any more than it's yours that millions of people hate you."

I said nothing. I do not know what you call it when you are so full of rage all the time that you appear outwardly lackadaisick. I have tried hunting up a word for it in the dictionary and have found nothing. She combed her hair with her fingers, wiggled all the fingers on her other hand beside her face.

"Look at the birdie," she said. "Do you want me to apologize because I've made adult concessions in order to be successful at what I do? Do you realize how petty, how privileged, you sound, smarting over some human-interest piece? Thank you for watching, by the way. We depend on viewers like you."

She took a drink of wine.

"I received a visit," I said, trying to steer the conversation back toward solid ground. "From a very strange man."

"You don't say," Misia said, sounding disinterested. She signaled to the waiter that we were ready then ordered for us both. The waiter disappeared.

"Is this about the story you're pursuing?" she finally asked.

"Couldn't possibly say."

"What *is* the story you're pursuing, anyway?" she said. "You can't possibly think that anyone will give you a byline."

"Really really really," I said, "you needn't concern yourself with what I do or why Misia. That's one of the fringe benefits of pushing me into the Hudson and divorcing me."

She eyed me now much the same way she'd earlier eyed the waiter.

"Listen, Thomas." She lowered her voice. "I can pay you. If you hand whatever you have over to me and my staff. I can't give you story credit, obviously, but—"

I exhaled.

"You've got a crack team of researchers every day turning up dirt on Environmental Activists and Make-A-Wish kids, reallocate some of those fine-tuned resources," I said.

She grimaced.

"Just an offer," she said. "Just trying to be nice."

"To make nice, you mean," I said.

"*Make nice* for what, in your mind?" My ex-wife has a California drawl that comes out only when she is annoyed. "For being a woman with opinions. Or being unapologetically successful. Or having the gall to be both at the same time."

"Maybe," I hazarded dryly, "you'd feel some measure of guilt, or chagrin, over the award-winning journalism that launched your television career."

She laid a palm flat across her sternum.

"Did I miss something? Did I hold a gun to your head and *make you lie* about your experiences in a war zone Thomas?"

"I'm not here to relitigate anything," I sniffed.

"Because if so yes, clap me in irons, if I forced you to claim a bunch of things in writing that were *embarrassingly easy* to debunk. I finally understand how unfair this has all been to you."

"I wrote a bunch of stories back when I was a foreign correspondent, when I was still drinking," I said slowly, keeping my voice steady, looking her directly in the eye. "I know of no alcoholic in the history of recorded time, Misia, who was not also a compulsive liar." The waiter came, delivered the food, retreated again without a word. "I was five years sober when I told my spouse about a bunch of false stories I'd filed before I'd gone into recovery. I did not anticipate—and this represents a lack of imagination on my part—that my spouse would years later use that information to springboard her own career."

"You're so maudlin in retirement Thomas."

"Early retirement."

She played with her food.

"The fact of the matter is, this is a business where people get destroyed. You see an opening, you take it. There used to be a version of you that could exist in perpetuity, as a sort of Emeritus Chair of High Journalism. No longer. You lie, I catch you, I destroy you. I don't care about the tangled weave of the human heart or any of that Gay Talese shit. It's not personal because none of us are personages anymore. We're people with jobs and bosses and incentive structures. You're part of the old coalition and I'm part of the new one, and the new coalition disdains liars and alcoholics and emeritus chairs, but more than anything else it disdains *losers* Thomas. You want to cast yourself as victim? Great. Be the Patron Saint of all Losers. Go and find your people so you can lead them."

She gestured with the fork in her hand. I stared at her and wondered if she found it as difficult as I did to be happy. She was correct that the world had moved on from me, and that there is nothing sadder or more embarrassing than the sort of actor who pompously frets over some imagined past glory. As if reading my mind she recited some well-bred California prep-school rote:

"*The king grew vain, Fought all his battles over again*
And thrice he routed all his foes, And thrice he slew the slain."

I forced a smile, thought once more of how I had planned to give Goober away, throw myself into the ocean. Leave the whole project to someone else. Then I said:

"The man who came to my door, you're saying you did not hire him. To raid my phone. To rattle me."

"What man?" she did not look at me.

"These are people's lives here you're playing with," I said, hearing my own temper creep surreptitious into my tone. I bit back self-recrimination, idiot guilt.

"Water seeks its own level," Misia said flatly.

"What does that mean?" I said.

"It means whoever the woman is that hired you probably is not the ingenue you imagine her to be."

"I didn't say I was hired. I certainly didn't say there was a woman."

"I've never known you to be protective of another man," she said.

I did not reply to this.

"The fellow, the one who's missing toes on his right foot."

"Neizar," she said.

"You hired him."

"I didn't say that," she said sipping from the wineglass. "You mentioned a man missing toes on one foot, I told you the name of someone who fits that description."

"Neizar," I said.

"Imagine the resources one would have to have, to be able to hire Neizar. Above my paygrade. He barely works anymore. He doesn't exactly need the money."

"He told me a story."

"I'm sure he did, he's full of them."

"You've got national security people, private security people, at the network, you could run something by?"

"You don't know anyone in national security?" she said.

"Not that would take my call," I said.

"Ah yes." She looked wan. "They take stolen valor fairly serious over there, I expect."

"Does he have connections at Langley?"

"Neizar? I'd imagine he has connections everywhere," she said.

I shook my head. "Has he ever *worked* with anyone over there?" I tried again.

She peered at me.

"Jesus Thomas what did he say to you?"

I shifted in my chair.

"He told me some things I did not want to hear."

She said nothing.

"I'm just trying to figure out how reliable he is," I tried.

Her gaze softened a moment. She shrugged.

"He's certainly plugged in," she said frankly, "but he's also become quite eccentric in retirement. He's got the same unfortunate nervous condition as you and my father."

I weighed my options, then said: "He as good as told me that what happened Upstate was staged. Maybe by Company. Or by some private... I don't know... cabal."

She smiled in a way I did not like.

"Neizar told you that?"

I nodded.

"What vested interest would anyone have in a little pissant berg upstate?" she said.

"That's what I said." I nodded. "But it makes a certain sort of sense. Certainly explains why an entire little town seems to be suffering such reticence about an event no two of them can seem to remember the same."

"I think Neizar was having a little fun with you," she said.

"Why would he do that?"

She inhaled, recited pompously: "I know of no alcoholic in the history of recorded time who was not also a compulsive liar."

I bit the inside of my cheek. She really did look gentler now. Conversing with her was like keeping out a constant eye for the tidal changes. "You remember the first thing I ever said to you Thomas?"

I ran my hand through my hair.

"You asked me this already on the phone," I said. "You're repeating yourself like a T.V. person."

"You never answered."

"Yes, I remember."

"I walked up to you at a party and I promised something."

"Yeh," I said.

"And you decided to fall in love with me," my former wife added.

"People don't decide to fall in love," I said. "It's like going broke: happens gradually, then all at once."

"Maybe *people* don't but I think you do. I think you *decided* the way certain people decide to be vegans. And that made you weak, because there is nothing more enfeebling than treating your own heart like a piece of real estate."

"And you disdain weakness," I said, "and emeritus chairs and something else I can't recall."

She smiled.

"Nothing is all bad, all the time, Thomas. Nor all good. Nothing is anything, really. Our brains are such seething machines aren't they."

"All that Gay Talese bullshit," I said. "Smells like the museum."

"Everything in its place," she said. "I like museums."

I got up without touching my food.

"I hope you can bill this as a client dinner," I said, kissing her on the cheek.

She looked peculiarly at me for a moment, then blurted out: "My advice Thomas, if Neizar is reading your tea leaves, is to stop. Don't readjust. Don't reassess. Stop."

I stood awkwardly for a moment, thrown by this comment.

"You said he was joking," I said.

"Boys with magnifying glasses sometimes joke with ants."

"Well, I have my job, he has his," I said, draping my coat over my arm.

Misia paused, seemed to consider what she was saying very closely now.

"Certain organisms Thomas—I work for one—Neizar for others, certain organisms learn to sup on themselves."

I opened my mouth. I felt my jaw flex and unflex, my tongue go dry. This was my wife. Had been my wife, once.

"You walked up to me at a party and you said you knew who I was."

"You know the line on such organisms? Wrath is their meat, Thomas. They starve by feeding. Do you understand?"

"You walked up, and leaned in very close, and said so that only I could hear, '*I will completely absolutely wreck your heart.*'"

She gave me some ghastly look, of importunacy or terror or maybe, it is possible, regret.

Our hearts are such seething machines.

But no, she had not said that. She had said *brains*.

Our brains *are such seething machines.*

"I will completely absolutely wreck your heart."

I kissed Misia on the cheek a second time, looked at her awhile, left knowing that I would never see her again.

CHAPTER 41

Leanne Swinburne had killed her child. Her baby daughter. That's what she had done. That's what the papers said, at least. Leanne herself said that the little girl had hit her head on the curb. That she had been running toward the house one day and tripped and her little head had impacted against the corner of the sidewalk, bounced off the concrete, and she had begun wailing, her eyes and nose running mucus. That Leanne had ushered her inside and pressed ice against the little girl's brow and cooed in her ear but had not taken her to the hospital because it was a work night, and the E.D. trip would be exorbitant, and the girl seemed fine.

Leanne got pregnant while she was still in Junior College and carried to term right after finals. The father, if you wanted to use that word, might as well have had a chest tattoo that said *Pull, Pray, See You Someday.* She took a semester off, ate away at her paltry savings, then came back part-time to finish her associates, worked the cash register at a car wash with an open nursing textbook underneath the counter, then had to arrange a sitter while she went through clinicals. Her mother could take the baby some of the time, but she herself worked the deli counter at Waldbaum's, so Leanne had to figure out a way to pay someone to come three times a week and watch S. in addition to car payments, tuition payments, keeping the lights on.

She lost all her pregnancy weight in two months on account of stress and not always being able to afford groceries. The manager at the deli would let her mother take home the spare Boars Head when her shift was up. Leanne would wolf down a pound of leftover turkey standing over the sink, listening to her daughter cry in the next room. The doctor warned she couldn't breastfeed on account of malnutrition, so S. was a formula baby, which was another expense, in addition to diapers, in addition to baby food, on account of you cannot feed a toothless infant child discarded deli-counter turkey.

Her arches and knees were like superfund sites. When she went for her first post-partum physical the doctor had, unusually, asked to take an X-ray of her feet, then informed Leanne that she had not one, but *two* untreated stress fractures running across all three cuneiforms. Leanne would not accede to them rebreaking her feet there in the hospital and putting her in two orthopedic boots for going on a month and a half, and so she lived with the discomfort. So much of being poor, you will find, is the learned behavior of living with discomfort. The X-ray was 120 dollars, which jumped up to $500 when Leanne missed the first payment in order to be able to afford the sitter for the week.

Leanne's daughter had been born with chronic epilepsy. Epilepsy, in case you are not aware, is a group of disparate neurological disorders that are all characterized by the fact that they cause their sufferers to shake uncontrollably. A man or a woman (or in this case a child) afflicted of severe forms of epilepsy will—even when properly medicated—suffer attacks sometimes as often as 10 times in a day. While seizures are not painful *in and of themselves*, generally speaking, when somebody who suffers epilepsy returns to consciousness after having suffered a Gran Mal seizure, the bodily sensation they experience is roughly akin to having competed in an Iron Man without prior training. I am told by a friend with a more mild version of the condition that occasionally, a person living with severe epilepsy will spend days unable or scarcely able to move, that his or her body has been so wracked with the exertion of the condition, the muscles so wrung out, that all they can do is lie in bed and shake.

Nobody could explain why a perfectly healthy young woman, with no known family history of neurological problems, should have given birth to a severely epileptic little girl. Leanne did not smoke or consume alcohol during her pregnancy. She did not skimp out on prenatal vitamins or drink too much caffeine. But Leanne was, not unlike Robert Vicaray, born in the wrong zipcode, in the wrong decade, on the wrong side of a municipal line that designated who counted as fully human and who did not. Irving County, where Leanne lived, experienced a rate of premature birth, and asthma, and congenital defects, and infant mortality, just around five times that of the national average. That there should ever be such a thing as a Cancer Cluster, a Suicide Cluster, a Maternal Mortality cluster, anywhere in one of the richest nations in the world, without a major national emergency being declared, is a sign of exactly who has the power and exactly where their priorities lie. Leanne's daughter was lucky insofar as her epilepsy was on the milder side of severe—she had about one Grand Mal seizure a week. Luckier, meaning, than other children who had been born poisoned, or whose entire lives were spent hooked up to frightening machines, or in a constant state of unabating pain on account of a bunch of decisions made in far off conference rooms to increase marginal shareholder value or slough off cumbersome regulatory obligations. And so at least, in Leanne's story, we have finally attained an understanding of what it means, of how it feels, to be lucky in the year 2012, in the United States of America. How it feels is: you shake all day.

When you are a working mother and your child seizes a little over once a week, your threshold for what situations merit an Emergency Department visit, slowly, imperceptibly slides farther and farther away from the perceived mean. There is no other way to financially survive your child's chronic illness—between the money you already pay for medication cocktails, for the specialist visits, you cannot on top of all that, have a hair-trigger when it comes to visiting the ED.

That, despite smacking her head, her daughter had appeared O.K. only a little worse for the wear, sporting a large, kiwi-sized welt, for going on two days, but just as happy and active as ever before Leanne out of the blue got a call from the Sitter while on her shift at the hospital. The Sitter was screaming. The little girl had had a brain bleed and collapsed. The Sitter had put a pillow under her head and called 911. Leanne's daughter was dead before the ambulance arrived.

Leanne does not know what precisely an angel is, but she privately, unsentimentally calls her daughter her angel. She thinks of her, now, as a little toddler-ish ghost-angel that hovers overhead watching everything Leanne does, teaching herself to play the zither and smiling beneficently at the silliness of it all. Who understands that her mom is flawed and a sinner but still is sympathetic and pulling for her, anyway. There is no one else pulling for Leanne. There is no word for certain sorts of pain. Certain sorrows eclipse the language, mock its aspirations to describe with their continental vastness.

The little girl, in autopsy, showed bruises that were consistent with a forceful Mom who did not spare the rod. Leanne's defense lawyer argued the little girls' bruising was consistent with a child who'd frequently had to be held down because she was seizing. It was the lawyer's one good moment in a trial where he frequently showed up late and unprepared and continuously coaxed Leanne to take a plea deal, which she did not do.

The group of 12 people empaneled to sit in judgment of Leanne as a mother, were declared by the court to be her peers. Though Leanne had never worked nights beside them at the hospital, had never commiserated with them over the constant strain of seeing your child suffer, these retirees and scowling church ladies were deemed, by consensus, qualified to decide if Leanne had the look and aspect of a child murderer. The doctrine we nominally espouse in this country is that it would be better to let 10 guilty people go free than to see one innocent jailed for a crime she did not commit. But the nuts and bolts reality of a criminal trial is that if the Prosecutor can successfully burden the jury's imagination with the heinousness of the alleged crime, jurors will be markedly more skittish about letting someone who Might Be A Monster go free, than about locking up an innocent person.

The prosecutors had trotted out text messages where Leanne said to friends that she wished her daughter had not been born (what mother has not expressed, at least had, that thought?). They trotted out bad old boyfriends. They could not locate the girl's father to make him testify, but this absence seemed a testimony all on its own. Leanne was not allowed to go to her baby's funeral. She was arraigned on a Friday and outside it was raining. Her daughter was buried that Sunday and only Leanne's mother was there to watch the little coffin go in the spongy ground. Do not ever say you know where sorrow's floor is. It is someplace down below where a sane person could think or breathe. The jury of her peers voted, unanimously, to put Leanne Swinburne in a cage.

So Leanne had gone to jail maintaining her innocence and it had not mattered one iota to her jailers. There were the text messages and the weary comments to friends, and the constant nagging poverty that pawed so insistently at her door. There was a story offered by the prosecution, about standing in your small kitchen at the end of a 12-hour shift, and watching your daughter seize-up on the carpet. About feeling that things ought to be better, feeling that this was no sort of way for a life to unfold. That somewhere along the line a wrong turn must have been made, some divine wire crossed, that little girls should be made to suffer so, that their mothers should have to watch and slave and hurt and never once win anything of value.

I wish that I could tell you categorically that Leanne Swinburne was innocent of this crime of which she was accused but I cannot. I wish that I could flatten the creases away from reality for you, and leave you with something smooth and clean and good and easy but I should not be much of a reporter if I did.

What I can say, is that very often in your life, you will be asked and tempted and coaxed and enticed, to sit in judgment of someone whose situation you cannot hardly know. That as long as there exist rich and poor, lucky and unlucky people, as long as there exist Leanne Swinburnes, so too will there exist actors and institutions whose sole job is to encourage you to render these sorts of judgments, to rapidly redraw your lines, set your standards, and unflinchingly cast-out those who fail to meet them—to put people away into boxes where they cannot complicate the story you are all-the-time telling yourself, about what it means to be good or lucky or free in America.

That on this one occasion, uncomfortable though it might be, you and I are going to sit with the living uncertainty of

Leanne Swinburne of Irving County, NY. We are going to forfeit our holy right to judgment. We are going to say that in this one single solitary instance, in the second decade of a new millennium, there was a little-marked, disremembered window, erected like a roadside shrine, where you and I briefly together abstained from meting out guilt or innocence. And afterwards you closed the book and went back to your regular life, and I went for a swim and never came back to mine. That by remaining quiet we could, for a time at least, stave off a force just as natural as the spring tide or the coming of the cicadas. To arrest the commission of all fates 'til the rules are rewritten in our favor. You have followed me this far already. Together perhaps we could manage it. Separately I do not think we would.

CHAPTER 42

Thomas Entrecarceles sits in his car outside an upstate cemetery listening-but-not-listening to a corporate country song, watching the headstones in a gauzy half-focus. After weeks of going blind on whatever the digital equivalent of microfiche is, he'd suddenly had a hunch, a stroke of dark inspiration. Thomas had searched a first name and a birthday.

He'd found one news story, then another, then another. He'd sat with a strange dread aching in his chest, unable to keep from reading story after sordid story. And eventually all roads had pointed him here.

He'd already stopped in town with Goober and spoken with the proprietors of both the town's flower shops. This was not Littoral. Not the cute little vacation town for weekenders. This was Irving, the small, sad industrial outpost over which Littoral claimed jurisdiction and dominion. The sky today was a bleached white but the air gave no sign of rain. Both of the florists had shaken their heads at Thomas' inquiries. A blind woman? No. No such person, sorry.

But of course, that was just another hunch of his. You would not go back and resettle in the town that'd made you a fugitive. Still, Thomas had come here to this public cemetery. He had sat outside here in his car, every day for a week now. Knowing as he does the importance of the day. It is the anniversary of the death of one of the cemetery's occupants. He shifts in his seat. It is coming about time to put away this particular hobby horse, to follow some other yarn, but he will wait here a while yet. To see if anything comes of it.

He waits a while. He waits a while longer. Waits long enough that the radio station begins to play the same songs over again, which Thomas thinks is bold, after only an hour or so. A shameless admission that they are indifferent to their own programming. That it is all just as indistinct to them as it is to a casual, out-of-touch consumer.

Thomas sees a beige sedan pull up, he sits up straight at the wheel and he sees a woman get out of the driver's seat clutching flowers. She walks into the cemetery without use of a cane. She cannot be the person he seeks, then. Still, as a matter of Best Practice he clips on Goober's leash, gets out of the car, and walks with his dog into the cemetery. He follows the woman from a way back, partly to respect her privacy and grief, partly to not let on that he might be following her. Goober sniffs some lichen. They trod past two beds of well-kempt forget-me-not. The figure with the flowers has entered the section of the cemetery where Thomas knows the grave to be. She does not seem at all concerned that she might be followed. It has been years, after all.

Thomas picks up his pace. The woman halts in front of a certain headstone, bowing her head or reading it, Thomas cannot tell. He trots closer. He is more sure now. *But.* Goober strains at the leash in every which direction. But she is not blind. He can tell from her movements: this woman can see.

He draws closer. She is halted in front of an unattended grave. Goober makes a pathetic noise in his doggish throat and she looks up. Thomas raises a hand. The woman raises her hand.

"Sorry to intrude," he says.

He takes a few more steps toward her. She watches him, unafraid, unblinking.

"Leanne," Thomas says, making his tone neutral.

The woman says nothing. She seems to recognize the name at least.

"I'm not a cop or anything. My name is Thomas Entre-carceles. This is Goober."

She clears her throat, looking at him.

"If you're not a cop, then who are you."

"I'm—" he starts, stops. His face looks rough. He has not been sleeping. "I sort of fell into this whole thing. Whole mystery."

"What mystery?" she says blandly.

"A while ago, years ago," he says. "When you first esc— got out—I think you met a girl. I think you helped her with something very strange. I think an animal and some people got killed."

"Animals and people get killed all the time." She gestures at the headstones around her. "That's only a mystery if you fool yourself thinking there's a difference."

"You met a young girl. You ended up in a sort of field hospital with her. Some people died," he continues, stepping closer.

"I don't want to talk about any girl I met."

"Well she hired me. She says she doesn't remember a thing that happened."

"Really?" Leanne's smile is chilly. "She says that does she?"

Entrecarceles nods. Goober, fixed on his own idiot frequency, flops onto his back and rolls around in a bed of flowers. Flips over again and mashes his wet nose against his master's hand.

"My advice to you, Mister Andrecarcell, if that girl hired you, is to run."

"Entrecarceles."

Leanne squints at him.

"You look strange," she says.

Thomas Entrecarceles says nothing. He does look strange—too skinny. And he looks sad, standing with his clueless dog in the middle of this empty cemetery on a weekday afternoon, examined by this woman who should be blind, but can see him quite clearly.

"How," he begins slowly, almost feeling embarrassed to ask, "did you get your sight back?"

She shrugs. "Guess it was temporary."

Entrecarceles says nothing. She looks at him.

"You ever read the bible?"

He shakes his head.

"Someone spoiled the ending for me."

She laughs at that.

"Well, there's a story in the bible about a blind man, Jesus heals. He covers the man's face in mud and spits on him. It's the only time he spits on anyone. And he says to wash. And the man washes his face and the first thing he—the blind man—says is: *I see men as trees, walking.*" She halts, then carries on. "I can't figure what that means, or why it'd be the first thing you'd say after being blind your whole life. It doesn't sound pleasant, though, does it? *I see men as trees, walking.*"

"Yeh," Thomas agrees lamely.

"Maybe it means he felt luckier being blind," she says, almost to herself. "Maybe it means we don't get to say what a handicap is."

Thomas blinks. Goober looks up at the people, who are the bosses of dogs.

"That girl can say she remembers what she likes. I know what she did. You know the name that's on this gravestone?"

She gestures at the plot she's standing before.

Entrecarceles says that he does.

"You know what day today is?"

He says that he does.

"Then if you're not calling the police on me, I'd ask you to please give me a little bit of privacy now."

She turns back toward the small headstone bearing the name of her only lost baby.

SAIRY SWINBURNE

OCT 1 2009 – MARCH 26 2012

Thomas Entrecarceles turns to leave her in peace.

"You should read it though."

He turns back around.

"Sorry?"

"The bible," she says. "I don't truck with all of it. But there's good parts." She stares at him, smiling. "Just that it might help you feel less lonely."

"Who said I feel lonely?" Entrecarceles says.

"Nobody I guess." She turns back to the grave. "Goodbye."

"Goodbye," he says.

CHAPTER 43

Owl-eyed Oscar Louder knew exactly what he had seen. Of course he hadn't admitted it to himself, not at first, but by the time their small three-man boat made it back to the edge of the flooding, back to where they could walk toward the Pavilion of the Abandoned Future, he was certain, his mind was set. He had, as soon as the craft was beached, leapt across the pavement and tackled Dave Boggs. He'd restrained him, found some rope, and left him in the custody of Sam Herbert (who had, you might have guessed, promptly abandoned him).

Then he'd run fast as his feet could carry him back toward the Pavilion of the Abandoned Future. He'd sprinted through the halls of the Pavilion panting, shouting, looking for Robert. He'd found some of the galley workers dragging propane tanks down the hall.

"Have you seen Robert Vicaray?" he'd nearly shouted.

"Last I saw," said the nonplussed kitchen hand, "he was laying tape on the east side of the building."

Oscar had found him, conversing in hushed tones with that strange girl and her mother, previously objects of suspicion, now of so little concern to Oscar. They had walked out as he entered the small closet where Vicaray stood looking gaunt and wretched.

"Hey," he said, looking at Oscar. "What's up."

"What's up," Oscar said, his skin erupting to goose flesh, "is that it was you."

"It was me what?"

"You caused the explosion." Oscar touched his glasses. "You're a mass murderer, Robert."

Vicaray's eyes widened, then he laughed. Oscar thought he could see something else working behind the flash of teeth and tongue, some panicked jerking thing, like a fish caught on the line.

"Oscar, what the…?"

He studied the insurance man's face.

"Your lackey, Sam Herbert was asking me about arson," Louder said slowly, "and I realized that I was forgetting to tell him something. Something a friend told me once."

"Yeh," Vicaray was still smiling pathetically, trying to muster some delicate laugh, some easy dismissal that would not come. "And what would that be?"

"Firefighter's arson," said Oscar.

"Sorry?"

"About a hundred times a year, it turns out that the person who set a blaze was a volunteer firefighter, Robert. They set the fire so they can come in and save the people."

"O.K." Vicaray would not stop smiling. It took on the character, suddenly, of a leer to Oscar. "O.K. so I'm confused. You're telling me Oscar you think I set some fire, so I could come swoop in here, because I have some hero syndrome? Is that it?"

Oscar shook his head, no.

"Those firefighters maybe, not you," he said. "I don't think you want to be a hero, Robert. I don't think you care about whether people know your name. But I think you kept imagining you'd cracked the code. First you thought it was volunteering with Green Peace or whoever, then it was bank-rolling solar fields, then it was showing up to disasters with band-aids. I think each time you discovered you were getting juked. Outflanked by some corporate poltergeist. Every time. And I think, quietly, you started to go insane."

Vicaray shook his head back and forth like a marionette, still flashing that horrible frozen grin.

"I was in Oklahoma when this happened, Oscar. We came here together, man."

Oscar raised his leg a little and tugged on the cuff of his pantleg. There were dark red spots of what looked like blood, speckling the ankles.

"Red wine," he said. "Up on top of that still, we found a thermos."

Vicaray said nothing. Oscar didn't realize he was rolling a cigarette between his fingers, fixated as he was on what he heard himself saying.

"You sent Boggs up there with some—I don't know— some can of lawn fertilizer or chlorine bomb or something. You're a smart guy, Robert, you say yourself, you like to read. You sent him up, you probably didn't think the explosion would be as big as it was. You probably—"

Oscar laughed coldly.

"—counted on the syrup company being good corporate citizens, not cutting corners, and figured you could stage your little victimless catastrophe. But they were cutting the syrup with molasses. Trying to bring down unit price. *Molasses has fumes the way jet fuel has fumes.* That blind woman said. The company probably got the rubber stamp from some retired chemist and figured if the chemical composition was a little more volatile, so be it. There were other fail-safes in place. But they didn't see you coming. Maybe you weren't even sure why you wanted it. Dipping your toes in the water. But you knew you wanted the company to be responsible. You knew you wanted your group to be the only ones on the ground after the tanks blew."

"*My* group," Robert Vicaray said slowly, tremulously, "is your group too. It doesn't belong to me. That's the point."

"No." Oscar shook his head. "The point is that it was *you*. And you didn't do it because you wanted to be the hero. You did it because it was a spectacle. That's why, isn't it? Because you could feel yourself getting used again. And you wanted to make something happen *out loud* and *on T.V.* Isn't that right?"

Robert Vicaray did not respond. He had been radicalized, whatever that meant. Become an extremist. And suddenly to him the civic peace did not seem civil or peaceful. Not where so many were doomed to drown or starve or lose their livelihood inch by undignified inch.

"I didn't," Robert croaked feebly. "I didn't Oscar."

Perhaps he believed it. But the truth was that whether or not he had set the explosion, that Robert Vicaray was glad that it had happened, for the horror of it. That he *enjoyed it*. That was the disgusting secret that played across his face as he stared at Oscar Louder, whose eyes might as well have been of chiseled stone for all they yielded. Perhaps, as I say, he was innocent of this crime. But if so, he could not bring himself to say it.

"Goodbye Robert," Oscar said, walking out of the closet back to the main atrium. And it was just about then that the Pavilion of the Abandoned Future erupted into chaos.

CHAPTER 44

Sairy had cried out among the beds.

She had walked out into the center of the auditorium on the first night of the Littoral Disaster and she'd cleared her throat, and said, self-seriously: "Please raise your hand if you or someone you know has been maimed or killed in this industrial accident."

It had been quiet. There had been some coughs, some blinks. She had repeated herself, like a census-taker almost:

"Please *raise your hand* if you or someone you know has been maimed or killed in this industrial accident."

And some hands had gone up.

Then she'd nodded, and said:

"Please raise your hand if you feel that the country you live in is too-big and no-good, and scary and you'd rather maybe have died or never been born in the first place."

And like some kind of electric current or catalyst, a ripple had gone through the crowd, and a few of the refugees from the Littoral Maple Disaster had tentatively raised their hands, glancing around, laughing nervously.

More and more questions had kept coming from this strange twelve-year-old girl, the sorts of questions you never actually ask out loud, out of politesse or social cowardice or the desire to seem well-adjusted:

"Raise your hand if you wish we could all quit this and start the whole thing over from the beginning where it wasn't ruined."

She had not deigned to specify what The Whole Thing was, and the crowd did not seem to need her to. Someone shouted *"Fuck!"*

"Raise your hands if you think the people tasked with protecting your health and well-being have completely abandoned you in favor of naked self-interest."

Some murmurs, some more hands.

"Raise your hand if you think those people who abandoned you have completely insulated themselves from any liability or responsibility or blame."

A few shouts now.

"Raise your hand if you're not happy at all, most of the time."

And more hands.

"Raise your hand if you feel you're not good and you're not happy and that all the qualities normal people seem to have in spades—the things that make you a good employee, or a good partner or a good son or daughter—that none of those are there, that God left them out of you on purpose, and how lonely it is all the time."

Now there was a great deal of noise. Peculiarly, more hands went up than stayed down. And Oscar Louder was shocked to see *his own* hand go into the air and stay there, quivering, in the middle of the crowd.

"Raise your hands if you don't think any of these avoidable disasters have added anything more to your lives. If everything feels just as lousy and silly and strange and too-expensive as before. If none of your morning commutes or doctor's appointments carry any sort of added meaning, the way bosses and public figures are always telling you they will. If you feel your whole life to date has been a steady series of subtractions."

And you can imagine how Sairy saying something like that got all those people recuperating in the Pavilion the Abandoned Future really jazzed. Even Oscar Louder, against his exactingly rational will, felt his skin break into gooseflesh, his hand still thrust in the air. And she said:

"Raise your hand if you don't think what happened at the maple processing plant was an accident at all."

At these words, the crowd fell quiet. The girl in the banana-print dress stood in the middle of a thousand faces swirling. You could hear a pin drop in the auditorium, just then.

Just outside, the first of the Rude Mechanics was noticing a long train of trucks labeled LITTORAL COUNTY ZOO beginning to pull up toward the side of the building, with confused PERT volunteers hanging bug-eyed out the passenger side windows gesticulating wildly to one another.

"Well it was not an accident," Sairy said to the crowd inside. "And I know who did it. And I can tell you."

A murmur went through the crowd.

"I will tell you," Sairy said slowly, "if you'll all agree to let me kill Beebop, the town's rhinoceros."

"What," somebody said.

"A rhinoceros," said somebody else.

Sairy looked deeply annoyed by the crowd's fickleness.

"I'm telling you if you don't vote for this now, you're going to regret it later," he said.

Some people shook their heads in disappointment. Someone said "For chrissakes!"

Then Sairy made her three haughty predictions (which I have already detailed) and told everyone one last time that they must vote to kill a rhinoceros. And the whole crowd (which had been hanging on her every word until that point) completely lost the thread and began to walk away, shaking their heads. Leanne Swinburne, for her part, stood idly by, listening to the little girl inveighing against a bunch of forces that Leanne herself found so abstract she couldn't even gin up the will to get angry about them.

"I guess your plan failed," said Leanne.

"That wasn't my plan," Sairy said. "That was table-setting."

About three minutes passed.

And then, as if on cue, someone called out panicked from the front entrance. It was Burt Orley. The fellow who would eventually speak the last word, and drive the nail into poor Beebop the Rhinoceros' coffin.

"The police are outside!" cried Burt. "They say they got an arrest warrant. They say Robert Vicaray is wanted for murder!"

"The police aren't setting foot in here," called Oscar Louder, looking around at all the nervous faces that had begun to stir at the word *police*. Louder looked at Robert Vicaray.

Glen Aurech said:

"Jesus Christ Robert what did you do?"

The words came out so flat and mean and accusatory that Glen could hardly believe it himself. All the trust and reciprocal charity of spirit between him and Robert Vicaray had evaporated in the very instant of his accusal.

Just then, in the midst of the chaos of the moment Dave Boggs came staggering into the room with his mouth clamped shut, blood pouring down his chin, with one hand held out in front of him, as if in sacrificial offering.

"Jesus fuck," someone cried. "It's his *tongue*."

Boggs staggered madly further into the room, smiling crazily, stabbing his meaty finger toward Vicaray, his mouth redly agape. "Someone cut out his *tongue*."

"What the fuck did you do Robert?" said Glen. "Why are the police here?"

"*Nothing*," said Vicaray shaking his head. "This is completely absurd."

But even as he said it, he felt two pairs of hands grab and restrain him.

"This is *absurd*. I didn't *kill* anyone."

Elver Bryce, a large man with a great chiseled block head, stepped before Robert, eyeing him up and down and began in a friendly businesslike way, to pat first his left leg, then his right. Robert heard the man gasp a little and withdraw his hand quickly. He straightened, looked at Robert with judicious dispassion, reached back into his pocket, more carefully this time, withdrew the object that had lanced him, and said, holding it up, "Do you want to tell me why you got a syringe in your pocket Robert?"

Someone wailed.

Just then, Sam Herbert slipped back into the Pavilion unseen, smelling strongly of sweat and butane, his fake nose pointing the wrong cardinal direction on his face. At the same time, Burt Orley, helpful relayer of information, shouted again from the entrance.

"The police say they got a bomb threat!

All inside the Pavilion of the Abandoned Future became bedlam. People wailed and stampeded and clutched each other tightly.

"Let them in!" someone yelled.

Oscar Louder, who was perhaps the only person everyone still trusted, repeated, louder this time:

"*The police are not setting foot on these premises.*" Then he began pointing at the volunteers who were not already restraining Robert Vicaray and said, "*Lock the doors.*"

And perhaps just because he sounded so calm and sure, while everyone else was running around like chickens with their heads cut off, people responded, they sprinted to the doors carrying mops and spare planks, anything that could jam them shut. Several more coordinated the piling of beds and heavy furniture in front of the main entrances.

And so the doors were locked with everyone inside. And Oscar Louder breathed deep and began to walk slowly toward the roof, where he could hopefully converse with the police assembled outside, and calm everyone down. And that is when he began to hear it: slow, steady tack-tack-tacks, bouncing off the windows and anodized roofgutters. Oscar Louder, now taking the stairs two at a time, shook his head, cursed, wondering just how much bad luck one town could have all at once. He stepped out onto the roof and held out his palm to the naked sky. It had begun to rain.

CHAPTER 45

Sgt. Dan Volsky, just outside, leading his jackbooted navy-blue troops into battle, shook his head in horrified wonderment. Rain had just begun lightly falling which, paired with the fact that the only aid organization in Littoral was currently under siege, meant that an additional 60 people would die from the city's flooding that night.

"Lackwits," Volsky said softly. "Vicaray has got that whole place rigged to blow, and they're barricading themselves inside."

Someone fetched Volsky a bullhorn from one of the huge armored cars that the police bring with them to de-escalate conflicts.

"O.K.," Volsky called into the bullhorn dryly, "we have an arrest warrant for Robert Vicaray. We have no interest in compromising in any way. If you do not allow us into the building we will enter by force. If he blows half of you up, so be it."

Dan Volsky felt very brave at that moment, volunteering half of the people inside the building to die in an explosion. As he saw it, anyone who threw in their lot with cop-hating murderers deserved exactly what they got, which is to say: mass death. Volsky's politics were simple and refreshingly arithmetic in that way. He believed that the holy recompense for most forms of moral failure that hadn't personally touched his own life was violence.

Oscar Louder appeared on the roof then, shouting something.

"What's he saying?" Volsky asked someone.

"I think he's saying there's no bomb."

Volsky returned the bullhorn to his lips.

"Are you trying to tell us there's no bomb inside?"

The black fellow on the roof nodded that, yes, that was exactly what he was telling them.

"Of course there is a bomb," one of the police officers beside Dan Volsky (the soon-to-be-late Leonard Dormer) said confidently. Dormer was annoyed by the idea that they should have lugged all their beautiful siege equipment across town under false pretenses.

More people joined Oscar Louder on the Pavilion's roof, staring down at the police, waving their arms frantically.

"Of course there is a bomb," repeated Volsky into the bull-horn. Then, "Either way we are coming in. If you do not open up we will assume you are armed. What the fuck is this?"

This last part Volsky accidentally said into the bullhorn as his gaze was drawn right, toward the long line of trucks pulling idiotically up to the entrance so that they sat squarely between the siege weapons of the Littoral P.D. and the Rude Mechanics inside the building.

"*Get the fuck out of here,*" shouted one of the frontline officers at the pickup truck. The PERT volunteer, nodding idiotically at the trailer he was towing behind him, said, "*Jaguar.*"

Oscar shook his head and shouted as well, but he did not have a bullhorn like the cops did, nor guns, nor siege equipment, so there was no way he could ever win the argument. Several of the Littoral PD put down their face shields and unholstered their weapons the way they had seen other cops do in movies or on the news.

Police officer Leonard Dormer was right, of course, there *was* a bomb. But it wasn't sitting underneath the feet of Oscar Louder or any of the other Rude Mechanics. It was rigged up inside the hollow interior of the model of the Challenger Space Shuttle, not fifty feet from where the Police stood in a neat martial line, at deadly parade rest. And it hadn't been planted by Robert Vicaray. No, it was Neizar Muntasser, on orders from Sairy Wellcomme, who had stolen the propane tanks from the galley kitchen and hooked them up to a trip wire the same way you might a bounding mine or a bouncing betty.

"Alright fuck this," someone said, and Volsky nodded, knowing that the time had come to stop exchanging polite words with a bunch of people who were essentially scum. That the time had come for Men Of Action to serve as the battering ram of History. That *these here surrounding him* were just such men, through whom History's whims moved with a fury.

"Fuck this," said Dan Volsky excitedly.

So it was that just as Dan Volsky and the rest of the Littoral P.D. charged the outside doors of the Pavilion of the Abandoned Future, guns already drawn, that one of them (Officer Tim Green, to be exact) tripped the wire that ignited one of an estimated thirty propane tanks clustered in the belly of the fake Challenger Space Shuttle, setting off a chain reaction inside it that built and built until finally the collecting pressure from the propane ripped open the rectum of the fake spaceship and sent it along a deadly parabola, flames blooming psychotically from its fake shuttle doors and cockpit, 'til it landed with and unholy BOOM right on top of the shock troops of the Littoral P.D., flattening them like human pancakes, at which point the impact of the crash, combined with the flames spreading within the shuttle's interior, caused a half-dozen of the remaining gas tanks that had not initially detonated to erupt in a *second* explosion, spewing shrapnel from the flanks and the nose, in every which direction, decapitating officer Matt Foley where he stood just in front of where the shuttle had come down, thanking any number of Christian saints (prematurely, as it turned out) that he'd been spared. The force of the second explosion was strong enough that it shattered the glass on the Pavilion's barricaded front doors and sent the furniture barricades skittering and scattering back into the auditorium's interior, careening across the concrete floors, bowling over all the people standing nearby and knocking over a couple empty hospital cots in the process.

As the explosion expanded and caught more and more objects in its violent tremble, it sent the PERT trailers of the Littoral County Zoo tumbling sideways, breaking their latches and in some cases killing or injuring their occupants. The terrified animals began, for the first time in their short unhappy journey, to rail against the confines of their portable enclosures, and the beasts of the land spilled out among the flames and began darting every which direction, mauling their captors, or the officers of the Littoral county P.D. Beebop the rhinoceros, dazed and greatly upset by the explosion and the overturning of his own trailer, staggered out, gained his footing, set sights on Dan Volsky who was standing in shock before the flaming lawn of the Pavilion and charged directly toward the august officer of the law, slamming against his abdomen, goring him with a horn and trampling him with three odd-toed feet 'til Dan felt his ribcage crack and one of the bones of his sternum go plunging into his left lung, collapsing it instantly as he lay there on the ground, with the rain pricking his cheeks on a dark strange night.

Oscar Louder stood there in shock. He thought: *Jesus Christ almighty.* But that's not what he said. What he said, almost too quiet for anyone else to hear was: "Act of man."

The rain pattered against the parking lot asphalt, trying to suffocate the propane fire but instead spreading rivers of licking flame around the crevasses of the lot, threatening the wooden struts jutting from the Pavilion's exterior. The model space shuttle roared and crackled. It groaned like a baleen whale.

And no one said it, but Burt Orley swears *he at least* was thinking about the girl's predictions, amongst the beds, and how it did not seem so crazy now, that they might all come true.

The people on the roof cried out at the mayhem and carnage unfolding below, at the sight of officers of the Littoral Police force being so violently dismembered by the second Challenger Space Shuttle explosion—and that was when Sairy Wellcomme called out in the auditorium, and said:

"If you allow me to hunt that rhinoceros, then I'll tell you who caused the maple explosion."

And the people of Littoral were so angered by the senseless violence unfolding outside, they began as one to gin and bustle and surge and push toward Sairy just as the fire alarm was triggered by the flames licking the outside of the building.

Someone cried out: "Tell us."

Here is what happened when Sairy said Robert Vicaray's name out loud, to the people of Littoral, New York: Their blood became toxic, their minds went crazy, and their hearts stopped working. And by virtue of the size of the crime of which Vicaray had been accused, he became in their eyes, incontrovertibly guilty.

The mob pushed past the various volunteer doctors and orderlies and other Rude Mechanics, and they grabbed an orange extension cord from the makeshift Janitor's closet, and muscled past a few shaking, pale-looking volunteers. They hauled Robert Vicaray by the scruff of his neck up the stairs to the second-floor roof, past Oscar Louder who was still calling out for everyone to remain calm. They wrapped and cinched the extension cord around Vicaray's neck, and right before everyone's eyes they stood him on the edge of the roof, and asked him rhetorically what he had to say for himself. Robert began to cry, big childish tears, teetering without his cane on the edge of the Pavilion's roof, and he tried to muster some important adult last words significant enough to lend meaning to his life (or at least his death). But instead, here is all that his words sounded like to anyone who should have cared to listen: a child, babbling to his mama. Here is what the crowd did: they bayed with delight. Then they dropped him off the edge with the cord hugging his throat.

Unfortunately, unsurprisingly, and rather gruesomely, a poorly tied electric cord is no substitute for a government-issue noose. Robert Vicaray's neck did not snap. Though his lower mandible broke and his trapezius and sternocleidomastoids both tore from the sudden violence of the fall, so that, as he gasped in vain for air, the fibrous knots of muscle in back of his neck became nothing but a limp bundle of ruptured tissue yanked away from bone. He passed in blaring agony, unable even to jerk with his dying, or assert where his face should point as he went. His eyes bulged. The blood vessels in them ruptured. His purpling face pointed straight upward, toward the sky. The townspeople of Littoral, NY strangled Robert Vicaray, with the weight of his own body, just before midnight on the same day that 119 years earlier they'd hanged Charles Guiteau for the crime of being born mad. And Robert, as he died, looked up blinking toward the deserted heavens, and in death, could scarcely believe what he saw. The strangled boy from Oklahoma flailed, casting his eyes skyward and gurgled: *"The man in the moon!"*

You might be excused for thinking that this was just parei-dolia, the lunatic imaginings of a mind on its way out the door,

with all synapses firing at the same time, except that Oscar
Louder, too, was gaping skyward, pointing slackly toward that
ghostly pale galleon, the earth's dead grey pet rock, and so
several more faces cast upwards just in time to see the face on
the moon, impossibly, turning away from the earth.

The truth, mind, is that the face in the moon did not turn
away at all. The truth, as contemporaneous NASA records
can attest, is that for some unknown reason (due to gravity
or electromagnetism or sun spots) the moon for the briefest
moment on the night of June the 30th, ceased it synchronous
ministrations and for a startled and brief celestial moment,
stood more or less still in the night's sky. Nothing was greatly
affected by this sudden about-face. The great satellite did not
come plummeting toward earth, nor go spinning off into
space. The tides of the Oceans did imperceptibly change by
about six inches in a span of three minutes, as some seaside
observatories noted. Those shifts were felt from the mouth of
the Hudson Estuary in Manhattan Harbor all the way up to
Troy, New York and the faraway shores of the Spice Islands.
But as miracles go, it was quite brief and quite unmarvelous.
And shortly thereafter, without much theatricality, the moon
resumed its rotation once again, appeared much the same as
it always had, as it still does, to you and me.

Of course, questions about why this briefest lacuna from
its rotational obligations occurred in the first place, without
any sort of prior warning, still abound, are still the subject of
any number of Doctoral Theses in the cosmological field. But
it is all rather academic. One thing everyone can agree on is
that the brief cessation or resumption of the moon's 27-day
synchronous rotation had absolutely *zero* to do with machinations or petty barbarisms of the denizens of one small tourist

town in Upstate New York (though it would prove reliably difficult to convince some of those denizens of this same point). The man in the moon does not care much for the affairs of men and women, even men and women so supremely modern and well-appointed as we.

Oscar Louder looked up alongside the dying Robert Vicaray, and the both of their eyes lighted on the same body, which Oscar had obsessed over ever since he was a little boy. And Oscar whispered, "I'm sorry things turned out like this, Robert." But of course, his friend Robert Vicaray could not hear this.

Here is what the journalist Thomas Entrecarceles has to say about the whole incident in his notes:

"It is useless to ask why the Man in the Moon turned away, just before midnight, on some specific night, June the 30th, say, of 2012. It is like the extinction of some obscure species in the newspaper or the heat death of a faraway planet. For you did not make a note every day previous, when the moon reliably spun in its place, the species clung to its mantle, raised its babies, and labored heroically in biologic obscurity. You did not consider it marvelous then. You did not count it as a miracle every night when the tides ran up the Hudson and spiked the pulses in your blood and set your heart on fire with their very pull. How self-centered, then, to ask why the Man in the Moon turned away, finally. You'd might as well ask how it was he could stand to keep looking for as long as he did in the first place." So there is that.

In Littoral, New York, in June of the year 2012, just as the clocks were striking midnight bringing a close on the first day of the infamous Maple Syrup disaster, a rain cloud sailed over earth's satellite's pallid face, obscuring it a moment from view, casting the people amassed there into torment and shadow.

The people teemed toward the exits as the Pavilion of the Abandoned Future burned. As, all over town, chemical fires that had burned independently got spread by the rain and the wind until the buildings surrounding them were all in flame, until every building in Littoral was burning. Every building except the Maple Refinery, and the Jail and the Zoo. Robert Vicaray died then, choking for air, thinking about his mother, looking up at the alien moon. All was quiet save for the rain. Nobody spoke. Until, finally, Sairy Wellcomme emerged into the night air, Leanne Swinburne in tow, to discuss, now, her half of the bargain. The thing she had been promised.

Sairy cleared her throat on the dark pavement, all business while behind her the city burned, and asked in measured tones, "Are you all ready to vote now?"

CHAPTER 46

The whole town is assembled here now. Sairy has made sure of it. They have all voted and now they will see the result of their vote.

Everything is exactly to her specifications. She is standing in a little curtained backstage area she had someone erect in the reptile room of the Littoral County Zoo. The name is a bit of a local joke. The zoo is technically located in neighboring Irving County but on account of a long-ago property dispute following the redrawing of the county line in the 40s, it is still called the Littoral County Zoo.

After the vote had passed, Frank Orr who ran Sportsman's Reserve, had helped Sairy select the exact Bow & Arrow from the sporting goods section for her to use today. Frank who is an avid big game hunter himself, and feels quite bad for having helped hang a man, was enthusiastic about assisting this strange little girl who spoke so eloquently about expiation and culpability and all that business.

The animal had not been difficult to track. It turned out, in his agitation, or panic, or what-have-you, he had cantered frightenedly back toward the only place in town he knew, one of the only places that was not on fire: they had found Beebop standing contentedly inside his enclosure. With the whole wide night blown open in front of him, walls of flame screaming on all unhappy sides, the poor old rhinoceros had decided he was happier back in his cage.

An owlish black head pokes in through the back curtain. "Are you quite ready?" Oscar Louder asks dispassionately.

The little girl sighs a horrible sigh.

It should go nearly without saying, but does not, that the Great African Blue Rhino is not actually blue—no more than the fearsome White Shark is afflicted of albinism, or the Australian Koala an actual bear. In reality, it (the rhino) is closer to dark gray in color. Nor does it appear at first glance to be all that Great.

The last living Blue Rhinoceros on earth is called Beebop. All the Blue Rhinos that came before him got sick or were murdered or accidentally galloped off a cliff or something. Beebop is 13 and they have stored almost a gallon of his seed in the hopes that somewhere along the line, field biologists missed a feral Rhino, that there is one wild female still out there somewhere, roaming around untamed, unaccounted for. And that they could use her to restart the species, like a sort of Blue Rhinoceral Eve. They have tried crossbreeding with other kinds of Rhinoceroses—female Black Rhinos, female Indian Rhinos—but the pregnancies never took, Beebop has sired no heirs. By most clear-eyed estimates, he is the final, the last of his kind.

"You're going to let me assassinate the rhinoceros then?" Sairy Wellcomme says slowly. It feels like it has been such a long journey to get here, she is nearly disappointed by Louder's accession. The former insurance man shrugs.

"They put it to a vote."

"That's right. They did." Sairy says eyeing him strangely. "And how did you vote, Oscar?"

He does not answer, looks around the small sparse staging area. He is startled to see Leanne Swinburne sitting nearby, tucked in a corner.

"You just knock twice when you're ready to come out," he says dryly and withdraws his face.

Beebop lives in a 500 square meter enclosure in the Littoral County Zoo. His habitat is hemmed-in by ten feet of rebar and pre-form concrete. He lives by himself. His environs are 9 inches of topsoil turfed over with fifteen types of imported African endema, a small artificial watering hole and a grated drainage pipe of unclear purpose. Beebop is blind in one eye, the only son of the zoo's previous Blue Rhino, named Daisy, whom he murdered during childbirth. At 4,200 pounds his weight is a little shy of what would be considered normal for a male Great African Blue Rhino, but also, since he is the last ever Great African Blue Rhino, you could say that he is exactly normal for his species in every way—that the average Great African Blue Rhino is 4,200 pounds, blind in one eye, and has killed his own mother.

Leanne Swinburne stirs almost imperceptibly in her corner. Sairy Wellcomme's head snaps sideways at the sound, she studies the other woman, sitting there in the dark.

"Yes Leanne?"

"I didn't say anything."

"But you want to."

"It's a dreadful show," she laughs, face upturned.

When Sairy was just a little girl there were over 100 Blue Rhinoceroses roaming freely hither and thither across the wide-stretched Savannah. She used to buy and read every book she could get her hands on regarding the great exotic creatures. She knows, even still today, that they are odd-toed ungulates, that their prehensile upper lip distinguishes them from so-called "grazer" rhinoceroses (like White and Indian varieties), that rhino horns are made of keratin, not ivory, and that Great African Blue Rhinos have poorer eyesight than any other subspecies—so poor that anything farther than ten meters away from them might as well be in China. She knows that we have systematically slaughtered them all as part of a larger strategy of ending all life on planet earth, which started around the time we hung Charles Guiteau from a Gibbet in Washington D.C.

"They're all cowards," Leanne says.

Sairy nods circumspectly.

"Maybe. Maybe there's only so much you can expect from people. Maybe it is cruel and unusual, Leanne, to look down on those who have to choose between death and depravity."

"What's your plan now?"

Sairy Wellcomme, or maybe some evil spirit inside Sairy Wellcomme, blinks her eyelids.

"It feels like my plan's pretty much come to fruition, no?"

Leanne leans forward.

"You're actually going to kill him. You're serious."

"Well I don't know if I'm serious Leanne but I'm definitely going to do it."

"What purpose would that serve. To kill a rhinoceros."

"The last rhinoceros."

"What purpose would it serve?"

"What purpose does any death ever serve?" Sairy says shaking her head.

"None. Never."

"Well." Sairy lightly fingers the grip on the bow and arrow Frank Orr had been so friendly helping her pick out. "If he's already going to die, which he is. And if, when he dies, it will be true that we murdered him, which it will." She looks at the blind woman. "Then I think it ought to be me that does it."

"Why?"

She shrugs, which Leanne cannot see, but which makes her look her age suddenly. Just a girl of twelve. "Because I love him so much."

"Don't try and play this like you're some kind of environmentalist here, when you feel entitled to some poor animal's life, just because your parents died in an accident," Leanne snaps.

She is not afraid of Sairy Wellcomme anymore. She is not afraid of anything anymore, that she can think of.

"I don't feel entitled to it," Sairy says. "It's you all. You're the ones saying 'I get to have this rhinoceros, and whatever takes it from me is wrong.' You're the ones who feel entitled to his life. I just feel entitled to his death."

Leanne looks revolted.

The girl, or the creature inhabiting the girl, breathes.

"Do you understand, Leanne, how much pain I am in, all the time? How I do not want to be here at all, how painful I find it to be in this body, and how I would do anything to get out? Sometimes I can hardly breathe from how it feels, being trapped in here."

"Yeh well welcome to the club," Leanne says.

"I'm sorry you can't understand."

"I understand fine," Leanne says, then, looking strained. "I'll stop you."

Sairy shakes her head, looking sad. "No you won't."

"And how do you know?"

"Because I'll tell everyone who you are. Because you love your freedom more than you love a rhinoceros. Because *everybody loves everything* more than any of us loves a rhinoceros, and that's how we wrecked it all. And that's why we don't deserve to have him anymore."

Leanne does not say anything more, just shakes her head in disgust. Sairy knocks twice on the wall, and the both of them are led out.

It is obviously a bit of a strange scene. The townspeople are all gathered on bleachers that've been dragged across town from the High School. There are great floodlights illuminating Beebop, the star of the show, milling aimlessly around his paddock, clearly irritated at having been woken up. The Littoral County zookeeper is in the back office crying and being given a sedative by a kindly doctor.

Sairy takes to a platform that gives her a clear view of the enclosure. She has had the chance to practice with the bow several times now and she is quite good. She has got three arrows in hand and more in a quiver which she lays on the ground. If she is indeed, as she says, some evil spirit, accidentally transported from some netherworld, she must be thinking just how close she is to going home now. The townspeople are all perched on bleachers' edges, hungry to forget the role they had in hanging Robert Vicaray, and also, loathe as they are to admit to themselves, in the grips of some dark titillation, some horrible macabre thrill, at the thought of what they are about to witness. Local bigwigs and the village priest have all turned out. Families with young children bouncing on their laps, staring in at the doomed rhinoceros.

Some A.V. whiz has rigged up a microphone so that it is jacked into the Zoo's main P.A. system. Young Sairy approaches and says, slowly:

"There is one Blue Whale who sings his song at 52 Hertz, even though all the rest of whales sing at 24 Hertz, so no other whale can hear this one."

Nobody says anything. Someone coughs.

"They call him 52 Blue," Sairy continues. "He is an infinitely gentle, infinitely suffering thing."

With that, she steps away from the microphone, clearly under the impression that this represented a satisfactory eulogy for a rhinoceros. Everyone in the stands looks sideways at his/her neighbor, confused but not saying anything.

Hortations done, she halts, staring down past the railing at the half-blind rhinoceros. Beebop looks bored, standing there, chewing listlessly on some imported African leaf. Twitching his ears to shoo off flies. He does not look infinitely gentle, or infinitely suffering. Sairy leans down, nocks an arrow, and straightens. She pulls back on the string of her bow.

People hear but do not really see the first arrow, it travels so fast. It sort of zips through the air, and sticks with a horrid thwap in poor Beebop's side. The world's oldest Blue Rhino lets out a bellow and some people begin to turn their heads or gasp. But Sairy, crouching next to the bag, is already loading up a second arrow.

Then there is a shout, and a gasp goes up, and Sairy Wellcomme's face looks taken aback as she is thrown to the ground.

The blind woman at her side is trying to wrest the bow from the girl's grip. Sairy Wellcomme's face betrays something, what is it? Admiration? Love?

But her grip is strong and, anyway, a few men have rushed out of the stands to restrain the crazed blind woman. They had a vote after all. The girl spoke convincingly and they all decided to allow her to kill the rhinoceros.

"*Don't!*" Leanne shouts as she is dragged away. "*Don't! I can see. I am awake now. I am fully awake.*"

There is some uncomfortable shifting in the stands but nobody says anything. The prevailing sentiment is Lets Get This Over With Yeh?

The girl retrieves her bow and looses the second arrow.

It whizzes through still air and sticks Beebop through the neck. The rhinoceros brays and tries to charge but he cannot ascertain from whence this new enemy has sprung, he cannot figure out why he feels so much pain, who or what has made him to hurt so bad. He charges in a circle, flashing Sairy his blind bulging eye. Sairy Wellcomme has loaded a third arrow.

A groan goes up in the stands. A few children begin crying. The rhinoceros makes a horrible agonized lowing sound. "Make her stop!" someone demands and many people will later claim it was them that shouted it. But it wasn't. It was Neizar Muntasser. It was the first time he ever experienced regret.

The third arrow releases with a crisp thwap—the bowstring accidentally flaying open the skin on Sairy's forearm—and sings viciously through the air of the enclosure, over the water and past the tall imported grass, and catches Beebop the rhinoceros directly through his jaw, straight up into his forehead, slicing between the eyes, and the pain-mad animal, still loosing inarticulate brays of murky objection, of uncomprehending pain, staggers, and halts, swaying a moment, before lowering himself, breathing heavily, to the ground.

All is quiet then in the enclosure with just the soft swell and fall of the poor beast's belly, barely visible above tall grass, to signal there is any occupant left alive inside. Sairy drops the bow. Children, gazing in the enclosure, keen loudly. Mothers clutch their babies to their chests.

Everyone, seemingly coming to their senses at the same time, realizes that this is a girl, a twelve-year-old girl, they've just allowed to kill this zoo animal. That the girl looks very pale suddenly, and she is bleeding from her forearm. Several adults rush forward toward her, trying to pull her away from the enclosure, get some gauze on the nasty cut on her arm.

"No," she says.

She says it softly, not taking her eyes off the belly, which rises then falls below view. They are draping a blanket over her shoulders, pulling her gently from the scene of the crime she just committed. "No-o." Sairy raises her hands to clutch at her head and moans the word, but they pinion her small arms back down to her sides to try and treat the wound.

"Please I'm sorry I take it back."

Beebop the Rhino's belly swells pregnant with air then collapses again.

"No. No. No. I take it back. I'm sorry."

She is jostled backwards, as if buoyed by strong waves. It is a mild and starless night under the kliegs and—if not for the girl screaming and all the people now crying—an idyllic one. *"I take it back please just let me take it back please."*

As she says it, Sairy looks not towards the faces of the adults surrounding her, or up at the Man in the Moon, nor even at Leanne Swinburne who—having been released—has already slipped through the crowd and melted away into the night. Sairy looks instead toward the cage, and the rhinoceros lying still there, just outside of view. She looks determinedly at Beebop and says

"Please get up please let me take it back."

And like children, or those who believe in miracles, the rest of the onlookers credulously trail Sairy Wellcomme's grief-mad gaze, back into the enclosure, where that gray belly softly rises, then softly falls. Where grass sits unswaying in still air. All there stand in expectation. But I do not have to tell you, reader, that the great beast never stirs.

CHAPTER 47

I knocked three times on the front door before it opened. Sairy Wellcomme looked surprised to see me.

"Thomas."

"Hello."

She stood back and allowed me into her apartment, her eyebrows went up, up, up.

"Should you be coming here, if you're being followed?" she asked.

The apartment was not decorous. It seemed almost ascetically dedicated to the idea that its occupant used it for sleep and nothing more.

"I'm not being followed," I said. "I'm being played with."

"I'm afraid I don't understand."

I let go of Goober's leash and he padded around happily.

"I suppose I shouldn't leave him in the custody of someone famous for killing animals, but I don't really have anyone else, so."

She winced at that.

"Please don't be cruel to me."

"Your name isn't Sairy Wellcomme," I said. "You stole a dead girl's name. A dead child."

Her face drew back.

"What?"

"There is no Sairy Wellcomme. There's a Sairy Swinburne. Buried in Irving, New York. And there's a bookish little twelve-year-old from a deeply unhappy family, who, when her parents died in an unforeseen accident, suffered some kind of a psychotic break, and stole someone's identity, and decided to begin a new life as them."

"That's not true, my name is Sairy Wellcomme." She shook her head. "I don't know what's gotten into you."

"Your mother tried to kill you once."

Her face contorted. She said quietly

"She did not, and how dare you say so."

"There's a police report. She tried to set your house on fire. Your father stopped her. She had a daughter named Eleanor. Eleanor Wellcomme. It is right there in the police report."

"It's a misprint. Or some cop didn't listen properly," she said. "Since I was a child people only ever called me Sairy."

"She tried to kill you. And you read in the paper or saw online about another girl whose mother tried to kill her—"

"*Stop saying that.*" She shouted now, Goober whimpered, Sairy Wellcomme's face was stretched white, trembling. She said, "My *mother* had *post-partum*—I guess you'd call them fantasies. Things she wished she could do, to make me… go away. I didn't know any of this, I was just a little girl."

She paused, fingering her throat.

"But they lasted quite a long time. Longer than normal." She smiled without any warmth in it. "She was so sweet to me when I was young. But she went to a therapist, secretly, and the therapist had said that what she—my mother—needed to do was to record herself saying all those things. All the things she fantasized about. That she needed to listen to that recording of herself saying them over and over and over. 'Til they didn't mean anything to her, I guess.

She would walk around all the time with headphones on. *Ignoring me.* Me. The most important little girl who'd ever been born. Well, all little girls are." She laughed harshly. "She was so caring whenever she wasn't wearing the headphones and she was so distant whenever she was wearing them, and I was so *young*.

When I was just about seven or so, one day, I found her head-phones laying on the counter, unattended. I was so jealous of the attention she lavished on them, on whatever she was listening to. What could she be listening to that was more important than me? So I put them on and pressed play. *I want to strangle my daughter. I want to stab my daughter. I want to put a pillow over my daughter's face and smother her. I want to stove my daughter's skull with a pool cue.* I stood there listening to my mommy's voice reciting all the things she wanted to do to me. Then she walked into the kitchen, and saw me there, with those headphones over my ears. And she yanked them out and slapped me in the face. That is the only time my mother ever laid a hand on me. And I ran out crying. We never talked about it. I don't think she told my father. And from that day on, from when I was seven, I mean, she wasn't kind to me anymore. She was cruel all the time, or indifferent. And she still listened to that recording but she couldn't find it within herself to fake loving me anymore."

"You remember everything that happened. You remember all of it."

"No I don't. Honest, Thomas I swear to God I don't remember anything. That's why I called you. I needed to know."

She was crying.

"You terrorized some poor woman, exhumed her daughter's name, wore it like a Halloween mask, then killed a rhinoceros as some final ritual to end your old life."

"But none of that is true Thomas, please," she cried. "Please you can't tell anyone that you think that, it will ruin me. Why would I hire you if that were true?"

I didn't say anything.

"Thomas. Please, Thomas, I'm sorry that I was evil O.K.? I'm so horrified and I'm so *sorry*. I don't do that anymore. I just act like other people now. I try to be good. Every day I try and be good, please don't do this."

I waved a hand.

"I'm not going to tell anyone anything. You hired me. I made you a promise."

It is horrible watching a grown adult weep like a child.

"I'm not evil Thomas I'm not. I don't remember. Please, you've got to believe me that I don't remember. I came from an unhappy family, O.K. I remember that, I should have told you that, but nothing after."

I waved a hand.

"I'm not doing any more favors," I said. "I already said I won't tell anyone. I can't bring myself to believe you. It's too much hard work and I detest hard work, and I'm too tired already." I lay down my notebook on her bed, patted the cover: "If any journalist comes knocking, I'm sure you can dissemble your way out of it. As far as I'm concerned you all deserve each other. Take care of my dog, please."

I let myself out. The night was dark. Sairy Wellcomme's block was quiet. I traveled down the staircase block angling toward an escarpment. I breathed, then heard a stirring to my left in the front garden.

"Lo?" I said.

Nothing. I took another step. Another.

A great weight came rushing through the air. I felt something impact against my skull, just below the ear. Pain exploded somewhere behind my eyes. The impact spun me and my body went tumbling down the last six stairs. I twisted my ankle and grunted. Tried to straighten and dash away but I couldn't put any weight on it. I leaned against the rail, panting, peering into the dark for some sign of what had clubbed me.

Nothing moved.

"Sairy," I called out. "Call the poli—"

Then a body was on top of me in the dark, pinning me with its strong knees, pulling some dark mass out of its interior coat pocket. It leaned close and I could smell the stink of its breath.

"Poor poor pretty thing."

I could feel some sticky hot mass dripping quiet from the left side of my head, and felt a hard cylinder inserted against the soft of my stomach.

"I'll blow you wide open pretty thing. Open open wide open. No more questions."

My hands searched around in the dark for some stone or rock or railroad spike. Anything to save me from what was pressed into my stomach, but of course there was nothing and no one. Just me and this stinking mass hulking above me in the dark.

Just then I heard another shape move, somewhere to the right. There was a grunt and a flash and both shapes toppled sideways. There was a loud report in the dark, and chipped concrete went flying past my face, scorching my cheek. The shapes rolled on the ground together. I crawled away toward my car panting, knowing I would not be able to stand. I heard another loud report and saw one of the two masses straightening.

"It's you," I said.

But it was impossible of course. I had seen the face in old photos, looking daft and friendly with one arm around a Too Tall little girl. But the person the face belonged to had died in a horrible accident, almost ten years ago. The man smiled apologetically at me in the dark, waved with one hand and slipped away down a side alley.

The shape on the ground lay still.

Inside I could hear Goober barking. Sairy Wellcomme came out of her front door.

"Thomas?" she called in the dark.

I said nothing. Lay there, thinking.

"I heard gunshots," she said again.

If she'd hired whoever it was that was lying face down on the ground, she might try and finish me off. But why would she have hired someone to kill me?

"Someone attacked me," I called hoarsely from my car. "He's dead."

"Oh my God." She sounded alarmed. "I'll call the police."

"Good idea," I said. "I'm going to the beach."

The Hudson River is not a river at all of course, it is an estuary. And Hudson Beach barely deserved the distinction of being called a beach in the first place. It is a small sad spit of land abutting Echo Bay staring out at the five islands. The sand is grey and in the winter and early spring it can be quite dingy, especially at night. But as I say, I am not particular about aesthetics.

I parked in the empty lot and limped out onto the sand. As I walked, I put my hand to my head and drew it away staring at the syrupy mass sticking to my fingers in the dark. I sat down clumsily with both my legs stretched out in front of me, it was low tide and the water was about five feet from me. I took off my socks.

So this was where I would meet my own illustrious ending, out under the stars in the cold tidewater. From here I could crawl into the water and swim out out out, 'til I was plopped deadeye in the middle of the great swallowing Atlantic. There was almost no boat traffic that I could see.

I lay back creakily. Or. The waves came in and went out again. Or I could just wait for the tide to come up. My body felt quite tired. Too tired even to carry itself. I could lay here in the sand and wait for the moon's pull to cause the tide to climb up the continental shelf, up the legs of my pants, carry its chill into the marrow of my bones, and I could float there in my clothes in the dark, and then maybe paddle out a little farther and a little farther yet, 'til I was out beyond the buoys, then out beyond all land, 'til I could see nothing but the great blue expanse all around me welcoming me, capacious enough to absorb whatever strange frequencies the land, my land, could not bear to abide in myself. It would not be an interment, I thought. It was a great cold homecoming. Yes. Why should grace ever have been anything but bloody? One very great body meeting one very small one and discovering there was room yet, before all the icebergs calved and the horse latitudes filled up with recycled trash, that I could myself occupy some small space in it, some middle depth, without feeling that my very presence had polluted it. I could do that. I could wait on the spring tide now in neap, and whenever it arrived I could know that it welcomed me, that it had made its preparations. I began to doze. Slapped myself on the cheek. While I waited, I thought, I could at least give a cursory re-examination to the facts of this strange case. To keep myself awake. That a young girl should kill a rhinoceros. How perfectly strange. That a town should help her do it. That so much of this should get buried or mixed up, the wrong parts emphasized, that our infinitely complex brains should so easily lose the thru-lines of creation, or hitch and sputter at the appearance of some loose thread, or imagine they saw a face in the moon looking down judiciously over these funny little lives, catastrophically spent. We have such seething hearts, do we not?

ACKNOWLEDGMENTS

THE IDEA THAT A BOOK OF THIS LENGTH, of any significant length, is a singular work, down to singular authorship is a fabulous illusion (albeit an illusion that benefits the author enormously) to that end, this book owes a debt of gratitude to its first readers Dominic Ciofalo and Logan Gee, Kiera Salvo, Katie Pearl, Juan Bisono, and Andrea Delgado. It would be difficult to overstate the editorial contributions of the indefatigable Patti Rice whose heroic work on this book kept me mostly honest. Great swathes of this novel were written in confinement in the Spanish city of Seville. That very dim time was made considerably brighter by close friends, namely Brendan, Sean, Maria, Justin, Ayesh, Johnny and Jennie and Katie and Claudia. I'd like to thank Ben Drevlow at BULL for giving me my first editorial post, and a thousand acts of generosity besides. And finally I want to thank my family, Kiera, Kelsey, Kala, Patrick, my grandfather Pasqualino Salvo, and my parents Barbara Breen and Joseph Salvo. I am nothing without them.

ABOUT THE AUTHOR

JESSE SALVO is a native New Yorker but now lives in Santiago de Compostela, Spain. His short stories have been published in over a dozen literary journals including *Hobart, Maudlin House, Barren Magazine, X-Ray Lit, Menacing Hedge,* others. Before that, he spent three years working for online comedy magazines. He is a senior fiction editor for Bull Magazine. This is his first novel.